Lying Ways

Rachel Lynch grew up in Cumbria and the lakes and fells are never far away from her. London pulled her away to teach History and marry an Army Officer, whom she followed around the globe for thirteen years. A change of career after children led to personal training and sports therapy, but writing was always the overwhelming force driving the future. The human capacity for compassion as well as its descent into the brutal and murky world of crime are fundamental to her work.

Also by Rachel Lynch

The Rift

Detective Kelly Porter

LYING WAYS

RACHEL LYNCH

CANELOCRIME

First published in the United Kingdom in 2021 by

Canelo
31 Helen Road
Oxford OX2 0DF
United Kingdom

A CIP catalogue record for this book is available from the British Library.

Print ISBN 978 1 78863 871 5
Ebook ISBN 978 1 78863 761 9

Look for more great books at www.canelo.co

Printed and bound in Great Britain by Clays Ltd, Elcograf S.p.A.

Chapter 1

'Enjoy your holiday, Dinger, don't rush back.'

The prison officer's farewell was laced with affection for the older man. Jack Bell had been a quiet and respectful convict. What you might call a good sort. Unlike some of the offenders inside Her Majesty's Prison, Highton, Dinger's eyes didn't suggest a violent or sadistic past; in fact they were more like sparkling portals to a grand old soul, more suited to a kind grandfather. His hands were huge, but gentle, and he spoke to the prison staff respectfully, especially Jeanie. She was his favourite. He spent most of his time banged up in his cell, like the others, shuffling around in his burgundy slippers, sent to him by his loving niece. But he was also let out more than most, thanks to his library job, delivering books and papers up and down the corridors.

Jack had been known as Dinger most of his adult life, and inside prison was no different. Tags and labels made existence easier on the inside. Dinger Bell. It was about the least clever or original sobriquet a bunch of heads could muster up, but then these were criminal minds, and lads at that: they were just babies, some of them, which is why Jeanie was so popular. She was a mother figure to them, from the sixty- and seventy-year-olds who'd never leave here, to the teenagers, arriving pale and terrified, bulging at the seams with regret and the realisation that they'd just made the biggest mistake of their lives.

On Dinger's first morning, thirteen years ago, she'd spotted him at breakfast, as she patrolled the room, chatting to the lads about what they missed: good food, family, football and the like. She'd welcomed the new arrival warmly and they'd chatted for a while about his family and his love of fishing. Dinger, like Jeanie, was a Cumbrian born and bred. As a girl, Jeanie's father had taken her to catch trout from his boat on the lakes which had licenses, and there were plenty of them. Munching on warm ham sandwiches, wrapped in saved greaseproof paper, tied with string, staring into the clear water below, looking for ripples to indicate where the rainbow-coloured fish were feeding, was the overwhelming memory of her childhood, and it was a happy one.

Dinger looked a bit like her father. But that's where the comparison ended. He was about the same height: six foot four, with broad shoulders, a wide jaw and grey hair. Even in his issued grey sweatpants and jumper, he looked smart. Jeanie figured it was a generation thing: they took pride in what they wore and made the best of it, like they were taught by their mothers. She felt safe when he was around. In the midst of the constant male threat that was part of her job, despite all her training and skills, Jack Bell was a source of comfort and security. Nowadays, Jeanie saw the young ones coming in with jeans around their hips, hoods over their faces, and tattoos all over their bodies, and they gave off a different vibe to the men of Jack's era. No matter their crime, there was something about a man who stood tall and proud, wearing cleaned and ironed clothes, that made one think him more innocent. In Category A prisons like Highton, the men weren't allowed to wear their own clothes, because of the potential opportunities to conceal weapons and contraband, but they could still turn themselves out nicely, like Dinger.

A final farewell look lingered between them as they said goodbye.

Jeanie saw something in Jack's eyes and threw him a warning glance. CCTV was everywhere, and they'd kept their feelings for one another hidden from questioning stares. She was warning him not to let his guard down now, at the eleventh hour, upon release, when, finally, they had the chance to meet up on freedom's terms. He got the message and turned away, taking in the view for one last time. He'd seen snippets of the desolate moor from his tiny cell window, and now he took in the whole thing and breathed the free air deeply.

HMP Highton was an institution that not many folk knew about. Of course, if you lived within a five-mile radius of the tiny village, and shopped at the local Co-op, then you'd be familiar with the high-security sprawl of concrete, metal and wire, built on peatland and heath, in between the rivers Esk and Irt. But the vast majority of the millions of visitors who crammed onto the Ravenglass steam railway every year, or hiked the western fells, had no idea. Neither did the tourists flocking to the nearby beaches on the coast of the Irish Sea. It existed in a bubble: sitting proudly on the ancient land that no one in their right mind would want to develop now. It'd be too expensive to dig adequate foundations into the edge of Hallsenna Moor, and, besides, it wouldn't be allowed. The wildlife habitat was protected. Back when the Victorians were looking for remote places to lock up their prisoners and forget about them, no one worried about preserving nature, just shooting, stuffing and framing it. So the prison had been built in 1843 and had stood on the windy, desolate moor ever since, welcoming some of Britain's worst offenders. The adult male population was made up of murderers, rapists, armed robbers and terrorists.

Jeanie loved her job.

She'd miss Jack Bell, though, brightening her shifts, though who knew where their relationship might go now he was free. He was inside for armed burglary; he'd ended up in HMP Highton because the use of weapons had elevated the crime to Category A. Jeanie couldn't imagine Dinger being armed and dangerous, but then most of the stories from the lads were the same: they were all in here because of some misunderstanding. Jeanie wasn't gullible or stupid, she knew the score, it's just that she also saw the boys behind the men, and felt empathy towards them. Even the ones who refused to acknowledge their own humanity, burying it so it didn't make them weak: she still treated them the same. There were the real bad 'uns, of course, the ones who'd committed the worst crimes imaginable; sometimes even Jeanie had trouble picturing some of the offences. But, to her, they'd once been little boys, loved by their mothers and looking up to their papas. Along the way, something had gone wrong.

With Dinger, it was his naïve trust of folk that had got him in to trouble. Until he met Rickie Burton, who hunted for foot soldiers to do his bidding. During his thirteen-year stay at Highton, Dinger had clawed his way up the pecking order and created a comfortable life. He'd quickly worked out who was in charge and made the system work for himself, and he kept out of trouble. Dinger was street clever like that, and Jeanie watched how he observed those who'd put themselves in charge of the wings. Like Rickie. Prison wasn't much different to the outside, really, not when you looked at it: it was an almighty test of survival, like a primary school playground. The only difference was that the physical boundaries were smaller, but the rules were the same. Dinger knew how to play the game, and thus he endured.

Now he was free of all that, and unchained. Free of Rickie.

But the prison population was changing. Some of the old rules were not just being bent but broken entirely, and Jeanie noted a certain stench infiltrating the wings; more attacks on prison officers were being logged, and they'd become more sinister and well planned. The atmosphere of the typical clink had developed into something altogether more violent and disrespectful lately, and Jeanie knew it was because of alcohol and drugs. As well as staff shortages. There simply weren't enough officers to prevent substance abuse and the inevitable violence which followed. The hours of boredom, always a constant component of incarceration, hadn't changed, but the demographics of the penal population had, in conjunction with a decrease in funding. Less money and more bodies, along with brain-altering poisons, all combined to create a more uncertain environment for Jeanie to do her job. Dinger was getting out at the right moment. And that made her happy.

In the fifteen years Jeanie had worked at Highton, she'd been assaulted five times. Each time had been worse than the last. Every time she'd witnessed an assault on a member of staff, the convict had been intoxicated on something. They made hooch by mixing hand gel, fruit, and bread for yeast. It smelled vile but it did the job. Other popular drugs were spice and weed. The wings stank of it. The method of ingestion grew more and more ingenious with every restriction put into place by the governor. E-cigarettes were their latest problem, because they were used to burn any drug the cons could get their hands on, creating an instant heat medium for inhalation. They'd become one of the new currencies inside, alongside spice, replacing cigarettes and shampoo.

She and Dinger had talked more and more about this changing dynamic, and the circumstances outside that were producing it. For every prison is a reflection of the condition of the society beyond the wall. Theirs was not looking good. This was what Dinger's plan was on the outside: getting the message out to those in the community who still gave a damn. He had a message about broken souls who ended up lost and forgotten, with no chance of rehabilitation. For this, Jeanie was proud of the man before her. He was committed to improving himself. He'd begun to write letters, with Jeanie's help, to professors, psychiatrists, educators and politicians, lobbying them about why young men ended up behind bars. And he'd received invitations to meet some of them.

After one final job for Rickie Burton.

The thought cast a shadow over her brow and she looked up at the sky, beyond the huge wall separating Dinger from his freedom.

'Take care, Dinger,' she said. CCTV didn't record conversations, but one couldn't be too careful.

He looked at her and smiled. His eyes were deep brown and he had wrinkles carved into his face, more than he had when she'd first met him thirteen years ago. His arms were still lean and his body hard and bulky, but his shoulders hunched over a little more, and silver hair stuck out above his T-shirt. She wanted to hold him but knew it was out of the question.

Dinger held the belongings he'd handed over thirteen years ago, when he'd been fifty-three years old; they were forgotten and dated now. He chuckled at the size of the mobile phone, and the quality of the photographs he'd carried in his wallet: they were of his daughters who no longer spoke to him, and one of his pet dog, who'd died seven years ago in a kennel. There was a Zippo Venetian silver lighter and he handled it, watched closely by Jeanie. It always amazed her, at this moment of release, how humbling the ritual was. These guys had been on the wrong side of a locked door for so long that when they reclaimed their possessions, if they came in with any, it was a poignant moment.

'Bye, ma'am,' he said, with a cheeky glint in his eye.

She looked up at him and beckoned him to the final set of doors, beyond which he'd start his new life on the outside.

'You'll be all right,' she said gently. 'You've got a lot of important work to do,' she added and she didn't mean the temporary job, set up by the parole agency at a local Co-op in Workington.

He looked at her and she thought he might cry. Inside his huge frame, she knew he was a good man. She'd never been scared of him; she had no reason. She was intimidated by very few of them. There were a handful who she kept her eye on, like a teacher who knows her class, keeping the naughty ones at the front where she can see their hands. Jeanie and her colleagues used an array of strategies to keep the bad sorts at bay, and she had to admit that there were some men who were beyond such tolerance and leniency. Jeanie hated giving up on anyone, but she'd witnessed, during her long years of service, that some of them had suffered such poor starts in life that left them too tough and hardened to turn back, and no amount of kindness or understanding would ever change that. But Dinger wasn't one of them.

His lip twitched and his eyes looked glassy. It was as if he wanted to tell her something. She touched his arm softly and he turned to go. They'd already said everything they needed to, about the hotel, and what they wanted. The guard of the outer perimeter opened the huge iron door and the clanks of the locks turning grated on Jeanie's nerves. He walked towards it and Jeanie turned away from the incessant wind that assaulted her senses. The damn gales never gave up in these parts.

And then he was gone.

Chapter 2

Kelly balanced a piece of toast on her lap as she fed the baby. Lizzie was strapped inside a bouncer, balanced on the kitchen table. Kelly sat in front of her, trying to coax her to take more formula. Her partner, Johnny, was in bed. They took turns feeding in shifts, like a tag team, passing the baton to each other, barely talking, until the day was over, and they had time to assess what had worked well, and what not so well. Johnny invariably took responsibility for the night stretch, so Kelly could continue with her job, as the detective inspector responsible for serious crime in the north Lakes. So far, the arrangement had worked pretty well.

For the baby.

Their lives had changed. Where once they'd made their own decisions about what set the rhythm of their days, now it was this tiny nuclear rocket in a pink bodysuit who called all the shots. Lizzie made gurgling sounds and her little voice went up and down in pitch, as if she were singing. Kelly smiled and joined in, matching the confusion of notes, thrilling her daughter and adding to her masterpiece. Lizzie kicked her legs and bounced up and down, making it harder to feed her.

Kelly's phone buzzed and the toast slipped off her lap onto the floor, jam side down. At least it hadn't stuck to her suit trousers.

'Shit,' Kelly said. She should know by now that phones and babies don't mix.

Lizzie giggled and stopped springing, pausing, waiting for her mother to turn her attention back towards her. It didn't happen fast enough and she batted her hands around, kicking herself up and down in the bouncer. Kelly put her phone down while bending over to retrieve the toast, and the bottle was knocked out of her other hand by Lizzie's enthusiastic foot. It clattered onto the floor and opened, and milk sprayed all over the cupboards. How it missed the two of them was a miracle. Lizzie giggled and sucked her fingers. Kelly exhaled and remained hanging upside down, deflated, eyes closed to the mess. She remained there for a few seconds, desperately trying to muster the energy required to sit back upright.

Between her and Johnny, she knew she had the easier life. She'd ached to get back to her desk at Eden House in Penrith, which is where, nowadays, her life was at its most peaceful. The problems caused by crime to other families were a welcome diversion, no matter how obscenely contradictory that sounded. A case that had a beginning and an end, as well as some evidence in the middle, was infinitely more straightforward than a baby. Their cobbled-together routine was holding for the time being, but each was as stressed as the other, and she knew that Johnny missed the mountains, as well as trying to fit in PTSD clients. He'd worked with veterans for five years now and it was something that gave him peace. An ex-soldier himself, he knew the impact war could have for decades after. They were only now seeing the fallout from the Second Gulf War, almost two decades later.

He'd been with the mountain rescue for eight years now too, and she knew that he longed to get back out there, in the wild expanse of endless peak and lake, doing what he did best: saving people. The trauma therapy work was just as essential to his make-up and she heard him holding Zoom calls late at night, talking veterans out of suicide. They were both exhausted.

But Lizzie was an entirely different mission. Johnny wasn't a first-time father, but he'd missed much of Josie's early life, being away on army operations for chunks of it. However, it also meant that he wasn't coming into this blind, like Kelly. It had been pointed out to her, by her own father, that she could be too hard on herself at times, and that babies didn't come packaged with user manuals. But she couldn't help feeling overwhelmed sometimes.

It was almost nine a.m. and time for Kelly to hand over. Sure enough, she heard Johnny's alarm go off upstairs and felt a flood of relief that she'd be able to spend her day with predictable adults, even if they were poring over horrible crimes, rather than in the company of a mercurial two-month-old, sophisticated in the art of chaos. She heard Johnny go into the bathroom and wash quickly and she looked up at Lizzie and slowly got to her feet, thankful she didn't have to change. It was always risky, the decision to shower and dress before breakfast rather than after it. She gave Lizzie a teddy bear and approached the mirror in the hallway, checking her long auburn hair for detritus. It was clear and she tied it up. The skin around her bright green eyes looked tired and dark. She applied some lip gloss and rubbed a bit of blush on her cheeks. At forty, she was considered an older mother. And sometimes she felt it. These days, wherever she was, she noticed every young twenty-something pushing a pram, and envied their energy. She went back to the kitchen to wipe up the milk.

'Who's coming?' she said excitedly to her daughter. Lizzie kicked so hard that Kelly thought she might fall off the table. The simple sheer delight of the child was something that made Kelly equally full of maternal wonder, but melancholy at the same time. Her job involved interviewing plenty of children who had never known how it felt to be the object of parental tenderness. She picked up the bouncer, Lizzie and all, smiling at her, and placed her on the kitchen floor, while she cleaned up the mess. She still had time, and would feel bad for Johnny if he had to start his day mopping up milk.

The relatively smooth morning routine hadn't been properly tested yet by a challenging case at work; Kelly had been able to maintain her nine-thirty starts. And so, usually, she handed over a clean baby, and one which was fed, happy and ready for a doze. At first it was hard to stomach, arriving at Eden House last, when the whole of her team was already assembled, but nobody grumbled. In fact, Kelly reckoned they rather liked it. Giving up a little power had been liberating, and she thought she was altogether more relaxed as a result. Lately, though, in the two weeks she'd been back at work since her maternity leave had ended, Kelly had noticed a few resentful remarks coming from Johnny.

She'd put them down to tiredness, and missing his job in the mountains.

Weekends were trickier. They both wanted to exercise, and Kelly was particularly keen to regain her strength and looked forward to feeling fit again. But they were lucky if just one of them found the time, let alone the energy, to get out even for a short run.

'Lizzie!' A female voice carried down the stairs and the baby kicked ferociously. Josie, Johnny's daughter from his only marriage, had lived with them since moving out of her mother's house four years ago, and she was almost seventeen years old now. Every morning, without fail, Josie sang out to Lizzie and played with her whenever she could, in between college lessons and friends. Josie had spent her whole summer either fussing over Kelly's pregnancy, or doting on the baby after her August arrival. Her return to college had been a wrench. It had also been tough not having her around to help with mundane chores. Kelly had already spoken with Johnny about getting some paid assistance so he could go back to work. They both thought it would ease things. But Lizzie was still so young, and they were wary of childminders. What they really wanted was a nanny.

Lizzie's eyes widened at the sound of Josie's voice, and Kelly laughed. Her feet started to bounce the chair up and down again.

'Who is it?' Kelly asked.

Josie appeared and surveyed the disorder.

'Little accident? If you need to go, I'll clear up,' Josie said. Kelly smiled and nodded, looking at the milk-sodden tissues in her hand.

'I was trying to read my phone and I dropped my toast. I think I've got most of it.'

'Have you got time to make some more?' Josie asked.

Kelly shook her head, looking at her watch. Without saying anything, Josie went to the fridge, took out some packets and threw together a sandwich in record time, wrapping it quickly in tinfoil.

'Here, take this,' she said.

Kelly took it gratefully. Josie kissed Lizzie and picked up her bottle, putting the lid back on tightly. She sat on the floor next to the bouncer, holding the bottle to Lizzie's mouth. The baby sucked peacefully.

Kelly heard Johnny on the stairs and popped her sandwich into her bag. He came into the kitchen smelling fresh and beaming at his small family. He kissed Kelly first.

'Morning, gorgeous. Ready? Have you got some food?' he asked.

'Thanks to Josie – she saved me, as always,' Kelly said. Below them, Lizzie had begun arching her back again and squealing at the sight of her father. Johnny knelt down and unfastened his daughter's buckles, and threw her in the air.

'Watch it, she's just eaten,' Josie said. Kelly knew that it was time to leave them to it. The whole rough and tumble on a full stomach debate didn't need her input. Kelly watched the three of them together, and the stress of spilt milk, early mornings and disturbed sleep began to fade.

It had been hard to admit that when she wasn't on shift at home, she wasn't needed, and the wheels wouldn't fall off. It was a bit like being the senior investigating officer for north Cumbria. Inquiries didn't stop because the boss had gone home for a well-needed kip for a few hours. It was the same with Lizzie. With Johnny and Josie at the helm, Lizzie was in good hands. Accepting that, as a mother, she didn't need to be there all the time, had been challenging at first. The societal pressure to be all things to everyone as a woman – homemaker, lover, provider, sister, daughter, and now, mother – was a matter of balance; of ego especially. Eight weeks in and it was becoming easier to manage, though it was still a challenge.

Johnny whizzed Lizzie around and plonked her on his hip to say goodbye.

'What's on the agenda today?' Kelly asked.

'A bracing hike up Blencathra. The weather is amazing. I'm meeting Tom Gorman and we'll go up there together.'

'Is that too high for her?' Kelly asked. Blencathra was around 3,000 feet but a safe hike. She knew as she said it that she shouldn't interfere. Johnny looked at her oddly.

'Sorry, I'm not getting involved. I'm sure it will be great. Will you use the harness?' Kelly asked.

The look again.

'Sorry! I'll go now. Wait, Tom? Do I know him?' Johnny knew a lot of people.

'I told you about him, he's ex-army. Good soldier. He's recovering from PTSD up here in the Lakes.' He was irritable and it was her fault.

Kelly recalled the conversation about Johnny's old colleague. They had yet to meet, what with the birth and Lizzie taking over. He sounded like a nice guy. She was relieved that she remembered him, as it was more likely these days that she'd forget names and places that didn't make her urgent list. She found that simple information, such as remembering her purse or where the iron was kept, had slipped down the pecking order behind the needs of the baby. It was only at work where she seemed to be able to count on her memory bank. At home, her mind turned to mush and she forgot the simplest things. It was on the tip of her tongue to suggest that her daughter might not be safe around an ex-soldier suffering with PTSD, but she knew it would make matters worse. Johnny wasn't stupid. She let it go.

'Have a good day,' Josie said, looking awkwardly between her father and Kelly.

Kelly smiled and left the kitchen, reminding herself not to be so worrisome. She decided not to take a jacket, as the autumn sun had been shining through the windows all morning and the forecast said it was likely to stay that way.

She shouted a final goodbye and shut the door behind her. On a fine October day like today, the backroad to work, along the B5320, was her preferred choice. It snaked across country from Pooley Bridge, through Sockbridge, and on to the south edge of Penrith. Autumn in the Lake District was spectacular and she stole glances at the ever-changing leaves as she drove. The different hues of orange, brown and red framed the surrounding lakes and mountains like a cosy canvas. The bronzes and coppers contrasted with the rich deep blues and greys of water and rock, and the lack of tourists created a pause in time, a perfectly serene landscape. Artists flocked here all year round, and it wasn't difficult to understand why. If Kelly could choose the perfect time of year to launch herself back into fitness, it would be this one. October was midway through and the sun was still high enough in the sky to get a bit of heat from its rays when it poked through low-lying clouds. It calmed her woes.

She and Johnny were transitioning through a new phase in their lives, that was all. Kelly was just jealous that Lizzie's first long serious hill climb was going to be without her. But she couldn't have it all ways. It was her choice to carry on working. She didn't have to. Johnny's pension, as well as hers, should she wish to take it early, was more than enough to live on. The cost of living in the Lake District was relatively low, compared to other places in the UK. House prices were modest, unless you desired a pad overlooking a lake, and you didn't have to spend tons of cash on entertainment: a walk cost nothing.

The sun was low in the east still and shone directly into her eyes. She lowered the visor as she left Pooley

Bridge, past the steady queues already building up at the steamer quayside. The bridge had been renovated this year and as a result, the steamer hadn't been loading at this end of the lake. It had still chuffed its way between Glenridding and Howtown, and Kelly had missed it. The village had needed a new bridge since the destruction of the old eighteenth-century stone structure during Storm Desmond in 2015. Since then, a temporary metal monstrosity had plugged the gap. But the new construction was beautiful. It followed the lines of the original, with its graceful arches and lines, built out of eighty tonnes of stainless steel. It was a marvel. Kelly and her family had been some of the first to walk over it during the opening ceremony.

Today, she headed the other way, away from the lakes and fells, which faded in the distance behind her. She hummed along to the radio and felt her body unwind. The irony of her using her job to relax wasn't lost on her, but it had come as a shock to find that as much as she loved her daughter, she also yearned for the simplicity of work. Kelly had had no idea that the interrupted sleep, the incessant feeding, the noise of a crying infant in the night, and her own broken body would have such a profound effect on the way she viewed her job – an occupation that had her dealing with drunks, killers, wife beaters, child abusers and rapists. It wasn't that she *preferred* the company of nasty bastards, just that it was a welcome break.

Chapter 3

'I don't want any bullshit answers or fancy pleading, Dinger. I'm just here to break your arms,' the man said. 'I'll put a bolt through your knees too, if you last long enough.'

'I haven't done anything,' Dinger mumbled from behind the material filling his mouth.

'It doesn't matter. If you fancy yourself as some saviour of young lads – or what you really want to do is get them alone to have your way with them – I don't much care. What I do care about is what happens to my dad's money, Dinger. Because you know what? It's going to be mine one day. Now, be quiet, I'm trying to concentrate.'

Jack's breath was heavy and the pain caused him to shake. He stared at the bolt gun in the man's hands and shook his head ferociously. He was naked and bound to a chair and he'd checked the restraints: they were bloody good, and doing their job – he could barely move. The cloth in his mouth was stuffed in tight and it prevented him getting full breaths; he felt slightly dizzy. In the man's other hand he held a small knife, and he jabbed it superficially into Jack's chest. It stung like hell.

He'd known pain before, plenty of it. There was the time he'd got his nose broken by a guy in prison who was the size of a house. They called him the Shed. It had been a case of mistaken identity. The Friday consignment of canteen had been delivered but the Shed's vapes weren't in there. This caused him to kick off and blame somebody. Dinger had been sat next to him at slop time – that's what they called their dinner, on account of it being so appalling. Every item on their trays merged into one: the over-boiled peas, the bits of stuff fried in breadcrumbs with no sign of a particle of salt, along with the insipid gravy, which was like dog shite, just without the aroma. That's why Friday canteen was so important. It was the day when parcels arrived from the outside, with treats for the inside. Most of the lads used money sent by family, or the little they earned inside doing jobs, to order their favourite things: chocolate, cigarettes, vapes, porn and shampoo. Dinger maintained a constant supply of Himalayan rock salt to flavour his food. It was more important to him than toilet roll.

The prison officers understood what it meant to fuck with someone's canteen and it was no trivial matter. The lads depended on the bags of stuff they waited for, week in, week out. Some of the blokes rarely got canteen delivered, because they had no family to send it. Poor bastards. Dinger shared his around.

The man twisted the knife and Dinger gasped. He didn't want to make a sound and reveal weakness, but he couldn't help it. The pain was seeping into his brain and making it ache. A thousand prickles of searing heat tormented him as the blade went deeper, and tore his skin apart. Dinger had seen all sorts of home-made weapons inside. Now, the man took out a new one and held it up to Dinger's face, smiling. This one was a thicker blade, a type of hunting knife. Dinger used something similar to gut fish. The guy lowered it and stuck it into Dinger's hip. Dinger closed his eyes and groaned.

'What? You wanna say something?'

Dinger nodded. They were inside an empty garage in his home town of Workington. He knew that much, but he didn't know if anyone could hear him outside. Was it worth screaming? Dinger had been out of the slammer for two whole days before a car had pulled up beside him last night and knocked him clean over. He'd been staggering home from the pub, where he'd entertained some new pals about his time inside. There were three hefty blokes in the vehicle, including the driver, who he could see through bleary eyes, and it took all of them to bundle him in to the back seat, and he'd ended up here. But now only one was left, and Dinger had come to the speedy conclusion that it was this man's job to extract information and torture him. The others were just muscle to get him to where he needed to be. Not everyone had the stomach for torture, but this bloke enjoyed it, Dinger knew that much. The problem was that Dinger didn't know what he wanted. The job for Rickie had gone to plan. He hadn't stolen from him. He could think of nothing he'd done to double-cross the guy. Rickie was also his friend.

The larger hunting blade was placed near his eye.

'Come on then, lad, tell me what you know.'

Dinger winced at the man's terminology, because he appeared twenty or thirty years his junior. Dinger could tell that he loved the authority that he exerted over his victim. Which led him to also believe that he wasn't going to get out of this alive, even if he told the man everything he knew. The man had mentioned his father's money, but that didn't make sense to Dinger either; he'd never stolen from a pal.

It only left one explanation. Somebody had double-crossed him, and there was only one candidate: Dean.

Sweat trickled down his face and he blinked fiercely. His breath came furiously, and his chest heaved up and down as the gag was removed. Faces and conversations whirred around in his head. He knew a lot, for sure, about a lot of people, but he'd never been a grass. He had enough information inside his skull to put several people behind bars for many lifetimes, if they weren't already there doing time at Her Majesty's pleasure.

'I made the drop like I was told. It all went smoothly, I swear, you've made a mistake. You've got the wrong man, just check, you'll see,' he begged. Charity wasn't something Dinger was used to asking for, but it seemed his last chance. His legs were going numb. His dodgy hip ached like buggery and he found little relief in the small breaks in between the agony of torture. Where was the blade going next? Not his eye? What was it that the Shed told him? They'd become firm pals after the canteen incident. It turned out that some big shot on another wing had commandeered several canteens that day. He thought he'd planned the whole thing meticulously, bribing guards and porters, making sure that at least twenty bags went missing and ended up in his cell. He'd soon been exposed, and the Shed simply waited for the right moment to corner him in the mess hall. The tray snapped clean in half when the Shed bashed it against a gurney full of trays of pissy gravy. The sharp edge was lethal and in the blink of an eye, the Shed had sliced the guy's face from temple to chin. Blood gushed everywhere, and cons surrounded the warring duo, shouting 'Blood! Blood! Blood!' It had been the highlight of the day – of the week, in fact. Unfortunately for the fella, the CCTV camera had been covered by a hoodie.

'*Breathe and glare*,' is what the Shed had told him. It was his worldly advice for what to do when faced with abominable pain, and the Shed had suffered his share of that. He wore the scars to prove it. A long ugly wound just under his eye and the remnants of half an ear were just the ones most visible.

The man sat back, as if to admire his work, and Dinger looked at him in panic. In that moment he realised that the man before him wasn't interested in what was right, just his orders – and he was enjoying what he was doing. Sure, it might be that he had the wrong man, but he'd started now, so he was going to finish.

Dinger went to shout, but the guy's fist silenced him.

He didn't much feel like breathing and glaring right now, and he reckoned the Shed wouldn't either. Every fibre of Dinger's body gnawed away at him and let him down. His muscles, honed by years of press-ups and pull-ups inside his cell, weren't going to save him now. His strength was waning. He'd witnessed horrific violence inside prison walls, where men were reduced to babies during bouts of brutality designed to do just that. Relationships were forged through pain and its incumbent followers. But then the softness of the woman he'd come to love washed over him and he saw Jeanie's face. They'd never have the life together they'd planned. He struggled, but felt the vitality leak from his body. Jeanie.

A single tear rolled down his cheek as he contemplated surviving this long, in one of the toughest prisons in the country, only to wither away in silent terror, days after release. Each new opening of his skin rendered him lifeless and inhuman: something he'd fought so doggedly for inside prison. The irony was what hurt the most. All he could do was watch as his body yielded to the wounds.

He tried to concentrate on the only person who might wish him such an unhappy end, and what he'd done to deserve it, but then he gave up. What was the point? An answer wouldn't change his fate.

'Don't be fooled, Dinger, it's definitely you I'm to be working on today. And tomorrow perhaps too. If you last that long. I do so hope that's the case, otherwise I wouldn't enjoy my job so much, would I? What'll it be? Are you a pussy? That's not what I heard. I heard you'd last for days.'

Dinger gulped. He had no idea how long he'd be able to put up with the physical suffering. He guessed it might be a long time; longer than the average law-abiding civilian.

He closed his eyes.

'Don't do that,' the man said. 'I was just getting to them.'

Dinger flinched and squirmed as the blade sank into his left eyelid.

Chapter 4

Eden House sat pompously on top of a sloping hill in the centre of Penrith. It was made of local red sandstone, quarried in the early eighteenth century. The structure was originally a Victorian workhouse, and had been converted into a police station in the nineteenth century, when it was renovated and extended. Now the whole of the policing for the northern Lakes was centralised here, and Kelly was in charge of the serious crime investigation team. In the south it was Barrow-in-Furness that took on the role, and similarly, the station there was an early Victorian pile of splendour.

There was no such magnificence on the inside, and Kelly drove around the back into one of the parking bays. Parking was a nightmare in town and so the staff was thankful to have an off-road space so close to the centre. Penrith was built on a series of hills, like Rome but less grand. A lot of the roads were cobbled and it gave an air of quaintness to it, which came in handy when they were touting for summer cash from tourists. There was a handful of rateable pubs and some lovely cafes selling interesting food. But the standard fare in town was pasties and fish and chips. During her pregnancy, Kelly had filled her face with carb-loaded treats. She couldn't get enough of them. Her cravings had all been related to bread or potatoes in some way and she worried at times, asking

Johnny if it was normal. Her team had never witnessed her tucking into crap before.

'Of course it's normal!' Johnny insisted. 'You need the energy because there's something growing inside you, using at all up without your permission.' It was a reassuringly gentle way to put it.

Weaning herself off the carbs had been hell over the last few weeks and she could smell the bakery down the road. At lunchtime, she'd pick up the drifting aroma of the chippy, open for the afternoon. It was torture. Gradually, with sheer stubbornness and willpower, she'd begun to eat more as she had before, and the pounds had begun to fall away. That and work, which helped. She was the one who insisted on going out to do house visits when they needed doing. It was way below her rank as detective inspector, and she should task a detective sergeant or constable with it, but sitting in the office all day would turn her stir-crazy.

Kelly checked her watch again; she just had time to take the stairs rather than the lift. It wasn't as if she'd get disciplined if she was late to her own briefing. She locked her car and checked her bag, realising that one of Lizzie's teddies was in there, left from a walk to the pub at the weekend. She'd realised that taking a baby out in to a social situation required some prior planning and preparation. Pre-empting mood-swings hunger, and taking into account changing facilities and entertainment, was key. She found that Johnny's army background came in handy at these times. He loaded everything effortlessly into a backpack and slung it over his shoulder, except this time the teddy had gone into hers. She smiled: never mind, she could sit it on her desk for the day.

The lower floors of Eden House were taken up by admin staff, as well as uniforms dealing with walk-ins and overnight custody. Kelly walked through the main entrance and greeted the staff at the front desk. She heard shouting from downstairs, which is where the cells were, and the female officer at the desk informed her they'd had a drunk in overnight, and he'd now woken up. If he wasn't careful they were going to charge him with affray, instead of just letting him go home to cool off and sober up.

'Good luck,' Kelly said. She walked past other offices and saw people sat at desks, busy behind computers. There wasn't much talking going on. A lot of police work was done in silence: writing reports, checking them or updating files. Even emails took up vast chunks of time, as everything had to be formally recorded and watertight, in case some aspect of a situation that had been documented here in Penrith was ever challenged. Other reports were stored here from smaller stations, which were no longer open to the public. Most stations around the Lake District were staffed solely for the purpose of being present, rather than patrolling or interacting with the community. All calls went to central pods and remote officers sat behind desks, like they did at Eden House, looking after their communities from behind walls. Of course, squad cars still patrolled, and officers on foot could often be spotted walking about Penrith, but, for the main part, police work was done like many other jobs now: online. Unless a visit was necessary, and that's where Kelly came in. It was the job of her team to open an inquiry when needed, and to look into local crimes committed on her patch. Occasionally, north and south Cumbria worked together, and they did so happily.

The mood upstairs in her own office, which was open plan except her room, was casual and relaxed. They had no major cases active at the moment, and so it was an opportunity to catch up on paperwork and look into some of the more trivial local offences, such as theft, minor assaults and drugs. Narcotics was something that had become more and more prevalent during Kelly's career, and now it was downright depressing. Drugs took up the majority of their time; if it wasn't the buying and selling of the substances themselves, it was that the perpetrator of a crime was high on something before committing it. People did stupid shit on drugs that they never would sober.

Kelly greeted her waiting team.

'How's Lizzie, today, boss?' Rob asked. DC Rob Shawcross had returned from paternity leave just as Kelly went on maternity leave, and it was good to be in his company again. She'd missed them all.

'Cheeky,' she replied. It was standard that her team was more interested in her daughter than they were in her. She'd got over it. Rob had a little boy of his own who would turn one in the new year. Rob and DS Kate Umshaw were Kelly's go-to agony aunts for trivial baby inquiries about milk formula and sleep routines. Kate was a little rusty on those things, as her girls were all but grown up, but Rob was bang up to date.

'How did the race go, Emma?' Kelly asked DC Emma Hide, a keen young officer whose pastime was racing hundreds of miles up and down fells. Kelly didn't judge: before Lizzie, she and Johnny had considered all sorts of extreme races. There was something about having the mountains just outside the door that made you want to run up them.

'Go on, Emma, tell them,' said DS Dan Houghton, their newest addition. He'd begun working with the team earlier in the year. He was a broad Glaswegian with a

27

gruff voice that belied a warm compassion. He was deeply intelligent and perceptive.

'What?' asked Kelly.

Emma looked shy.

'She was the first woman home, out of more than two hundred,' Dan spoke for her. Kelly noticed a frisson of appreciation between the two, but moved on. Dan was married, but that was none of her business.

'Jesus! Emma, that's amazing. And now I can drink I insist we go and celebrate. What about this Friday, everyone? A quickie at The Bell after work?'

The general murmured consensus was affirmative, and it gave them something to look forward to.

'What was it like?' Kelly asked, wanting more information. Emma had entered the October Scree Challenge, which was a race over the screes of the Lake District. Over two days, camping in between, participants covered fifty miles and a total of 5,000 feet elevation. It attracted more male applicants than female, and around 700 in total. Kelly felt a burning desire to get out and train for something awe-inspiring herself, but she feared that those days were gone for now. She looked at Emma, with her fresh face and tight skin; Kelly felt tired already.

'It was bloody hard, and the weather was proper shit,' Emma said.

'You're tough, and I bet you coped,' Kelly said. Emma had been training for months, not touching a single drop of booze and managing her calorie intake. It was a favourite source of conversation in the office: what Emma was eating, especially how much meat she seemed to put away, and if she might have a small glass of wine at the pub when they made it there occasionally after a quiet day. She certainly didn't eat the stodgy carbs favoured by pregnant women.

'Right, let's get going, anything overnight I need to know about?' Kelly asked. Every morning they gathered to assess what jobs needed prioritising. On a Monday, it was usually all the drunken-fuelled antics of the weekend, which sometimes turned into extremely violent crime, but by midweek, which it was now, it was fairly quiet.

DS Kate Umshaw arrived late, breathing apologies. Kate had three grown-up teenagers, all girls, and she was something of an oracle for Kelly. She'd confided in Kate early in her pregnancy, when no one else knew about it, and she held regular check-ins with her in her office at work, which had become a bit of a regular routine. They'd close the door, put work aside and Kelly would offload. Kate, ever patient, would always have a solution, or at least a suggestion. She'd become a rock for Kelly. They'd spent more time together out of work too, with Kate driving them to Manchester to shop for baby clothes, amongst other things. Kelly smiled at her.

'No worries,' Kelly assured her. 'I don't think you've missed anything crucial, apart from Emma winning the women's scree race.'

'Oh my God!' Kate hugged her younger colleague. 'Blimey! You put us all to shame. On that note, I brought in some cake.'

There was a collective groan, but secretly they all loved Kate's cake, and it wouldn't last long with Rob and Dan picking at it for the rest of the day.

'Good time?' Kate asked.

'Twenty-one hours, give or take a few minutes – my watch stopped working,' Emma replied.

'Bloody hell, I'd give up after the first mile. Well done you, Emma,' Kate said.

Kelly restarted the briefing and got through it quickly; there was little new of note to report, and the conversation turned to their most recent case, which was a local suicide. The man had been working from home, on MS Teams, and had exited a meeting with twelve colleagues. Only he hadn't switched off his camera, and was still live. His aghast co-workers had shouted to warn him as he proceeded to get a box of tissues out of his drawer and google a porn channel. Some had turned their computers off in horror, others had exited the meeting or closed the programme, while others had tried to phone him. Some watched, glued inexplicably to their screens, hands over mouths, as he pleasured himself. Their cries of panic had gone unheard and it was only a text, seen after the event, that informed the man that he'd been live the whole time. He'd left his desk, gone upstairs and hung himself. His wife had wanted a full investigation into how MS Teams could be held accountable for manslaughter. They were expecting to hear from the CPS to see if the wife had a case for them to investigate.

'Dropped,' Kate said.

'Poor bloke,' Kelly said. It was a tragic case. According to his GP, the man had suffered from general depression for years, and this incident had simply tipped him over the edge. After his death, the wife discovered that he was also in line to lose his job. They were mortgaged to the hilt and faced ruin. At least she'd get a handsome insurance payout now, though even that was being disputed because it was unclear if his policy covered suicide.

Apart from that calamity, it was a relatively quiet period at Eden House, and for that they were grateful. There'd been some notable unrest inside Highton prison, over near Seascale. The prison population teetered around nine hundred to a thousand, but it was built for six hundred. Conditions were appalling and Kelly regularly checked in with the police liaison officer at the prison. Discipline was a prison affair, but they had plenty of suspects on remand there, as well as sentences coming to an end: convicts who might cause them a headache on the outside. Several of the prison officers were ex-military and Johnny knew a couple of them. Kelly knew from conversations he'd had with them that overcrowding, disorder and threats of violence were a lot worse than the governor let on. Legislation was due to be debated in Parliament later this month, which could potentially lighten the load. But it was highly unlikely to be passed. The general public didn't like the idea of reform, just punishment, and Kelly had little hope that funding to improve the environment inside would be forthcoming. Why spend money on criminals?

'I'm briefing the chief constable at ten,' Kelly moved on.

'Charming man,' Kate said. What she really meant was that the new chief constable, Andrew Harris, appointed this year, was alarmingly attractive. He was also a decent bloke, something they all found refreshing, compared to some superiors they'd had in the past. Andrew Harris was in charge of the whole of the Cumbria Constabulary and had vowed to make changes. They'd heard it all before, and anything likely to make a difference to their effectiveness cost money, lots of it, so the seriousness of his promise lacked guts. Instead, they hoped to be pleasantly surprised. One thing was certain: Harris valued Kelly Porter's opinion, and had invited her to HQ to discuss it several times.

'Good, thanks everybody,' Kelly finished up. Jobs were dished out for the day and everyone moved back to their desk spaces and got to work. There were no site visits or interviews today, though a phone call from Barrow had put them on alert about a man who'd been reported missing this morning. All units in the county had been notified to look out for him. His last known location was Seascale beach, where he'd been with his girlfriend's dog. The dog had been found wandering around the sand dunes, whining for its carer, a man called Dean Kirby. Technically, Seascale was kind of in between north and south Cumbria, but the man was a Barrovian, and quite a distance from home just to walk a dog. He'd been reported missing by his girlfriend, who saw an appeal for the owner of the dog on Facebook.

The team dispersed and went back to their various tasks for the day, and a hush fell on the office once more. Kelly went to the coffee machine and took a cup to her private office and sat down to catch up on emails. The window was open and she heard the traffic below in the street. If she strained her neck and sat up in her chair, she could see the castle ruin. She did so when she was idling for a distraction, which, amongst mountains of paperwork, was often.

When she was satisfied that she'd sifted through the most important communications in her diary for the morning, Kelly called to Kate through her open office door. She never liked being shut away, as if she were some aloof boss; she preferred being accessible, and everybody knew they could walk into her office anytime. If her door was closed then it was a different matter entirely. But it rarely was. Kate poked her head around the door.

'I'm done here, I'm off to Carleton Hall soon,' Kelly said to her deputy.

'Fancy some company?' Kate asked.

'Why not? If you like. Purely professional, of course?' Kelly smiled.

'Of course, I have a vested interest in the future policing of this county, with three grown-up daughters to worry about,' Kate added. She turned to leave. 'Come and get me when you're ready to head out?'

'Will do,' Kelly said, and smiled to herself as she rooted for her bag under her desk. Chatting to Kate in the car might be just what she needed. As she bent over, her stomach felt bulky above her skirt and she wondered if she'd ever get back into shape. The pregnancy had left her hair weak and dull, her once honey-coloured waves lacked bounce and shine, and her nails were brittle. Lizzie had literally sucked the life out of her. She'd bought new clothes to return to work, but two months off had caused her to become used to joggers and vest tops. The summer had been glorious, and one to remember in the Lakes. Tourists had flocked to the beaches, lakes and fells and she'd eaten a lot of ice cream. Summers like that were usually spent hiking, swimming and taking the *Wendy* out on Derwent Water, but not this year.

A tiny seed of doubt entered her head, and it concerned Johnny. A vision of them, this time last year, watching the stars above Ullswater as the *Wendy* bobbed up and down on the lake, taunted her. They'd just made love. He was the Johnny she'd fallen in love with. Since the birth of their daughter, though, he seemed emotionally absent in small ways that she couldn't put her finger on. He was a different man to the one seventeen years ago, who shortly after the birth of Josie, had left his first wife to go on operations to Iraq. That time, he'd been away for nine months and shortly after, his marriage fell apart. His own PTSD, as well as her numerous affairs, saw to that.

But was he fully healed?

Chapter 5

The new chief constable had arrived in post like a whirl-wind. The first thing he set about doing was requesting accounts on all aspects of crime: its investigation, the gathering of CPS data, and its evaluation, which had sent section chiefs like Kelly into a flat spin. She hadn't had to justify her position in such a manner since she'd worked in the Met. Their first meeting had been nerve-wracking, but she'd instantly warmed to the man. He'd transferred from Manchester – after a messy divorce, or so the gossip alleged – and the common ground between them of having worked crime in a large metropolitan area encouraged an instant connection. He was quick-witted and didn't bullshit.

Now she looked forward to their meetings. She closed her computer and went to find Kate, who was busy applying lipstick. Kelly raised her eyebrows, and Kate shrugged. She was an attractive woman, in Kelly's opinion, and had been stuck in an unhappy marriage for years. Kelly guessed Kate put up with it because of the girls, but Kelly knew from experience that couples who remained together simply for the kids could do even more damage than if they separated. More recently, something had finally broken and Kate's husband had moved out to trial a separation. Kelly suspected he wouldn't be welcome back. Kate was free to appreciate any man she chose. Besides, if Kelly thought that Kate wouldn't pay attention or add value in a professional capacity just because she fancied the bloke, then she wouldn't be taking her. Let her have her bit of flirty fun, she thought. She had to admit, Andrew Harris was good company.

They took the stairs and found Kelly's car in the car park to the rear. From the hill, they could see the ruined Penrith Castle that Kelly saw from her window, and they saw tourists queuing to get inside to look around. The unseasonably warm weather had prolonged the holiday period, to the delight of shop owners and taxi firms, but Penrith was essentially a working town, and Kelly thought about her mother again. Wendy had lived all her life in the small town bordering the national park before her untimely death to cancer. What would she make of Lizzie? She'd no doubt be pushing her around in her pram all day long, should she have been given half the chance. Kelly smiled to herself. Wendy would have made an amazing grandmother.

'That's a mother's smile,' Kate said as she got into the passenger seat. Kelly climbed into the driver's seat and stared at her colleague.

'What?' Kelly asked.

'It's like walking around with a secret, isn't it? I remember, even though mine are now almost adults. You never forget, you know.'

'I don't want her to grow up,' Kelly said.

'I think "grow up" is slightly over-egging it. *Survival* is a fairer goalpost. Aim low and surprise yourself, that's what I say. Wait till she's two, *then* you'll want her to grow up,' Kate said. She winked. Kate often did this: dropped golden nuggets of droll wisdom into a conversation to bring Kelly back down to earth.

'You fill me with maternal inspiration, Kate,' Kelly said. She started the car.

'Oh, I do hope not.'

They drove out of town and the landscape turned from sandstone listed buildings, hotels and council estates to leafy suburbs. Carleton Hall nestled in between the trees, dignified and silent. It was originally built in the early eighteenth century, with restorations culminating in the 1950s with it being partially rebuilt. Its listed status meant that many of the original features were still present, and its pretty sash windows added to the character of the place. It was a pleasing place to work, near the gorgeous Eamont Bridge, another listed Cumbrian monument, dating back to the fifteenth century. The outside was well looked after, with flower planters and tended gardens. They parked to the rear.

Their neck tags allowed them to pass security and they made their way to the office of the new chief constable. Increased rates of people-trafficking in the provinces had put Cumbria back on the crime map, as had a huge emerging drug problem that didn't seem to want to go away. Barrow-in-Furness was the new hotspot for dealers and factories and the police struggled with the work-load. They had help from neighbouring boroughs such as Manchester and Lancaster, but it still wasn't enough. Criminals have always been good at staying one step ahead of the cops, and lately, moving drugs, sex workers and hard cash to the sleepy villages of the Lake District had become a thing. It was always a consideration underlying any conversation about increased funding, and there was a balance to be struck with all the normal functions of policing too.

Chief Constable Harris wanted to know what Kelly's plan was. The problem was that without extra resources and funding, the job was impossible. Kelly didn't shy away from telling harsh truths – her ego wasn't her sole priority, like it was with some other officers desperate to win medals. A small department of detectives trying to battle the problems facing a county in flux was never going to be enough. They didn't have their own drugs squad, they didn't have enough helicopters, they didn't have a dog squad and neither did they have adequate officers spread significantly enough on the ground. She lacked boots, pure and simple.

Add to that the lingering spectre of burnout hiding in the shadows behind every police officer in the country, due to staff sickness, abuse from the public and, of course, the relatively hostile terrain of the Lake District to contend with, and they faced a constabulary on the brink. And they weren't the only ones. Cumbria was low on the pecking order. The big cities took priority.

So, Kelly figured, it was her job to convince Chief Constable Harris that she could make it work: she could put square pegs into round holes. No matter what happened, she'd do her best, and that's all he could ask. He was a reasonable man, and not political, which was a bonus. Any chief constable who tried to woo the public with false promises and white lies didn't help the constabulary in the long run. Knife crime had doubled since last year, the effects of synthetic chemical drugs on young offenders was horrifying, and the county's stats on crime were all up.

The chief constable's secretary asked them to take a seat, but it wasn't long before he came out to greet them, shaking their hands and asking if they'd like coffee.

Andrew Harris was in full uniform, except his hat, and it always struck Kelly how attractive it was seeing a man in uniform. She'd never had the pleasure of seeing Johnny in his, only in photographs. Working in plain clothes, as detectives did, she missed the fleeting charm. Andrew had the air of an old-fashioned copper, tall and commanding, but Kelly also knew him to be fair and gracious, a rare combination.

They both accepted and followed him into his office. Inside, with the door closed behind them, he swung his chair in front of his desk and plonked himself down. He was a large man, six foot or so, and broad; a bit like Rob and Dan, but twenty years older. His face was worn by the marks of experience and he had a deep glare; Kelly wagered he had seen a few nasty situations in his time. He'd moved back to Cumbria because it was his original home: they had that in common.

'Nice to see you again, ladies. Shall we get straight to business? I've read the whole of your report, Kelly, and it's candid, I give you that. You don't pull punches, do you? But that's a commendable thing when we face unprecedented times. There's no more money coming, I can tell you that. And no more boots on the ground. Our recruiting levels are at an all-time low. No one wants to be a copper any more, too busy wanting to get on celebrity reality shows, no doubt.'

'Safer, sir,' Kate said. He nodded, agreeing with her.

'Attacks on officers have risen sharply in the last five years, usually drunken yobs on a Saturday night, but recently more sinister. Why is it always drugs?' he asked wistfully. 'It's a scourge, and I'm determined to push into schools and colleges and get kids talking about the alternatives. Banging them up when it's too late is nonsense, we need to be motivating them sooner.'

'I agree, sir, the reoffending stats make for dismal reading, but when Young Offender Institutions are so overcrowded that seventeen-year-olds are being sent – albeit temporarily – to places like Highton, we're losing the battle,' Kelly said.

'Damn right. Here's our coffee.'

'Sir, can I make a suggestion?' Kelly asked.

'Sure, go ahead while Kate and I tuck into those chocolate biscuits.'

Kelly had made the mistake of telling him, last time she was here, that she was on a post-baby diet. She tried not to dwell on not being offered a biscuit. Kate tucked in. Kelly turned the conversation back to work.

'Can't we argue for lesser sentencing? Highton is already wildly overcrowded. We're the only nation in Europe who hands out such hefty sentences for first-time offenders for what might be considered rehabilitative crimes, related to childhood trauma and lack of good luck, to put it bluntly. I'm happy to liaise with the governor on it,' Kelly said, grabbing a biscuit for herself, sodding the diet. The chief constable dunked his and so did Kate. Kelly had yet to have the pleasure of meeting Governor Brian Taylor in person.

'Lovely idea, Kelly. But I've spoken to him myself several times. He's firefighting. He told me last week that on most shifts, there are two prison officers per wing at some points of the day – that's one to fifty men. If we go in suggesting cosy training days on how to be nice to the prisoners, I don't think it would be received well.'

'Like I made clear in my report, financially, the situation is bleak,' Kelly said.

'It's bleak indeed, but I know your team will deliver the best they can. I'm hoping to steal some officers from Carlisle and Lancaster as drug running smudges our county lines from their neck of the woods, and it's happening more often. We'd be perfectly reasonable to ask. Barrow did. Also, we're going to have to change the way we prioritise work. We simply haven't got the resources to dedicate to the thousands of minor offences tying up our time. A lot of it is admin, and I intend to apply for apprentice administrators to input much of our work. It's an extension of the model tested by Manchester last year. They had a huge uptake and for very little extra money. We're talking about administrators who input data, freeing up people like you to do what it is you're supposed to do, investigate.'

They sipped coffee and crunched biscuits. It was an amicable meeting where both sides were on an equal footing – that's how Kelly felt, at least. As a chief constable, Harris listened, which was more than a lot of them did.

'Did the governor mention the current mood inside Highton, sir? The morale?' Kelly asked.

He nodded. 'Bloody dire,' he replied. 'He reckons they're one scrap off a full-blown riot in there,' he finished.

'Have they got the manpower to deal with such an incident?' Kelly asked.

He raised his eyebrows; that was the only answer she was going to get. She shook her head. She'd been inside plenty of male prisons in her time, mainly liaising with defence lawyers, and they were grim places, devoid of hope. The electric charge of latent violent testosterone sat heavy like a stench the whole time you were in there. Kelly knew first-hand that there were some serious offenders who should be put away for good, and others who perhaps should be rehabilitated in separate facilities. But it didn't work like that. The general public didn't give a toss about bad 'uns, and so the government forgot them.

They moved on to another topic and by the time their meeting drew to a close, though Chief Constable Harris had offered them very little, Kelly left his office buoyed by the fact he appeared to have their backs. It was enough to put a spring in their steps. Kate especially had enjoyed the meeting.

'Call me unprofessional and tell me to bugger off, but did you exchange a few sultry looks in there?' Kelly asked.

'He's gorgeous,' Kate replied.

'So things haven't improved between you and Derek, then?' Kelly asked. Kate shook her head.

'My sex life is dead, I'm a slave to three witches of Eastwick, and I think Andrew Harris is single.'

'I heard that he was. Do you know for sure? It might be just gossip.'

'I can tell. Besides, I googled him. He's got a profile on Match.com and he's divorced.'

'Kate!'

'What?' She smiled. They reached the car and got in, carrying on their conversation. 'Derek moving out was the end, I know that now. Who was I kidding? He accepts it too. It's mutual and amicable. It feels too good, and I don't want him back. I've just lost fifteen stone of worthless flab and I only have to cook, wash and clean up after four now.'

Chapter 6

As the traffic lights turned green, Kate read out loud from Andrew Harris's profile on Match.com.

'I feel guilty for doing this,' Kelly said.

'It's just a bit of fun, I'm not going to wink at him or anything,' Kate said.

'Wink at him?' Kelly asked.

'I know, I'm new to it too. There are all sorts of symbols and signals that alert the person if you're interested. A wink lets them know you're interested in getting to know them. The final stage is actually meeting them. I've learned all of this in the past few weeks, by the way, I wasn't on it the minute Derek left, though we haven't slept in the same room for three years.'

'Oh, Kate, I had no idea things were so bad. I wish I could have been there for you recently, I'm sorry.'

Kelly drove across the junction and indicated to turn left, back towards the town. The suburbia of Penrith was quite pleasant, with its stone houses and stunning backdrops. Something about the mountains created its own microclimate and the sky at this time of year shone bright blue. It framed the greens, oranges and purples of the hills and fells and made one feel at peace. Sure enough, Kelly's bad start to the day, which had put her in a depressed mood, dissipated, and her conversation with Kate about Andrew Harris distracted her. Kate had gone through a lot recently, and Kelly was genuinely disappointed that she hadn't been available for Kate to reach out to; even if it had been sharing a drink at the pub, or a meal at her house, she would have liked to have been there more for her friend. Looking after three teenagers alone must be tough, but then, Kate said it had always been like that anyway. Kate often described her husband as her fourth child. What if he really was like that? Then she was better off without him.

She thought about Johnny and what sort of a partner he was and felt a wave of guilt. He was daddy day care, left holding the baby while she got on with her life. She felt lucky. Here she was, at work, chatting to a close colleague, having meaningful adult conversation, after gaining praise from the head of the whole constabulary, meanwhile, her baby was being looked after – no, spoilt – by relatives falling over themselves wanting to be with her.

'I think you've already caught his attention,' she said. Now it all made sense: Kate had a new hairstyle, she wore more make-up and she'd bought some new clothes for work.

'What do you mean, I've caught his eye?' Kate asked.

'I think he appreciates a strong, attractive and intelligent woman, and I think he enjoys your company. Some things can't be solely professional, you know, there's chemistry between you two.'

'I'm not sure it's allowed, is it? Superiors fraternising with the minions?' Kate asked.

'I think that's bollocks. Neither of you are in a relationship,' Kelly said.

They were both distracted by an incoming call on Kelly's phone. It was connected to Bluetooth and on loudspeaker. It was from Eden House.

'Ma'am, are you free?' said the switchboard operator.

'I am now, I've finished at Carleton Hall.'

'Right, ma'am. I've had a call come in from a pod in Kendal who received a 999 call from the mother of a boy who was playing with his friends, over in Workington, on wasteland near an industrial estate there. A detective is requested on scene. An ambulance is heading over there now.'

Kelly threw Kate a glance, who raised her eyebrows and looked at her watch. It was almost lunchtime.

'What details have we so far?' Kelly asked the operator.

'The boy and his friends were kicking a ball and it smashed a window. They went to retrieve it and saw something through the broken frame.'

'Go on,' said Kelly.

'They said it looked like a man who was hurt.'

'Is he injured?' Kelly asked.

'They reported a lot of blood but were too scared to go inside and scarpered, telling their mums when they got home.'

'How long ago was that?'

'The call just came in.'

They hung up after confirming the address and Kate punched it into the satnav.

'Let's go,' said Kelly.

Workington was a fifty-minute drive in good traffic, and midday on a Wednesday was about as good as it got.

'Why were the boys not in school, is it half-term already?' Kelly asked.

'Term restarts on Monday for a lot of schools,' Kate confirmed.

'Right, let's find out what these boys saw,' Kelly said.

The drive along the A66 took them along the shore of Bassenthwaite Lake, and the mighty Skiddaw scowled at them from the east. The hills surrounding the four-mile-long body of water were rolling and grassy, not craggy like some of the others. It was a peaceful part of the Lakes and there were no other cars on the road, but soon they came across a group of people having a picnic on the tables scattered around Blackstock Point. Once they left the lake behind, the journey was bleak, as they cut through Cockermouth and left the national park.

The old coal and steel area of Workington had been rejuvenated. Sliced in half by the River Derwent, they were heading to the northern district of Seaton. Kelly munched on a nut bar as she followed the navigational instructions and they came to an industrial estate sign-posted 'Central Way', about as generic as they come. They were looking for North Avenue when they spotted an ambulance. Its lights still flashed but it was stationary and silent. Kelly and Kate saw two paramedics exit the warehouse outside which it was parked. A few people had gathered far off, to the edge of the street, in front of a warehouse that boasted MOTs and a car wash, though it looked run-down and unused. The gate was shut. They drove up to the address and parked next to the ambulance, attracting suspicious stares from the ambulance crew, until Kelly flashed her neck tag.

She switched off the engine and they got out. The air was slightly cooler here than in Penrith. There, the red sandstone seemed to warm the town up. Here, they were close to the brutal Irish Sea and its biting westerlies. She was thankful that she remembered they had spare jackets in the boot. She grabbed one and went to introduce herself, passing another to Kate to wear. The medics looked grim, and Kelly knew that this wasn't just a bunch of schoolboys fooling around.

'What have we got?' she asked.

'Confirmation of life extinct at,' he looked at his watch, 'twelve-oh-five p.m. Caucasian male, in his sixties perhaps. Skin cold to the touch, extensive trauma around the whole body, which is naked.'

'So it's a homicide then?'

He nodded. 'Yup.'

'Have you called for a perimeter?'

'I was just about to.'

Kelly turned to Kate. 'Get a forensic team here too. Let's get covers, gloves and masks out of the car.'

They walked back to the rear of Kelly's Audi. She glanced over at the small crowd of people watching from the car wash, which was closed, and they pointed when she brought plastic overalls out of her boot and began putting them on.

'Kate, can you call Eden House and get Emma to trace the 999 call and get the address of the mother who called. We need to interview all the boys. I want a list of working businesses in this industrial estate too. Half of them look abandoned but someone might know something. Who is this building registered to?' she asked. Kate took some overalls and the rest of the protective equipment she'd need to join Kelly inside, and made the required phone calls. Once she'd done that, she busied herself with covering up her clothes and anything that might contaminate the scene. Hairs, oil from hands, dirt from shoes or fibres lingering on their clothes could all transfer to items inside, potentially endangering the integrity of the crime scene.

The forensic team would gather and log evidence once they arrived, but Kelly wanted to assess the scene first. It was always fortunate when one got to attend a scene when it was relatively fresh. The ambulance crew had taken the man's pulse and run a few other checks, to confirm life extinct, but they wore protective gear too. They left the medics to pack away their gadgets and tubes, designed to save lives, which wouldn't be needed here today; Kelly caught the eye of one of them and noticed that the young woman looked as though she might throw up. Ambulance crews see some alarming sights, especially at the scenes of road traffic accidents, but attending a gruesome murder scene was quite rare. Kelly braced herself for what she'd find inside. This would be her first sight of a dead body since giving birth to a vital vibrant child, one who was at the beginning of her hopefully long journey though the shitstorm that is humanity. The irony wasn't lost on her; she saw Lizzie's smiling face in her head.

She went in.

The warehouse, which was more a series of storage garages, was empty, apart from a chair towards the back wall, in which sat the slumped figure of the victim. Kelly could see from all the way over by the door that there was a lot of blood, like the boys said. She noticed smashed glass on the floor; that was where the boys' football must have hit. She went to the broken window and peered out, careful not to step on the glass. The shards would all be dusted for prints later. Outside she could see waste ground, perfect for a kick around. She examined the floor all the way up to the man, looking for any clues as to who – or what – might have been here. There were stains on it

48

and she saw a cigarette butt next to a chocolate wrapper, which was blowing about in the wind coming through the window, and the now open door. It was the packaging for a Snickers bar.

An aroma of metallic sweetness reached her nostrils behind her mask and she knew that the poor guy had already begun to rot from the inside out. Blowflies had no doubt already done their work and laid the eggs of their young inside his cavities, to feed off his flesh when they hatched. All mothers want the best for their children. As if on cue, a big fat purple shiny fly landed on her arm and she shrugged it off, repulsed by it. It buzzed off and landed on the floor.

As she approached the man, Kate entered behind her and exclaimed.

'Jesus, looks like an execution,' she blurted. Kelly continued to look at the scene. She flipped open a notepad and began sketching the location of various items, so she could remember before the forensic team took everything away. She took photos to send to Ted, the coroner for the north-west, who'd no doubt be given the grim task of performing the post-mortem on the unfortunate fellow. Who knew – perhaps he wasn't a nice person. But no one deserved to die like this: alone, stripped and beaten to death. She was used to seeing blunt trauma on a body, but the man's flesh also showed signs of sharp wounds. It was ugly. There was a lot of violence in this act, she thought. It was personal.

The man was tied to the chair. His body was swollen and mottled from the bruising he'd suffered. Bruises continue long after human expiry and only Ted would know how long he'd been here. His hands were behind his back and Kelly noticed that blood pooling had begun to occur. Kelly looked at her phone and saw that the ambient temperature was twelve degrees Celsius. The temperature of the body would continue to decline by the hour, until it matched the air. Standard body temperature varied depending on a person's activity, but in this scenario could be assumed as around thirty-six degrees, which would mean a drop of twenty-four to match the environment. But he could have been here overnight, when temperatures fall much lower. It was a clear night last night, without a cloud in the sky, and she and Johnny had sat out on the terrace with blankets, picking out constellations across the sky.

Kelly noted that the blood pooling was extensive in his feet and abdomen, where it had become trapped on its journey south, due to the generous nature of the man's girth. His gut wasn't green, as far as she could tell, and this was a sign, perhaps, that putrefaction hadn't yet begun in earnest inside his bacteria-infested digestive system. So he was somewhere in between early post-mortem changes and the decomposition stages. In other words, it was a recent kill.

She couldn't easily make out his facial features because his face had been bludgeoned and cut up, with bits of skin hanging off. His hair was white-grey and he was balding. The man's genitals looked like black pudding and she felt sorrow for him. At a moment like this, any good detective saw the victim of such a savage crime as a real person, with family, desires, hopes and dreams. Somebody (or several people) had taken his life on purpose and he'd suffered. His eyes appeared closed, but then she moved closer and she realised that they just appeared that way because the lids looked drawn together, as if in repose. On closer inspection she saw that the cavities were empty. The eyes had been removed.

'Fucking animals,' said Kate. 'He went through a prolonged and sustained attack. Poor bastard.'

At the moment, they had no clue as to the identity of the homicide victim.

'Not much evidence,' Kate commented. The clean-up (except the body itself) had been thorough, and there was no clothing to search for ID. He was intended to be found, just not identified, or at least not quickly. Unless the perp, or perps, were disturbed before they had chance to get rid of the body. It was certainly ballsy, leaving a dead body to be found like this.

'Right, I'm done, let's call the coroner,' Kelly said, walking towards the door. 'Let's have a look at the perimeter for fresh tyre tracks, litter, drinks cans, evidence of food and cigarettes, or alcohol. How could anyone do this sober?' Kelly asked. The she stopped. 'Wait,' Kelly said, stopping. She'd spotted something in the corner. It reflected light and she walked towards it and stopped, bending down.

'It's a Zippo lighter.' They got close and Kelly took a photo on her phone. It had beautiful swirls and patterns engraved on it, as well as some initials.

The lighter would be bagged for evidence and hopefully might give them some prints.

They went out into the sunshine to wait for the forensic team. Shadows danced and jumped amongst the buildings and Kelly noticed that the crowd had grown bigger, but a perimeter team was already here dealing with that. A blue tented entrance had been erected between the warehouse door and a van, from where it would be extended once forensics were here. The body would be removed once they'd got what they needed, which wasn't much. Perhaps the only way to tackle this job was to swab the whole place, especially the body. A great deal of contact had happened between this man and his killer (or killers), and Edmond Locard's exchange principle held that a scenario such as this couldn't happen without transfer. It was microscopically impossible. Sometimes Kelly thought about this when she was lying on the sofa with Johnny, Lizzie in between them: how many fibres, spittle particles, oils and skin cells floated around and ended up on Lizzie? Survival despite contamination was a wonder, and she prayed that whoever this man was, he had taken enough tell-tale signs with him into death to nail the bastard who did it.

Chapter 7

Johnny drove along the A66 towards Keswick. The day was perfect for a leisurely hike up Blencathra, one of the oldest mountains in the park, also known as Saddleback due to its shape when seen from the east: that of a ridge with a dip in the middle, where a saddle might be put on a horse. It was Alfred Wainwright who popularised the old Cumbrian name of Blencathra, meaning 'top seat'. Johnny preferred the even older interpretation that the word in fact meant 'working horse' in old Welsh.

Lizzie gurgled and played with her toes, strapped into her car seat in the back of the car. She took in the sounds around her and listened to the voice of her father as Johnny told her names of things.

'Look at that hill, Lizzie!' She had no idea what he was saying, of course, but his attention was all she craved. Her replies were single syllable utterances mimicking his tone, and he smiled. Every parent wanted their child to be the first to reach milestones, and Johnny took enormous pride in pointing them out to Kelly after work over a glass of wine. He sang to the radio and Lizzie cooed. Kelly had bought a series of podcasts suited to babies for the car, but today they listened to Bay Radio. It played classic old rock tunes and foot-stomping pop, as well as delivering comforting news from around the region, unlike the big channels which only reported doom and gloom.

They were to meet Tom at one o'clock, and Josie had made sure that Lizzie was fed before they left. That way, she'd likely nod off in her harness strapped to Johnny's front. He liked to have her facing him, but when they went walking he turned her around so she could begin to appreciate the beauty and wonder of her home. Johnny had only moved to the area about eight years ago, after retiring from the army. Ever since, he'd made it his mission to familiarise himself with every boulder, beck and beach. He intended the same for his daughter. Blencathra was a majestic walk on a day like today. The views would be magnificent. It stood at the top end of the national park and, when the skies were clear and still, one could see all the way to the Isle of Man to the west, the Yorkshire Dales to the east, and Blackpool Tower to the south.

He pulled off the road and saw Tom in the car park. They'd served together in Germany fifteen years ago when they were both senior captains. Since then, Tom, who was a Household Cavalry officer, had served in Afghanistan on a particularly tough tour. It had been shitty. Discharged last year, Tom was looking for meaningful employment, and tracked down his old pal. Soon after, Tom approached him about his mental state, and he became a welcome addition to Johnny's growing client list.

The collective supposition amongst Johnny's clients was that he himself had escaped the agony of being haunted by the past. It was a flattering assumption, but not accurate. Johnny had his fair share of memories associated with Helmand Province. No one knew why some soldiers became crippled by flashbacks, while others didn't. If the experts had an answer, then there'd be a drug for it. All Johnny could promise his friend was that the air and expanse of the Lake District had soothed him, and still did, every day. There was something about the serenity of the mountains that healed. They were a magnet for the damaged. So, after a long drunken call together late at night, Tom had agreed to visit. That was at the beginning of the summer, and Tom had now made the Lake District his home. In three months, Johnny had watched Tom grow stronger and stronger.

Lizzie recognised him, and kicked her feet. Johnny parked the jeep and got out, holding out his hand for Tom to take. He was a little taller than Johnny, but with shorter hair, which had turned grey. His shoulders were just as broad as they had been in his soldiering days and he was still as fit, but his eyes had lost some of their lustre. Johnny had noticed that, in quiet moments, Tom would drift off somewhere private in his head, and his eyes would lose their sparkle. But those incidents had become less and less frequent. Trauma work was messy and painful, and Johnny knew that Tom was far from being out of the woods yet, but the move to the Lakes was having a positive effect on his friend.

'Mate, she's grown in two weeks! Hey, Lizzie, you ready for our walk?' Tom asked. Lizzie smiled and babbled something to him.

'I agree,' Tom said.

He was a natural, thought Johnny. He knew Tom had several long relationships under his belt, but none of them had lasted. His battle with his mental health always got in the way. Maybe up here, surrounded by peace, he stood a chance to change that. Early results were promising. Johnny lifted Lizzie out of her seat and gave her to Tom, who jiggled her around and pretended to tickle her.

'Typical,' Tom said, watching Johnny gathering everything he'd need for the walk. 'Like a military operation.'

Johnny laughed. 'It has to be, mate. It's the only way.'

'How's the missus?' Tom, asked.

'At work. She's good. She misses Lizzie during the day, but it's good for her to get out too. And I get to have this one all to myself.'

Tom passed her back and Johnny strapped her into the harness.

'You make that look easy,' Tom said.

'Great day for it,' Johnny said. 'It'll be perfect up there.'

Johnny locked the jeep and they set off up the steep track. That was one of the joys of hiking in the Lake District: a lot of climbs started from the base of the mountain. There was something about starting at the very bottom that made a walk so satisfying.

'I did Sharp Edge last week,' said Tom. Sharp Edge was a ridge that provided an alternative route up Blencathra for adrenaline junkies. It was exhilarating, and Johnny and Kelly had done it several times. There was a drop either side of the spine of about a thousand feet, and steady footing was essential. Johnny had made plenty of rescues up there.

'What was the weather like?' Johnny asked. It was a common and fundamental part of any walk in the Lake District and was hotly discussed. It could make or break an afternoon.

'Proper crap. It started off all right but came in quick,' Tom said. Lizzie had gone quiet and Johnny knew that she'd nodded off. So much for her experiencing the grandeur of the scenery, he thought. He put a hand over her head and adjusted the position of the harness tenderly so it made her more comfortable. They'd walked upwards for perhaps 600 feet already and paused to look back towards Keswick and Derwent Water. 'That's where the *Wendy* is moored,' Johnny said, pointing to the large glistening sheet of water in the distance. Derwent Water was a pretty uniform shape, like a lake should be: oval. Many of the lakes in the park were oddly twisted, thanks to the ancient glaciers that had constructed them, but this one was satisfyingly regular.

They sipped some water and carried on.

'I had an interview last week,' Tom said.

'That's awesome!' Johnny was genuinely thrilled for him. He knew that Tom wanted to buy a house so he could get out of the rental market, and a job would put him in a stronger position.

'Where?'

'Highton prison, it's near here.'

'Yeah, I know it well,' Johnny said. 'I know a few of the prison officers.'

From army to prison was a well-worn career path for a soldier. The work suited the discipline and standards of ex-forces personnel. 'Some hard fuckers in there, mate,' Johnny said, making his expletive quiet, as was his habit now so he'd hopefully avoid teaching Lizzie bad language by the time she was old enough to understand. He stopped and turned to Tom.

'Do you believe you're ready?' he asked. Tom put his hands on the straps of his small rucksack, hooking his thumbs through, as he stared across the national park. They were close enough friends that the question wasn't taken as a challenge, or indeed a moment of faithlessness. Tom looked at him.

'Yeah, I do.'

'Well, then, you are,' said Johnny. They carried on. The feeling of being out amongst nature, with the warm wind blowing the grass in waves, and the sun shining her last murmurs of autumn before she went to bed for the winter, was exhilarating, and Johnny felt at peace. He wouldn't swap positions with Kelly any day: he was perfectly content looking after Lizzie and doing this with old friends and clients.

'Is Liam Fawcett still there?' Johnny asked.

Tom nodded. 'He's a custodial manager.' He laughed. 'Is there anyone you don't know? He was on my interview panel and showed me around.'

Johnny walked in quiet reflection. He'd known Liam Fawcett for years, and the guy had been beset with problems throughout their acquaintance. They still met occasionally and went for walks, in fact it was Liam who'd sent other ex-soldiers his way for therapy; soldiers who still struggled with what they'd seen and done. Johnny wasn't keen on the man but he felt sorry for him. Liam was the type of person who always gave the impression that they were plagued by bad luck, when, in fact, they simply made terrible choices. Liam was immature, and the prison service suited him because it kept him contained. In the army he'd been a liability. There was talk of him executing Iraqi prisoners back in the Gulf War, though it never saw the inside of a courtroom. But it wasn't Liam's track record that made Johnny fall behind Tom at an easy pace, so he could take a breath, it was the recollection of another man, introduced to him by Liam. Another former brother-in-arms, who Johnny also still met occasionally, and had in fact based his first scholarly article on. The paper had gained international acclaim, though the world of trauma work was relatively small and so it wasn't big news in that sense. Even Kelly didn't know. He tended to keep his PTSD work away from her. She had opinions that weren't helpful at times, and it created tension between them that he often worried about. As a law enforcer, Kelly's orbit gravitated to punishment. Johnny's trajectory was at odds with this; his priority was trying to repair the damage that led to behaviours that wider society saw as deviant and criminal. Johnny couldn't accept that humans were born bad. Take Lizzie. Perfectly formed, innocent and sponge-like in her desire to learn from her parents. Anything that was injurious to that bond could serve to ruin her development at crucial stages of her life. The worse and more prolonged the harm, the more her growth would stall and even fail completely. That was the essence of trauma. For some it was so bad that they never recovered; they were simply too fragmented. Kelly *said* she understood the importance of an offender's history but he didn't think she really got it.

After another 600 feet of rapid ascent, they came to their first false summit. Over it, they could see the peak in the distance. It was gentle hiking from here and they could take it easy, discussing the views, as well as Tom's interview.

'When do you find out if you got the job?' Johnny asked.

'I'm hoping today, which is why I told you. If it's good news, maybe we could get a pint later?'

'You'll walk it,' Johnny said.

Chapter 8

Seventy-one-year-old Ted Wallis, after a fall last year and a wobble of faith in his physical ability, had not slowed down. He'd felt his old self come back as his granddaughter, Lizzie, breathed new life in him. As chief coroner for the north-west, he had no intentions of handing over the reins just yet. He walked with purpose and went over the notes in his head. Kelly Porter had called him as soon as she'd examined the crime scene at the warehouse in Workington, and that was where he was now. He'd parked his car close to the vehicles surrounding the location, and stretched his legs. It was a relatively long drive for these parts from his stone cottage in Keswick, and Ted was more used to working at either Carlisle University Hospital or The Penrith and Lakes. Jaunts like this were pretty rare because he wasn't called to each and every death recorded in the county. But this was different. When Kelly had rung him to tell him that he needed to attend a crime scene, he'd known that it must be an important one. But she also happened to be his daughter, and he took much pleasure from working with her when he had the opportunity, even if it did involve examining some poor sod's body.

The building had been surrounded by a flurry of activity since the 999 call had alerted the authorities. Police cars, forensic vans and a few unmarked vehicles sat in the space, which looked as though it was normally abandoned. He glanced around and watched the crowd he'd driven past on his way to the blue tent, erected at the entrance. The people standing there, hoping for a glimpse of grue, studied him; he saw them asking one another questions about his importance. There were several TV cameras too and they pointed them at him as he got out of his car. He knew a few of the regular Cumbrian journalists because of some high-profile inquests over the course of his career. They came and went, often cutting their teeth locally and moving to the bright lights of Manchester or Leeds eventually. His name would be associated with major crime, so the gossip would have already begun.

He showed his identity lanyard to the young PCs guarding the entrance and paused. Once inside the cover of the blue tent, and away from the prying eyes of the public, he accepted gloves, overalls and shoe covers and put them on easily, used to having to wear such equipment. His hands were steady and true and he felt ready for the task ahead. He went in and found Kelly inside, chatting to a forensic officer. She waved at him and he went to her.

The warehouse was huge, but separated into smaller individual storage units. Ted recognised the sweet aroma of death and he looked over to the point of focus for everybody's attention: the body. He could tell even from where he was standing that the manner of the man's passing had been terrifyingly traumatic. Ted often contemplated what might motivate one human to defile another so earnestly, but he'd never found a satisfactory answer.

The mood inside the building was quiet as people concentrated on their jobs, and in between the click of a camera, Ted heard the buzz of a lone fly. Kelly finished up with the officer and turned to her father.

'Hi Dad.' Under more formal circumstances, she'd address him as Ted Wallis, but not here. They both turned their attention to the body. 'It's one of the most violent crime scenes I've ever seen,' she said. 'Whoever did this is a bona fide fucking nutcase with zero humanity. There are differently aged wounds and we reckon he was tortured for some time. Take a look and see what you think.' They walked together to the body.

'Do you think Lizzie's first word will be an expletive?' he asked.

'Some of the most intelligent people swear. It's a fundamental part of our rich heritage, showing emphasis and epic comedic timing, when used correctly,' she replied.

'Granted, but will her teachers see it that way?' he teased. She ignored him and led him over to the body. She'd ordered it kept in position until they'd collected every scrap of evidence they could squeeze out of the crime scene. When, as senior investigating officer, she was satisfied that they'd reached that point, then the coroner's office vehicle would bag him up and take him to the closest facility for Ted to perform the post-mortem operation – in this case, The Penrith and Lakes Hospital. Kelly had already made up her mind that she'd watch this one. She attended occasionally, when she felt that the key to the crime was in the actions of the murderer, or murderers, in the moment. That seemed an obvious point, but it wasn't. Crimes of passion, like those involving rage and the use of a deadly weapon, such as a knife or firearm, told their own story, but torture was a unique proclivity. This was no accident. This was a crafted sequence of harm, and the application of those acts of aggression was what identified the death as merely the end state of what had come before. It was chilling.

'This is horrendous, Kelly,' Ted said.

'I told you. I was thinking that it's reminiscent of a scenario you might find in the field of war,' Kelly faced him. They stood perhaps a few feet away from the victim.

'In what way?' he asked.

'I'm thinking about people who witness bloody civil wars and the like, or a military invasion or occupation. It's not just an execution, it's a litany of pain. This guy was truly hated by somebody,' she said. 'But it was committed with dispassion.'

Ted paused and looked at the body. 'Or he meant absolutely nothing,' Ted added.

She nodded. 'Carrying out a job, then.'

Ted walked past her and knelt down, first checking that no evidence markers were in the area so he didn't disturb anything. Kelly told him what they'd found so far. As well as the Zippo lighter, they'd also located various series of blood spatter patterns, a clump of hair, and a tiny metal ball, about the size of a pea, with a hook sticking out of it.

Kelly watched her father. She knew that this was a pivotal moment in his understanding of how this man had met the end of his life, and why. Motive was usually alarmingly straightforward in violent crime. Humans normally kill one another in rage. This was different, and she was keen to get Ted's opinion. He had forty years of experience looking at death and getting to know it intimately. Often something that he spotted at this stage ended up cracking her cases later on. She waited patiently.

The camera clicked and the fly buzzed. It turned her stomach but she had to let nature take her course: fly and maggot activity could help pinpoint a person's exact time of death and, from there, they could piece together his last hours and days alive.

'His eyes were taken when he was still alive,' Ted said.

'Jesus,' Kelly said.

'Some of his fingernails too,' he added.

Anger burned inside Kelly's body. This was the part of the job she hated. She found it difficult to process why somebody would go to these lengths to take a life. In her world, there was no single possible explanation, apart from that the perpetrator was a fucking animal. But before she found her why, she needed to ID the poor sod in front of her.

'I think his genitals are burned,' Ted said, leaning far over to examine the penis and testicles, which had turned black.

'The testicle hair is singed and, wait, there's a cigarette butt under there,' he said.

'Great, we'll leave it and have it wrapped when we bag him,' Kelly said.

'Why take his gag off?' Ted asked.

'What?' Kelly asked.

'He'd have been fairly loud, I wager, when he screamed in agony, as I imagine he did, so he must have been gagged, or unconscious,' he said. 'Look, you can see friction marks around his mouth.'

'Or extremely used to pain?'

'You think this was a bizarre game?' he asked. 'Like sadomasochism?'

'No, not really, it's just that I read that there are some very rare people who are immune to pain, and it takes a lot to make them react. There's a chance that because his wounds are so horrific, it was done to him to push him to his limit,' she said.

'It's possible, of course. There is such a thing as congenital insensitivity to pain,' he said.

'We're not far from a housing estate here, and it's a risky place to conduct such a prolonged attack. There are working businesses ten yards away,' she pointed out. She'd been over to the car wash and found it manned by a single mechanic working on an engine. It wasn't a car wash at all, it was a garage for doing up classic cars, and the man had slid from underneath an old Aston Martin to speak to her. He was covered in grease and had a broad smile.

He hadn't heard a thing.

'What else did he say?' Ted asked, peering at the victim's hands.

'This place has been empty for months and he saw no one coming in or leaving,' she replied.

'Any other witnesses?' he asked.

'Just the boys who found him.'

Ted nodded.

'I'm having some of them interviewed this afternoon,' she said.

'I presume you're bagging the chair too?' he asked, peering underneath the man's torso at the chair he was still fastened to by some kind of strap.

'It looks like a seatbelt,' Kelly said.

'It looks more like a winch strap to me,' Ted said. Kelly knelt down.

'What makes you so sure?' she asked.

'I'll have a proper look when I get it off, but it's the fastener. It looks medical,' he said.

'We'll use two bags taped together and transport the whole lot together,' she said.

Ted stood up and walked around, careful not to disturb the forensic officers placing evidence markers and logging details.

Kelly joined him. 'We found tyre tracks outside on the verge, so we can at least compare them to any vehicles owned by businesses.'

'Ma'am,' an officer shouted to Kelly. They both turned to where the sound came from and an officer on her knees waved them over. When they reached the corner of the building, the officer pointed at what she'd found. It was a gold signet ring, the kind men wear on their pinky fingers. Kelly knelt down and looked at it, flung on its side, abandoned and lost. It could have been there some time, as it was pretty dirty, and Kelly couldn't make out the insignia on the front. It might be irrelevant.

'It looks heavy and valuable. Get it dusted,' she said.

'Yes, ma'am.'

Chapter 9

Kelly arranged to meet Ted at the Penrith and Lakes mortuary later that afternoon. Meanwhile, she and Kate headed to an address in Workington, close to the industrial estate, to the home of the boy who'd run home to tell his mother about the man who was bloody and hurt inside the warehouse.

The mother, worried about what her son had told her, had gone to the warehouse herself to check out their story.

'Boys can be full of tall tales,' Tania Carter said.

They'd been shown into a clean and tidy lounge and now sat with cups of tea on a table in front of them as Kate took notes. The woman exuded calm. She was quiet and spoke softly. They'd met the boy briefly before he was allowed to go to his room. Interviewing children had to be done carefully. They'd get information from the mother first.

'So you went to the warehouse yourself. Was that with the boys?' Kelly asked.

'Yes, they went with me, babbling about how they'd heard noises – that's why we thought he was alive. I never expected to find him that way.' Tania paused and looked down at her hands, and picked her cardigan.

'It's a horrible shock,' Kelly said. 'I'm sorry you had to witness that. We have people who can help you. If you feel that you might need to speak to somebody, I can make sure an officer in our liaison team visits you to check in. Did the boys go into the warehouse with you?' Kelly asked.

'I stopped them as soon as I went in. I ushered them back out behind me. I went in alone and shouted out to him. I could see the blood around him and that he was strapped to a chair. I knew it was bad, and that's when I left and dialled 999 on my phone.'

'And tell us what you noticed over there in the run-up to this morning,' Kelly asked.

'There was a lot of coming and going over the weekend. I can see the car park in front of that building from my bedroom and I always forget to close my curtains. I generally leave the light off and close them late, it's a habit.'

Kelly allowed her to babble; she was still in shock.

'I read my book with a little lamp,' she carried on. Kelly took a sip of tea. 'Anyway, I'm going on. I heard loud voices and I went to the window to look. We sometimes get druggies over there and I was annoyed. But it wasn't kids up to no good, it was three big fellas. One of them looked, and sounded, as though he was defending himself, and the other two were trying to get him inside the warehouse.'

'Defending himself how?'

'Like verbally, you know. Reasoning with them and the like. But for some reason, he didn't just walk away. All three of them ended up going inside. That's when I shut the curtains.'

'And what day was this?'

'Sunday night.'

'Can you give us a description?' Kelly asked.

'Yes, one of them was the poor man in there dead. I'm sure of it because of his white hair and his build, you know. I'm good like that.'

'Did you see their faces?'

'Sure.'

'Can you show us upstairs and take us to the window and show us where they were?' Kelly asked.

'Of course, come on up.' Tania got up and the officers followed her upstairs. The hallway was narrow and the landing tight, but they filed into a single bedroom. Kelly knew the young mother lived alone with her son and admired her toughness. From the little they'd seen of the relationship between mother and son, she was doing a great job on her own. Tania's room was decorated with flowery wallpaper and more flora was embroidered on the bedspread. It was a singularly feminine space. Tania took them to the window; they had a clear view of the warehouse.

'Is there much light at night?' Kelly asked.

'Look, there's a street light there. His hair shone silver.'

Kelly and Kate looked down at the scene. The entrance to the warehouse was in plain sight and three large men entering it would be clearly visible under the light at night. Kelly felt a thrill of hope rush through her – Tania could be their key to finding the two strangers, and also possibly the ID of their white-haired victim.

'Did you see the men carrying anything?' Kelly asked.

'Well, that's the thing. Later on, I was woken up by a bang and I realised that it was a door. It was loud, but I had my window open, it was muggy that night.'

Kelly thought back to Sunday; it had been hot.

'What was the bang?' Kelly asked.

'I got up and went to the window. It was a van door slamming. The same two men were unloading something. The white-haired one wasn't there. I went back to bed.'

'You didn't see what they were unloading?' Kelly asked.

'Yes, it was just a bag,' Tania replied.

Kelly thanked her and asked if they could see her son. She agreed and led them to his room. The lad was shy, and well he might be – it wasn't every day the police come to your house to ask you about a dead man. He confirmed what his mum had said, but Kelly wanted to know more about the days between Sunday and today, and if they'd seen anyone around the area they didn't know. Anyone who stood out, perhaps.

He looked at his mum, who nodded.

'I saw a man going in there with a shopping bag,' he said.

Kelly looked at Kate. They'd driven past a Co-op around the corner. Maybe that's where the murderer had bought his Snickers bar.

Chapter 10

Brian Taylor stood in front of the window of his office, which overlooked the whole of Highton prison. He'd been a grade-four governor for five years, and the role hadn't been without its challenges. The Prison Governors Association had put enormous pressure on the justice system to improve conditions, but there was no money, pure and simple. They had to make do with what they had. Some prisons had been farmed out to private security companies such as G4S, and they had more investment for sure, but it didn't necessarily follow that standards were higher.

Punishment was something that the public expected, whether inside a private or public institution, but unfortunately, just locking people up didn't seem to work, and reoffending rates were getting worse. They said goodbye to a con one year, and he returned the next. To Brian, prisons had become containment facilities, period.

Despite this gloomy summarisation, Brian saw his prison as like a family. The officers were like parents, and their children were the cons. The parents set the rules and implemented them, and the children did as they were told, most of the time. The children had the right to the privacy of their own rooms, and a balance was struck about behaviour and boundaries. Occasionally, the children might have a valid reason to complain, such as poor food quality, loss of privileges or the unreliability of the heating or internet. Then there would be level-headed discussions about what the parents would allow by way of improving the comfort of the children, within sensible limits. Meanwhile, the house ran smoothly and everyone got along. It was similar to how he ran his own home. Sure, there'd been arguments with the kids as they grew up, but, by and large, they bloody well did as they were told. He hadn't seen his kids in a while.

The problem was that nowadays, there was no discipline. A lot of the lads inside started to go off the rails as youngsters. Every copper could tell you the local toerags who'd end up inside. Kids needed to be controlled, or else they'd end up in here. They soon learned that if you didn't follow the rules then somebody would get to you eventually, and you'd pay for it. However, recently, he'd sensed an increase in tension. The prison officers had snitches on every wing, who'd tell you how things were going. D wing was a growing problem. One female officer had faeces thrown at her last week, and there'd been a quasi sit-in inside the cells, with inmates refusing to follow orders and barricading their doors. The stand-off had been diffused by another female officer, who talked the ring leader into opening his cell. Four guards had gone in and dragged him off to solitary, but not before he'd kicked out at an officer. That officer was now in hospital with a punctured lung. There was a time when Brian would have said that female officers in a male prison were worth their weight in conciliatory gold. They had a calming effect. However, all too often nowadays, female officers were attacked as frequently as males, and it was a concern.

He'd once seen himself as a visionary: he listened to opinions, and he was fair. But when inmates resorted to violence, he had zero tolerance. The bottom line was that the cons didn't run the place, he did, and if they wanted to reverse that, then they shouldn't have got themselves banged up in the first place. To counter that, though, Brian had learned over the years to accept that prison was a con's home. An inmate's tiny cell was his piece of turf, and a delicate dance of push and shove enabled every prison officer to go home unharmed to their loved ones at night.

Brian moved away from the window and sat behind his desk. He liked the young man they'd interviewed last week, and so did Liam Fawcett. They were both ex-army and had that in common. When he had time, he'd call Tom Gorman and offer him the position. They were desperate, and another ex-army chap was just what they needed. He was aware of the young man's past, that he'd been discharged on mental health grounds, but to Brian, all that rubbish was irrelevant. The lads who fought for the country saw some seriously horrible stuff. It was to be expected that they'd struggle with it. A good straightforward job would sort him out.

D wing was on his mind. Every wing had a big cheese, a dick swinger who controlled everyone else. D wing was no different, but the punk dragged off to solitary after injuring one of his officers had not been the main man. Brian knew this because there was no main man on D wing, there were two. And they answered to him. They went by the names of Lofty and Titch, due to one being very tall and the other short. The short one was called Lofty and the tall one Titch. Prison humour. D wing contained sex offenders, child-murderers and mental cases, and as a result it was the roughest place in the prison. Rape offenders had become more accepted by the general prison population of late, and Brian allowed them to mingle more freely with other wings. It was a sign of the times: on the outside, rape was being downgraded.

Brian relied on cons like Lofty and Titch to keep the status quo. On A wing, that man was Rickie Burton, otherwise known as the Shed. However, all it would take was some kind of shift inside the wings and Rickie Burton could become a lot less powerful. Dinger had already gone, after his release on Friday, and he'd been another stabilising influence on the youngsters. Brian sensed a change in the old guard, and he didn't like what was coming up to replace it. He certainly didn't want the sex cases on Lofty and Titch's wing taking over. For now, they were keeping a lid on things, but for how long? The old-timers like Rickie Burton didn't do drugs and they dished out discipline fairly and swiftly. Of course, Rickie had his fingers in many lucrative pies, and some of them paid the governor a cut, but that was a fair trade. The new wave of cons were addicts and damaged dropouts. That could spell disaster for the delicate equilibrium inside Highton.

Perhaps a reshuffle was in order? He could divide and conquer, all but D wing, of course. The problem with spreading sex cases around was that they wouldn't last long, and the beating of a paedo (well deserved as it was) could light the spark that could bring down the whole prison. A few trusted officers were used to feeding back information from the wings, and they'd informed him that Dinger's absence hadn't caused much notable change in behaviour. However, some of the youngsters missed his father-like presence and a few were on suicide watch. Rickie Burton seemed to be holding it together, but the events on D wing had rattled the governor. He sensed a precarious teetering on the edge of something, like a sickening feeling in his stomach, warning him that they'd had a very close call. Prison officers were going off sick at an alarming rate, and they couldn't keep up with the smuggling; it was like a tsunami of illegal substances and weapons, all aimed at gaining more control and independence. Brian happened to believe in the rule book, but he also had a few clauses of his own.

Only the restoration of order would cheer him up.

His secretary sent a call through to his desk phone. He answered in a gruff voice.

'Sir, it's HMP Altcourse on the phone, they want us to take fifty prisoners off their hands, they're twenty per cent over capacity and they're Cat A inmates. It's been approved by the prison service. They're struggling, sir,' she said.

'*They're* struggling! Where are we going to put them? Jesus H. Christ!' he ranted, and his face turned purple. He knew he needed to cut back on the whisky and cigarettes, but with muppets like this on the end of the phone, how was he expected to handle stress? He felt his heart pump in his chest and slammed his fist on the desk. The telephone line went dead.

Chapter 11

Kelly's team at Eden House was instructed to stop what they were doing and attend an emergency briefing. Kelly and Kate made their way back from Workington, leaving the local searches for witnesses in the capable hands of Workington coppers. It would be Kelly's team of detectives, though, which would chase the evidence found at the crime scene. They had close relationships with several labs in Carlisle who'd drop their workload and shunt samples up the queue for Kelly or her father, the chief coroner. Lab work cost a lot of money, but solid forensic evidence was the only thing that stood up in court. The opinions of witnesses could be explained or argued away, so they chased the stuff under microscopes. It wasn't glamorous but it was vital. Anything with an integral surface, including the victim's hands, had been brushed for prints at the scene, and they'd found several. They were dealing with a fairly public space and so any prints found could have been there for weeks, even months, but chemical traces of people were a good place to start. Anybody with a criminal record had their fingerprints and DNA on record, so straight away that gave them access to thousands of potential suspects. With murder, one often found that the suspect had offended before. Crime, Kelly believed, was like a graduate course: thugs usually started with killing cats and ended up at murder. And in this case in particular, somebody with the stomach and the skill to torture on such a scale must have done it before. If they were lucky, he'd have left a trail.

Coffees were distributed and the team perched on tables or sat at desks. Kelly went to the front of the room and sat on the edge of a desk. Behind her was an interactive white board. She tapped the keyboard, linked to it, and an arrangement of boxes appeared on the large screen behind her. Photos of the body were positioned in the middle. The detectives not present at the scene with Kelly and Kate exclaimed their disgust.

'Jesus, guv, what a mess,' Emma said.

'Yeah, it's nasty. This is what Kate and I have gathered so far. Forensics have finished up now and the body is on its way to The Penrith and Lakes. I'm going to sit in on the autopsy.' Kelly pressed some keys and information boxes popped up one at a time, forming the beginning of their investigation. Going forward, new information would be added to the system electronically, linking any key information. It was a form of dynamic reasoning, based upon the systems used across the whole of the UK. It meant that information couldn't get lost across county borders. It also did the work of hundreds of officers. Before Kelly's time, laborious Kardex systems were used to solve crime and it could take years to find suspects; meanwhile they were free to continue to commit offences. The modern information technology system could be applied to any serious malfeasance and was used by the Royal Military Police as well. Touchingly, the acronym was a nod to Arthur Conan Doyle's Sherlock Holmes. HOLMES stood for Home Office Large Major Enquiry System. It was easy to use and any detective could update it at any time of the day, making the management of a serious inquiry less onerous and more likely to succeed. Humans make mistakes, and keeping an eye on thousands of pieces of information, not just the evidence found at the scene, could frustrate an investigation.

Kelly went through what they had so far, using the images on the screen to clarify. She explained her working theories of a military element, a group attack, and the possibility that this wasn't the first murder in the killer's career.

'Let's get to work. Emma and Dan, take the physical evidence – the Zippo, the signet ring etc. Kate, you and Rob chase the lab on prints as well as tracing the van seen by Tania Carter on Sunday night. Contact me on my mobile if you need me, otherwise crack on and update HOLMES as you go, we really don't want any delays on this. We have the witness statement from Tania Carter, who reported seeing several men at the warehouse. These guys have families somewhere. Emma, run a check on missing persons from the surrounding counties too.'

'Yes, guv,' Emma replied.

Emma and Dan cleared a space at a double desk and drew up a plan for who'd take what. Kate and Rob did the same. By the end of the day, they all hoped that the limited information they had so far would grow into something that made sense. The next forty-eight hours would be crucial in gathering as much information as possible to generate leads to chase.

Kelly went to her office to freshen up and gather what she needed for the hospital. Mortuaries were cold places, and she grabbed a sweater. She opened a drawer and rooted round for a small pot of Vicks VapoRub tossed in there a good while ago. There was a knock at her door, which she usually left open, and she looked up as Emma peered around it.

'Hi, Emma,' Kelly said. She continued to feel through the drawer and found the miniature container.

'Guv, could I ask a question?' Emma said.

'Of course. Talk to me, what is it?' Kelly said. She sensed that Emma was reticent and so she stopped what she was doing, popped the Vicks into her bag and sat down.

'I was wondering if I could accompany you to the post-mortem,' Emma said.

Kelly thought about it for a second and realised that she'd never suggested it to her team before, and equally never asked for volunteers. Had she assumed that they didn't have the stomach? How narrow-minded of her. But then her enthusiasm waned as she thought of her brand new investigation and how much work they had to do. Could she spare Emma?

'Tell you what. Come with me, and let's see how long it goes on – it could be hours – and keep in touch with Dan about the leads I gave to you two. If something comes up, you can always head back over here,' Kelly said. She watched as Emma's face lit up.

'Meanwhile, go and see if there's a budding inspector downstairs who wants to get in on some action, they can help Dan out,' she added. Emma nodded. Kelly knew that all good detectives came from the ranks, they had to, but they didn't often get the chance to see what working a case was really like until they were qualified. Kelly had been given an opportunity to join an investigation when she was a uniformed copper and it had been this that had planted the seed in her head. She'd been given tasks that junior detectives normally get to do, such as interviewing witnesses and handling evidence. There was always a uniform hanging around who fancied themselves a detective, but who was seen as too young and inexperienced. It was an opportunity to see who was interested in making the jump. But Kelly rarely ventured downstairs, apart from to say hi, or to use the interview rooms.

'Make it quick,' she told Emma, who left the room, still smiling. Part of becoming a detective was crime scene investigation, that was pretty obvious, but real live autopsies were hard to come by. At the end of the day, they were expensive, and why go to the trouble for the vast majority of deaths in Cumbria, which were old people dying from degenerative diseases? Coroners only ordered autopsies in special circumstances, like murder. Kelly had come to take her position for granted. It helped that Ted was her father, of course. It meant that her positive relationship with the coroner was convenient when she needed it. That wasn't always the case for detectives. Some pathologists didn't appreciate intruders into their work spaces and felt they got in the way.

She took her bag and left the office, just as Emma walked back in with a young uniformed officer. Kelly smiled and nodded to Emma, indicating she was ready to leave.

'Guv, this is Fern Brown,' Emma said.

'Ma'am,' the young woman said. Kelly could see from her epaulette that she was a police constable.

'Have you finished your probation yet, Fern?' Kelly asked.

'Just about to, ma'am.'

'Right, come on then,' Kelly said, walking over to Dan.

'Detective Sergeant Dan Houghton, this is Police Constable Fern Brown. She's interested in crime detection and I want her to shadow you today. I'm taking Emma with me to the hospital,' Kelly said.

Dan raised his eyebrows and looked at Emma and winked.

'I see this has been discussed before,' Kelly said.

Dan smiled at her. 'Leave it with me, guv,' he said in his strong Glaswegian accent. 'Come and sit down, constable,' he said to Fern, who relaxed a little at the friendly welcome.

'Dan, Emma's on standby if you need her. Let me know if anything important comes up,' Kelly said. They headed to the door and took the stairs.

'Have you got something warm?' Kelly asked Emma.

'Just my jacket,' she replied.

'I've got sweaters in the car, mortuaries are freezing. I've got Vicks for under your nose too.'

Chapter 12

'Are you ready?' Kelly asked Emma.

'I think so,' she replied.

'Here, put this under your nose, you'll need it,' Kelly said, passing her the Vicks. They'd parked the vast multi-storey car park run by a private company, and made their way through the labyrinth of corridors, down into the bowels of the hospital, to the mortuary. They'd been led into a changing room where they were given overalls. Ted would be inside already, she reckoned. He'd be scrubbing up and preparing everything he'd need to carry out his investigations inside and outside of the body, going through a checklist in his mind to help him to establish what had finally killed the man.

To get to the operating theatre, they had to walk through the cold storage room where dead bodies were kept at a steady two to four degrees Celsius; the same as a fridge. It slowed decomposition down to make the medical exam more accurate. But their stranger was already on the slab, ready for his turn. They proceeded to the main theatre and opened the metal door. The inside was a collection of everything industrial-grade steel, and the silver colour of the metal captured their attention. The only other colours belonged to the paintings on the walls, hung by Ted, and Kelly was familiar with all of them. Her favourite was the one depicting an eighteenth-century operating theatre. A wooden table was in the middle of the floor with some poor woman on it, knocked out from alcohol or a punch, with maybe a hundred men gathered around to watch the anatomy lesson. The men smoked pipes and the surgeon wore a dirty apron. There was a kick box full of sawdust on the floor to catch the blood and a collection of knives for amputation. Kelly pointed it out to Emma, who went to study it.

'Christ,' she said.

Another door opened and Ted came in, fully suited and booted for the operation. Many coroners weren't medical at all, and were appointed from the legal and judicial services, but Ted was a skilled physician and the combination of the two roles saved much time. He could perform the operation, take the samples, examine the results *and* write the report. Kelly noted that Emma was quite star-struck and it made her feel proud of her father. They'd only had a relationship as father and daughter for two years, since Wendy had told her the truth about her biology. The man she'd grown up with, John Porter, had believed that he'd fathered both of his daughters, but Wendy had embarked on a brief but passionate affair with the handsome young pathologist and had never told a soul. At first, Kelly had been judgemental of her mother's secret, but then she realised that she had no right to question the choices of another woman. How dare she? It was her ego that had been damaged, because the news changed her perfect image of her childhood. In fact, under examination, she'd realised that it wasn't flawless after all, and the arguments, John Porter's temper, and her mother's stoicism all came back to her. Wendy had sought the arms of another man because she was bloody miserable. The fact that her mother had found love again with Ted three years ago warmed her and gave her peace. It had also brought joy to Ted's life, even though it was cruelly taken away again so soon when Wendy had lost her battle with cancer.

'I'd shake hands but I'm a bit indisposed,' Ted said to Emma. She nodded and smiled profusely.

'Kelly, nice to see you again,' he added. They didn't discuss their relationship at work and kept it professional.

'Ted. We've still got no ID. Did you come up with a time of death for us?' she asked. Time of death was an inexact science. The cadaver's body temperature had been carefully taken every hour for several hours, so they could establish how quickly his body had cooled.

'The entomology department is working on the specimens from the warehouse; we should get a definitive answer soon. In my experience, given the conditions, and that he hadn't been in water, or moved, I'd say twelve to twenty-four hours. Rigor mortis was established in the same position as he was found in and it's now subsided – I've had a look and the muscles have begun to relax.'

'So we're talking yesterday up to the early hours of this morning. It's a small window and is supported by Tania Carter's statement,' Kelly said.

'Who is she?' Ted asked. Kelly knew that he was keen to follow investigations closely when the victims ended up on his slab. He had a sharp mind and a natural investigative brain, plus the added benefit of understanding what the human body went through during the transition from life to death. He also had an impressive grasp of psychology, having nearly gone into psychiatry mid-career. She happily shared details with him and welcomed his theories. He was usually right.

'A witness on the estate next to where the body was found. She said she saw two men clearly persuading a third to go into the warehouse on Sunday night. The view from her bedroom window is excellent, with a street lamp close by. She identified our John Doe as well.'

'Good stuff,' Ted said. Then he turned to Emma. 'So, you want to see an autopsy? Is there something wrong with you?' He asked her. He joked easily and caused no offence. It always amazed Kelly that a man who was so gentle and kind had his hands on bits of dead tissue all day. But then she hoped people didn't meet her and think *murder detective* straight away.

'I do, yes. I suppose it's the part that puts everything together for me. I work with the photos all the time, and we watched recorded versions in college, but I thought I'd ask. The actual body of the victim is important, and I think it'll make me more connected to the case,' Emma said.

'I think you're a very smart young detective. That's exactly what it does. It also makes you want to catch the bastards that did it,' he said. 'Right, let's get started.'

Ted called his mortuary technicians via an intercom and they came into the room and greeted the detectives. Kelly knew them both and introduced Emma, and they got to work. Ted ran the show and it was his orders and instructions that the technicians followed. Kelly and Emma were mere observers, and Kelly showed Emma to a metal stool out of the way, where they perched and watched. Emma wore one of Kelly's sweaters and she noticed her hugging it a little as the process began. Ted spoke calmly into his mic and placed his goggles over his face. The squelch of his rubber boots, the clicking of the camera as the technician checked his equipment, and the suction of the sluice were the only noises, until the metal gurney was wheeled in, on top of which sat a large black mortuary bag.

'He's still attached to the chair,' Kelly whispered to Emma, who looked puzzled by the size and shape of the body bag. The technicians transferred the bag to the large metal mortuary slab, which was connected to a metal sink and the sluice. There were holes all across the slab where fluids could drain into the sluice, and Kelly peered at the painting again, pondering what hellish nightmare surgery in the eighteenth century must have been.

The sound of the zip caught their attention. Kelly reckoned Emma was holding her breath. Once the body, and the chair, was fully exposed, it was photographed while still inside the bag and examined by Ted. Clear plastic bags covered the victim's head and hands. Vital evidence from the crime scene could lurk inside the bag and they wanted to be sure they had samples of everything. Emma glanced sideways at Kelly, who asked if she was holding up. Despite being experienced police officers, the sight of brutality was never easy to stomach. After all, that's what made them human: the need to empathise with somebody who'd been through unspeakable trauma. If they couldn't, they'd be as bad as the killer. Emma whispered that she was okay.

'It's different to the pictures,' she said. Kelly thought about it and realised that Emma was right. It was a privilege to witness a person in death, as it was their last chance at communication with the living. They watched Ted walk around the examination table. He went close in and then stood back and instructed photographs to be taken. From their vantage point, Kelly and Emma saw the man's whole body now as well as the chair he was strapped to.

They watched Ted take a cigarette butt out of the bag with tweezers, and place it into a plastic bag. Ted examined the binding holding the man to the chair carefully, and Kelly watched and waited. It was black and looked as though it was made from some kind of hard-wearing nylon.

'It's robust. The shape is inconsistent with a standard car seatbelt. It's too thick. It's not a type of bungee, or like any industrial winch strap, and it doesn't look like a climber's winch. This is designed to be attached to something, like a hoist,' he said.

Kelly leant over to Emma and explained Ted's theory, filling in what Ted had shared with her back in the warehouse.

'So it came from a hospital?' Emma asked.

'Or a care home. Hoists are used to bathe the elderly,' Kelly said.

Ted cut away the bindings and handed them to an assistant, and then he lifted off the chair, which still had dusting residue all over it where forensic officers had hoped to lift prints. Next he carefully removed the clear plastic coverings. The man's hands were black, from taking prints, and his skin was flaccid. Kelly was used to the familiar thud and squelch of dead limbs being picked up and dropped back down, even when done gently. She sensed Emma relax and was pleased she'd come.

It was time to get the man out of the bag, and the technicians performed a well-practised manoeuvre to do so. The guy looked hefty but they expertly got him lying on his back. That was when they noticed the tattoo. It was a large spider's web around his left elbow.

'Interesting,' Kelly said. Ted looked up at her and stopped talking.

'Tattoos of spider's webs are associated with incarceration. I wonder if he's an ex-convict. That would sure make our lives easier,' she said.

'I'll request an emergency DNA profile for you,' Ted said, and carried on working.

'I'll chase his prints too,' Kelly said.

'Have his eyes been taken?' Emma asked Kelly.

'Yeah, I was going to share the finer details with the team later on. It could be significant, or it could just be another form of torture. Of course, it can be associated with knowing your killer, but also with not wanting to be watched while you're hurting somebody.'

'Or trophies,' Emma added.

'Yup.'

'God, he suffered, didn't he?' Emma said.

'Yeah, he did. Whoever did this enjoyed it and has a lot invested in the process,' Kelly said.

'We've got old wounds here that have dried up, as well as fresh. I'd say he was held for a period of time,' Ted said. 'Can I see the exhibit of the small metal hook please?' Ted requested. A technician brought a photograph up on the computer screen of the small object found by forensics and bagged and tagged to be sent to the lab. Ted did some measurements and searched a couple of puncture wounds on the victim's torso.

'I reckon you've got something like wounds from a cat o' nine tails here, Kelly,' Ted said. 'Little hooks have been used to tear the flesh and rip bits out. It also indicates that some clearing up was done at the scene, because we didn't find bits of matter, did we?'

'No. Tania Carter said she saw him enter the warehouse on Sunday, so whoever killed him could have had him for two days,' Kelly said. The thought made her shudder. 'It's an unusual choice of torture device. I wonder if it has a religious connotation,' she said.

'Because Jesus was whipped with one?' Emma asked. Kelly nodded.

'There could be something significant about the Catholic practice of self-flagellation,' she added.

'Here,' Ted said. The technician had got up a photograph of a cat o' nine tails from the internet. It looked like a short whip with strands of leather or plastic coming from it, on the ends of which were attached small metal balls with hooks to flail human skin. It was a barbaric form of brutality and it indicated to Kelly that their torturer was fascinated by pain. They heard Ted log his notation of the cigarette butt that they'd spotted at the crime scene, underneath the body. The smoker's DNA might still be on it. However, again caution was required, because it could have been lying on the warehouse floor for months.

One of the technicians wheeled a metal table over to Ted. On it were the implements of his work: saws, scalpels, scissors, probes, small hammers, dissection pans, a biopsy punch and a rubber block. Kelly knew that evisceration would begin soon. Ted collected samples of the victim's hair and cut his finger and toenails, putting all of the samples into small containers and placing them carefully on another metal table to his side. As he did so, one of the technicians peeled labels off and attached them, one by one, to each receptacle.

'Every toe is broken,' Ted said. He used sticky tape to remove suspected foreign particles from the victim's skin and noted other trauma. The man had pincer marks on his chest, burns from what looked like a handheld lamp that one might use to look inside a car engine, as well as a broken nose. Ted bent over to look behind the man's genitals. Kelly stiffened. She didn't know why, she'd seen it a thousand times before. Rape was something that coroners always looked for with any murder victim. Sexual violence was often a part of an attack, and Ted had already mentioned the possibility of a sex game. Ted stood up and looked at Kelly, shaking his head.

Thank God, thought Kelly. The man had endured enough. The room suddenly felt airless and silent as the grave. However, the lack of evidence of actual assault didn't mean that there was no sexual motive. The awful injuries to his genitals were enough to indicate a sexual interest. Sometimes deranged killers can find fantastical satisfaction in the acts of dominance over another without having sex with them. Nothing could be ruled out at this stage.

Next it was time to weigh and measure him, and then clean his skin ready for the Y incision. Ted counted the wounds: there were forty-seven.

'I haven't seen this kind of torture since my days in Northern Ireland. It's paramilitary in its viciousness and style,' Ted said. He looked over at Kelly. 'Another possible lead for you when we get his identity?'

'You think it was an interrogation?' Kelly asked. Kelly knew that Ted had worked in Northern Ireland, in Belfast, in the 1970s, before moving to Carlisle after becoming increasingly burnt out by the autopsies he witnessed during his training. It was the closest he'd been to an actual war zone.

'Or whoever did it is ex-army, or worked as some kind of mercenary. Those lads who saw stuff like this were pretty messed up,' Ted added.

The odds were stacking up for this crime being personal.

'Is his tongue intact?' Kelly asked. 'Sorry, Ted, I shouldn't interrupt you, I know you'll get to it,' she added.

'Just going in now,' Ted said, probing the man's mouth and lifting his tongue up to look under it, down his throat. 'It's here, and intact. He's got good teeth. There are contusions around his mouth – as I expected, he was gagged at some point. Nothing around his throat, so he wasn't strangled. Ah, here we go,' Ted said, lifting up the head.

'Here,' he added. Kelly and Emma went over to take a look. 'Well, I didn't expect that,' Ted said. They looked to where he pointed and realised that as Ted held the man's head up, there was a single trauma wound to the base of his skull. The hole was about an inch across and covered by his hair. The body had been so bloody that they'd missed it in the warehouse.

'That's a puncture wound, not blunt force. Something has been forced in there, maybe with a hammer, and then removed. It'd be quick, I'll grant you that. Maybe they got what they needed, or maybe the poor man was unconscious and of no more use. In the absence of a gun, it's a completely efficient way to bump someone off,' Ted said. Photographs were taken.

'I wager this is our cause of death. You can't torture with this wound, the victim wouldn't survive. It's a mortal wound.'

He took the rubber block and placed it under the cadaver's back, causing the chest to protrude upwards and its arms to splay out, improving access to the chest. He took his scalpel and made an incision from the pubis up to the sternum, then up to each shoulder, creating a Y shape. Then he peeled back the skin, the soft tissue and the muscles, a bit like filleting a fish, exposing the ribcage and neck muscles. He removed the larynx, oesophagus, main arteries and ligaments and separated the spinal cord, rectum and bladder from the main organs. The flesh and sinew sat in a pile in a metal dissection tray.

'He looks to be a healthy chap to me. His liver is of normal size, as is his heart muscle. Kidneys look good, spleen good colour, pancreas nice and soft… Let's see what's lurking inside, shall we? Both lungs have collapsed, and that is likely down to the beatings he received.' There was a bit of tugging and jerking, but Ted managed to get the whole organ sac out in one go. Kelly peeked at Emma, who returned her look. Her eyes were wide and she mouthed, 'This is amazing.' It was obvious to Kelly that the woman had a strong stomach. There were plenty of times that Kelly wanted to vomit while watching the operation being performed. She started to notice the smell and reached into her bag for more Vicks and offered it to Emma, who said she was all right without it.

The long and heavy collection of organs was placed on the waiting dissection tray and Ted had a look inside the cavity. 'Apart from heavy bruising, I can see no other internal wounding. I'm afraid to say that I think they got what they wanted and executed him, plain and simple. But it took a lot of time and pain to get there. It's a horrible crime,' Ted said. He turned back to the organs and began separating them and weighing them. The rest of his afternoon would be taken up by slicing thin slivers off and examining them under a microscope before sending samples to the pathology lab.

'I'm pretty much done, ladies, if you need to head off. There are no surprises really, from what we discussed at the warehouse, Kelly. You're looking for a very cruel and emotionless group of people, I'd say.'

'He must have wronged them in some way,' Kelly said.

Kelly gathered her things and Emma did the same. 'Call me later when you're done,' Kelly said to Ted. They left the room and went back through cold storage into the small changing room, where they removed their protective equipment.

'That was incredible,' Emma said.

'Do you feel a bit closer to our victim?' Kelly asked.

'Yes,' Emma said. 'It's weird. I saw every one of those injuries being inflicted, and I'm imagining what type of person could possibly go through with it all.'

'A coward,' Kelly said. 'It takes no balls to torture someone who is tied up and can't fight back. My guess is whoever did this is damaged themselves and feels no empathy for others at all. They've had to survive using violence and it's all they know. Whoever it is, they're a mean motherfucker.'

Chapter 13

'Two developments, guv,' said Kate Umshaw as Kelly returned to Eden House.

Emma had asked questions about what she'd seen all the way back to the office, and Kelly longed for some peace and quiet. She'd always worked well in a group, but she also valued quiet time, when she could just think and process.

'I'm listening,' she said to Kate as her second in command followed her into her office.

'First, a man has been reported missing today from Workington. Released from HMP Highton on Friday, and matches the description of our John Doe. His name is Jack Bell.' Kate paused and allowed Kelly to absorb what she'd just said. She was in the middle of taking off her jacket and she stopped.

'Second?' she asked, finishing what she was doing and fully alert.

'The guy who went missing on Seascale beach – the one from Barrow, Dean Kirby – has turned up. Dead.'

Kelly had her hands on her hips and she now folded her arms across her chest and perched on the edge of her desk. Kate waited.

'And that has what to do with us?' Kelly asked. 'Isn't Barrow dealing with it?'

'That's the thing. They called us because it's a similar MO to our John Doe. He was tied to a chair in an abandoned warehouse. Barrow also told me that Dean Kirby had done time in Highton prison.'

'You have my full attention now,' Kelly said. Her mind whirred. If somebody was going round killing off ex-cons, why was it so public and brutal?

'I thought I would,' Kate said.

Kelly looked at her watch; it was gone five p.m. The chances of the lab in Carlisle having a DNA profile from the corpse yet was slim. However, they had the missing person report.

'Let's pay a visit to the person who reported the convict missing. Who is it? Are they reliable?'

'Jeanie Clark. She was his prison officer at Highton. They were meeting up to check in, but he never showed,' Kate said.

'Meeting up to check in? Isn't that the job of his parole officer?'

Kate shrugged.

Kelly pondered the scenario. The female officer obviously had good cause to meet an ex-con after his release from prison, but Kelly wanted to know what that reason was.

'Give me five minutes to check in at home, and are you all right to come with me?' Kelly knew that Kate's girls were pretty self-sufficient now, but she still checked. It was getting late, and if the officer was on shift and they had to drive over to HMP Highton, they wouldn't be back until later tonight.

'All three have got tutors or clubs on a Wednesday, and it's orange night,' Kate said.

'Orange night?' Kelly asked.

'The night they can have anything coated in an orange crumb that goes in the oven with chips,' Kate winked and walked out.

Kelly took a deep breath and called Johnny, who was exhilarated from his walk with Lizzie and his friend.

'Hey,' he said. 'Good to hear your voice. Lizzie was amazing – I think she appreciated the scenery despite being asleep for most of the time.' Kelly laughed. She felt a twinge of guilt but quickly pushed it away.

'Something's come up,' she said.

'Serious?' he asked.

'Yep. Murder. Kate and I have to work late, I need to interview a witness and it can't wait. I'll grab something to eat on the road,' she said.

'I'll get Josie to look after Lizzie, I arranged to meet Tom for a pint. He found out he got a job that he was interviewed for last week,' he said.

'That's great news! Sorry to be a pain,' she said.

'It's no problem, Josie loves babysitting, don't sweat. It's an early drink, I won't be late. I'll see you whenever,' he said. They hung up. Kelly repacked her bag and went into the incident room to update the team.

'Don't bust balls tonight. Do the work and chase the leads we have, but then go home and I'll see you all tomorrow at nine thirty,' she said. Kate was ready and they left the office, heading to the stairs.

'Can you get the prison officer on the phone and ask where she is?' Kelly asked as they walked to her car. Kate did so, and the female officer answered her phone promptly. Kelly listened to the exchange as they got into the car and Kelly started the engine. Kate hung up.

'She's at home in Whitehaven, I've got the address,' Kate said.

'Well that's great, we don't have to drive all the way to the prison. So what does Jeanie Clark sound like?' Kelly asked.

'Concerned, as in personally worried.'

Kelly pulled away. 'Did the file on Jack Bell arrive?' They'd emailed the prison requesting the details.

Kate checked her iPad. 'Yep. It's here.'

'Is there anywhere nice to pick up some food between here and Whitehaven?' Kelly asked.

'Why don't we get something there?' Kate suggested.

Whitehaven was an attractive small coastal village and it was bound to have a cafe open for takeaway in the early evening. The drive west would be a pretty one as the sun went down over the Irish Sea. They'd take the A66 all the way and turn south just before Workington, for the second time in a day. But that was police work.

'So, who is your liaison in Barrow on the Dean Kirby case, is it Craig Lockwood?' Kelly asked. They'd worked cases together before, ones involving county-wide crime, and she liked him. He was an old-school copper who trusted his nose.

'Yep. He's sent me everything he has so far on Dean Kirby,' Kate replied.

'Let's have it, then,' Kelly said.

Kate opened the file and began reading out loud to Kelly. They drove past Blencathra on their right as they neared Keswick, and Kelly imagined Lizzie, in her harness, close to her father, nodding off to the sound of hard breathing and chatter to his mate. It was a pleasing thought.

'Dean Kirby. Fifty-eight years of age, been in and out of prison at Her Majesty's pleasure since the age of seventeen. His girlfriend who reported him missing was a pen pal to him when he was at HMP Highton. This last stretch was twenty-two years for manslaughter, but he was released after fourteen years for good behaviour. His release date was last month. After that, he moved in with his girlfriend in Barrow, and it was her dog that was found on the beach wandering around on his own,' Kate said. 'He has an exemplary file from Highton,' she added.

'How long had he been gone before she reported him missing?'

'The preliminary interview with her from today says she was with her mother, who has Alzheimer's, at her home in Millom all last week and over the weekend, so she has no idea. The dog was in good health when it was found but it's perfectly feasible that a dog can get by outside for days or weeks on its own. The last time she spoke to him was last Wednesday. She says she was busy with her mother sorting out nursing home possibilities etc. so they didn't speak all weekend. She saw the appeal for the dog on Facebook this morning.'

'So he could have been missing all weekend? Which fits more with our MO: prolonged torture. What's the crime scene report say?' Kelly asked. Kate scanned the file on her iPad and read out the important bits.

'A group of kids was fooling around on waste ground, near the old waterworks at Seascale, when they went inside some derelict buildings, doing what kids do, but they got the shock of their lives when they came across a dead man strapped to a chair,' Kate read.

'Does Craig think we're dealing with somebody with good local knowledge? Both men were found quickly and in relatively open locations with unlimited public access.'

'By kids,' Kate added.

'In places popular for kids playing, yes. If that element is planned that is disturbing,' Kelly said. 'State of the body?' she asked.

'He's only just been taken to Furness General Hospital in Barrow, where he's being stored, so cause of death as yet unknown, but the notes from the crime scene, signed by Craig Lockwood, state multiple trauma wounds, loss of blood and splatter consistent with the scene being the place of death, bound to a plastic chair, naked, and eyes removed.'

'Fuck. That's pretty conclusive. Can you get Lockwood on the phone?'

Kate dialled the number and the call came up through Bluetooth. Detective Inspector Craig Lockwood answered.

'Craig! Good to speak to you again, but not under such circumstances,' Kelly said.

'I agree, how are you keeping? I saw the internal. Congrats on the birth of your daughter,' he said.

'Thank you. Bit of a baptism of fire at my age, Craig,' she said.

He laughed. 'I guess you're calling about Dean Kirby,' he asked.

'Indeed. I'm on my way to interview a prison officer by the name of Jeanie Clark who lives in Whitehaven. She reported another ex-con missing this afternoon, called Jack Bell. If it's our man then they were at HMP Highton together for thirteen years,' she said.

The sheer black rock of Skiddaw nestled to the east of them as they drove along Buttermere again.

'Technically you should take this one and I'll help where you need me. I'm happy for you to become the senior investigating officer at the Seascale site. Meanwhile,

I'll do the legwork on forensics and witness statements etc. and feed it in to your team,' he said.

'I'll have a clearer picture when I speak to Jeanie Clark. If I get a positive ID on Jack Bell being our victim then I think there is no denying that the same perp committed both homicides. Can you work on how we think Dean Kirby got to Seascale with the dog? Your report says there was no vehicle or cash found at the site. Why was he that far north of Barrow, and how did he get there?' Kelly asked.

'Sure,' Craig replied. 'His photo is going out in the local press tonight. If he hitched or got the train, somebody must have seen him, and with a dog, he'd stand out,' he said.

'Exactly. Thanks Craig. I'm going to make arrangements for the body to be transferred to The Penrith and Lakes, I want the same pathologist who examined our man to conduct the autopsy on Dean Kirby,' she said.

'I was going to suggest that. If your medical examiner is free, and if you think your body is Jack Bell, then he should be the one to perform it.'

'I'll give him a call,' Kelly said. They hung up and Kate requested Ted's number via Bluetooth. The computer confirmed the number and it rang a few times before being answered by the commanding voice of the coroner.

'Hi Ted, I'm afraid I've got another body for you. It's in cold storage in Barrow. There's a strong chance that there's a link to our John Doe from today.'

'Goodness me,' Ted exclaimed.

'I know. We're following a lead that suggests they both did time together at HMP Highton. I'll fill you in when I know more. I know you can't perform another post-mortem tonight, that's out of the question, but do you think you could make time tomorrow morning?' Kelly asked.

'If you think they're linked then for consistency, I'd want to perform it myself,' he said. 'It's a shame I won't have the chance to view the body where it was found,' he added.

'I know. I thought you'd say that. Can I call you when we finish up tonight? Have you got plans?' she asked him.

'I was actually going to pop over to see my grand-daughter, so why don't I wait up for you?'

Kate glanced sideways and smiled. The team knew Kelly's personal link to Ted Wallis, but it was rarely discussed.

'Perfect, I shouldn't be too late once we've finished over in Whitehaven,' Kelly said. She ended the call.

The sun was dipping in the west and as they neared the town of Workington, they could see the dying light sparkling on the surface of the sea. A severe wind was whipping up the surf, giving it a wild look. Then they turned south, to Whitehaven, and the sea disappeared from view.

Chapter 14

'Congratulations, mate. When do you start?' Johnny asked Tom. They sat in front of the fire in The Crown at Pooley Bridge. They didn't need the heat, it was more for the ambiance. Having said that, there was a nip in the air and their cheeks were rosy from their earlier exploits.

'Tomorrow.'

'That's quick. What's the governor like? A good sort?'

'He's a big fish in a little pond, mate, reminds me of the old quartermaster in Windsor, rationing supplies of webbing and camouflage cream,' Tom said and laughed. Johnny rolled his eyes.

'Will you cope with that?' Johnny asked, knowing he could never work in a large institution ever again, it would kill him. But he believed Tom to be more suited to following the rules, and he could handle tricky characters better. Johnny was more likely to wear his heart on his sleeve and get into trouble. The mountain rescue better met his requirements for a pastime and a job. Firstly it was outside, but, more importantly, he made split-second decisions on the mountainside, rather than waiting for a tin-pot dictator to call the shots. It was instant grat-ification. The same was true when he'd been company commander: he was in charge.

'We'll see, mate, it's money. I'm not in it for the long haul. Apparently burnout can happen after about five years. I don't want to get to that stage,' Tom said, finishing his first pint.

'Another?' Johnny asked.

Tom nodded. 'Good pint, is that,' he said.

'Real ale around here, mate.' Johnny made his way to the bar, which was quiet due to it being midweek and the season tailing off. Pooley Bridge wasn't a huge tourist destination but business was steady. The little town centre boasted excellent ice cream shops and pubs like this one, with bar meals on offer, and outdoor seating overlooking the river. It was also an excellent start point for walks and a drop-off point for the Ullswater steamer. Visitors could go around the whole lake, stopping off when they fancied and hopping back on to get back to Howtown or Glenridding. There were book and art shops too, and the town relied on summer cash to get through the winter. Tom had got a cab from his rented flat in Keswick and would catch one back.

'So what sort of prisoners will you be consorting with?' Johnny asked as he came back to the table with fresh pints.

'There are different wings for different severities of crimes. You've got your high-risk wing with paedos on it, your murder wing and your rapist wing, then the rest are gun, drug or finance related. There's kids in there on remand and they should be kept separate but they're not, there's no room. The serious sex cases are kept apart because they'd be beaten to a pulp by the non-sex cases should they be allowed to mix.'

'I heard that. So it's true, then?' Johnny asked.

Tom nodded. 'I was shown some files by the governor and I guess he was watching my reactions. Honestly there's some sick people in there,' he said.

'So why aren't they in mental hospitals?' Johnny asked.

'That's the point. The prison service is buckling under the strain of mental health problems because these people should be in psychiatric wards, but they haven't got the room, so they end up in a regular prison, on meds, but with no kind of rehabilitation or therapy. A prison officer's job is pretty much containment, making sure the conditions don't get so bad that the balance is tipped and the shit hits the fan,' Tom said.

'So what you mean is, they're already at crisis point and on the verge of collapse, and your job is to firefight? Mate, you really think this is a good idea? You don't need that crap in your life.'

'Maybe it's just what I need to get some perspective. I feel as though I'd be giving something back to a system that's broken and letting so many people down. Do you believe in nurture or nature?' Tom asked his friend.

'Oh, Jesus. Okay, here's one for you. This is what Kelly would say. It takes a hell of a lot of nurture to change nature.'

'Clever, mate. When am I going to meet her?'

'Too clever. I was thinking maybe you could come over for Sunday lunch this weekend, but then I got a call from her this afternoon and a big case has just landed on her desk today. When that happens, I hardly see her for weeks, until they wind up the investigation.'

'What happened?'

'Murder. Come over anyway and meet Josie, my seventeen-year-old.'

'You old git, she's seventeen already? I thought that hair was going a bit grey,' Tom said, and laughed. 'I want a family one day,' he added, changing the mood.

'You'll have one, wait and see. Kelly and Lizzie came out of the blue for me. I never expected either,' Johnny said.

'But my illness always gets in the way. I meet someone, and I think it's all fine then, *crash*, it all goes Pete Tong.'

'Don't put pressure on yourself. It'll work out. So what happens tomorrow?' Johnny asked.

'I go through my paperwork and sign the contracts, and then I shadow someone for three weeks. Apparently I'll be wound up a treat by the cons when they know I'm new,' he said.

'Of course you will be. I bet they're cunning as hell. Watch your back,' Johnny said.

'I'll be put on one of the soft wings at first to see how I get on. Every wing has a big cheese, and I need to get to know the politics and groupings. I've got no kudos whatsoever in there, so I need to build up slowly.'

'And do you know who is Le Grand Fromage?' Johnny asked. There was always someone running criminal gangs inside prison. It was the same with soldiers. Any group living in close proximity, whether at war or in prison, brought out the natural order of things. The weak fell by the wayside and the strongest emerged as leaders.

'Apparently he's called the Shed, real name Rickie Burton.'

'Don't tell me, he's massive?' Johnny had heard the name before, and was again reminded of the favour Liam Fawcett had asked of him. He took a long drink to avoid Tom's eyes.

'You guessed it. Then on another wing, which I won't be on yet, as it's got some of the worst offenders on there, things are run by Lofty and Titch: one's small and the other's a big fella.'

'Imaginative. At least you can keep up with the nicknames. It'll be the same as the army. There'll be one who sells stuff, gets stuff, takes the bets, handles the cash and exports to the outside, fucking watch out, mate,' Johnny said.

'Don't worry, I'm going to be shadowing a long-timer who has got my back. She's called Jeanie.'

'A woman? In a male Category A prison? Hats off to her, she must be tough as old boots,' Johnny said.

'Liam told me that all the fellas respect her.'

'Sounds like you'll be in good hands.'

'Don't worry, mate, if it gets too much, I'll walk away.'

'What about your own treatment?' asked Johnny. He referred to Tom's ongoing medical plan for conquering his PTSD. It involved a combination of pills and therapy. 'Does the governor know?'

'Yeah, I was open with him, he wasn't fazed by it. It's a condition, like autism or depression, it's not debilitative.'

'It can be,' Johnny said. He'd had plenty of experience working with sufferers of PTSD and only now was it being recognised as the sometimes fatal, traumatic affliction that it really was.

'Watch out for triggers in there,' he warned. 'You never know what could take you back.' Inside the highly charged environment of a prison, violence, threats to safety, mentally unstable inmates or fights could all potentially generate a trigger response in Tom. Johnny didn't want to mollycoddle him, but he'd made such progress recently.

'All prison officers have free access to counsellors, and weekly check-in sessions,' said Tom.

'Good, they need to look after you,' Johnny said.

'What's this murder, then? I heard something on the news about a body down in Seascale,' Tom said, changing the subject.

'That'll be it, then, she didn't go into details,' Johnny said.

'Does she tell you about her cases, though?' Tom asked.

'Sometimes, if she needs to get things off her chest. She sees some pretty shit stuff,' Johnny said.

'I bet she does. The reason I ask is because the guy they found murdered was released from HMP Highton last month.'

'That'll make your job more interesting,' Johnny said.

'I don't know how coppers do it,' Tom said.

'What?'

'Keep their heads when they see murder victims and stuff.'

'I think we've seen worse, mate. I've never told Kelly about some of the things we saw,' Johnny said. He didn't make a habit of getting personal with clients, but Tom was a friend, and they'd known each other a long time. Tom's surprise that Josie was seventeen made him realise just how long that was.

'Why not? She'd get it,' Tom said.

'No, mate, I don't think she would. She's pretty black and white, like most law enforcement officers, they deal in right and wrong, guilty and not guilty. What we did was more complicated than that.'

Chapter 15

Kelly parked outside the address they had for Jeanie Clark.

Earlier, they'd stopped at the lovely Whitehaven marina and grabbed the last two crab sandwiches from a fish stall on the quayside, which was about to close. The sky was getting darker when they'd arrived, and the boats bobbed up and down like corks, with the steady ebb of the tide. The moon was bright in the cloudless sky and cast a fresh silver light across the harbour.

Jeanie lived just five minutes from the quay. It only took one ring of her doorbell to get the attention of a woman who opened the door and smiled at them warmly, though she looked more than a little concerned. She confirmed that she was Jeanie Clark and beckoned them inside. She was a small woman but Kelly didn't underestimate her; she was well aware what these prison officers put up with. Jeanie had a generous face and was softly spoken. They were taken into a modest lounge and Kelly began to piece together a picture of a character who appeared to live alone. The place had a welcoming feel. Framed photos sat on tables and everything was neat and tidy. There weren't any pictures of children.

They sat down. Kelly and Kate perched on the three-seater sofa and Jeanie sat on an armchair opposite them.

'Have you got news about Jack?' she asked.

'We were hoping to ask you a few questions about him, actually.' She hadn't gone into detail about why they wanted to see her during their earlier call, indicating that it was just a follow-up on her missing person report. Jeanie nodded.

'I'll be completely honest with you, Ms Clark…' Kelly said.

'Jeanie is fine.'

'Right, Jeanie, thank you. I'll be transparent with you; the body of a man matching Jack's description was found in Workington this morning,' Kelly said.

Jeanie put her hand to her mouth. 'Oh my God! You think it's him?' she asked.

'From what you said about Jack, we think there is a possibility, but let's make sure, shall we? Did Jack have any obvious tattoos?'

'He didn't have many, not like some of them. The one he regretted most was the big one on his elbow, it'd be his left elbow, of a spider's web. It symbolises doing time in prison, and he said he got it years ago, the last time he was inside. Does that help?' Jeanie picked her nails nervously.

'Yes, it does. Also, do you recognise this?' Kelly showed her a photo of the Zippo lighter.

'That's Jack's, where did you get it? I handed it back to him myself, the day he left Highton,' Jeanie said. Kelly saw that the woman's chest was expanding and contracting heavily.

'We were sent Jack's file this evening,' Kelly said gently. She'd already studied his photo, and now she was sure. Even though his face had been badly disfigured, it had been the hair that confirmed it. Jack Bell had no registered next of kin to inform. 'Pending DNA and fingerprint confirmation, we have to inform you that we are sure that

Jack is the man we found in Workington,' Kelly went on, as gently as she could.

'Oh God,' Jeanie said. She let out a cry, and it was one of real pain. Kelly wondered what type of relationship the two had struck up in HMP Highton. She gave her a moment.

'You two were close?' Kelly asked.

'He was a decent man, and this was his chance to make good,' Jeanie said. She got up and went to the kitchen for tissues. When she came back her eyes were red.

'How did he die?' Jeanie asked.

'All I can share with you at this time is that it was murder,' Kelly said.

'But he's not been out a week! Who?' Jeanie asked.

'At this stage we need to keep the investigation confidential as we work through,' Kelly said. 'I would ask, though, that you think about any possible rivalries or fallouts Jack had in prison.'

'He kept himself clean, I can vouch for that. I don't understand why anyone would want him dead, he didn't know anyone on the outside, apart from a niece in Barrow.'

'So she could be his possible next of kin? His file had no details for her. Perhaps we could get them from you?'

Jeanie nodded and wiped her eyes. 'I'm sorry, it's a terrible shock,' she said. Kelly and Kate waited.

'Perhaps there is someone who is inside the prison who might have wanted to harm Jack?' Kelly suggested.

'What? Like an order?' Jeanie asked. She was horrified, but Kelly noticed that she stopped crying and went into deep thought, as if she remembered something.

'Jack's wing ran smoothly, and there's not much mixing with the others,' Jeanie said. She'd closed up.

'We'll need an outline of his routine, who he associated with, who might have had a grudge against him, for example. We'll also be looking at ex-convicts who were released before Jack, and if they were associated with him,' Kelly said. She took a deep breath. 'Did you come in to contact with another inmate called Dean Kirby at work?'

'Yes, I know Dean. He was released last month. Has he got something to do with this?'

'I'm afraid that Dean Kirby was found dead today at Seascale. It too was murder,' Kelly said. She watched Jeanie take it all in. As far as next of kin were concerned, she was the nearest thing they had at the moment. The next twenty-four hours would be spent getting to know the two victims and how they were linked.

Jeanie was shaking her head. 'It's unbelievable.'

Jeanie Clark's reaction to the news of Dean's death was more in keeping with somebody who knew him professionally, and now Kelly was convinced that Jack Bell had had some sort of personal relationship with his prison officer.

'You think they're connected?' Jeanie asked.

'We don't know at this stage, but we'd appreciate any information on them both from you. So far, you're the closest we've got to knowing either of them. Did they interact?'

'Yes, all the time. Dean was transferred to A wing three years ago and he and Jack became close. They were pals.'

Kelly could see that Jeanie's mind was whirring.

'A minute ago, you said Jack didn't know anyone on the outside, apart from a niece in Barrow. Why didn't he arrange to see Dean if he was a friend?' Kelly asked.

'Because I had no idea that Dean was still in Cumbria, and I didn't hear Jack say as much either. They might have met over the weekend,' she added.

'Ms Clark – Jeanie – just what was the nature of your relationship with Jack Bell?' Kelly asked. She watched the prison officer carefully. At first, she was lost for words.

'Jack always had time for a chat. He always included you in his thoughts, and liked to stop to talk on his library rounds. I suppose I knew him better, that's all. I wasn't the officer discharging Dean.'

'You said when you reported Jack missing that you had arranged to meet. Why was that?' Kelly asked. There was a lengthy pause.

'We were friends. I offered to meet him to check up on his progress.'

'And what were your plans for the afternoon?'

'Lunch. Fish and chips,' Jeanie replied. Kelly thought it too quick a response, and the woman had become nervous.

'Does the governor of Highton approve such informal check-ups on prisoners? And did Jack's parole officer know?'

'Jack was no longer a prisoner.'

'I'm sorry, of course.' She changed the subject, not wanting to push the witness away entirely. 'Do you have any information on Jack's family?'

'He didn't have any contact with his daughters. The niece wrote to him and sent him presents. That's all I know.'

'We'll be visiting the governor of HMP Highton tomorrow. It'll be an opportunity to interview any convicts who knew Jack and Dean well. Could you give us the heads-up?' Kelly asked.

Jeanie gave them half a dozen names and Kate wrote them down. She also gave them a brief precis on each man, detailing how she thought Jack or Dean had known them and the nature of their relationship.

'Thank you for your time.' Kelly and Kate got up to leave. 'I'm sorry to be the carrier of such awful news. If you think of anything else, here's my card.' Kelly handed it to her and turned to the doorway. Jeanie showed them out and they walked back to Kelly's car.

'What do you think?' she asked Kate.

'Odd for a prison officer to be so close to a con. It was almost touching,' Kate said.

'We need to find out what contact the cons are able to have with the outside,' Kelly said. 'There's also the email address that was set up by his parole officer – I'll have Rob check it out.'

Chapter 16

By the time Kelly had dropped off Kate and got back to Pooley Bridge, it was gone ten o'clock, but she didn't feel sleepy. In fact, her senses were alert and she felt as though she could stay up all night. On the way back to Penrith, Kelly had called Craig in Barrow to request that he interview Jack's niece and find out where his daughters lived, but in the meantime, she had plenty to think about. Her mind felt fully charged, like a battery, ready to tackle the hundreds of questions racing through her head. However, she also knew that staying up all night wasn't an option. She had to stick to some kind of routine, otherwise she'd eventually sabotage her health and her family. Besides, she'd learned the hard way that she wasn't a machine, and investigations just took time.

She opened the front door and went in, and was immediately greeted with the smell of cooking. The entrance opened up to a lounge, which was in semi-darkness; no one was there. The fire was laid to be lit. She closed the front door and heard voices in the kitchen. Johnny, Ted and Josie were busy talking and they stopped when she went in. Johnny came to her and kissed her, Josie gave her a high five and Ted hugged her.

'Lizzie asleep?' she asked. This was the first bedtime she'd missed, and she had a feeling that it'd be like that for a while.

'She took her bottle and went straight off,' Johnny said.

'How was your pint with Tom?' she asked. She approached the hob and peered into the pan. Dirty plates sat on the side and Ted and Johnny had wine glasses.

'Nice to get out of the house,' he smiled. 'Do you want a bowl?' he asked, going to the cupboard. She took off her coat and put her bag down, and Josie pulled out a chair for her. 'He starts his new job tomorrow,' Johnny added.

'That's great,' Kelly said, sitting down.

'It's great he's got a job, but maybe not so great where it is,' Johnny said.

'Why not?' she asked, glancing at Ted. He knew something she didn't.

'He's starting as a new prison officer at HMP Highton,' Johnny said.

'Oh dear,' Kelly said. 'It's not a great time to be starting there. My current case, the one I told you about, is tied up with the prison. I'm going there tomorrow – will I see him?'

Johnny raised his eyebrows. 'Maybe. Will you have to interview any of the officers?' he asked.

'I would imagine so, we're getting background on the victims, who were both inmates there,' she replied.

Johnny placed a bowl of food in front of Kelly and got a fork. She tucked in and the subject changed to Josie going back to college after half term. It felt normal, to be sitting with family, talking about ordinary stuff. It was the distraction she needed. She finished her food and sat listening to their voices, and it soothed her. After Josie announced she was going to call her boyfriend from her room, the three adults went to sit in the lounge, and Johnny lit the fire.

'Can I speak freely?' Ted asked. 'I didn't want to bring it up in front of Josie. It's about work.'

'Of course, go ahead,' Kelly said.

Johnny sat back and watched the flame take. 'I don't mind,' he said.

'I've been sent the photos of the other body, and it looks the same,' he said.

'I know,' Kelly said.

'You've got a sadistic bastard on your hands. Be careful,' he said.

Kelly stared into the flames and sipped red wine from a large glass. 'What time can you do the operation tomorrow?' she asked. There was no way she could make the time to attend it, and they agreed she didn't need to. She'd seen inside the mind of the killer this afternoon and had no desire to repeat it. Besides, Ted would give her his preliminary conclusions as soon as he had them.

'I'm aiming for ten o'clock. This time I'll know what to expect, but I'll let you know if I find any surprises,' he said. 'Will you warn Johnny's friend?' he asked.

'That's a good point. Johnny? You can tell him what the press has been told, which is that two ex-cons from there were found murdered today, in separate locations, in abandoned buildings. One in Workington and one in Seascale. They were released from HMP Highton a month apart. It might just put him on his guard when he starts. We don't want him thinking he's going to walk into an ordinary situation. The prison population will have already heard, and you never know what kind of reaction news like this can bring in response.'

'I'll call him now, it's getting late,' Johnny said.

Kelly turned to her father. 'What do you think?' she asked. 'You saw the first body, and the photos from the crime scene in Seascale are almost identical. Why do killers remove eyes?' she asked.

'Fear of being watched? A message that the victim has seen something of value?'

'That was the path I was drawn to: that Jack Bell and Dean Kirby saw something, or knew something, and were ordered killed. But why wasn't it done inside prison? That's so much easier and less risky,' she said.

'Because then you'd know who did it, and who wants extra time on their sentence? This way, it's thrown the authorities off,' he said.

'What's really driving me nuts is the fact that the bodies were found so easily, as if they were meant to be. Why go to all that trouble? Someone is taunting us. I mean, it's brazen, and defiant. Do you think it's a lone killer?'

'Yes. He needs muscle to detain his victims, which indicates that the killings are on orders, but the torture pattern and the methodology is uniquely depraved, and I'd be very surprised if the actual wounding was done over a prolonged period by several people.'

Kelly stared into the fire. 'He's committed. He enjoys what he does.'

Chapter 17

The morning brought drizzle to the Lake District and it matched Kelly's mood. She'd barely given Lizzie her breakfast when she had to pack up and leave again. She kissed her daughter's nose, making her giggle, but when she went to the door, the child began to scream.

'Hey!' said Josie soothingly, but Lizzie continued to bounce angrily in her rocker. They heard footsteps on the stairs and Johnny came down.

'You better go,' he said. 'It's hard, but it's tough love.' He kissed her and told her she looked gorgeous. Kelly didn't feel even slightly attractive but smiled at him anyway. They seemed like passing ships and she felt an urge to sit and talk with him, about nothing much, but about everything too.

Apparently he felt the same. 'I need to speak to you about something, but it can wait,' he said. She raised her eyebrows and looked at her watch. They'd stayed up last night in bed, talking about her case. He'd stroked her hair and listened. Now she couldn't return the favour and it irritated her. She never seemed to find time for him. Lizzie continued to scream as she left the house and banged the door behind her. The abrupt thud drowned the baby out and she got into her car. Starting the day in a bad mood wasn't wise. She needed a clear head.

She drove away and her heart rate slowed. The drizzle created fog and it made the view a bleak one. She'd been notified late last night that Jack Bell's fingerprints were a match to their body, and she'd sent confirmation to Craig, who she called now.

'DI Lockwood.' His voice was firm and abrupt.

'Give me some good news,' she said. The drizzle turned to rain and her wipers sped up automatically. It wasn't a day for climbing, but they had to be grateful: the rain was the reason the Lake District was so lush and green, and the lakes so full.

'Morning, Kelly. I spoke to Dean Kirby's girlfriend. I got the impression from her that our Mr Kirby might have been earning money from less than legal means since his release,' Craig said.

'Really? What kind of thing?'

'She didn't know, and frankly wasn't interested. She said he went out at odd hours, and came back with money in envelopes.'

'Great. Could she be a little vaguer? Did she show any emotion over his death?'

'Not really,' he said.

'What about her flat?'

'It's being searched this morning, but she's had plenty of time to clean up anything that might attract our attention. The search warrant only came through this morning. Any luck with Jack Bell's?'

'He was living alone, so we might have a cleaner scene,' she said.

'Kirby spent so much time behind bars it's going to be virtually impossible to trace all the ex-cons he could be in touch with on the outside,' Craig said.

'Well, we can start with the recent ones and work back-wards. And cross-reference the ones which Jack might have also known. I've spoken to the police liaison officer at HMP Highton, he's a good egg. He's the best chance we have at mediation with the governor. We need to get him onside if we have any chance of entering the premises to conduct interviews. The governor's name is Brian Taylor. I've never met him. Both Jack and Dean were residents of A wing,' she said.

'I've put a few officers on Dean's last movements, but it'll take time,' he said. 'As far as him getting to Seascale, we've had a few calls from the public since his photo appeared in the local press. One is interesting. A man matching Kirby's description was seen last Friday hanging about the Ravenglass railway, at Saltcoats, with a dog. He was in between the railway station and the road and it looked as though he was waiting for a ride. It was about two o'clock in the afternoon. The reason our witness remembers him is because it was chucking it down and the dog looked miserable. The woman almost stopped to offer the stranger a lift, but thought better of it.'

'Do you have CCTV for that stretch of road?' Kelly asked. It was a remote part of Cumbria. In fact the exist-ence of the railway line owed its survival entirely to the Sellafield nuclear plant – otherwise it would have gone bankrupt years ago.

'There is at Ravenglass station, but not the Salt-coats area. We're looking at tickets bought at Barrow for Ravenglass. There were seventeen purchased on Friday and we've obtained Barrow station's CCTV. If we can spot him then we can work out what time he arrived in

Ravenglass and made his way to Saltcoats, to verify the witness statement.'

'Where is there to go from Ravenglass railway?' Kelly asked.

'HMP Highton, for one,' Craig replied.

'Seascale for another,' Kelly said.

'Yup.'

'Did you talk to Jack Bell's niece as well?' she asked.

'I did. The last time she saw her uncle was at a visit to prison two weeks ago. She said he was excited to get out and showed no signs of fear or worry. She was pretty cut up. She also said there's no point contacting the daughters. They haven't spoken in years. Some family dispute apparently.'

'All the more reason to contact them,' Kelly said. They agreed on that.

'She gave me their numbers. One lives in Ulverston and the other in Workington.'

'We'll take one each. I wonder if he tried to make contact,' Kelly said.

'When's the autopsy?' Craig asked.

'Ten a.m. From the photos, the coroner is aware of the similarities. Let's hope we don't get any more bodies turning up in the same fashion. I've got my team checking who was released from HMP Highton during the past year to see if any of them went missing, or can't be accounted for. Meanwhile, I'm off to see the governor. He's agreed that I can meet with him; I'm yet to hear if he'll allow general interviews.'

'You driving down there? I'm tempted to meet you.'

'Oh, please do, if you're looking for something to do,' Kelly said.

'Everything is in hand this end, so I'll meet you there. What time are you aiming for?' he asked.

'Should take me an hour, so midday?'

'See you there,' he replied, and hung up.

Chapter 18

Kate popped her head around Kelly's door. The morning briefing was complete and it had been a grim reminder that they were now working a double murder case. It was a stark jolt of realism after a period of respite from such crimes. Their first task was to get to know their victims. Anybody and everybody connected with them had to be chased down and interviewed. Kelly knew that time was crucial, and she had PCs up and down the county, with Craig's help, doing the legwork to try and piece together the two ex-convicts' last movements.

'I brought you a coffee. We've got a brand name and profile of the tyre tracks found at the scene of the Bell murder.'

'Van?'

'Yup,' said Kate. 'However, they're bog-standard Bridgestones used on transit-sized vans all over the country, and available online as well as at every backstreet tyre place that exists.'

'Great. Any unique features?'

'Yes, a mould was taken, and there are the cuts and stone imprints that you'd expect any used tyre to have, but first we have to find a vehicle to match it with,' Kate said. 'We'll keep working the CCTV and come up with a list to check over.'

'Good, thanks, Kate. Have you got a minute?' Kelly asked.

'Yeah, sure,' Kate replied. She sat in the chair in front of Kelly's desk.

Kelly took a deep breath. 'Did you feel guilty coming back to work when your girls were young?' she asked.

'That's deep,' said Kate. 'Yes, I did. I still do.' She sighed, as if regretful. 'I used to wonder what my relationship with their father might have been if I'd been a stay-at-home mum, but then I realised that Derek had his own choices too, and he could have helped more with the girls. You do your best, and that's got to be good enough. It's never going to be perfect for everyone, that's not how families work. You just need to keep most people happy, most of the time.'

'I think Johnny misses the mountain rescue,' Kelly said.

'So hire some childcare. Or find a childminder. My daughter, Millie, would do it. I know she's not a professional, but she adores babies. She's decided to take a gap year but hasn't really defined what that is yet. At the moment, it involves lying in bed and watching Netflix. I think she thought that the bank of Mum would fund her travelling to Asia with her mates, but I put an end to that fantasy. I told her to get a job to fund it. There's loads of people who could give you testimonials, she's been babysitting since the age of fourteen.'

'Really? I never even thought of that. Can I meet her?'

'Well, technically it's morning, so I doubt she's conscious, but I'll ask her to give you a call, or do you want her to pop in?'

'I'll run it past Johnny first,' Kelly said. Kate lingered for a few moments and looked deep in thought. 'Sorry, I shouldn't burden you with such rubbish,' she added.

Kate looked at her. 'No, you're not. My mind drifted off for a second there. It's not you at all. Millie needs something to do to get her arse out of bed in the morning. No, I'm thinking about something else.'

'Go on, I'm intrigued now,' Kelly said, waiting.

'Last night, late, I mean it was gone eleven for sure, I couldn't sleep, my mind was on the case, pieces of information just wouldn't get the hell out of my head.'

'I know what you mean. I dream about all sorts of weird crap when we're working a case,' Kelly replied. Kate agreed.

'I was thinking about the victims. Their last moments. I don't know. You'll get this when Lizzie is older, but being a mother makes you terrified sometimes, you feel as though something is going to happen. Some maniac is going to take them and torture them and you won't be able to do anything to stop it.'

'Jesus, Kate, that's awful. I do look around sometimes when we're out, worried that someone will take Lizzie,' Kelly said. It was true, she'd become almost paranoid about her child's safety and the evils of the world had suddenly become more real lately.

'It's amazing what pops into your head when it's dark. When I woke up this morning, I felt silly, and wondered where all the worry came from,' Kate said.

'You've got a lot on. Why don't you go easy on this case – you don't have to be on the front line, you know,' Kelly said.

'I know, I appreciate that, but at the same time, I enjoy it. If *enjoy* is the right word. You know what I mean.'

'I do. It's the buzz of getting nearer to taking one more nutter off the street,' Kelly agreed.

'I did actually find something to distract me last night,' Kate said conspiratorially.

'Go on,' Kelly said.

'Well, I kind of got into a Match.com conversation with Andrew Harris,' Kate said.

'You what?!' Kelly had to fight to keep her voice down. She went to the door to close it. 'Tell me!'

'I winked at him,' Kate said.

'I know what that is, then what happens?' Kelly said.

'He winked back and then liked some of my photos.'

Kelly waited, eager to know more. Kate went on.

'So then we started a private conversation, and we were talking for two hours.'

'Real talking, or by message?' Kelly asked.

'Message,' Kate replied.

'Two hours. That's a long message. So when do you talk for real? Have you arranged anything?'

Kate paused. Then nodded. 'He's taking me to dinner on Friday. But what do you think?'

'Why does it matter what I think?' Kelly asked.

'Because he's a senior officer, and it might be seen as a conflict of interest?' Kate said. Kelly saw that she was worried about how it might look.

'You barely know him. If it turns into something, and you want to see each other, then I'll look into the College of Policing guidelines. Yes, he's senior, but you don't work with him, and you're not in the same building. I'm your line manager, too, so he doesn't report on you.'

'Thanks, Kelly. I woke up this morning feeling a bit embarrassed.'

'Well I'm glad you told me, I'm excited for you, really. I am. And I want to know how tomorrow goes. You'll miss drinks with Emma, but that'll depend on how work goes – you know what she's like once we get into a big case like this,' Kelly said. 'I might have to force everyone to down tools for an hour.'

Kate got up to leave.

'Maybe keep it to yourself for now,' Kelly added.

Chapter 19

Tom Gorman followed senior officer Liam Fawcett to D wing for his first tour. Officer Jeanie Clark was off sick after the shocking news. The heads-up from Johnny last night had dampened Tom's mood somewhat. It wasn't something one wanted to hear on the first day of a new job. With the rank of custodial manager, Liam wore three bars on the shoulder of his shirt, compared to Tom's one. Fawcett was the officer tasked with babysitting him on his first few days, and it was a bit like his first day in battalion, as a fresh-faced second lieutenant out of the military academy at Sandhurst, meeting his platoon sergeant for the first time. He'd known nothing.

Just like today.

When he'd asked Johnny what Liam was like, he'd told him that he was tough, but fair. And Tom saw that the cons respected him. The job of the CM was to run a wing, with each wing occupying its own floor. The CM was aided by three supervising officers and a handful of prison officers. Liam Fawcett was called 'boss' by both cons and his subordinates. No wonder so many ex-soldiers ended up working in prisons, thought Tom, but how many army officers did it? Maybe he was crazy to take this job, like Johnny believed he was. But he wanted to go back to basics. He didn't want some fancy role in the city, or a security role in the Middle East. He wanted a normal job, and some peace and quiet. Any kind of emotional stress could bring on an attack, but physical stress, such as a prisoner kicking off, didn't tend to have the same effect. Complex PTSD was more about being transported back to the fear of an incident, rather than the physical shock of it. The stress that made him regress to the horrors of his past were all mental. Relationships were the worst. No sooner had Tom begun dating a woman, if she asked questions about him and began to pry in to his character, it was over before it had a chance. The same was true of high-pressure jobs. Jobs his parents thought he should go for. His father had given thirty years of his life to an investment company in London. He'd had grey hair by forty-five, and a heart attack by sixty. Tom was looking for something simple, and he believed that prison was just that. You did time for something. That was it. His job was to attend to the basic needs of the inmates.

'You know my friend Johnny Frietze?' Tom asked.

Liam stopped and turned to him and smiled. 'Yes, I do. I knew you were all right. Johnny's a good fella. He's helped me in the past,' Liam added.

As they entered D wing, Liam explained that it housed their vulnerable persons. That meant those liable to be attacked by other inmates for the nature of their crimes. 'Some call it the nonces' wing,' Liam told him. 'Welcome to Highton.'

The men on D wing were locked down all day, though a few of them who cleaned were allowed to keep their cells open. A couple of prisoners glared at him.

'Lofty and Titch,' Liam said. The men, one tall and thin, the other short and fat, greeted the officer and sized up the newbie. Tom felt protected enough behind his stab vest, but one hand went to his bodycam and the other to his PAVA spray, as if for comfort.

'These two keep everything in order, if you know what I mean,' Liam said.

Tom knew of their crimes: one was a serial rapist and the other a paedophile. Both had found God inside prison, apparently.

'You two got yourselves a nice flat-screen TV in here,' Liam said, indicating their open cell. 'And plenty of burns by the smell of it in here,' he added. Burns was prison slang for cigarettes, but in this case it was vapes. Tom smelled something other than tobacco. Regular drug tests in the army meant that Tom had stayed away from substances, but he still recognised the stench. The whole prison stank of it.

Tom had been given several documents to read before his first day on the job. He'd spent his evening reading policies and current literature about the drug problem in all UK prisons. It was something that was endemic and difficult to control. Walking around the wings, seeing the living conditions with his own eyes, looking at what twenty-three hours of incarceration a day did to a man, Tom began to realise that the situation was more than desperate. His job as prison officer was more about fire-fighting than rehabilitation. Keeping everyone safe and breathing was about as much as they could achieve with the resources they had. He listened and watched as Liam banged on doors and chatted with various inmates of D wing. It was a holding exercise. Prison was a giant container store, keeping the dangerous at bay for as long as possible so they didn't bother the rest of society. It was depressing, and Tom thought about what Johnny had said. Was he ready for this?

He was aware that Lofty and Titch were still watching them. Liam opened a cell and went inside. Tom waited in the doorway, looking back over his shoulder at the two men.

Liam filled the small cell. The officer was around six foot two, and Tom reckoned he worked out at the gym. He was what Tom imagined as the ultimate stereotype of a prison officer. Tom felt exposed and vulnerable, like the boys hanging around police stations in Afghanistan.

'Who's the pretty boy, boss?' an inmate asked Liam.

'Put your claws away. This is Officer Gorman, you can call him boss.'

Liam looked around the cell, but didn't touch anything. 'You hear anything about my officer getting hurt?' Liam asked. Tom was aware that there had been an incident on D wing recently. The officer was still in hospital.

'You have a visitor this weekend right? Both of you?' Liam asked the cons. They nodded. It was all that was needed. It was a warning, that was all. Privileges were one of the few ways to control prisoners. The cellmates were silent and Tom peered over Liam's shoulder.

'Right, lads. Keep out of trouble,' Liam said, as he locked the cell behind him, backing out. Music was turned up and they carried on their tour.

'Come and visit me, pretty boy,' a voice said.

'Show's over, ladies,' Liam said, winking at Tom. If the purpose of the visit had been to send a tingle down his spine, then it had worked.

Their next stop was A wing, where Tom was introduced to the Shed, real name Rickie Burton. The man was huge. He actually held out his hand for Tom to shake and Liam nodded his approval. Tom noted a long scar along his jaw; he was also missing half an ear. Tom was reminded of a film he'd seen on great white sharks, gliding gracefully through the deep blue, the oldest ones sporting wounds of battle along their sleek bodies. Lesions, gouges and evidence of attacks were worn like medals of honour and implied time served in the mighty ocean. The same could be said about Rickie Burton: he wore his injuries with pride.

'Welcome to Highton, boss,' he said. Tom nodded. Was it a trick? He wasn't sure if he should take the situation at face value or if Liam was testing him. He shook Rickie's hand. Liam didn't react, he simply chatted with Rickie for a few minutes about the news, the weather and the football. Rickie informed them that the wing was quiet and the lads were content. More privileges were afforded this wing than any other, and it was down to the discipline of this man. The doors of A wing were kept open more than on any other wing too, and violence against officers was minimal. Of course, there was brutality between inmates, but that was controlled by Rickie and dealt with accordingly.

'No Jeanie?' Rickie asked. Tom flinched at the use of a prison officer's first name, but Liam didn't.

'She's pretty shocked about Dinger.'

Tom knew that they were talking about Jack Bell, who'd been found murdered five days after being released. He also knew that it was Johnny's girlfriend, Kelly, who was investigating it, along with the murder of another inmate released last month. They'd both been residents of A wing. He was thankful to her that she'd asked Johnny to call him last night.

'I wish I was on the other side of that wall. I'd find the bastards and chew their nuts off,' Rickie said. He had the physique and the menace behind his eyes that convinced

Tom that he would indeed do just that, given half the chance.

'I know, pal, right?' Liam agreed. Quickly, Tom was realising that the relationship between prisoner and guard here at HMP Highton was a delicate balance of rules and needs. It was clear that Liam was in charge, but it was more of a compromise than a penal arrangement, and it seemed to work, from what little Tom had witnessed on his first day. But not always – as demonstrated by the recent events on D wing.

It was relief when they left the wings and Liam showed him the stores, the electrical plant and the library. Then they had tea with the governor.

'And what do you think of our little family?' he asked Tom.

'It all runs smoothly, sir,' he replied. 'I've learned a lot from the custodial manager, sir.'

'I'm sure you have, there's no one better than CM Fawcett to show you the ropes. Of course, we hope Jeanie will be back soon. Watch your back when the CM isn't around. They try to separate you. Have you run through the emergency procedures?' he asked Liam.

'Yes, sir. That's the first thing we did this morning,' Liam said. The practices referred to by the governor were a series of codes used by officers in certain threatening scenarios. For example, there was a code for a fight between prisoners, one for a knife attack and another for a drugs-related incident, and so on. It was how the staff dealt with disturbances on a day-to-day basis. It was just one of the systems that Tom had familiarised himself with over the course of the morning and last night.

'And how did you find our friends on D wing?' the governor asked.

Tom was taken aback, not only by the familiar and casual way the governor approached the question, but also by Liam's clear collusion. It would appear that this was how they spoke to one another.

'I'm not sure what to think of them if I'm honest, sir. I would have thought that my personal opinion of prisoners is irrelevant and unhelpful,' Tom said.

The governor nodded. 'Right you are. Sensible chap. We do tend to get a little institutionalised in here. Day one for you, Tom. We've probably been inside these walls too long, which is why it's good to have a fresh pair of eyes. They're all scum in the end.'

There was a brief silence that Tom thought he should fill, but he didn't know what to say. He looked at Liam, who sat back in his chair with his legs crossed and arms behind his head. He was very comfortable around the governor.

'Have you both worked together for a long time?' Tom asked.

'Too long!' Liam said, and the governor laughed. Again, the lack of appropriate professional boundaries took Tom by surprise. In the army, overfamiliarity preceded presumption and led to disrespect. Rank was a necessary check on the structure of everything they did. If there were chinks in the hierarchy inside Highton, Tom wondered what else was sloppy about how things were run there. 'Was Mr Burton in good spirits? His horse came in yesterday. That means I owe him fifty quid. Can you believe it?' The governor slapped the desk in front of him and his tea cup rattled.

'Jesus, do you ever learn?' said Liam.

Tom looked between them. Triggers were beginning to light up in his head. He heard Johnny's words.

'Don't worry, Tom, you'll get used to it,' the governor said, bringing him back to the moment. 'Think of it like keeping prisoners of war in check, there are always those who you need to keep onside. Rickie Burton is our Saddam Hussein. He keeps order in a small country. In return we allow him certain privileges.'

'What kind of privileges, sir?' Tom asked tentatively.

Liam laughed and the governor smiled.

'All men need certain things to thrive, Tom. They need to feel as though their place in the world is important, valued and useful. You'll get to know Rickie in your own time. Don't let his size put you off, he's actually a very decent chap. He's resourceful and clever, and I like that. He plays a game, and it's my game. In return I generously allow him to continue the pursuits that make him feel as though he is all of those things I just mentioned. Now, to me, he's none of them, but he *thinks* he is, and that's why it works.'

'What if you give up your place in the world because you committed a crime?' Tom asked.

'Precisely!' the governor said. 'We get sent all the ones who can't play on the outside, so they come and play in here, and it's our job to make sure they stick to the rules.'

'The rules?'

'My rules. Liam will fill you in, there's no rush. This ship keeps afloat because there is compromise on my terms. Sometimes, it's impossible to stick to certain protocols laid down by politicians in London, who have no idea how things work. Sometimes, you have to come up with better solutions. All I'm saying is that to get the best out of the cons, you need to make them think you're being fair. But that comes at a price.'

'They pay for privilege?' Tom asked. The question was out of his mouth before he could help himself. What worried him most about his outburst, though, wasn't so much what he'd just heard, it was that they'd somehow thought it timely to tell him on the first day of his job. Was this some kind of crazy recruitment ritual? His question wasn't answered.

Chapter 20

Kelly left her car and walked over to Craig. It had been a while since they'd met face to face and they shook hands warmly. Craig was one of those people who never looked stressed. There were men she came across in the force who wore their work on their faces, but that didn't apply to Craig. To look at him he could have been a banker, or a grocery store owner. You never knew what he was thinking – unless you knew him as well as Kelly did.

Kelly wore a trouser suit and low heels. Normally, she'd be more casual in the office, but a prison visit necessitated something more formal. She'd spoken to the prison police liaison officer over the phone and tried to sweet-talk him. She knew they had no jurisdiction whatsoever on the governor's turf. This was his prison, and she needed his permission to conduct interviews and searches. Legally, she wasn't allowed to enter a cell, but that's what she wanted to do, because that was the only thing that would allow her to rule in or out whether a serving con had had anything to do with the murder of Jack Bell and Dean Kirby. A cell search was a delicate affair, she knew that, but that's where cons kept their contraband, such as USBs and mobile phones.

'You're looking tanned,' she said to Craig. 'Been somewhere nice?'

'Italy,' Craig replied. He wore a grey suit and adjusted his neck badge on the end of his lanyard. A gust of wind took her hair across her face and she straightened it. Her heels clicked on the tarmac and they walked towards the prison gate.

'Whereabouts? I've always wanted to go,' Kelly asked.

'Tuscany. We stayed on an old farm and drove into Florence, Siena and Pisa. It was pretty impressive, though very hot,' he said.

'With the boys?' she asked.

'Only the younger two.'

Craig was divorced and gave the impression to anyone who asked that he wasn't interested in a relationship. He was an attractive man and kind. He cared. In that sense he was old-fashioned. A couple of years ago, before Johnny, he'd have been the type of man she'd have liked to get to know, which was funny, because her taste in men had changed so much since moving back from London. There, she'd been attracted to thrusting workaholics who worked murder squads for sixty hours a week. It was a million miles away from Johnny, who was a proper grown-up. Like Craig.

They chatted about the case.

'I went to see Jack Bell's daughter who lives in Ulverston,' he said. Kelly waited. They were nearly at the outer security door. The guard opened his hatch, ready to check their ID.

'She was unmoved by her father's death. It was quite depressing really. She didn't say much about what soured their relationship, apart from they were sick and tired of bailing him out when he had no money. She got her sister on the phone when I was there, the one who lives in Workington. So that'll save you a job. She said, "Dad's dead," in the coldest voice and put me on speaker. It was odd.'

'Families,' Kelly said. 'Did they know anything about him prior to his death? Did he contact them when he was released?'

'No. They'd had no contact for the best part of two decades.'

'That's devastating. Do you think we need to find out more? What about the niece? Did she elaborate on their relationship? If he was such a pain in the arse, why did she bother with him?'

'Every family has its own unique and special relationships, don't you find?' he asked. It was true, they were all dysfunctional in some way.

'Didn't she have plans to see him upon his release?' Kelly asked. If they were so close, then one would expect her to be excited for the date at least.

'Yes she did, this week.'

The guard took their names and found them on the list of visitors expected for the day. He passed them their visitor badges, which they clipped to their police tags, and he pressed a button to open the outer metal door. They pushed it and went inside, where they had to walk through a body scanner and hand over their belongings, except their lanyards. They were greeted by another guard who said he was to escort them straight to the governor's office; the governor was expecting them. The place smelled of cigarette smoke and the sweet aroma of weed. Kelly raised her eyebrows at Craig.

'Jesus, I hope they don't test my clothes when we get back to the office.' She winked. Random drugs tests were common in the police force, just like they were in the army.

'It's completely out of control,' Craig said. 'We had a case in Barrow recently, and when the guy was found guilty and sent down, he joked that he'd be better off inside because he could get drugs more readily than he could on the outside. I don't know what they're supposed to do. It gets smuggled in inside bodies, clothes, presents, babies and God knows what,' he said.

'Maybe it's something we don't bring up with Governor Taylor?' she said.

'I know you'd love to,' he said.

She smiled. He was right. She could hardly help herself poking her nose inside anything that raised her hackles. Her problem wasn't that drugs were common inside prison, but that no one seemed to care.

Prisons depressed her. It wasn't too difficult to see why; after all, they were full of violent, frustrated criminals. However, it was also the way they were run that got Kelly's back up. The police caught the criminals and spent thousands of hours putting together a case. Then the lawyers swooped like vultures, agreeing secret deals in wine bars, dismissing half their work. Then the judges waved their gavels from their lofty thrones and dished out sentences that were laughed at and ridiculed by anyone who knew anything about rehabilitation or effective incarceration. The governor, the man she was about to meet, was the next link in the chain: it was up to him how the prisoner lived from day to day. Most of them did their best, and then gave up. Prisoners being dependent on drugs, as well as suffering from untreated mental health issues, was wrong, plain and simple. The whole penal system was fucked. The notion that prisoners somehow had a chance of staying clean was a joke. Gangs ruled inside these walls, just like they did on the outside. What Kelly wanted to know was: which ones were Jack Bell and Dean Kirby affiliated with inside? Any questions she had about her two victims depended upon who they associated with on the inside, and Jeanie Clark had already given her an idea.

They were escorted through a series of doors and corridors, all caged in reinforced steel, and clunky when opened. Each bang of metal on metal jarred Kelly. The prison officers they saw were polite and respectful. They went up some stairs and were asked to wait in an area with a few chairs laid out. The place was generally dismal.

From a distance, they heard the occasional shouting and banging coming from the wings. The governor's office was self-contained inside the prison building. The wings were housed in a separate structure, joined by a series of walkways. There was something sinister about being so close to so many serious criminals; it chilled Kelly's soul. The last time she'd been inside such a place was Broadmoor, when she'd visited the Teacher, one of the most appalling criminals in recent history. Some people, like the Teacher, took well to incarceration, they were born for it. It was as if they worked all their lives to get there, to a place of safety and nurture, where they had no responsibility whatsoever, apart from to follow rules. Something clearly happened, Kelly knew, to human beings in their development, which divided the species into two streams. One half ended up in places like this, or Broadmoor for the true nutters. Kelly had never believed that the Teacher was crazy, but apparently the jury at the trial thought differently. It meant that rather than face the brutality of a place like this, the Teacher got special treatment at a glorified hospital. But there wasn't much Kelly could do about that – her job was to catch bastards, not judge them. That was the job of those in the white wigs.

They didn't sit down in the small waiting area. Kelly was too fidgety and Craig too curious. He read the flyers and pamphlets on smoking, sexual harassment in the workplace and venereal disease, which were pinned to a noticeboard outside the governor's office. They looked as though they'd been there ten years. The door opened and a man held out his hand. He went to Craig first. In Kelly's experience most men did the same, overlooking the outstretched hand of a woman in order to shake one belonging to another male.

'Brian Taylor,' he boomed.

Dick swinger, thought Kelly.

'Detective Inspector Craig Lockwood. This is Detective Inspector Kelly Porter, she's the senior investigating officer running the case,' Craig said. Brian Taylor turned to her, almost apologetic, but not quite, and held out his hand.

'Detective,' he said. She felt a sense of unease as his eyes wandered down to her blouse and back to her eyes. He was a middle-aged man who looked like a prime heart attack candidate, and he smelled of alcohol. His pot-belly made his shirt sit awkwardly, and he had dark circles under his eyes. But he attempted a warm, if wary, smile.

'Please come in. Can I get you a drink? Hot or cold?' he asked. Craig said he'd love a coffee and Kelly asked for water. They sat down in the chairs offered and Brian Taylor went behind his desk. There was a large window behind him and Kelly could hear the bounce of a ball, and shouting. It must be the exercise yard below.

'So, what a damn way to go, eh? We were sorry to hear the news. Both Bell and Kirby were good inmates. They were exemplary in fact. They shouldn't have really been here, a Cat B or C would have done them fine.'

'That's good to know,' Kelly said. 'So they didn't cause any trouble? They kept themselves out of fights and rivalries?'

'I wouldn't go that far. All our inmates have run-ins, but as far as general behaviour, yes. They were liked by the staff too.'

'Yes, we noted the close relationship between Jack Bell and your officer Jeanie Clark. Is that usual?'

'It's only a problem if it's inappropriate,' Brian said. Kelly noticed that he seemed uncomfortable at the notion.

'And it wasn't?' Kelly asked.

Brian looked at Craig, who said nothing.

'No, of course not. Jeanie is known for looking after her lads. I mean, she talks to them, mothers them a bit, you know? They like her. She makes things run smoothly, she's a calming influence on the inmates,' Brian said. 'In here, this is their home, and at the end of the day, my officers want no trouble, and to go home to their families unhurt.'

'Right,' Kelly said. 'But is it normal for her to meet them on the outside after release?'

Brian looked puzzled. 'Are you telling me that she met Jack Bell and Dean Kirby after their release?'

'I'm telling you that she had arranged to meet Jack Bell and that it was she who reported him missing, which is how we identified him and connected him to Dean Kirby, and Highton,' Kelly said. She flicked through her notepad. 'Jeanie told us that Dean and Jack were on the same wing, A wing. We'd like to speak to some of the men on that wing please. We have plenty of time so can fit in around their working day.' Kelly asked.

She waited. She found Brian Taylor too buoyant and chummy. A man in his position should be a little distracted, stressed, a tad gloomy even. Two of his ex-inmates had been brutally murdered, and one of his officers had planned to see one of them out of hours. Add to that all the pressures of running a Category A prison, and she couldn't help but reach the conclusion that he was either not suitable for the job, or hiding something. Or both.

He picked up the phone and dialled an extension number. 'Liam, I've got local police detectives here, they're investigating Bell and Kirby's deaths. They want to conduct some interviews with A wing inmates.' He paused. 'Today.' Another pause. 'Can you arrange it?' He hung up.

'That was the custodial manager of A wing, where Jack and Dean were held until they were released,' Brian said. 'I'll warn you, my prisoners don't take well to surprise police visits, so get what you need and don't stir up a hornet's nest,' he said.

'I appreciate the delicacy of the situation, and I'm very grateful for your permission. I came myself because the nature of the crimes is of the gravest level,' Kelly said. 'I'll go easy. I don't want to be responsible for any trouble after we've left.'

Brian nodded. 'How did it happen?' he asked.

Kelly saw a flicker of humanity and realised that Brian Taylor had probably seen some of the nastiest wounds inflicted on human bodies. Like the police, she knew that prison officers cauterised their emotions over such things.

'We're piecing it together. You'll appreciate that I can't share details at the moment,' she said. Brian looked at Craig again and it needled her. 'Is there an old-timer on

A wing who runs things?' she asked. Brian looked at her. She waited. Still Craig said nothing.

'Jack Bell would have been that man,' Brian said finally.

'Really?' Kelly said. 'That's not the impression I got from Jeanie Clark,' she said.

'Oh?' Brian asked. 'I'm assuming, of course, that the popular ones have more privileges and the senior ones are respected. You'll have to speak to the custodial manager about that.'

Kelly figured that assumption was the last thing a governor of a Category A prison would rely upon, but let it pass.

'Right. And how about communication between prisoners and the outside? I'm figuring the trade in mobile phone hardware is as buoyant as ever,' she said.

'The discovery of contraband is dealt with sternly, detective. No one wants two weeks in the block,' he said. The block was another name for solitary confinement, and it was a living hell. Being locked up in a dark cell in the bowels of the prison for twenty-four hours a day, with no fresh air or exercise, and maybe a radio for company for good behaviour, if you had batteries, was pure torture.

'When was the last search carried out for mobile phones?' she asked.

'I'll have to consult with my custodial managers, but I can assure you that cell searches are a regular and normal occurrence here at Highton.'

'Glad to hear it. And what sort of contraband do you usually find? How much does a mobile phone sell for in here, for example?' she asked.

'There's no trade allowed inside the prison, that's strictly against the rules,' he said. She could see that he was becoming flushed under his collar.

'Of course it is,' she said. 'Perhaps you could take advice from your police liaison officer as to whether a cell search, in the light of the current turn of events, would be something you'd consider.'

'I'll consult and get back to you. However, if you're suggesting a full wing search then I'll need to take legal advice. You appreciate that kind of thing can kick off a lot of trouble?'

'Of course. I thought that, in this situation, you'd agree with us, governor,' she said.

'I do, in principle. But full wing searches need to be handled with care,' he said.

'Do you track calls being made to and from the prison?' she asked.

'That's all very well in la-la land, detective, but in the real world, we don't have those resources. Like I said, contraband is dealt with sternly. If you'd like access to the mobile tower then I'm sure you can get it with a warrant. I'll have an officer escort you to the wings.'

The conversation was over.

Chapter 21

'S&M, or sadomasochism – a combination of two men's surnames. The Marquis de Sade, a French nobleman and the father of sexual cruelty, and Leopold von Sacher-Masoch, an Austrian writer who wrote about the fantasy of being sexually dominated.'

Kelly sipped her tea, which was insipid and vile. They were sat in the officers' canteen, which apparently served marginally superior food to that in the convict's mess hall.

'Where do you get all this stuff?' Craig asked her.

'It interests me. This case has got me thinking. The motive is elusive, but this fits. We can't ignore it.'

'With no sex?' he asked.

'That isn't ruled out yet. This type of personal prolonged harm is often linked to sexual gratification in murders.'

'I thought the point of S&M was to survive to do it over and over again. Isn't the addiction one of submission and dominance? They're not supposed to die,' Craig pointed out.

'Yes, correct, but it's the same *process*. The punishment of Jack Bell took time and it was enjoyed, indicating to me that this is a killer who derives pleasure from all kinds of pain. An obsession with pain, is there a term for that?' she asked.

'That's where your masochism comes in, isn't it?' he asked.

'That's inflicting pain on oneself,' Kelly said.

'But isn't the sadism part about inflicting pain on others? The whole *process*, like you say, depends upon having a dominant and the submissive – both are crucial for sexual gratification,' he said. 'This wasn't a partnership, this was an abuser and their abused.'

'Now who's an expert?' she said. 'Okay, so we're looking for someone who has formed an unhealthy bond with pain, so they must have either seen pain or experienced it themselves,' she said. Then she rolled her eyes. 'Isn't it lovely, having people like that in your life? I should transfer to traffic.'

'Are you getting tired of it all?' he said.

'I didn't think I was,' she said.

'Is it Lizzie? Now you're a mum, you feel a bit more mortal and vulnerable? The only thing parents want – well most of them anyway – is to protect their children, and we can't. Well, after a point, we can't. And we know, because of what we do, what some twisted psychos are capable of,' he said.

'And usually because they didn't have parents who gave a shit,' she said.

'That's normally the case, yes. But this is too deep for a Thursday morning, Kelly. I know you live for catching these weirdos, like I do, and don't worry, you'll get this one too,' he said.

A prison officer came towards them and Kelly noticed the three stripes on his shoulder epaulettes. He held out his hand to Craig, and introduced himself as Custodial Manager Liam Fawcett. Once again, Craig made a point of introducing Kelly as the SIO, but then Kelly guessed that CM Liam Fawcett already knew that.

'I've arranged for you to interview three inmates this afternoon,' he said.

'Great, can you sit down and join us? We'd like to get your take on Jack Bell and Dean Kirby. You must have known them well.' Kelly said. Liam looked at his watch.

'I appreciate you're busy,' Kelly added. She noticed a junior officer come into the room and look at her. Kelly reckoned it might be Tom Gorman. He only had one stripe on his shoulder.

'I've got a rookie in today, I'm showing him round,' Liam said, following her gaze.

Kelly nodded.

'We won't take much of your time,' she said.

He sat down. He was a big man and looked awkward perched on a prison chair.

'Tell us what you know. Your impressions of both men, who they hung out with, what they were like as prisoners,' Kelly said.

'They were pretty different. Jack was a kind of father figure to the young ones. He kept clean. Didn't do drugs, and surprised me; he didn't look like a criminal, he shouldn't have been here. Dean was the opposite, he was a naughty lad, always in the wrong place at the wrong time, and he had swagger. He got into a couple of fights in the early days, but then Jack took him under his wing.'

It was the second time she'd heard this morning that Jack Bell shouldn't have been here.

'So they were close?' Kelly asked. Liam nodded.

'What about enemies?' she asked.

'In here? Jesus, take your pick, it's not exactly a friendly place. Drugs, drink and being caged up all day aren't conducive to positive relations. Grudges get carried out on the wrong people, accidents happen,' he said.

'Accidents?' Craig asked.

'There'll be a disagreement about something trivial, like TV or cigarette papers, and one thing leads to another and it turns violent,' Liam said.

'And that happened to Dean and Jack?' Kelly asked.

'Dean mainly.'

'Who did he irk the most?' Kelly asked.

'Well, that's the thing, he got into scrapes and low-level threats, but there wasn't one person I could say he had a problem with, and besides, even if he did, how could they get to him outside?' Liam said.

'Easily, as far as I gather. A relative, a paid hit, it's quite straightforward,' she said.

'But you're assuming someone in here ordered it, for what? Jack and Dean weren't playing sides, they weren't trading goods, as far as we know, they were just doing their time, and mobile phones are banned.'

'Oh, come on, are you telling me that the men inside this prison don't have mobile phones?' Kelly asked.

'They're not supposed to,' Liam replied.

It was a weak argument and reminded her of the governor's attitude. She changed the subject.

'Is Rickie Burton on the list of people we're seeing this afternoon?' Kelly asked.

'He is. Is he important?' Liam asked. Kelly eyed him. If Jeanie Clark had told them that Rickie Burton ran A wing, then CM Fawcett would sure as hell know it.

'What do you think? You see these men day in, day out. We were told that Rickie Burton, otherwise known as the Shed, is unofficially in charge of A wing,' Kelly said.

'He might think he is, but I actually am. Whoever told you that has no authority or grounds,' he said.

'It was your officer, Jeanie Clark,' Kelly said. Liam Fawcett's left eye quivered momentarily, but his face didn't flinch. Now Kelly had two senior officers playing down Rickie Burton's role inside HMP Highton. Jeanie Clark had no motive to lie and they'd got to her before any of her bosses had.

'Were Dean Kirby and Jack Bell inside Rickie Burton's circle or out of it?' she asked.

'In it,' Liam said. His lips barely moved. He shuffled in his seat and Kelly knew that he was uncomfortable. She asked him one more question.

'Does Rickie have many visitors? Of course, we'll be requesting the CCTV from visitor days,' she added.

'I don't supervise visitor days, I remain on the wing making sure we get through the day without a serious incident,' he said. Again, his response was short and terse.

'So you run A wing, and Rickie Burton is a prominent character on the wing – your wing – and you never chatted to him about visitor days? I thought that was something all cons looked forward to, and couldn't shut up about,' she said.

Liam Fawcett stretched, as if bored. He went to get up. 'It's the junior officers who chat to the lads. I spend most of my time in the wing office. To be honest, cons aren't great company, and I'm very busy as it is,' he said. He stood up and towered over them.

'Of course. We'll talk to the more junior officers on duty, and let you get on with your day,' she said, smiling.

Fawcett called over the new officer.

'This is Prison Officer Gorman. Tom,' Liam turned to him. 'Change of plan. Can you take the detectives down to the gym? I've set up interviews with three inmates from A wing – you can escort them back and forth. If you need help, tell the supervising officer.'

Tom nodded and smiled at the detectives. Kelly held out her hand and he took it. They exchanged a knowing look, missed by Craig. Liam made his excuses and left, and Kelly and Craig gathered their things, ready to be escorted to the gym, where tables and chairs had been set up for them to conduct their interviews.

Chapter 22

Liam Fawcett made his way to the technical support room. He squeezed his fists together in a quiet rhythm. His polished shoes clunked on the plastic flooring and echoed down the halls of the prison. He made his way through a series of huge metal gates, which banged behind him. Officers greeted him with 'Sir' and he nodded his acknowledgement. He was *something* round here, and Kelly Porter had made him feel insignificant. His temper raged. Finally he made it to the tiny room to the rear of the prison, from where its guts functioned. There were several rooms housing boilers, electrical circuits, and the one he stopped outside, which housed the feed for the CCTV cameras. He went inside.

'Sir,' said a woman sitting at a desk, staring at a TV screen. She jumped up and went to speak, but he stopped her. 'Save it,' he said. 'I want to see the footage from Jack's last day,' he demanded. The woman was Jeanie Clark.

'That copper thinks you're off sick, with stress,' he added.

'Technically I am, I just came in to do something I forgot about,' she said.

'Fucking hell, Jeanie, why did you tell her that Rickie runs A wing? I looked a twat in front of her. She has this sidekick,' he said.

'Another woman, but older?' Jeanie asked.

'No, a bloke. He's docile, just sits there, and lets her whine on and stick her nose in.'

'I'm sorry. I made a mistake. I was shocked about Jack,' she said. 'They came to my house and started asking questions about the prison. I'd only just found out about Jack there and then – they identified his body from his tattoo. What the hell happened to him?' she asked.

'I don't get involved in all of that, it's none of my business, but if he deserved it, then that's the way of it. We don't know what these cons get up to, Jeanie. That's the bottom line and we stick to it, understood? I know you were fond of him.' He turned to the screen. 'Are you rubbing some CCTV?' he asked.

She nodded, and carried on searching.

'Let's see his last day,' he said.

They watched together and Liam drew up a chair. 'All the governor cares about is the status quo, he wants no trouble,' Liam said.

'It's a bit late for that, isn't it? Will they talk to Rickie?' she asked.

'Yeah, they're seeing him as we speak. He's too good for her though – that detective – she thinks she's clever and we're all stupid. I left the rookie to deal with her,' he said.

'Tom? I was supposed to do that for you, sorry,' she said.

'No worries, Jeanie. I'm sure it was a shock for you. You've got to admit, though, it's a bit sloppy hitting two ex-cons at the same time.'

'What do you think Jack did?' she asked. 'I thought I knew him,' she added.

'Jeanie, come on, he was a con. Surely you didn't fall that hard?'

He watched her and realised that she had. Her face said it all. It was strained, and she had dark circles round her eyes. He'd watched as their relationship went from amenable banter to close cosy chats and stolen glances. Liam had thought of stopping her but could think of no good reason to spoil it. Christ, it wasn't as if it was hurting anyone. But now, as he watched her, he understood how far things had gone.

The footage in question came up on the screen and Jeanie slowed it down. They kept digital records for a month and then it was sent to a central office somewhere in Swansea, to be filed permanently. Prison CCTV was often used in criminal cases. They kept the lot. However, working a month back, it could be deleted at source. Jeanie put her hand to her mouth as she watched her last conversation with Jack played back. Liam gently lifted her hand off the computer mouse and took over. There was no sound, just the ethereal and grainy footage of the man, when he had still been living and breathing.

'I'm not sure I can do this anymore,' said Jeanie. Liam looked at her and frowned.

'Look, Jeanie, all we're doing is making sure the system works. That's all we've ever done.' He grew serious.

'I know, I know, Liam. God, I know that.' She put her head in her hands.

'Maybe you should take some time off, and don't speak to that detective. You might slip up,' he said.

She looked up and he could see that she was worried, but he wasn't threatening her. He meant it, she needed a break, he could see that much. She gazed back at the computer screen and watched Jack say goodbye at the front gate, and then he was gone.

'Can you excuse me for a minute, Liam? I need to find something else,' she asked.

'What?'

'It's private,' she said.

'But it's on CCTV?' he asked.

'It might be,' she said.

'For fuck's sake, Jeanie, you were *that* sloppy?'

'Don't be stupid! Of course not! But I was on that wing, with him, a lot, and I mean a *lot*. Anyone trying to find an excuse to accuse me of getting too close could piece stuff together, and it wasn't like that. And I feel bad enough about it as it is, without you reading me my rights.'

'What was it, in his cell or something?' he asked.

'There's no CCTV in cells.' Their voices had lowered to a whisper and the assonance of the consonants rang around the small room in hisses, more marked by Jeanie's panic.

'No, I just think that if that copper goes digging, maybe she'll find some malpractice, you know, some days there's only me on the wing with eighty blokes.'

He stared at her and then to the screen. He knew it was the right thing to do.

'Do it, but be quick,' he said.

She rewound the footage of Jack speaking to her before he left prison and deleted it to make it look like he walked straight out after the final checks.

'That female detective is shrewd, she'll come after you if she suspects anything.'

'Aren't you worried what she might get out of Rickie Burton?' she asked.

'No. Not at all, his poker face is better than I suspect hers is. The big male with her is a dark horse, though, he's a watcher,' he said. 'Right, I'll leave you now. Make sure you cover your tracks. Can you replace it with something?' he asked. 'Gaps will beg questions,' he added.

'Leave it with me, I know what to do. I can loop it so no time is lost.'

'Jesus, were you a spy in a former life?' Liam asked.

'I worked in a photo lab for ten years. Why do you think the governor likes me so much? I'm useful.'

'Make sure you stay that way,' Liam said. 'He's getting antsy. He doesn't want his face rubbed in any shit. He likes to keep his hands clean, you know that.'

He left and closed the door.

Chapter 23

Ted went through the motions of booting and gloving up. Protective gear was worn during a post-mortem operation to protect the surgeon, not the patient. Joseph Lister might have revolutionised surgery back in the day, but germs couldn't bother a corpse. It was hot work under so many layers, but Ted was used to it and the mortuary was cold. He'd read through the notes on Dean Kirby, the man lying on his metal slab next door, inside a black body bag, waiting to be examined.

Kelly was keen to find out the time of death because the modus operandi of this killing was almost exactly the same as that of Jack Bell.

But.

And it was a big but.

If Jack Bell had been tortured for two days and finally killed on Tuesday, that didn't leave any time for the same person to carry out another murder twenty miles away, especially if Dean Kirby's body showed signs of prolonged torture as well. Ted's gut feeling was that Dean's body had been in the warehouse longer than Jack Bell's. Both bodies had been found yesterday but, whereas Jack Bell had lain there dead for around twelve hours, Dean's body looked more degraded. Putrefaction had begun, he saw that from the photos he'd been sent. Kelly hadn't had the opportunity to visit the crime scene this time and so neither of them had the benefit of witnessing the body as it lay. To an untrained eye, especially one looking at photographs, a dead body in the first stages of decomposition, around a time period of a week, depending on weather, surroundings and insect activity, looked pretty standard: colourless, bruised and whiffy. Dead flesh began to smell quickly but the activity in the first stages was all inside, out of sight, unless the body was gaping open. It's only when the insides have liquefied that the rot spills outside. There are many factors complementing this process, of course, and discovering which of them were at play here was just what Ted intended to do. It was crucial that he produce a timeline for Kelly, so she could work on finding either a serial murderer, or multiple killers. It would be vital to her case.

Ted had written on Jack Bell's post-mortem notes that he died somewhere between midday and midnight on Tuesday. He also knew that Dean Kirby's last confirmed movements were on Friday, at Saltcoats, and that was the day Jack Bell had been released from HMP Highton. It all indicated to him that these attacks were very well planned, and not at all random. His suspicion that Dean Kirby had remained on the warehouse floor for longer than Jack Bell had done had prompted him to call a forensic entomologist, who had agreed to Zoom in to the autopsy remotely. That way, instead of Ted waiting for insect evidence to be sent away to an expensive lab, he could get expert opinion live from an old pal, who he'd attended university with. Of course, some evidence would still have to be sent to a lab, but Ted trusted Professor David Tripp implicitly, and he could give his analysis on the call, thus saving them a little bit of money.

Once he was covered in plastic, Ted went in to the mortuary room and popped his goggles on, as well as his mic. He greeted his assistants, who had already laid everything out. They were a well-oiled team. It occurred to him that, this week, he'd been inside this room a little too often, and for the worst reasons. Kelly's job was to work out who did these hideous things to human bodies, and Ted was all too aware of the irony that he could cut up dead bodies for a living, but couldn't possibly face what it took to find out why they'd ended up that way. That was the real gritty work. Looking family members in the eye and asking questions no one wanted to hear.

The professor joined them from the remote invitation to Zoom, from his computer, and Ted nodded hello. They chatted briefly about how long it had been since they enjoyed a pint, and how their families were. A few comments about the news and politics followed, and then Ted turned to the pressing subject of the day: rot. He'd already sent the notes across to David and now Ted took a small camera, linked by Wi-Fi to his computer, and approached the body bag.

'How's the picture, David?' Ted asked.

'Clear as a bell,' David replied. He sat in a fancy office and Ted could see paintings, books and a hearth behind him. David leant forward as if he were in the room with them, for a better look.

Unfortunately, the chair that Dean Kirby was strapped to had been removed before he was zipped up inside the bag. However, there were a few exhibits taken from underneath him. It would have been helpful for Ted to witness the position of the chair first-hand, as well as to see how he was fastened to it, but that moment had been lost. The same kind of strapping had been bagged and tagged, though, which was another aid for Kelly. The attending officers hadn't known about the body in Workington. At least he had the photographs. Unlike Jack Bell, this body had been on its side and the blood pooling was consistent to his expiry happening in that position. The poor guy had had enough, no doubt.

When they were all ready, Ted checked his mic and unzipped the body bag. The first thing they all noted was the smell and, sure enough, a fat maggot fell onto the floor. Ted bent down and held the camera close.

'It's a *Calliphoridae* larvae for sure. You say he was inside a warehouse? Was it protected from the elements?' David asked.

'Yes, it was pretty cosy in there, from what I've learned,' Ted replied. DI Craig Lockwood had visited the site and explained to him that the warehouse was closed up and the ambient temperature in there was thirteen degrees. Insect activity would be pretty standard at that temperature, especially with nice fresh carrion to feed on, and an absence of other curious beasties, not interested in a concrete shell. Other flies would be attracted of course, but *Calliphoridae* was always first to the party.

'Our friend the blowfly,' Ted said.

'Indeed. So-called for the old assumption that's how they turned meat bad, by blowing their breath over it,' David said. 'Adults lay their eggs within minutes of death, if they're in the area. They can detect carrion from two kilometres away. It was by a beach, you say?' he asked.

'Yes, less than a mile inland,' Ted said.

'Many sheep?' David asked. Cumbria was famed for blowfly strike because of its huge sheep population, especially between the months of May to September.

'There are several farms in the surrounding area,' Ted said. He'd already looked this up when assessing the crime site.

'Makes sense. So the initial larva stage would begin about twelve hours after death. The larvae go through two more stages, as they grow and shed their skin, and then emerge as adults after about three days. Were there any burrowed nearby?'

'No, the warehouse was clear of any other organic matter so there was nowhere to burrow. Several specimens were located surrounding the body, though.'

'So they'd reached maturity and were looking for somewhere to tunnel in, to pupate. That takes about three days, so that's what we're working on here.'

Ted was almost relieved. That fitted with the timeline in his head. If Dean Kirby was taken somewhere on Friday, when he was spotted at Saltcoats, then he likely died on Saturday or Sunday, four days ago, and before Tania Carter saw Jack Bell being forced into the warehouse in Workington. It could be the same killer.

'That makes sense, because from what I can see, his body is on the verge of going into bloat. So three days adds up for me. Can I send you some samples to confirm?' Ted asked.

'Of course. Are there any open wounds?' David asked. Putrefaction was accelerated should a corpse be badly damaged.

Ted turned to the metal slab and further revealed the body, taking the camera close for David to see the wounds. One of his assistants took photographs and another took measurements. None of them showed any reaction to the increasing stench. They were used to it. Ted always used a scented ointment under his nose, but it was more out of habit than anything else. It didn't really mask the perfume of decay. He took a pair of tweezers and removed several maggots from the body, placing them into tiny tubes. An assistant labelled them.

'I can see several stages there,' David said.

As corpses rotted, more and more flies were attracted to the site and it could quickly get crowded. Ted almost had the body bag fully off now and it was clear that flies had colonised much of the body. Orifices and lacerations were the obvious host sites, and Dean's eyes were full of larvae of different sizes. His mouth and ears had also been colonised. But what Ted noticed, and showed David with the camera, was the movement inside his body. It was clear that the whole organism was providing a meal to thousands of larvae, eager to feed and grow. The body lay on its back now and Ted noted that the abdomen was green, as a result of fermentation. It had also begun to swell, and that was what Ted referred to as the bloat stage. The man's internal organs were literally disintegrating, and Ted knew that there'd be little left to weigh or document. It was all part of the expiry of the human biome. At this stage, Ted knew that he'd have to turn to bacterial community composition, instead of complete organs, for answers. Lactobacillus in particular declined exponentially alongside decay, as more robust bacteria like proteobacteria thrived, and it was an accurate predictor of time of death. It was a sad but helpful fact that the science of gut microflora had come on leaps and bounds in the twenty-first century, indicative of the commonality of murders. Ted would still need to examine the cadaver, because he still needed to establish the cause of death. Sometimes, in specimens at this stage of deterioration, cause of death was impossible to ascertain, especially if the deceased died of cancer or heart attack, or indeed anything to do with the internal organism. But this was blunt trauma. Ted could see clearly that the man had sustained a serious head wound. Unlike Jack Bell, there were few other wounds, indicating that Dean Kirby had not been tortured for as long. Ted could see that one nipple was missing, and there were restraint marks around his wrists. Ted looked closer at the head wound, and gave the camera to a colleague, who was asked for close-ups on the larvae.

Upon closer inspection, Ted was able to state conclusively that a head wound of this severity would kill a person. He could see the man's brain and bits of skull embedded in the matter. In his experience, the shape of the trauma and the way the skull had caved in was consistent with a severe fall, or something like a head-butt. He couldn't help but reach the conclusion that it looked like an accident. No one would torture a man like this, because it simply wouldn't work. No information could be gleaned from a person after suffering such blow.

'I've got enough,' David said. Ted left the corpse and approached the desk where he'd placed his computer, and thanked the professor. They promised to meet up, as old friends do. Ted went back to his work and he began surveying the body, ignoring the insect activity. It was difficult to distinguish between rot and trauma, but Ted had enough experience to do so with conviction. He noted that the victim's genitals were black, and bruising consistent with force rather than decay was present all over his lower body. The guy had taken a beating for sure.

When he was satisfied that everything had been documented from the outside of the body, Ted prepared to eviscerate and go inside. It would be messy, that was certain. That was what the rim around the gurney was for, to collect body fluids. He fully expected a tsunami of maggots and gunk to flow out of the cavity as he opened it. He just hoped that there was enough of the man's heart and brain left to answer his questions about how he'd eventually died. For now, at least he could tell Kelly the news that they probably had a serial killer on their hands.

Chapter 24

Rickie Burton looked like a stereotypical hardened con from a Netflix documentary. Prison seemed to suit him, and he swaggered across the room to meet Kelly and Craig. He wore prison-issue dark grey joggers which looked odd on an ageing man; they were too baggy and better suited to a teenager. His hands were cuffed together, which made his gait even more pronounced. His dark grey sweater matched the bottoms. Category A prisoners generally had to wear issued clothes. Inmates in other prisons, there for lesser crimes, were allowed to wear their own clothes for good behaviour. Here, the less chance someone had to hide a weapon the better. His sweater was pulled up at the elbows and Kelly observed that his arms were covered in tattoos. She noticed the spider's web on his left elbow straight away. It encircled the joint, just like Jack's. He grinned at them and Kelly was struck by his confidence. It was like meeting with someone in their own home, not a formal request in a Category A state prison. But then, getting out of your wing for an hour, even if it was to meet a copper, was like a little holiday. The guard was remarkably casual too, but that could be part of the act of all prison officers: they made their wards feel comfortable. The guard accompanied Rickie to the chair provided and Kelly and Craig remained seated.

'Mr Burton, ma'am,' the officer said. Kelly nodded. Rickie Burton sat down and looked at the detectives. He sported a long unsightly scar down his jawline and Kelly noticed that he had most of an ear missing. It looked mangled, like that of any respectable English rugby league player from the 1970s. Her eyes lingered on the scar and she felt repulsed and fascinated at the same time. He touched it and she darted her eyes away. Burton was looking at Craig, and so he didn't seem to notice her indiscretion. The guard stood by the wall and put his hands in his pockets. Tom had gone off to return to duty.

'Do you want a chair?' Kelly asked the officer, who replied that he was happy standing for as long as it took. Fair enough. He was a pleasant enough chap who unfortunately had to stay, it was prison protocol. Kelly didn't expect any trouble, but she did want to ask some pertinent questions about prison routines and leadership. No doubt it would all be fed back to CM Fawcett. She had nothing to hide, though it would be interesting to see how Rickie Burton acted in front of prison staff.

'Mr Burton, may I call you Rickie?' she asked. Burton looked at her and shrugged. He touched the skin where the rest of his ear should have been, often.

'I don't mind,' he said. His accent was local and his voice gravelly.

'Thank you. This is DI Lockwood and I'm DI Porter, and we'd like to ask you some questions about Jack Bell,' she said.

He shook his head and looked at his feet. Kelly reckoned he'd been interviewed by police more times than he could remember, and to him, this was all a game.

'Bastards,' he said.

'Pardon?' Kelly asked.

'Bastards,' he said, louder.

'Who?'

'The fuckers who killed him,' he said, as if Kelly was stupid to ask.

'Plural? What makes you so sure?' she asked.

'We might be in the nick, but I still read the news, and get told stuff. I heard he was beat up bad. It'd take more than one man to do that to Jack Bell and get away with it,' he said.

'And do you know of any people who might want to do just that?' she asked.

'Plenty. You want to take a look on D wing. The nonces in there had it in for Jack. They always did. They hit him hard one day, I'm going back a few years now. That's when I told him to ask for a transfer to my – I mean – A wing,' he said.

'Why was he allowed to do that if he was on a sex offenders' wing? I thought they were kept separate from other prisoners, or that's how I understood it,' she said.

'Jack was in for rape,' he said.

'That's a sex offence,' Kelly said.

'Not if she was asking for it.'

Kelly's throat constricted and she felt acid swirl in her stomach. She looked at Craig, who sat forward and spoke quietly.

'Watch your mouth,' he said. Burton smiled. He was enjoying himself. He was the sort of person who loved a good bombshell. Especially if it shocked a woman.

'DI Lockwood, would you check that conviction for me?' she asked. Craig nodded and checked his notes. The governor had allowed them access to Rickie Burton's file as well as those of Jack Bell and Dean Kirby, they just hadn't had time to trawl fully through them yet and she was under the impression that Jack Bell was a burglar. Kelly turned back to Rickie.

'It was our understanding that he was doing time for aggravated robbery,' she said.

'Ah yes, but the rape was before that. The first time he was in prison. If you get done for rape – and he was framed mind, the fucking bitch made it up – then you'll always land yourself on a sex offender's wing, even if you go down for something else. That's how it works, they don't want troublemakers mixing on regular wings,' he said.

'So rapists aren't sex offenders in your book?'

'Not if it was fair dos,' he said. His mouth curled slightly at the edges and the tiny hairs on Kelly's arms stood up.

She changed the subject.

'Did you and Jack get those tattoos together? They're very similar, almost identical,' she asked, pointing at his elbow.

'Yep, there's a lad on the wing who trained up and charges the lads for work. He's good.'

'So, you and Jack were close friends? You got him on your wing and you got matching tattoos?'

'He was like a brother,' he said. Kelly saw his eyes go red and watery, but something about the way he talked made her uncomfortable, and hesitant to believe anything that came out of his mouth. Emotion does very specific things to a human face, and she was seeing little evidence of authenticity here. Maybe it was just because he was a con, and subconsciously, she couldn't trust him. She'd learned over the years that criminals rarely give anything away for free, especially to coppers.

'So, it's your theory that certain prisoners from D wing ordered people on the outside to kill Jack?' she asked.

Rickie nodded. 'That'll be right,' he said. He leant back and stretched out his legs, putting his arms behind his head. He took up a lot of space and Kelly got the impression that he enjoyed throwing his weight around.

'And where do they keep their mobile phones?' she asked.

He smiled and shrugged. He was enjoying the break to his routine.

'How much does one go for now?' she asked.

He shrugged again. 'I don't deal in contraband,' he said. She let it go.

'When do you get out?' she asked.

'Never,' he replied.

'And you're not bothered by that?'

'Why should I be? I've got everything I need in here,' he said.

'Except your freedom,' she said. He grinned again and she saw well-worn teeth stained yellow. She thought of her father. They were around the same age, but one was dignified, quick-witted and kind, and the other still behaved like a little boy. The man before her was beyond immature; he was undeveloped. He'd most likely been the wrong side of the law all his life and had never carved a satisfactory and legal existence for himself. He lived comfortably at Her Majesty's pleasure and clearly felt safe here. He didn't want to leave. Maybe he didn't want Jack to leave either. Or Dean.

'Were you disappointed to see Jack released? You must have dreaded it,' she said.

He sat up and flicked something off his trousers. 'You get used to it,' he said. 'People come and go all the time. That's prison life.'

'You're local to Cumbria, like Jack? I can hear it in your accent,' she added.

'Yup, I'm a Workington lad, like Jack was,' he said.

'And the people on D wing, who you said are responsible for Jack's death, they're Cumbrian too?'

'Nah, they're southern poofs, from Kent or somewhere,' he said.

'So, there are specific individuals on D wing who you think might be behind this?'

'Like I told you, the two nonces in there who are in charge, Lofty and Titch, they're called, but I can tell that you now they're not their real names.' He winked.

'Thanks, I'm sure I can find out. Officer?' she asked.

'Yes, ma'am,' he responded.

'Lofty and Titch on D wing? You know them?'

'Yes ma'am,' he replied.

'Good, can you arrange for me to see them too? I'm sure the governor won't mind,' she said. He nodded and radioed a colleague to come and replace him. She turned back to Rickie.

'They call you the Shed? I guess that's due to your size? Everybody has nicknames in here, don't they? Dinger Bell. It's like the army. Coppers do it too.' She chatted easily and calmly. He rolled his eyes and she knew that her reference to coppers being anything approaching normal lads and lasses amused him.

'So if Lofty and Titch run D wing, who runs your wing?'

'I do,' he replied.

Craig looked up from his notes. 'Jack Bell did three years for rape between 2001 and 2004. He was incarcerated on D wing for the whole stretch and the same men were incarcerated with him at the time.'

'Lofty and Titch?' Kelly asked.

'Yes,' Craig replied. Kelly watched Rickie smile again. This must be the highlight of his year, she thought. He was having such a good time that he'd completely forgotten to keep up the grieving act for his dear friend, and he'd begun so well.

Chapter 25

'Have you tidied up after yourself?' Brian Taylor asked his custodial manager. Liam shifted uncomfortably on the spot. Suddenly his new shoes hurt.

'Always, guv. There's nothing you should be worried about, the police are just on a fishing trip,' Liam added.

'Me, worried?'

Liam watched as his boss's temper bubble under the surface. His voice was becoming louder and louder and Liam expected an imminent explosion. The governor's capacity for rage was legendary. All he wanted was a smooth-running ship. If anything went wrong, Brian Taylor hunted for blood until someone was punished. Liam got the feeling that he was next in line.

'I tell you what, sonny, if any shit hits the fan, it'll be you covered in muck, not fucking me, is that loud and clear?'

Liam nodded. 'Yes, sir,' he said. 'I didn't mean to suggest that there was a problem for you, at all, sir. I mean, there's nothing to worry about in any way, that's what I meant to say.'

'What the actual fuck is Jeanie Clark doing telling a copper that a con runs one of my wings?'

The governor paced up and down in his office, and when he asked this question, he stopped in front of his prison officer and eyeballed him. Liam was wider, more muscular and taller, but that mattered for nothing when faced with Brian Taylor's wrath. Everybody who worked in HMP Highton was used to the governor's colourful language. It wasn't uncommon. Who could cope working in such an environment without some form of release? Not many, that was for sure. It didn't offend anyone, it was just something you got used to. Of course, the equal opportunities officer had to massage his reports. On paper, Highton was a model of official inclusion. The fact that most officers were white males didn't look good, but Brian was working on that. Jeanie Clark was a valuable member of the team because she was a woman working in a man's world, and that looked good. They couldn't afford to be seen firing women, but Jeanie had fucked up, and now it was about damage limitation. Liam had seen first-hand what the governor was capable of, and he was not the kind of man who ever got caught out.

'Sir, if I might point out. The coppers are just looking into Jack Bell and Dean Kirby's records, they're not here for anything else,' Liam said.

'And now they're interviewing Rickie *fucking* Burton!' Now Brian was shouting, and Liam winced at the emphasis on the expletive. Brian loved the word 'fuck'. Everybody knew that the governor's daily mood was indicated by how many times he used his favourite word and with what level of volume. Today it was repetitive and loud.

'I briefed him before the interview, sir. He's going to lay everything on Lofty and Titch. It'll divert them. He's a natural, sir, trust me, it'll work out,' Liam soothed. Brian began to calm a little and sat down behind his desk.

'I hope you're fucking right,' he said. 'She was asking about the trade in mobile fucking phones!'

'Sir, if there's a thorough enough search for wing phones, it'll cause a full-blown riot,' Liam said.

'I know that!'

'They're a thousand quid a pop now,' Liam said. 'Sir, let me go and check everything is in order. The female copper wants to interview a few of our nonces on D wing now, so it looks like whatever Rickie said had the effect we wanted. He's a good one, that one, he's on our side,' he said. 'Maybe I can get him to deliver up some drug addicts who've traded spice for phones and that'll put her off.'

Brian nodded and Liam felt relief that he'd averted disaster, for now.

'Did anyone see this coming? Is it anyone we know? Somebody from another prison perhaps, or an old enemy getting even?' Brian asked.

'That was my thought, but both of them? It's an odd one,' Liam said.

'I don't like that fucking woman nosing around my business,' Brian said.

'I know, guv, let me handle it. Rickie knows what to do and it's not as if he's going to prison for it, is it?'

Brian smiled at the joke.

'What's going on with D wing? Have things settled down? The last thing I need is Lofty and Titch being chased on this and the wing descending into chaos again. I had a long conversation with the prison service about the injuries of the inmate. It's not enough to say we're under-staffed. His family was considering suing us but they've been talked out of it by some fancy barrister working for the CPS.'

'Privileges have been cut for everyone involved, sir. Lofty and Titch have it in hand. Don't worry about them being distracted. We've upped the meds of a few of them as well so they won't cause trouble,' Liam said.

'If only we could do that with all of 'em. Needles, that's the way forward! Rehabilitation, my arse, drug 'em up and lock the door! Right, Liam. I feel better.'

Liam nodded. 'Good, sir. Can I get you a cuppa?' he asked.

'Yes, good lad, you can,' Brian said. He sat on the chair behind his desk and opened his computer. The fifty extra inmates from Altcourse were arriving this afternoon.

The timing sucked.

Chapter 26

Kelly felt decidedly uncomfortable. It was rare that she met someone who freaked her out to this extent. The man sat in front of her was skinny, what her mother would call lanky. He looked insipid, if that was an adjective that could be used to describe a human being. It was all she could think of. She looked at his hands, which were long and thin, like him, and at his clean nails, which were feminine and dainty. A shiver travelled up her spine when she glanced at his eyes. They were black and dead.

His nickname was Titch, but neither Kelly nor Craig found that ironic or funny. It was simply revolting. There was nothing minimal about him, apart from his mouth, which was small and pinched. No matter what she told herself to think, or how she hoped she'd manage her emotions, when faced with a prisoner of his ilk, she couldn't help but imagine his crimes. Craig had examined the file of the two men who allegedly ran D wing. This one was inside for raping five children aged between three and twelve years old.

Bile threatened to escape from Kelly's duodenum; her head told her that she had no control over the organ and its collection of the substance from her liver, but digestive physiology wasn't important here. It was simply that she felt as though she was going to throw up. The very notion of this man's hands on a child made her feel violently wretched, and angry. She wanted to rip his fucking head off. She sensed that Craig felt the same, but, as good coppers do, they both kept their feelings hidden. Even working with the worst offenders like Titch, detectives had to remain calm and impartial, just in case they decided to confide in you and let a few nuggets of information slip. It had happened many times before. A case could be cracked wide open by a bastard like this trusting you, even for just a second.

With some, of course, you knew you'd never breach their defences. Some enjoyed the game. As she looked at Titch, she knew that he'd keep his secrets to the grave. He was suspected of murder too, but that had never been proven. Craig had given her all the information she needed to know from his file and that was more than she ever wanted to hear.

'We'd like to have a chat with you about how well you knew Jack Bell and Dean Kirby,' she said, introducing herself and Craig.

He held a vape in his cuffed hands and sucked on it, and a white cloud of vanilla shrouded him. Something about the combination of sweet and acrid reminded her of the aroma of a ripe corpse. She was struggling to rid herself of images of what this man had done. Spittle left his mouth and stuck to the mouthpiece as he puffed. Kelly knew that the fine balance of power inside a hardcore prison such as this was between those who relied on drugs, and those who didn't. The addicts were the mules, trading anything they could get their hands on for the spice that was imported into the prison via increasingly ingenious methods. The latest was by drone, controlled by someone on the perimeter and delivered into a broken window, while cons guarded the cell doors. Once inside, the big guys, who stayed clean, traded the shit for favours. A drug addict could be paid in spice to start a fight on the landing outside the cells, which was essentially a diversion, while debt was settled in another cell.

Kelly could tell from his face that Titch didn't do drugs.

'I knew Dinger from the last time. He was on D wing,' he said. Kelly knew that he was from the West Country and the drawl almost made him sound like a jolly farmer. It was an odd paradox.

'And did you get on?'

'No, I'm a paedophile, I get on with no one,' he said. He smiled and Kelly felt her fist clench around her pen.

'What about Lofty?' Kelly asked. Slowly, he smiled once more.

'Yep, he's like me. We're cellies.'

Kelly knew this was the common prison term for cell-mates. It sounded childlike and thus apt for such a man to use it. Maybe part of being incarcerated was that these criminals never grew up and took responsibility, like the rest of us did.

'Did Jack get into any trouble here when he was on D wing?' she asked.

'There's always fights on D wing, on account of the crimes.' He held her stare.

'Why was he moved to A wing?'

'Rickie wanted him.'

'Can I clarify that you mean Rickie Burton?'

He nodded and took another drag of his vape.

'Why did you allow it? You're in charge of D wing, aren't you?'

'Jack was simple, you know, backward,' Titch said. 'He weren't no use to us.'

Kelly had read that Jack Bell would qualify as having special educational needs. In contrast, Craig told her that Titch's IQ was a staggering 132, which qualified him for Mensa.

'He was studying for GCSE English, every Wednesday, with the prison teacher, trying to better himself. That doesn't sound backward to me, as you put it,' Kelly said. She found herself defending the dead man.

'Rickie knows.' He smiled again and sucked on his vape. His fingers were stained yellow from when he was allowed the real thing.

'Knows what?'

'That Jack will do what he's told. On the inside, that is.' He smiled again.

'You know Rickie Burton implicated you in Jack's murder? Remotely, of course,' Kelly said, noting the inference in Titch's statement.

He let out a high-pitched howl and slapped his thigh, chuckling like a child telling a joke. He doubled over and continued to guffaw. It was an ugly sight. Kelly looked at Craig. They waited for the chortling to subside.

'Is that funny?' she asked.

'Hell, yeah. It's so funny. Me? Why would I do that? Dinger Bell saved my life.'

'How?'

They listened as he told them the story from years back, when he'd been set upon by paedo bashers. Jack Bell was painted as a hero.

'I told him not to go to A wing, but he'd been promised something on the outside. Money probably, or a job and a house, whatever it was. I told him he was an idiot and it was a trap, but I couldn't stop him. And now look. Dean followed him not long after.'

'What?' Kelly asked.

'He was promised the same thing.'

Chapter 27

'You're playing piggy in the middle,' Craig said as they left the building and walked back to their cars. They planned to drive to Seascale and grab a drink over a chat about what they'd learned from their visit to Highton. They could also visit the scene of Dean Kirby's murder.

'You've got the gaffer of A wing blaming the gaffers of D wing, and vice versa. I'm wondering if any of them really knows what happened and they're just deflecting from any heat coming their way on our behalf,' he said.

'You mean, they're just playing games to divert any attention at all from their own wings, like children when taken into the headmaster's office and asked who started the fight. They'll say anything to get themselves off the hook,' she said.

He nodded.

'So we might be looking in completely the wrong place,' she said.

'It's possible. Until we have a motive, it's difficult to know. Maybe we should concentrate on who they both served time with, who is on the outside now, and has been for some time. These big cheeses in here are really small fry,' he said.

'Really? I'm not so sure. I've got officers working on that back in Penrith. I'm not ruling out the dynamic inside Highton,' she said, stopping to look back to the prison.

'I'm not convinced by the governor or the custodial manager. All they seem to care about is keeping the prisoners happy, and I wonder why that is. I understand how delicate the situation is, but we need a cell search to find the ways the prisoners communicate outside. I assume that any burner phone used to order a murder would have been destroyed by now, but we could concentrate the search on the signals bouncing off the local transmitter over the past couple of weeks,' Kelly said.

A car drove past and Kelly glanced at the driver, who was a woman with a scarf over her head, sitting low in her seat.

'That was Jeanie Clark,' Kelly said to Craig. The car sped off towards the exit and disappeared. 'She told me she'd been signed off sick. Why would she be coming in to work today?'

'She forgot something?' Craig suggested, dubious.

'Likely story,' Kelly said.

'I wonder if she knew Jack did time for rape,' she added. 'Do you think people can change?' she asked Craig. 'He was a model prisoner when he was here. Do you think he was manipulated by Rickie Burton and then used to carry out something on the outside? Something no one else knew about?'

Movement caught her eye and they watched as Liam Fawcett walked out of the prison towards his car. He acknowledged them tersely. They approached him.

'Knocking off shift for the day?' Craig asked.

'Yep, that's me done,' he said, taking off his jacket and opening the back door, throwing it on the seat. He looked perturbed.

'I thought Jeanie Clark was off sick, I've just seen her leave,' Kelly said.

'Yeah, I saw her, she needed to come in to get something for her laptop,' he said.

Kelly eyed him. 'I thought she was in shock,' Kelly said.

Liam opened the driver's door and got in.

'Can I ask you if you think it odd, a prison officer meeting up with an ex-prisoner for lunch?' Kelly asked.

'No, I don't find it odd at all, plus it's none of my business,' he said. He slammed his door and started his engine. Craig beckoned for him to put his window down, which he did. Craig leant in.

'This shouldn't be a "them and us" scenario, pal. We're on the same side, remember. But it does look suspicious when the boundaries between prisoners and their guards get smudged and everyone seems to be withholding potentially important information.'

'He speaks. What information? You're jumping to false conclusion after false conclusion. Highton's no different to any Category A gaff up and down the country. These fellas are pure fucking evil and they'll sell your granny if you let them. They need a firm hand, and we, as guards, need insider allies. That's all, end of. Do your job, *pal*, and I'll do mine.'

His window went back up.

He pulled away and Kelly watched his car leave the same way Jeanie's had. 'We've ruffled some feathers here,' she said.

'Yep, we sure have,' Craig said.

–

In the pretty seaside village of Seascale, Kelly looked for somewhere to park. Craig had told her that the centre of the small village had a car park near the railway line that split the hamlet in two. The coastal rail route was rugged and windswept and Kelly had once taken it with John Porter, who she believed at the time to be her father, years ago, when he took her and her sister to Ravenglass, to go on the steam train. The car park was near a children's play area and some kids were there with their parents, who eyed the unfamiliar car suspiciously. It was quite obvious that strangers didn't often turn up here. With less than 2,000 residents, Kelly guessed that everybody knew everyone's business. So Dean Kirby, with a dog, should have stood out.

There was an ice cream parlour and Kelly was reminded of her pregnancy cravings. She used to always find an excuse to drop in on her favourite ice cream shop at Glenridding, ordering two scoops of whatever took her fancy. Now her mouth watered. Craig parked next to her. The people at the park stared at them. They must have looked official, or like two office workers meeting for an illicit affair. They locked their cars, took coats and walked to the shop, where Kelly ordered coffee and a slice of cake. She was peckish. Craig added his order and they took a table by the window and peered out across the Irish Sea.

Sellafield, the nuclear plant under decommissioning, was hidden a mile down the coast and the view was of a windswept wilderness, with no clue of the monstrous structure behind the vast sand dunes. The colours on this stretch of coastline were made up of gentle greens, browns and the pure blue of the sea. It was remote and isolated and most of the population was employed by Sellafield. Such a life wasn't suited to Kelly, and she wondered what business Dean Kirby had here.

'Have you been notified yet about Dean Kirby boarding a train to Ravenglass?' she asked. They sat opposite one another and listened to the wind whistling outside. The windows rattled in the background. Craig looked at his phone and nodded. The woman came across with their order and they thanked her as she unloaded her tray. Craig nodded again as she left them to it and showed Kelly an email. She took his phone as he buttered his tea cake. Kelly looked at the email and the attached photograph. Dean had boarded the 1:24 p.m. from Barrow, which stopped at Ravenglass at 2:13 p.m. That fitted with the witness statement. She read the information out loud.

'It'd take about twenty minutes to walk from the station at Ravenglass to where the witness spotted him in Saltcoats, so it's more likely to be three p.m.,' said Craig.

'And the coroner came back to me with a time of death of sometime on Saturday. Let's drive the route to Seascale and look for residential cameras. Do we have anything from the house-to-house enquiries carried out here?' she asked. 'Did you notice the way they looked at us when we parked? They're not used to strangers.'

'Yes, but the killers might have simply driven through, straight to the abandoned waterworks.'

'Are they close by?' she asked.

'Not too far, we can walk. There's still a police presence there.' They finished their food and drinks and Kelly approached the woman behind the counter, who smiled. Kelly showed her ID card and introduced herself.

'You here about the body?' the woman asked.

'Yes, we are. Have you heard anyone talking about suspicious vehicles or activity around last Friday or Saturday?' Kelly asked.

'He was a bad 'un from Highton, wasn't he?' the woman asked.

'He was an inmate there, yes.'

'I remember his dog. Poor thing was found wandering round on the beach. They brought him in here and I gave him a bowl of water and some bread. Miserable wretch was starving,' she said.

'Had you seen him before, with somebody?' Kelly asked.

'I drove past him on Saturday morning when I came to open up, and he was on his own then, but I had no idea he was abandoned.'

'What time was that?' Kelly asked.

'Seven in the morning. I went to check once I'd got the lights on and stuff, but he was gone.'

'He was definitely on his own?' Kelly asked.

'Definitely, I can see all the way down the beach from both directions from the back of the shop, I'll show you,' she said. Kelly and Craig followed her around the counter and through the back to the loading area. Sure enough, Kelly could see for miles in both directions.

'Where's the old waterworks?' Kelly asked.

The woman pointed north. 'Over those sand dunes.'

'Did you notice anyone from not round here coming into the shop that Saturday?'

The woman thought carefully. They went back into the shop.

'We do get tourists milling about, usually they're lost or have got off the train, thinking they'll grab an ice cream. There was a fella on his own. I remember him because he was so polite and quiet spoken. He looked as though he'd arranged to meet someone, and he waited around outside for ages, but no one came. He bought three ice creams over about an hour. He looked disappointed. I asked him if he was all right and he looked a bit confused. He asked where he could buy cigarettes and I said I could give him some, so he came back inside. He was a sad-looking fella,' she said.

'Did you tell the police at the time?' Kelly asked.

'They've been going door to door, but I've had no one in here asking,' the woman said. Craig tutted.

'Have I done something wrong?' she asked, worried now.

'No, not at all, I'm sure they'll get round to you. It could be extremely helpful information – could you describe him? And anything that might make him stand out?' Kelly asked.

'He was oldish, I guess, sixties, kind-looking. Shabby clothes, looked like he'd been hidden away for twenty years,' she said, laughing to herself at the memory of the man with such dubious dress sense. Craig looked at Kelly.

'Carry on,' she said.

'Erm, white-grey hair, Oh, I remember, he had a T-shirt on under his jumper, which he took off because he was hot. And he had a great ugly tattoo, here on his elbow,' she said.

'A tattoo of what?' Kelly asked.

'A spider's web,' she said. Kelly flicked through her phone and found a photograph of Jack Bell, and showed it to the woman. 'Is this him?' she asked. The woman nodded.

'Yes, that's him,' she said.

'Did you see him light his cigarette after you sold them to him?' Kelly asked. 'Did he by any chance use one of these?' Kelly showed her a photograph of the Zippo.

'He did! I remember the smell, it's peculiar isn't it? Like fuel. Is it important?' the woman asked.

'Yes, very important, thank you. I'll need you to approve our statement when I type it up, so I'll get your personal details.'

'Who is he?' the woman asked.

'He was called Jack Bell, and he's dead now.'

The woman put her hand to her mouth. 'But how can that be? He was such a lovely-looking man. That's so sad,' she said. She appeared to think about something. 'Wait, is he linked to your body up at the waterworks?' she asked.

'We think so,' Craig said.

'Holy moly,' she said.

'Did you talk at all?' Kelly asked.

The woman thought again. 'He said something about not worrying about life. He said if you get to his age then you have everything you need and don't want for nothing,' she said. 'Strange. He said that but looked sad.'

'And the person he was waiting for never turned up? Did you ask who he was waiting for?'

'No, I thought it rude.'

They took the necessary details from the woman and made their way to the old waterworks, a couple of minutes' walk away. It was sealed off with police tape and two uniformed police officers sat in a squad car at the entrance. Kelly and Craig showed their ID badges and walked towards the warehouse where Dean Kirby's body had been found. The water purification plant had operated up until 2018, and in a mere two years had grown over with unruly bushes and weeds, as well as become home to birds, foxes and insects. Craig opened the door to the room where the body had been found and Kelly followed him in. The outdoors hadn't quite reached inside yet and the concrete walls and doors were bare. As Ted had already told her, this slowed the insect activity on Dean's body to normal levels, which enabled them to get accurate results. Marks were drawn where he'd lain, strapped to the chair, and little circles were also drawn around where the exhibits had been found, including the dead larvae. Kelly visualised the photographs in graphic detail and cast her thoughts to Ted's preliminary autopsy findings, which he'd sent over to her. His official report would take a lot longer, but he'd given her the important facts via email.

'It's very isolated. I assume no one comes here,' she said.

'Apart from kids playing,' Craig said.

'Risky.'

They walked around. If you were looking for the perfect spot to torture someone to death, then this was it. No tyre tracks had been found outside, and no physical evidence of other accomplices, like at the other site in Workington, where Jack had died.

'Do you think they were supposed to meet?' Craig said.

'It looks like it,' Kelly said. She walked around the quiet room, noting how tucked away from the howling wind of the Irish Sea they were.

'It was well planned,' she said. 'This place was well chosen.'

Craig agreed.

Kelly couldn't help feel the terror of the victim's final moments, all alone and cut off from everything he knew and trusted. They didn't have much of a picture of either man, and less about Dean, who seemed a troubled soul, in and out of prison his whole adult life. The prospect of getting out must have been disconcerting. Perhaps meeting Jack would have been something he looked forward to. But who would know they were here, and who would betray them? She couldn't get Rickie Burton out of her head.

'Should we take a drive down to Ravenglass?' Craig asked. She nodded and took one last look around. They'd double back and go south again, past Highton, to Ravenglass, where Dean Kirby had got off the train from Barrow. She drove slowly, looking left and right, to see if any isolated old mansion might have CCTV at the bottom of their driveway overlooking the road. There were none. This stretch of the coast was deserted. Until they neared the A595 and saw the turning to HMP Highton, from where they'd come. This time, not distracted by searching for the turning, she saw that, over the road, with several CCTV cameras on display, was a petrol station.

Chapter 28

Kelly's drive back to Eden House was long and she felt fatigued. It had been a constructive day, to a point, but she was no closer to getting a motive for the crimes. She and Craig had agreed to split the focus of their squads into clear lines of inquiry. Kelly's team would pursue the physical evidence of the case, and Craig would take on the almighty task of finding ex-cons who'd served with Jack Bell and Dean Kirby.

The light faded as she pulled into the car park around the back of Eden House. She'd used the drive to catch up with Johnny, and he confirmed that he was thinking about restarting with the mountain rescue. She told him about Kate's daughter, Millie, and they agreed to invite her over to meet Lizzie.

Penrith was quiet, and as Kelly slammed her car door shut, the noise echoed off the walls. She'd changed back into trainers after her visit to HMP Highton, and so her footsteps made no sound. The silence made her aware of her breath and she went round to the front entrance. Her team was assembled upstairs, waiting for their brief from the boss to round off the day.

They'd all been busy.

She greeted them and they gathered in the incident room, sitting in groups, chatting about various details of the case, or simply about what takeaway they might get tonight. She felt a swell of pride that this was the team she'd created.

'Ready in five,' she said. She went to her office after noticing that the board in the incident room was filling up nicely. The lure of long hours tempted her to stay late tonight and work through it all. But the familiar knot of guilt sat under her ribcage and she told herself that she'd not stay too long. Her office was hot and she threw open a window, letting in the noise of the streets below, which wasn't much, but there was something about the evening air that cleared her head after the confinement of the prison. She sat heavily in her chair and logged on to her desktop computer. HOLMES had been updating all day and she hadn't had time to give it much attention. There was always a dilemma for a SIO over how much time to spend in the office and how much out chasing. In this case, Kelly believed that she couldn't have missed the autopsy yesterday, and equally had to go to Highton in person, and she was glad she had. It wasn't the sort of thing that could be easily linked by video. She'd gained the measure of the governor, Brian Taylor, and a few of his officers, notably Liam Fawcett. She'd be interested to find out how Tom Gorman's first day had gone.

Kelly went to the ladies' bathroom and washed her hands, which felt grimy after being out all day. She touched up her make-up and sprayed a bit of perfume on her neck. She felt somewhat revived and ready for what would most certainly be a very detailed and focused meeting. Her phone buzzed. It was a text from Johnny.

Any idea what time home?

She looked at her watch. Lizzie would be having her tea.

Just giving final brief now. 7?

He texted back a thumbs-up emoji. Now she'd committed to a time, she knew she had to stick to it. Unless something unexpected came up.

Back at her desk, she read the updates and made sure that any new information was checked and filed accordingly. HOLMES had revolutionised the way investigations were carried out. Miniscule pieces of information which could easily get lost or dismissed as irrelevant were never forgotten by the dynamic reasoning software. The easiest to solve were the crimes of passion, like a husband stabbing his wife to death in a fit of jealous rage. Or the gang-related deaths of vengeance, wrought on young men, spilling out from the cities into the provinces. Kelly held the common view that most murders were either too emotional and rash, or stupid. However, serial killers, in her experience, were different. They followed a pattern, and were often only caught when they made a mistake, usually caused by becoming complacent, and bored of their own modus operandi. To her, it looked like their killer was only just getting started.

Her phone buzzed and made her jump. It was Ted.

'Hi Dad,' she said.

'Kelly, are you home?' he asked.

'No I'm still at work, I've just got back from Highton and I'm about to give a brief. Have you some news?'

'Actually yes. Dean Kirby died from severe anaphylaxis. The head wound was inflicted post-mortem,' he said.

'What drew you to that conclusion? It's odd in a murder case, I have to say.' Kelly was stunned.

'I knew you'd say that. I've sent you my report. There was pharyngeal oedema alongside a standard heart attack, but no heart disease, as well as raised mast cell tryptase. It's pathologically sound.'

She regretted asking.

'Do you know what caused the allergic reaction?'

'I can find no insect bite, so he had to have been allergic to something at the scene, or he ingested something.'

'Our killer likes to torture for a prolonged period, so that would have screwed his plans. Maybe he cracked his skull open in a fit of rage for ruining his agenda,' Kelly said.

'My thoughts exactly,' Ted agreed. 'There was nothing associated with common food triggers in the remains of his stomach, nuts, fish and the like. I'm waiting for his blood to come back to determine if he'd been given some kind of drug or anaesthetic.'

'That would dull the killer's enjoyment,' Kelly said. 'What about latex? No sophisticated killer like this would be stupid enough not to wear gloves,' Kelly said.

'Possible. Without evidence of any of the other normal triggers for the fatality then latex should be ruled in as a promising alternative.'

'And if the kill was a disappointment, it's not surprising that another followed soon after,' Kelly said.

'Is that normally the case?' Ted asked.

'In a high percentage. Say a serial rapist and murderer fails to pull off his plan because he was disturbed, often you find that another victim is attacked successfully nearby not long after,' Kelly said.

'So he worked extra hard on Jack Bell,' Ted said.

'Exactly,' Kelly agreed. 'Were you able to determine if Dean Kirby had been sexually assaulted?' she asked.

'Inconclusive, but he did have similar genital bruising and burning,' he said. Kelly knew that this meant that there wasn't enough viable anal tract left for a swab. She had a sudden moment of grief. A feeling of loss washed over her, instigated by the horror of the passing of these two men. Whoever had done this to them was a certified fucked-up and twisted individual and she wondered what could have possibly happened to him to make him this way. Killers aren't born, they're made; of that she was certain. They were dealing with somebody who had suffered, and who wanted to revisit that agony on others. But the realisation made her head go round in circles. If the murders were paid hits, then why employ a deranged killer to do it, who might be messy? Surely contract kills were clean; wasn't that the whole point?

She sighed and said good night to Ted. She was weary. Catching a person capable of such gratuitous violence was never easy, and Kelly knew that she was potentially going to have to go head-to-head with a sadist and a risk-taker, and that was a recipe for an alarmingly dangerous investigation. It exposed herself and her team to the world of pure madness. She knew that many serial killers weren't technically mad, but their behaviour was. It was the FBI who first began profiling serial killers in the 1970s and the practice had come a long way since then. Serial killers were generally said to have personality disorders, usually psychopathy, and often had low-functioning amygdalas: the part of the brain related to consequence. Kelly knew that whatever this killer did, his killing would always be the single most important thing in his life, because he'd learned to get his kicks from it, for whatever reason.

That made him a formidable adversary. Maybe their only chance lay in finding who had helped him – as well as who had paid him.

She got up from her chair and went to the incident room.

'Thanks, everybody, I know it's been a long day. I've been looking at the work you've been doing in my absence, and I'm blown away. Thank you. I'll let you go very soon, and then I'll do the handover to the duty officer for tonight. Much of what we have achieved today now requires lab results and replies from witnesses to come back, so there's nothing we can do in the middle of the night. If you want to stay back and finish a few things off, then be my guest, but I want everyone fresh and rested for tomorrow. The next couple of days will be tough. Kate?'

Kelly perched on a table and allowed her second in command to speak.

'Thanks, guv. Me and Rob have been chasing the forensics.' She flicked a few keys on her computer and exhibits came up on the huge white screen behind Kelly. Everyone paid attention. Kate went through several physical pieces of evidence, but none that stood up to any cross-reference with their victims. It was essentially a collection of detritus and rubbish.

'None of the prints we lifted were matched on any of our databases, so they weren't from Jack, or anyone else who has served time.'

That was a disappointment, because Kelly was hoping that an ex-con was responsible, perhaps someone who had served in Highton.

'I'll interject there,' Kelly said. 'The coroner just called me, and he thinks Dean Kirby died of severe anaphylaxis. The working theory is that in the absence of food, drugs or an insect bite, it could be latex, and that would indicate gloves, explaining the lack of prints. Carry on, Kate.'

'The clump of hair was identified positively as Jack's. We also searched the CCTV requested from the local Co-op, close to where Jack's body was found. On Sunday night this man bought a Snickers bar at ten p.m.' Kate brought up the CCTV reel and paused it on a still frame of a man making a purchase at the Co-op.

The officers looked at the footage of a large man wearing a brown jacket and jeans, making his purchase.

'Have we a trace for the serial number of the Snickers bar?' Kelly asked.

Kate nodded. 'Yes, it matches the batch sent to this Co-op three weeks ago, and the wrapper found at the scene is from that box.'

'Fantastic. Do we know who he is?' Kelly asked. Kate paused the footage and tried to get a good still of the man. She rewound it and fast-forwarded it, settling on a frame where the man's face could be made out by its shape, though not in a great amount of detail.

'Was the server interviewed?' Kelly asked.

'Yes. She was working the late shift. There weren't many customers that time of night and she remembers a few men coming in, but not this particular one, and she couldn't identify him,' Kate said.

'Get this released to the press,' Kelly said, pointing to the photo. It wasn't great, but it was a start. Whoever ate that Snickers bar had left the wrapper at a murder scene.

Rob put up his hand and all eyes settled on him.

'Rob?'

'Boss, I was reading Jack Bell's emails on his account set up for him by the parole service. There aren't very many, but most of them are between him and Jeanie Clark. I'm no expert, but I'd say they were closer than she's letting on,' he said.

'Agreed. Go on.'

'One of them mentions how he's changed and he's working on providing her with the life she deserves. He talks of making a sizeable amount of money, soon. And that was an email sent on the night he was released.'

'So he had something in the pipeline, and it might be a motive. Thanks, Rob. Dan?' Kelly asked.

Dan stood up and spoke confidently. Emma gazed at him in admiration and nodded when he made his points.

'Me and Emma have been working on the signet ring. The insignia is military,' he said. Kelly raised an eyebrow, recalling something that Ted had said to her.

'It's the bugle and regimental motto of the Light Infantry. "*Cede Nullis*" means yield to none. The Light Infantry ceased to exist in 2007 and was merged into the Rifles, so we're looking at someone serving before that date,' Dan explained.

'And somebody who saw some action,' Kelly said. 'I don't think an infantry soldier would be up to no good if he'd served his time in the rear echelons handing out ammo,' she added. 'Do you know where the Light Infantry served regularly?' she asked.

'Between 2000 and 2007 they served in Bosnia, Northern Ireland, Sierra Leone and Iraq. After they became the Rifles, they were sent mainly to Afghanistan,' Dan said.

Kelly ran her hand through her hair, fiddling with the ends, and closed her eyes. She'd talk to Johnny about it tonight. There might be some infamous fuck-ups, known to serving soldiers, where things had got nasty in the field.

It was that type of thing that could unhinge an ex-soldier. Tom Gorman might be worth talking to as well.

'We've also been working on the winch strap. It's a standard design, heavy duty, used in hoists, generally for getting people in and out of the bath in care homes. You can order them off the internet, but that's its main use. The label had been cut off but we're making enquiries as to when this specific design and colour, as well as its properties of strength and efficiency, started to be manufactured, and where,' Dan finished.

'Brilliant, thanks, Dan.' Kelly said. It was her turn. 'I spent the day at HMP Highton, as you know, with DI Lockwood. We paid a visit to Seascale afterwards and spoke to an ice cream vendor who positively identified Jack Bell hanging around there on Saturday, waiting to meet someone who never turned up.'

She allowed the new information to sink in. It was significant because it linked their victims further.

'Rob, I want you to take a closer look at the finances of an inmate at HMP Highton. Rickie Burton seems to rule the roost, and it was intimated to me by another inmate that both Jack and Dean were manipulated by Burton into becoming some kind of foot soldiers. I want to know how he survives in there. To live a comfortable life inside, you need means.'

'I'll request a warrant to search his financial records at the prison. He must have direct debits and standing orders, and he must shop online from inside prison,' Rob said.

'That's what I'm thinking. Concentrate on payments to individuals as well,' Kelly said. 'If you're quick, you might catch the magistrates' office, so do you want to do that now?' Rob nodded and left the room.

'Moving on to the care home angle. We need to compile a list of care homes in the county. Emma? Can I give that to you?'

Emma nodded happily. 'Yes, guv. We've had it confirmed that the biggest distributer of care home equipment in Cumbria is Covey Care, a company based in Kendal.'

'Good job, keep on it,' Kelly said. 'Craig Lockwood is concentrating on anyone who did time with our victims in the last decade. In the case of Dean Kirby, there will be a lot of names. I'm hoping it will lead us to whoever helped transport our victims to the sites of their deaths. This might give us a clearer picture of what Dean and Jack were up to when they left prison.'

'Mules on the outside?' Dan suggested. Dan had served the Greater Glasgow division for Police Scotland for many years, and he'd seen his fair share of underworld criminality. He knew a thing or two about how gangs could control business affairs from behind prison walls. He'd even told them stories of gang members committing severe crimes to get incarcerated, thereby gaining access to traitors inside to settle scores.

'That's exactly what I'm thinking,' Kelly said. 'Have we had the reports for the flat searches yet?' she asked. Emma, who was sat in front of a police computer screen, beat them to it.

'Guv, they've both been sent across. They look pretty wordy,' she said, scrolling through the emails.

'Great, can you prepare a precis for me in the next half an hour?' Kelly asked.

'Of course, guv,' Emma said.

'Dan, can I bend your ear?' Kelly said. He nodded. 'Thank you everybody, wrap things up and get some well-deserved rest at home, and I'll see you all at nine thirty tomorrow morning,' she said. The officers filed away, back to their desks, chatting and comparing notes. When it was quiet, Kelly turned to Dan.

'This is your patch, Dan. What's your experience of convicts using mules on the outside?' she asked.

'It's rife,' he said. 'Money gets transferred by relations on the outside, who call their brothers, nephews and grandsons on the inside to confirm transactions. It runs smoother than if they were living outside the wall because they have the protection of the state – no one can get to them.'

'How ironic. But the relatives can be got at,' she pointed out.

'True, but why would you take out a granny and start a war? Money is going to shift around anyway, it's the *types* of business and the extent of turf control that is disputed, not who works for them, necessarily.'

'So we need to find out what Rickie Burton controls on the outside, and take a long look at his family,' she said.

'And then find out who his enemies are,' he said.

Chapter 29

By the time Kelly climbed into bed next to Johnny, it was gone midnight. It had been her turn to give Lizzie her eleven o'clock bottle. Feeding her daughter calmed Kelly and emptied her head. The biggest change to Kelly and Johnny's daily pattern was that they couldn't discuss issues as they arose; they had to wait. Bedtime seemed to be the most convenient moment to raise questions. Kelly was reluctant to ask Johnny about his time in the military so late at night, but it was her only opportunity.

'When should we invite Millie round?' she asked.

'The weekend?' he replied. He yawned but pulled her body towards him and held her. He smelled her hair. 'I missed you,' he said.

'It's my first big case since Lizzie, isn't it?'

He nodded and snuggled into her. His hold was firm. His hands travelled down her body but her mind wandered.

'How much do you think we should offer her?' she asked.

Johnny stopped his caresses and put his head into his pillow. 'Who?' he asked.

'Millie?' she said.

'Ah. Erm, I suppose we need to decide what hours she works first,' he said. He leant back and put his hands behind his head.

'What were you thinking?' she asked.

'I wasn't. I was thinking about this,' he said, putting his hand on her waist and slowly moving it towards her breast. She smiled and turned towards him. They kissed and she felt him relax against her. She smelled him and realised that she'd missed the mix of warm skin and clean scent after he'd showered before bed.

'What year were you in Iraq?' she asked.

His hands stopped moving again and he gave up. 'Which time?' he asked. He turned his light off and settled down to sleep.

'Any – what were the dates? Did you serve with the Light Infantry?' she asked. He sighed.

'What's this about?' he asked, turning towards her once more.

'Sorry. It's work. I might have a suspect who is ex-military. He might have worn a signet ring with the Light Infantry insignia and motto,' she said.

'*Cede Nullis*,' he said. She looked at him.

'You know it?'

'Of course. *Yield to none*. They weren't impressed when they were consumed by the Rifles. Three hundred years of history down the drain. The old-timers still call themselves *LI*, and they're sensitive about which regiment.'

'How many were there?' she asked. He rubbed his eyes and yawned again.

'Originally four, then cut to three. The originals were the Duke of Cornwall, Durham, Highland, Green Jackets, King's Own Yorkshire, Devon and Dorset, there are quite a few. It was in the sixties that they became first, second and third battalion. They all became the Rifles in 2007. Think Sean Bean in *Sharpe* and you have your Light Infantryman. Why?'

'I need to find a needle in a haystack,' she said. 'I thought I'd start with you. Can you remember any incidents in Iraq involving the Light Infantry, which weren't reported in the press, but that were quite messy – you know, damaging for the troops who witnessed them?' she asked.

'Take your pick. It was all messy. It was street fighting, close-quarter building clearance, IEDs under civilian roads, friendly fire, you name it. There were plenty of fuck-ups,' he said. Kelly noticed his body language change and she knew she'd hit a raw nerve.

'You don't have to,' she said. He ran his hands through his hair and propped himself up on his pillow.

'It's not me,' he said. 'I'm fine. It's a long time ago. It's just the lads we lost in one way or another. Not necessarily the dead, but the quadruple amputees, the ones who never got over the noise, the ones who couldn't forget the nightmares,' he said.

'I know,' she said. 'They're the ones I want to know about.' She sat up and faced him. 'I think I'm looking for somebody who was severely damaged. If they owned this ring then they'll be proud of it and upset it's gone, right? I know that the victims weren't military, but whoever wore the ring might have been.'

'Or they could be a fantasist, having bought it at a bric-a-brac store, pretending they're tough,' he said. He lay down again, and sighed. Kelly felt awkward.

'You're right, it could be nothing.'

She waited.

'I was there twice. The second time was worse. The first time was shortly after the invasion, in 2003, and things were positive. Everybody seemed to want it to work. Saddam was history, the locals were onside, and there was

205

a kind of buoyancy. By the following year, things had already taken a downturn. Things went to rat-shit quickly. It was more hostile and unpredictable. I heard several reports of soldiers going rogue. It wasn't their fault; it was just that they'd been pushed to their limits. There were a few kidnappings and stories of torture-related incidents that didn't reach the press.'

'Any specifics?' she pushed him.

He sighed and closed his eyes. 'I tell you what, I'll sleep on it and think about it more clearly in the morning. I'm tired. I'll talk to Tom as well, he saw some pretty serious shit,' he said. He tuned over.

'I'm sorry,' she said. He remained silent and she watched his back move gently up and down. She doubted he was asleep. She felt as though she'd crossed a line and wondered if her work was welcome in their home any more. Johnny always showed enthusiasm for her investigations and had helped clarify many of her thoughts when she'd been stuck, but now she sensed a shift in his patience. Should she be more concerned about spending time with her own family, rather than working out why somebody else's loved one had perished? But wasn't that hypocritical of him? Hadn't he once prioritised the freedom of strangers over his own daughter, Josie? Wasn't he still prioritising the mental health of his clients over his own?

But there was something else. He seemed defensive. He'd showed a kind of irritation that she was suggesting that an ex-colleague could be responsible for awful crimes, which, to her, was an anomaly. Didn't he come into contact with screwed-up heads all the time with his PTSD work? Wasn't that the whole point? Maybe he was defensive because he was protective of them. Could it be that his allegiance to those spoiled by war was preventing him from admitting that some of them were so damaged that they could commit horrible crimes? She pushed the thought away.

Surely not.

She turned off her light and settled down in bed, but she couldn't find peace. Her thoughts kept going to the chances of finding a ruined soldier somewhere who owned that ring and was missing it keenly, because it represented so much of what had happened to him. She decided to contact the Ministry of Defence tomorrow and ask them directly about soldiers who'd presented with PTSD after active service. It was somewhere to start, and took the pressure of having to ask Johnny every five minutes. She hoped that she hadn't opened some old wound for him, because it wasn't like him to shy away from handing over information. But then again, it was late, and they had a two-month-old baby.

Chapter 30

Kelly took her coffee into the briefing room, where there was a palpable buzz around it being Friday, despite there being an ongoing serious case to crack. The forensic reports were in on the two flats searched yesterday. The first was the flat Jack Bell was staying in, which was a parole halfway house in Workington regularly used by ex-cons. The problem with this was that, unless it was made spotless in between each user, there'd be forensic material from countless other people residing in the property. The second was the home of the Dean Kirby's girlfriend, in Barrow. Craig had overseen that and had sent through notes with his comments alongside. It came with its own set of issues, because Dean Kirby didn't own it and it was only his primary residence for as long as he was in a relationship with his girlfriend. She could easily argue away other DNA evidence, should she so wish.

So their focus wasn't so much on genetic material but on physical evidence that could link the two men after their release dates, indicating that they were pursuing the same line of work or activity before their deaths, and possibly giving their killer a motive.

Her whole team was punctually assembled and talked amongst themselves. Animated chatter was a good sign, it meant energy was high. Kelly walked to the front of the room. The awkward way that she and Johnny had said good night last night played on her mind, but seeing her team distracted her. She noticed some new uniforms, including Fern Brown, and was thankful for Andrew Harris. She'd requested further data crunchers. Unfortunately, the sexy side of detective work, the bits one saw on TV, was uncommon; officers mainly spent time at a desk trawling through the thousands of pieces of information that came their way, hoping to find a match or a new lead. So far, apart from her trusted inner circle of regulars – Kate, Rob, Dan and Emma – Kelly had been lent a further twenty-three uniforms to lighten the load, which would only get heavier as more information came in. It felt like they were racing against time, because this killer had a hunger for what he did; he enjoyed it.

This is how she started the brief. She stood in front of the incident board and brought up their ever-growing display of leads, suspects, persons of interest, locations, sightings and so on. It looked like an old-fashioned pinboard with photos and diagrams attached to it, but it was a digitalised version. Kelly checked it several times a day, hungry for developments.

'Let's take a step back,' she said. 'Those present stared at the photographs of what the murderer had done to his victims. This guy savours what he does. I had it confirmed this morning from Dean Kirby's medical records that he had a severe latex allergy, and so it would seem plausible that the killer's arousal was cut short by premature death. We surmise that he either booted Dean in the head out of frustration, or he shoved him over in his chair so hard that he hit his head with serious impact, it made him exasperated, and he went after Jack the same day. There are precedents for this kind of serial behaviour. The lead-up to a kill excites the perp to such extremes that he has to follow through. An unfulfilling kill, like that of Dean Kirby, would be highly unsettling, and he'd have to satisfy the urge to finish the job. I've been discussing sadomasochism with DI Lockwood from Barrow, and it doesn't have to involve sexual acts. The infliction of pain is enough to bring about orgasm.' She paused.

The officers took notes and the newcomers listened, transfixed. On cases such as these, when help was required from uniforms, fresh faces always arrived full of enthusiasm and excitement. Extra boots were made up of those thinking about jumping on a detective course in the near future. That's what Kelly had done in London. She'd found the twisted minds of murderers fascinating. She looked at Fern Brown, who was captivated, Kelly knew, by the thrill of it all. Based on that look alone, she wouldn't be surprised if the young PC applied for the detective course. She carried on.

'So, the signet ring and the trauma implied by this level of depravity both lead me to a military inquiry. A profile might take the shape of an ex-soldier, suffering with PTSD after an operational tour, where he saw unimaginable horror, acting out. The model fits our suspect with what we know so far. It would seem that the victims were selected, or given on order. The killer must have known the movements of both victims, so the question is, why didn't he kill them both in Seascale if they'd gone to meet there?'

'Maybe the meeting wasn't something the killer knew about,' Dan said.

'Agreed. The killer stuck to specific instructions. After the men were in his control, he had the time and the inclination to torture them.' She waited for people to finish taking notes. 'It's a theory. I'm phoning the MOD today to request a list of Light Infantry soldiers who served in Iraq in the Second Gulf War, from 2003, who were also reported as suffering with PTSD-like symptoms. Emma, can you take charge of this?'

'Yes, guv.'

'Dan, give her a hand, I'm expecting plenty of them. The PTSD rates from Iraq were through the roof. Look for people with links to Cumbria. Their recruiting ground was typically the north-east, but that doesn't mean an ex-soldier couldn't have retired up here. The mountains have the power to pull broken souls together.'

She briefly thought of Tom Gorman. And Johnny.

'Right, the reports from the two flats are in, and they've flagged up some interesting questions.'

She acknowledged the raised eyebrows.

'At this stage, that's all we seem to have: questions. We're doing sterling work. At some point soon, some of the dots will begin to join up.' She turned to the board, which was blank once more, and brought up the files on the two flats. 'Most interesting is this,' she said.

The reports appeared side by side, and she used a pointer to share her thoughts. She started with Jack Bell's flat. It appeared sparse and barely lived in, which was no surprise given that he'd only been out of prison for two days. His few belongings had been neatly packed in drawers and cupboards and there was little food or refreshment in the tiny kitchen. The bed was made and there was no contraband found at the scene, i.e. nothing illegal or obviously out of place.

'There was one thing that stood out, though,' she said.

She brought up a photo of a brown envelope. It contained a mobile phone and £2,000 in cash.

'I doubt Jack Bell came across this legitimately, and he certainly didn't withdraw it from a bank account. He hasn't got one. The phone is unregistered and was used once, for an incoming call. The IMEI number shows it was bought at a Tesco store in Workington the day of his release. The incoming call was traced to a tower near Seascale the day he was supposed to meet Dean Kirby, on Friday the fifteenth of October. It puts Jack about as close to Dean as we can get him and corroborates the ice cream seller's story. It's clear that after the use of the phone near Seascale, Jack went back to his flat and put it in this envelope, with the cash. It looks like we have an exchange here. Now, the ice cream seller said that Jack gave up waiting, but it would appear that he met *someone* – maybe just not Dean.'

She brought up another photo of a similar brown envelope, but it was against a different background.

'This is from the flat of Dean's girlfriend. It also contains a mobile phone, and around four thousand pounds in cash. Forensic analysis of the phone puts it at three locations before Friday the fifteenth of October, two in Barrow and one in Seascale, so he'd been up there before. This phone was bought from Tesco, Barrow, three weeks before, just after Dean Kirby's release. Unfortunately no calls were made on either phone, they only received them, but we do know that Highton prison uses the same tower as the Seascale calls. So, it's *possible* that the calls came from Highton.'

Kelly shuffled paper and checked the report on her iPad. It was complex data and she wanted to make the best sense of it. New technology enabled them to trace phones to within three miles, and evidence from this had put countless criminals away in recent years. But the exciting new development had been that they could trace actual phones, rather than just SIM cards. This was groundbreaking. Which is why she wanted a search of the wings at the prison, to see if communication had occurred between these phones and someone inside the prison on their crucial dates.

'The governor of Highton is understandably reluctant to order a full-scale search of cells. These mobile phones go for around a thousand pounds a pop, and that's big trade. He could have a full-blown riot on his hands should we discover extensive contraband to this effect. I get it, but with the evidence we have now, I'm coming to the conclusion that it's our only option. I want to manage it, and of course it would be the tornado team for Highton who would carry out the search, not us. But however much I push, I don't think I'll get the governor to agree to the search on my terms. The inmates see their cells as their home, and any invasion is rejected with every power they can muster. The prevalent trade in spice inside the prison enables the big guys to recruit foot soldiers to do their dirty work, and this is what Brian Taylor is worried about. Should the wings get prior warning about a raid by the tornado team, they'd simply go to ground and get rid of the contraband. We need the element of surprise, but Brian Taylor has warned us that some wings are at breaking point. Putting eighty men in solitary is not feasible, and if the tornado team feel threatened they'll simply withdraw, leaving the physical integrity of the prison in jeopardy.'

She let this sink in. Many prisons had a tornado team, deployed during emergencies, for example if a fight kicked off, threatening the stability of a whole wing. In extreme circumstances, such as a full-blown riot, national teams could be deployed. The last thing Kelly wanted to do was threaten the security of the whole prison; however, she needed answers, and she wanted to either rule in or out phone calls coming from the prison to either Jack Bell or Dean Kirby.

'I'm discussing this with Chief Constable Harris this morning,' Kelly added.

She noticed Kate shift in her seat.

'Both envelopes have been tested with ninhydrin solution and revealed some usable prints. We've had a match on both Jack Bell's and Dean Kirby's prints, but there are other not yet identified prints on them as well, so this could be an important lead. Kate, will you take this one?'

'Yes, guv.'

'Right, everybody, let's keep updating HOLMES. As always, any pertinent developments then I want to know ASAP. I'm going to hopefully be able to organise a search at Highton early next week. Of course, I expect any mobile phones linked to the murders to have been destroyed by then, but if there is generic communication with the outside, and it matches one of our leads, then we have a potential suspect. Any other business?' Kelly asked.

'Guv, the strapping found around both bodies,' Dan said.

'Fire away,' Kelly said.

'We've traced it to a company that supplies nursing homes with winching kit for bath hoists. It's common and widespread, and we found one hundred and forty-one care homes in Cumbria. We've had a fantastic response. Over a hundred have come back to us and thirty-seven use this brand. We're checking employee lists.'

'Well done, Dan. Good work. I'm thinking latex gloves, too. Shop-bought plastic gloves have a much lower percentage of latex, because it's expensive, but NHS and industry supplies are hardcore, containing enough latex required to trigger an anaphylactic shock. It makes sense.'

Kelly finished up and Dan set about modifying the case study diagram to include the hypothesis that their suspect could work in a care home.

They were making progress.

Chapter 31

'Sir, I know it's sensitive and I appreciate the risk, but we need to search those cells. Section four of the Regulation of Investigatory Powers Act specifically states that public authorities have the right to intercept communications, if it's in accordance with prison rules.'

Kelly stood in front of Chief Constable Harris. He rubbed his chin. He sat at his desk and swung to the left and back to the right on his chair. She'd come to brief him on the case, which was highly sensitive because of the nature of the deaths. Minimal detail had been released to the public, but those in the know wanted this bastard caught quickly. Chief Constable Harris had been more than generous in finding extra boots for her enquiries and he'd personally managed the mutual aid request to other constabularies, most notably Lancashire and Yorkshire. She let him think.

'And what type of governor are we dealing with?' he asked finally.

'Tight,' she said. 'He's wary. The prison is overcrowded and they had trouble last week. There's some nasty criminals in there, sir. He's scared of it kicking off, and technically we have no jurisdiction inside those walls without a section nineteen.'

'Correct. We need to go easy. The governor knows his prisoners better than anyone. By all accounts, and I have this on good faith, Highton is a tinder keg waiting to explode. It wouldn't take much to tip it over in to a full-blown reactive situation,' he said.

'I know, sir. Which is why I have an alternative plan.' She didn't add that Brian Taylor's intimate knowledge of his inmates perhaps wasn't as healthy as Andrew Harris might imagine.

The chief constable stopped twirling and looked at Kelly. 'I'm all ears,' he said.

'The main guy on the wing we want to search is called Rickie Burton. He's served twenty-nine years of a thirty-year sentence and he's up for parole in a year. He doesn't want to leave – he's got everything he could possibly want inside. I've got officers working on his bank accounts and family ties. There's only one reason why a man like him would be happy in prison, and that's because he has a thriving business on the outside. After all, inside, he's safe from rivals. Unlike Jack Bell. I think Rickie Burton was threatened by Jack Bell and Dean Kirby leaving prison.'

'So he had them killed?'

'It's a theory. I need to get inside those cells, so I have to come up with a workable solution for the governor. Anything that upsets Burton's racket is going to rile him, sir,' Kelly said. 'Apparently mobile phones like this go for a thousand pounds apiece these days,' she added.

Harris whistled. She showed him a photograph of a Zanco Tiny T1 handset. It was about two inches tall and an inch wide: perfectly sized to hide inside a rectum.

'Imagine he's got fifteen in his cell, or somewhere else on the wing, wherever his stash is – that's fifteen grand. That's a lot of money and a lot of favours. It's also a lot of goods from the outside. Add to that the potential that he controls the drug addicts by dealing in spice, and you have a very lucrative trade going on. I heard that the main guys always stay sober. I tell you what, chief, this guy's skin is as clear as a baby's proverbial – he doesn't do drugs and he doesn't drink hooch. There's only one reason why a seasoned con would look so good, and that's because he's wealthy and knows better. He wields power because he's organised. He can even order murder.'

'Do you have evidence of this?' he asked.

'Not yet,' she said. She saw his disappointment and acknowledged that it didn't look that convincing. Rob had yet to give her any solid evidence of transactions between Rickie Burton and people on the outside in the form of cash deals.

'Sir, cons run wings for a reason. It's to keep the status quo, and the screws are thankful for that. That way, everybody gets to sleep at night. Upset the apple cart and you get punished. Now, if we were to somehow let Rickie Burton know that a grass had handed information over to police, he'd feel unsafe and move any contraband, thinking a search was coming. So, if the search is an accidental result of someone's big mouth rather than the authorities imposing their force, then Burton would deal with it in-house, avoiding a revolt against the system. He's not stupid, I've met him. He's as steady as a rock, and shrewd. He'd know that all he needed to do was bide his time and wait it out, then move his contraband back when it was safe,' she said.

'I'm not following. How does that enable us to go in and conduct a search? Have you spoken to the governor about this?'

'We feed information from outside that a general search is about to happen, then we conduct a cell-by-cell search, staggered over time, keeping all prisoners inside their cells until it's done. That way, there's no opportunity for barricades, or for Burton to find out what's really behind the search.'

'Is that feasible?'

'I spoke to the prison liaison officer and he said it's unusual, but if we get the governor onside it might provide an opportunity to search cells in a measured and controlled manner. It would take a lot of uniforms, though, sir.'

'But you said that would cause a riot.'

'Not if we tested the phones in real time and replaced what we found,' she said.

He rubbed his chin. 'Have you run this past legal?'

'Like I said, compliance with RIPA is in accordance with prison rules, if we get the governor onside.'

Kelly watched him as he considered her suggestions. She'd caught Kate in the ladies at Eden House and they'd gossiped for ten minutes as they touched up their make-up. She had her date with Andrew Harris tonight. Kelly looked at him and swore he'd had a haircut. She'd smelled fresh cologne as she'd walked into his office too. She tried hard to keep her smile to herself. Christ, Kate deserved it. It meant that she wouldn't be available for drinks with the team to toast Emma's fantastic achievement on the October Scree Challenge, but it would only be quick anyway, they had work to do. Kelly would suggest that they nip out for a quick drink at around five thirty, and those who wanted to return to work were free to do so. She didn't encourage weekend work when they had a big case like this, although most of her team made an appearance at some point, and took their Toughpads home with them. Kelly did it, they all did. Trying to find justice was a vocation, not a job.

The chief looked at his watch and Kelly wondered if he was thinking about what Kate might wear, what they might talk about and if he still had it in him to charm a lady. Part of Kelly felt a kind of maternal protection towards her second in command. She hoped that Kate didn't get hurt. So far his potential relationship with a much more junior colleague hadn't come up in their conversation, but they'd have to cover it eventually because Kelly was Kate's line manager. It was just that she hadn't quite worked out how to raise it yet.

'I can see it working,' the chief said. 'I want it in writing, so I can sign it off, happy that we're not stepping on anyone's toes or getting in Governor Taylor's way. These governors are territorial, and rightly so. I wouldn't wish the job on anyone, and he gives his life to that place.'

Kelly doubted that Brian Taylor was as altruistic as the chief was making out, but she had what she wanted and so nodded politely.

'Can you manage that by first thing Monday?' he asked.

'Of course, sir. I'll try and talk him round today.'

'Wouldn't anything of significance have been destroyed by the prisoners by now?' he asked as she prepared to leave.

'Yes, sir, but evidence of phone use cannot be erased. The use of the signal will still leave a trace.'

'Good. Brief me Monday morning,' he said.

'Yes, sir. By then we should have a warrant for the tower records too.' She lingered a second more than was natural.

'Sir, changing the subject to a delicate topic.'

He looked at her and nodded. She thought his cheeks flushed. 'It's just a technicality, sir. I just wanted to say that I have read through protocol and wanted to let you know that I'm aware of the situation as per force recommend-ations for a senior officer such as yourself,' she said. Her words were chosen carefully.

'Thank you, Kelly. I appreciate it. I've sorted my end too.' He coughed. Kelly knew he was uncomfortable and she didn't want to prolong his anxiety.

'Have a nice weekend, sir,' she said, going to the door.

He smiled broadly. 'I will, Kelly, and you too,' he said. Kelly smiled as she turned away, dying to tell Kate that he was eager to get rid of her out of his office so he could prepare for his date. Kelly knew that he was taking Kate to a swanky restaurant in Ambleside, by the lake.

Something positive to cut through the shit was always welcome.

Chapter 32

The drive back to Eden House finally gave Kelly an opportunity to call Tom Gorman. He answered straight away.

'Tom? Hi, It's Kelly, we didn't have a chance to be properly introduced yesterday,' she said.

'Hi Kelly, I thought I'd better answer an unknown number, I was expecting a call from HR here at Highton,' he said. 'Nice to hear from you. Yeah, yesterday was a bit rushed, it would be good to meet you properly. It was mad at work.'

It made sense that he was at work, the line sounded echoey. 'And your first day? How did it go?'

'Different,' he said.

She laughed. 'I can imagine. A baptism of fire, I should expect.'

'It wasn't what I thought it'd be, coming in knowing that two ex-convicts had been murdered. Thanks for the heads-up, by the way. I was on their old wings all day, it was surreal. But there we go, that's what I should expect, I guess, these aren't woke wallflowers, are they?'

'No, that's one way of putting it.' She paused. 'I know that your loyalty is with your employer now, so you don't have to answer any of my questions, but can I ask what you thought of the relationship between the staff and prisoners?' she asked.

'I don't think I'm speaking out of turn. My first impressions were, they care. They see the prison as the lads' home, and I never thought of it that way before. It's their patch, and the only way the relationship will work and the prison can function is through cooperation. At the end of the day, there's probably three officers per eighty men. That simply won't work without some form of combined effort. If civvies on the outside understood this then maybe the penal system would get more sympathy. Society isn't willing to spend the money on proper rehab, so the alternative is keeping the status quo, and I think Governor Taylor, though a bit old-fashioned, hits the right notes,' he said.

'That's a lot to pick up in a day,' Kelly said.

Tom laughed, 'Yeah, it's a bit deep, isn't it? But that's why I applied in the first place. I want to be on the side that gives these lads a chance, rather than just writing them off.'

'But many of them are lifers, Tom. They're in a maximum security prison for a reason, because of their threat to public safety. Do they deserve your respect?' she asked.

'I think so. They're not animals. There needs to be some kind of functionality to prison. Locking them up and throwing away the key is something that undeveloped countries do, not democracies. It's one of our biggest hypocrisies as a nation,' he said.

Kelly reflected on his passion. He seemed to have put a lot of thought into it before even turning up for his first shift. It was admirable, but also potentially hazardous. Besides, her job was to find out what had happened to two ex-convicts, not ruminate about the penal system.

'This reciprocal relationship, then, how much do you allow the inmates to get away with before enough is enough? I'll give you an example. Say I want to search the cells for phones that could have been used to communicate with the outside to order a murder – when does that override the prisoner's right to privacy, when they've already opted out of society's rule book?'

'It's a tough one. When a police inquiry is on the table, then there has to be a compromise. It needs handling delicately, though.'

'I appreciate that. Did you see Jeanie Clark yesterday? I saw her leave, but she was supposed to be off sick.'

'No, I was told she was off, which is why I had Liam show me around.'

'Liam Fawcett?'

'Yes.'

'What did you make of him?' she asked.

'Good bloke. Proactive. Not afraid to make tough decisions.'

'Such as?'

'He thinks about what's best for his prison, and not the system as a whole. So he released two cons from the block yesterday because he knew that to keep them down there with no batteries or exercise was counter to what we were trying to achieve.'

'Which was what?'

'Preventing D wing from kicking off again.'

'Isn't that the lunatics running the asylum?' Kelly asked.

'Not if he now has favours to call in,' Tom said.

It struck Kelly that Tom was easily drawn in, which wasn't consistent with what she knew of soldiers, based on what she'd been told by Johnny. In her opinion, soldiers were rightly sceptical, and reserved judgement until they'd weighed up all sides. However, it was also possible that Tom was not being totally transparent with her and felt allegiance to his new boss. After all, two days was barely enough time for Tom to get the lay of the land inside Highton prison.

'I hadn't realised that Liam was an old pal of Johnny's,' he said.

Kelly tensed. 'Oh, right, yes, neither had I,' she said. 'And how's today going?' she asked, batting away the unwelcome information.

'It's canteen day, it's crazy. That's why I'm in, for an extra pair of hands, it's the most difficult day of the week. I'm on my break.'

'I suppose Rickie Burton gets plenty of canteen delivered?' she asked.

'You know I can't discuss specifics, but good effort for trying,' he said.

'Can I ask you about your time in the army?' she said, changing the subject. He was quiet and Kelly knew she'd hit a nerve. It had to be done. 'Sorry, it's none of my business, but I'm trying to trace infantry soldiers who served in Iraq and were discharged after suffering severe PTSD.'

Another silence.

'Tom?' she said.

'Sorry, I was thinking. It was a long time ago. I know plenty of soldiers with PTSD – it's endemic in the forces. It would be easier for me to tell you who didn't suffer from it. Liam Fawcett is one example. Did Johnny tell you he treated him too?'

'I'll get to that as part of my inquiry. I'm concentrating on ex-LI for now.' Kelly's breath quickened.

'Light Infantry?' he asked.

'Yes.'

'That's a blast from the past. I served with several out there. I know a few who are still serving if that's what you want, under the Rifles now, of course.'

'I'm more interested in those who left the forces. What dates did you serve in Iraq?' she asked.

'2003, 2004, 2005 and 2007,' he said.

'Four tours?'

'Yes.'

It was a terse reply, and Kelly sensed the conversation was nearing its close, but she'd established two important things. One was that Tom knew plenty of men who'd served in difficult tours of Iraq, around the same time as Johnny had said things got ugly, who had suffered from PTSD and now had been discharged. The other was that Johnny had lied to her.

'Perhaps you could put together a list of names for me?' she asked.

'Sure, I'd be happy to.' His voice was clipped. It reminded her of her conversation with Johnny last night. It was clearly a touchy subject, but they'd both confirmed that they were in the same area at the right time, and both knew veterans from the Light Infantry who'd served alongside them. She realised that both men were uncomfortable with her line of questioning and they both displayed a sensitive loyalty to comrades past and present. One thing she was sure of was that, when the military was concerned, there was a hidden layer of devotion between these men that was impenetrable.

Chapter 33

Rob and Kate sat in silence, each studying their computer screens. Rob was examining data from Rickie Burton's bank records, which had been requested by Cumbria Police. Burton would soon realise that access to his account had been frozen, in accordance with financial service law, and the bank was under no obligation to share the nature of the decision with him. This would be enough for him to kick off, and so Rob worked quickly.

Kate, meanwhile, scrutinised the burn marks on Jack Bell's body. It had been the coroner's report that first hinted that the burns might have been caused by some kind of lamp, in close proximity to the skin. Any lamp held too close to human flesh could cause damage, but this one had burned to the extent that the shape of the element was left on the skin. Kate had ploughed through hundreds of lamp designs, but the one she'd settled on as the most interesting was a treatment lamp, used for conditions such as psoriasis and eczema. She'd found a detailed picture of a Derma UVB phototherapy lamp, used in hospitals, and the pattern was similar enough to the untrained eye to raise suspicion. The lamps were also used in care homes. Emma was working on the list of care homes in the area and Dan was trying to cross-reference ex-army veterans who'd taken paid employment in the health services. It would likely be a short list, as many soldiers went into security work, but even so, it was taking a long time to compile. The Ministry of Defence had promised to do their best, but they weren't the quickest or most open of institutions, even when there was an urgent request for evidence under section 19, and Dan was becoming frustrated. All he'd asked for was a list of former Light Infantry soldiers who had links to Cumbria, which he could then use to start working out whether there were any likely suspects.

Kate was unable to concentrate, and looked for excuses to distract herself. Thankfully she received an email notification, and she saw that a new message had arrived in her inbox from the lab. Since the dissolution of the police Forensic Science Service in 2012, each constabulary had to hire private companies to do lab work. It cost a fortune, and they were only used in high-profile, serious cases, such as murder. Every police officer on the planet would like to send each scrap of evidence off to a lab, which would allow them to gain immeasurable insight into the crime scene and help them trace the perp as fast and efficiently as was possible. But it wasn't feasible. It wasn't anywhere near. Budgets meant that the forensic bill had to be handled carefully. Kate knew that Kelly would love to send each reel of CCTV, speck of gravel and partial shoe tread off to the lab, for every robbery, domestic and ABH, but she couldn't.

Kate opened the email. It was about the signet ring. They already knew that the ring probably didn't belong to Jack. It hadn't been part of the goods signed in upon arrival at HMP Highton thirteen years ago, neither his daughters nor his niece recognised it, and Jack had never been in the military. She scanned the email.

'Rob,' she said.

He peered across from his computer screen. 'Yup?'

'A print has been lifted from the signet ring,' she said.

'So all we have to do is find someone's finger to match it,' he said sarcastically.

'Tetchy?' she asked him.

'Sorry,' he said. 'Are you coming to the pub tonight?' he asked.

'I can't, I've got to get back for the girls,' she said. She didn't add that she also needed to get ready for her date.

Rob nodded. 'I'm going to sneak one in before going home,' he said.

'Are you allowed?' she teased. Kate knew that Rob's wife was sensitive about his working hours. It was no secret, and was probably no different to the arguments between all new parents over who did what, who needed the most sleep, who deserved a break and who was more tired. Kate no longer had to worry about such arguments; her girls were grown up and independent and Derek was living in his own flat, out of her way. Funny that now Derek was out of her hair, she didn't mind the house-work so much. Kelly's boyfriend was different, that was for sure. Kate didn't know if it was because he was a bit older and wiser, at fifty, or because he already had a grown-up daughter, or that he just had an understanding temperament. Some women might call him boring, but to Kate, he was a keeper. Kelly Porter belonged at Eden House, doing what she did best, and if her man's ego (or lack of it) was such that it made her decisions smoother, then bloody good luck to her. Kate wouldn't wish her life with Derek on anyone. Had she wasted her life? No. Everything happens for a reason, she thought. Plus, she'd never give up her girls just to go back and change history with a man. The thought of her date made her smile, and

Rob looked at her curiously. To avoid his questions, she went to Kelly's office and told her the news about the ring. She was clearly still struggling to concentrate, and it was a good excuse to move around.

'They managed to lift a print? Just one? And it was clear?' Kelly asked.

'Yes. It's a partial thumb. You know Derek wears a signet ring, and he constantly twists it with his thumb and middle finger, like this,' Kate said, demonstrating the fiddling motion. Kelly watched her and nodded.

'Makes sense,' she said. 'Are you off soon?' she added.

Kate gently closed the door behind her and smiled conspiratorially. She sat down.

'I'm nervous as hell,' Kate said.

'I can see that, you're like a loaded spring. Why? You'll knock him dead. Just be yourself,' Kelly said. 'Did you decide what to wear in the end?'

'Well, I didn't want to appear slutty, and I certainly don't want to look like a detective, so I'm going for a cream dress I bought for a wedding. Don't think shoulder pads and hat, it's elegant and plain.'

'Perfect. Not too booby? Though you should show them off.'

Kate was well endowed.

'Thanks. That's why I chose the dress. I want him to talk to me, not my chest,' Kate laughed.

'Quite right, though I'm sure they've got a lot to say. Do the girls know?' Kelly sat back in her chair, welcoming the diversion.

'They know I'm going on a date, but they don't know he's a copper,' she said.

'The copper who happens to be in charge,' Kelly said.

'I'm trying not to think about it. Did you inform occupational health?' Kate asked.

'I don't see why I need to. I spoke to Andrew this morning, as your line manager. It's not exactly anything serious yet is it?'

'Am I being stupid?' Kate asked.

'Of course not! Bloody hell, Kate, you deserve some fun. Go and have a brilliant night and stop feeling guilty. You guys don't work together, there's no conflict of interest. You fancy each other, that's all that's important. Order something expensive, though. Hasn't that restaurant got a Michelin star?'

'Apparently so.'

'How did he get a reservation so quickly?' Kelly asked.

'He knows the owner,' Kate said.

'Handy.' Kelly smiled. 'I'll remember that.'

'Will you be working the weekend?' Kate asked her boss. 'Or is that a stupid question?'

Kelly looked up and tilted her head as if to say, 'Are you kidding?' They both knew the answer. Kelly wouldn't take a full day off now until they'd gone as far as they could to secure a conviction for the deaths of the two ex-convicts.

'Did you ask Millie if she could come and meet Lizzie tomorrow?' Kelly asked.

'Yes, she's excited. She's coming to you about nine, is that all right?'

'Perfect. We've got a baby, remember, we'll have been up for hours.'

Kate got up to leave.

'Make sure you take a toothbrush tonight, you never know,' Kelly said.

'If it gets that far, it'll be a miracle. No one's been that far south in years,' Kate said. She left and Kelly got back to work. She'd work for another twenty minutes and then suggest they grab a quick beer at The Bell. She hadn't realised the disturbing irony of the pub name until now. 'Come on, Jack,' she willed. Let it be a sign.

Chapter 34

The pub was patronised mainly by a mixture of locals, with a smattering of tourists searching for a convenient bar, after a day sightseeing. When visiting the Lakes, staying in Penrith was cheaper than, say, Keswick or Windermere. If one didn't mind driving everywhere, it was just as convenient, if not as pretty. From Penrith, most walks could be started within the hour. Getting to the western Lakes was a bit of a hike, but then it was from anywhere in the national park, unless one chose to stay over that way, say in Eskdale or Wasdale. They were remote places where only serious walkers stayed, or couples looking for a quiet romantic escape. The sweeping valleys and plummeting rock over in the west meant that road access was limited, and thus visitors were low in number. But it was well worth the effort.

The small group was well known to the landlord and they'd already had a conversation about the two bodies. It went along the same lines as it always did when there was a serious crime in the papers.

'*Caught them yet?*'

'*No business them sort being here in the Lakes, tarnishing our good name.*'

'*Bad business, what you doing about it?*'

Next came the theories and unhelpful advice, becoming more outlandish as the night wore on. At some point, usually around nine, it would be time to leave them to it, discussing how they'd better handle the police investigation. Kelly usually got a pat on the back. 'You're all right, girl, even though you came up from *that* London.' Modern habits, such as sexual equality and right-on political correctness, took their time reaching Cumbria, but Kelly didn't take it personally. Local knowledge could be a powerful thing.

Emma drank Coke, Rob ordered two pints of lager, one for him and one for Dan, and Kelly accepted a small G&T. They found a table to huddle round and Kelly toasted Emma's efforts.

'In a rare moment of emotional mushiness, I'd like to take this opportunity to say how lucky I am to be surrounded by the team I've got. I couldn't ask for more, truly. You give me everything,' Kelly said.

Rob was clearly feeling good about himself and Kelly squeezed his shoulder; well he might. He'd made huge progress with the personal finances of Rickie Burton. He'd discovered hundreds of transactions in cash and thousands of account transfers for various amounts dating back years, and he'd already begun to compile a list of recipients.

They clinked glasses and Kelly enjoyed the moment as they took a well-earned break from work. They asked Emma questions and swapped stories of adventures and incidents in the Lakes. Dan told them about the highlands of Scotland and they teased each other about which country was more beautiful. The atmosphere was buoyant, after all, it was Friday night, and the bar was busy. Kelly's phone rang, and she took it out of her pocket to see if it was important. It was.

'Bloody hell, that's all I need,' she said. She answered but couldn't hear, so left the small group and made her way out into the corridor where the toilets were.

'Ma'am.' It was the on-call officer at Eden House. 'I didn't want to disturb you, but I thought you'd want to know,' the officer said.

'Go on,' Kelly said.

'After your handover, I received an email from HMP Highton, as requested, of CCTV footage of the family meeting room. Rickie Burton had three visitors over the last two months. Each time, the footage clearly shows Mr Burton being escorted in to the room, but each time, a convict or prison guard gets in the way of the camera angle. Ma'am, I don't think it's an accident. I can't make out the visitor on each occasion. And I think it was blocked on purpose.'

'By prison guards?'

'That's what it looks like, ma'am.'

'I'll be back soon,' she said, hanging up and making her way back to her team. Her face must have given away her concern.

'Something come up, boss?' Rob asked. She explained what she'd just been told and her intention to go back to the office.

'I'll finish my drink first,' she said. The alcohol warmed her body and made her head slightly foggy. Damn. She'd forgotten to eat. Booze on an empty stomach, even a small G&T, wasn't ideal, but she just accepted that she'd be a bit slow for the next half hour, then she'd grab something from the kebab shop, on her way back to Eden House.

Her phone went again; it was a text from Johnny. It was a photo of Lizzie, with the caption 'Hello Mummy!' She smiled and the image soothed her irritation, though she felt a small tug of guilt. She sent kisses back to both of them and popped her phone back into her pocket, listening to the team swapping stories.

Their laughter was a tonic. Rob's anecdotes about parenthood were always entertaining and Kelly laughed with them. Attention turned back to Emma, and she described the toughest parts of the race. Dan was rapt; Kelly noticed the way he looked at Emma. The two of them agreed to get another drink, but Rob said he'd pass, as he had to get back to put his son to bed and read him a story, and Kelly said she'd walk out with him. They left Dan and Emma in passionate conversation, and Kelly realised that he never talked about his wife any more. The evening air was cool and she wrapped her coat around her.

'When did your little one stop waking up in the middle of the night?' she asked him.

'I can't remember. I just know we woke up one morning without being up in the night and grinned like conspirator plotters. It was a great day,' he said. 'Does Lizzie wake up much?'

'She's definitely worse when I'm not there to say good night.'

'I get it. They know how to press your buttons.'

'Why are they so clever?' she asked.

'They're perfect agents of disruption. They're hard-wired to get what they need, any way they can. If only we stayed that clever, we'd all be geniuses,' he said, laughing.

They said their goodbyes. 'Try and get a good night's sleep,' she said.

'You too, boss.'

They parted company and Kelly went to the kebab shop, ordering a chicken special with loads of salad and chilli sauce, and made her way back to the office. With no-one around to watch, she devoured it and wiped her mouth. It was just what her body and brain needed, and she wiped her mouth. She looked at the photo of Lizzie again. It would be her bedtime soon.

Before she realised, she was fully immersed in the case and by the time she'd finished reviewing the CCTV footage of the visit days at Highton, she'd already been back in the office for almost three hours, and it was gone nine o'clock.

There was no doubt at all: on all the days that Rickie Burton received visitors at HMP Highton, the CCTV cameras which could have shown his visitors clearly were either covered up, or not working properly.

Chapter 35

Kate was shown to the table where Andrew sat. When he saw her, he stood up and beamed. The waitress smiled at them knowingly, it being obvious that this was a date and that they weren't a married couple, on the basis that they were so pleased to see one another, and so very smartly dressed. She pulled out Kate's chair for her and waited for them both to sit, waiting for Kate to get comfortable before handing her the set tasting menu, which consisted of fifteen courses, and paired wine menu. God, she'd be hammered if she tried all of the samples, but it would be rude not to at least taste them.

He looked different. But then, all coppers did out of uniform. His daily garb was made up of stiff white shirts, pressed black trousers, a smart black tie and epaulettes decorated with oak leaves and a crown to denote his superior rank. They drew the eye and reminded one where one stood. Not so tonight. Kate was drawn more to his face than his shoulders, and found it warm and open. Without the penguin attire, he was three-dimensional and very handsome. He wore casual light tan trousers, a nicely tailored blue shirt, with a few buttons open at the top, and he smelled of expensive cologne. He had personality, and for this she was relieved and grateful. She'd dated coppers before, years ago, before she married Derek, and found many of them as rigid as their trouser folds. This man wasn't like that.

'You look lovely,' he said.

'So do you,' she replied. Thought of his rank and position faded quickly and they fell into easy conversation. He made her laugh, and he reciprocated by delighting in her anecdotes. They didn't talk about work. Instead they talked about grown-up stuff like children, life's ups and downs, and maturing too quickly. Kate only noticed they'd gone through ten courses already because her dress was beginning to feel tight and she wanted to visit the toilet. She felt a bit squiffy and it was no wonder after ten sips of paired wines, red, white and rosé, as well as fizz. Each drop complemented the matching morsel perfectly and she wondered at the sommelier who was actually paid to study wine. She was in the wrong job.

She excused herself and asked a waiter for directions to the ladies. It was lavish. Gold mirrors adorned the walls papered with a bright scene of a rainforest. She'd heard once that the cleanliness of a restaurant's loos was a good indicator of the standards in the kitchen. The sinks were marble and fresh towels were laid out alongside toiletries, creams and perfume. Music played gently and the lighting was soft enough to make her skin look rosy but fresh. She topped up her make-up and stared at herself. It was a face she'd not seen for a very long time. It was the unmistakable countenance of excitement and thrill. The sort of thing one might witness on a seventeen-year-old, not a nearly fifty-year-old showing the inevitable signs of age catching up. She touched her fingers to her jowls and pulled them up, as if after a facelift. Fat chance. Money like that didn't grace the pockets of policewomen. She knew a woman who'd gone to Poland to get it done and it looked fantastic, after the swelling and bruising wore off. It had cost a fraction of the price charged in the UK, but Kate didn't have the courage. She went to a cubicle and then washed her hands, smiling to herself once more.

When she returned to the table, Andrew was on the phone and he gestured an apology to her. She couldn't help but overhear his conversation and it sounded to her like it might be his ex-wife. It was a conversation about one of his children.

'I appreciate that, but on a Friday night, when frankly I can do nothing about it, it can wait.' He hung up.

'Sorry,' he said to Kate.

'No worries,' Kate said. 'Problem?'

'Ex-wife, calling me about my son's A Levels. It's my weekend, I'll pick them up tomorrow and see what the problem is then. She does this.' His voice was tinged with frustration mixed with something else, an obvious sense of guilt and failure. He looked as though he was used to beating himself up on a regular basis about leaving his kids. Derek hadn't been struck down by that particular affliction, Kate noted.

She reached out her hand and put it on top of his. 'Hey, don't be too hard on yourself. Parenting is difficult enough without adding self-flagellation into the mix. Do yourself a favour and allow yourself some fun too,' she said. He squeezed her hand, and it surprised her.

'You're right,' he said.

'I'm glad we did this,' he said, out of the blue. 'Would you like to do it again?'

Kate said yes, she would.

'I might have to move you out of serious crime, though,' he said.

She shot him a sharp look. 'What?' she asked, her spoon poised mid-air.

'I'm joking,' he said, and she sighed. 'It's just that the more time I spend with you, the trickier it will be line-managing your team. Perhaps I'll move myself instead. I was actually thinking about retiring soon, I might bring it forward.'

Kate didn't know what to say. All she could think was that when she looked at his face and listened to him talk, she knew that he meant it.

Chapter 36

Kelly yawned and looked at her phone: it was eleven o'clock in the evening, and she sighed, frustrated with herself for allowing so much time to slip by. She turned off her computer and gathered her things, wondering if Johnny would still be up when she got home.

Her phone buzzed as she went to put it in her bag and she was surprised to see that it was Brian Taylor, the governor of Highton, returning her call. She remembered that he smelled of booze when they'd met and braced herself, wondering what he could possibly want at this time.

'Kelly Porter, good evening,' she said.

'Detective. I received your message. I'm sorry, I was tied up somewhat. How can I help you?' asked the governor.

Kelly loosely outlined her plan to him, trying her best to get him to consider the value of such an operation.

'It's the only way to find out if there was communication with the outside leading up to the deaths of your ex-prisoners,' she said.

'I've got fifty new prisoners who I really do not want. I don't even know where to put them,' he complained. Kelly listened, not knowing what he was going on about. 'It's not the best time,' he said.

Kelly noticed that some of his words were slurred. 'I understand,' she said trying to appease him. 'But—'

'There's always a but,' he interrupted her. 'You lot think you can waltz into my prison any time you fancy and put a cat amongst the pigeons, but I'm telling you there's no need for a full search. I'll have it in hand tomorrow, I promise you. I'll find out if there was illegal communication. I'll get back to you.' It was vague and Kelly felt frustration rise in her throat. She'd have no option but to secure a warrant, with Chief Constable Harris's permission. She sat on the edge of her desk and closed her eyes.

Brian Taylor said something muffled and hung up before she could thank him for his time. She put her phone away. It was time to go home. Her head was saturated with information. It kept going around and around, playing different scenarios, and she could no longer distinguish between what might be plausible and what might not be.

She actually felt pity towards the governor. She'd seen for herself how cramped it was inside the prison, and Tom Gorman had told her about it too. Conditions were at breaking point. She was reminded of Darwin's theory and it wasn't too far off what went on inside such institutions. Life was a case of survival. Justice was served in the showers, where there was no CCTV, and evidence washed down the drain. It was a harsh levelling ground, one that reduced grown men to tears as they were taken away to begin their life locked up. She'd seen it for herself. The van that took them was affectionately known as the ice box, because there was nothing in it apart from cold terror, not even a seatbelt to hang yourself with. Kelly had no idea where Brian Taylor intended to put fifty extra prisoners, but it made the task ahead of them even riskier.

She spotted a new email, a technical report on the two IMEI numbers of the mobile phones found in brown envelopes; one in the flat rented by Jack Bell, and the other owned by Dean Kirby's girlfriend. A brief list of numbers was attached to each device. Kelly read that one of the devices had been traced to a known drug dealer in Barrow-in-Furness. Butterflies fluttered in her tummy. It was too late to call Craig, but it was a great way to finish the evening.

–

She snuck quietly into the house and closed the door, but she needn't have bothered, because Johnny was awake and sitting in the kitchen with a glass of wine. She smiled at him, but didn't feel any warmth in return. She put down her bag and went to him.

'You okay?' she asked. She rubbed his shoulders.

'I spoke to Tom earlier,' he said.

'Right,' she said. She wasn't entirely sure where the conversation was going, so she waited.

'Do you mind if I sit down?' she asked.

'Of course, sorry. Is it that obvious I'm in a bad mood?' he asked, softening.

'Yes, it is,' she said.

He sighed.

'What did Tom want? Is he all right?' she asked.

'Yes. He's fine, it's just I'm not sure it's helpful for him to be interrogated by you.'

She was tired and took a moment to absorb what he was saying. She didn't know exactly how her conversation with Tom, who was a material person of interest because of his new connection with the prison, was an interrogation, but she waited for an explanation.

She got a glass and poured herself some wine and sat opposite him.

'What's up?' she asked.

'I'll be honest with you, spending time with Lizzie has made me re-evaluate a few things. Sure, I want to get back to the mountains, and I need to get back to work, but it's more than that. My work with veterans.'

'What about it?' Kelly asked.

'Well, that's just it, isn't it? I don't feel as though you take it seriously, until it benefits you and you hijack one of my friends,' he said.

Kelly digested the accusations but couldn't speak. She felt him glaring at her and wondered how many glasses of wine he'd had. His normally mild manner had evaporated and Kelly knew there must be more to it than her conversation with Tom. She forced herself to remain calm.

'Tom works at the prison now, so I had to speak to him. Did he say it made him uncomfortable?' she asked.

He shook his head.

'No, it makes me uncomfortable. You always have to find someone to blame, and this time it's a veteran. How many vets do you know who are hanging about the Lake District cutting people up?' he asked.

She could see his anger bubbling under the surface and didn't like it.

'It's not like that at all. I'm not *looking* for a veteran to be connected with my case. It's a line of enquiry, that's all. What is this really about?' She touched his arm. 'You want to protect Tom?'

He stared at her and Kelly saw that he was looking through her rather than at her.

'Johnny?'

'It's nothing,' he said.

Upstairs, Lizzie began to cry.

Chapter 37

'Mum had a bit of a sore head this morning,' Millie told Kelly. The sun shone through the whole house from the back terrace, the doors to which were thrown open. Kelly had her own throbbing head today as well, but it wasn't alcohol-related. They'd been up most of the night with an unsettled baby. She poured strong coffee and tried to engage Millie in conversation. She was a polite and friendly young woman and Kelly felt regretful that she couldn't mirror the girl's enthusiasm.

Johnny came from the kitchen and handed Millie a lemonade and she took it gratefully. It was a beautiful October morning and Kelly tried to concentrate on the sunshine, willing herself to improve her mood. She turned her attention to Lizzie to distract herself. She and Johnny hadn't spoken this morning, as they'd shared breakfast duty and other chores. Kelly's heart ached, but she figured he'd come round in the end.

She watched as Lizzie looked up at Millie and seemed thrilled to have a new face to examine and charm. Millie went straight to the baby, putting her drink down and kneeling on the floor.

'Can I hold her?' Millie asked.

'Of course,' Kelly replied. Millie unfastened the bouncer and picked the baby up, who wriggled with delight and played with the girl's necklace, pulling it and giggling adorably. Kelly watched in a bit of a daze, as her daughter showed no signs of being up all night. No-one would ever know, looking at her now. There seemed to be nothing wrong with her except perhaps a sixth sense that her parents were edgy.

Kelly thought that Millie looked like her mother and had the same open laugh. She was easy to be around and Kelly felt comfortable and happy that she would win Lizzie over, if she hadn't already.

'Have you got plans for college?' Kelly asked. She was aware of Johnny making himself busy.

'I'm taking a year out. The last twelve months has been crazy and I want to earn some money. I thought about travelling, but I can do that after my course. I want to do international politics and the final year is in Miami.'

'Wow! That'll be fun,' Kelly said. 'So have you already got a job?'

Millie bounced Lizzie on her hip and looked like she'd been taking care of babies for years. 'I work in a cafe in town but it's only part-time and I don't really enjoy it. The money is not great but the tips from tourists are good,' Millie said.

Johnny seemed to have stopped fiddling with whatever he was doing and came to sit down. Millie took a seat too and Kelly thought it might be a good moment to leave to go to work.

'Johnny wants to get back to work, but he works shifts – is that all right with you? I'm out all day,' Kelly said, as if smoothing the path to her retreat.

'It'll be about fifteen hours a week,' Johnny said. 'It's about time that Lizzie met some new faces, but we don't want her going to nursery just yet.'

'I'm happy to work around you. Do you want me to do some housework too? Like a nanny?' she asked.

Kelly and Johnny glanced at one another and said yes in unison. It was the first time Kelly had felt any connection to him all morning.

'I'll show you around,' Johnny said, standing up as suddenly as he'd sat.

'Right, I need to go, I'll just tidy the breakfast pots then,' Kelly said, kissing her daughter goodbye. She looked at Johnny but didn't go to kiss him.

On her own in the kitchen, she popped two paracetamol to ward off the threatening headache at her temple, and took a deep breath. It was going to be a long day.

Her phone buzzed; it was Emma.

'Guv, can you speak?'

She listened to the faint laughter of Millie from the living room, no doubt being entertained by Johnny, the perfect stay-at-home dad. The bitterness of the thought caught her off guard and she replied to Emma: 'Of course, what is it?'

'I'm in the office and I've received a staff list from a care home in Waberthwaite. It's an old Victorian place just off the A595. Dan and I were thinking about paying them a visit, we've got nothing better to do on a Saturday,' Emma said. Kelly couldn't help wondering why Dan might not wish to spend his Saturday with his wife, but she thought she knew the answer to that one now. They were both in the office very early, even by the standards of highly enthusiastic young detectives.

'I'm listening,' Kelly said.

'They use Covey Care kit, they have a contract with them to supply all of their clinical equipment,' Emma said. She paused.

'Including?' Kelly felt the tiny hairs on her arms stand up. The terrace door was open but it wasn't cold. The sun shone along the hardwood floor, through the crack in the door to the kitchen. The late summer roses in a vase on the windowsill moved gently with a slight breeze.

'Guv, they supply their latex gloves, their winches and straps, as well as therapy lamps. One of their senior members of staff is a guy called Ian Burton, and he's ex-army.'

Kelly grabbed her things and headed to the door, just as Josie came downstairs to leave.

'Where are you going?' Johnny asked his daughter.

'I'm going to a concert in Keswick Park.'

'What about my charity abseil?' he said.

Kelly stopped a foot from the door. It wasn't just Josie who'd forgotten that he was out all afternoon, and now she felt sheepish for disregarding the importance of it.

'I can stay if you need me,' Millie said.

'You're a star,' Kelly said. 'If you're sure?' She glanced at Johnny briefly and left, knowing that they'd have words tonight.

Chapter 38

Nathan Appleton apologised to his wife for the third time. He had no choice but to make a trip to Highton prison on a Saturday because he'd left behind some documents that were needed to mark GCSE coursework. He taught English in the prison library every Wednesday, and had done for two years.

'I don't understand why you need it today, though,' she complained. 'We'd arranged to meet the Barnes at The Fox, walk up the Lion and Lamb, then have lunch back at the pub.'

'I know, but it won't take me long. These grades need to be submitted to the board on Monday and I haven't finished marking them,' he said. 'I'm sorry, I won't be much later than we'd planned. If I drive down to Highton, I know exactly where I left them, and I'll be back to join you at The Fox car park.' They each had their own car. That was part of life living and working in the Lake District – public transport was fairly good but it took time to navigate the winding single-lane roads. Having your own transport was much quicker, even when there was a herd of cute Dexter cattle in the way. She sighed.

'This is a classic case of what I've been talking about,' she said.

He looked at her and knew what was coming. His wife had attended a time management course on behalf of the Nationwide Building Society in Kendal, where she worked, and now she fancied herself an expert.

'You left those papers on Wednesday, but it's taken you this long to realise. If you'd picked them up on Thursday then you could have had them marked by now and my day wouldn't be ruined!'

There was no point arguing with her, or indeed defending himself. He got his coat.

'Just go!' she said. 'We'll head off without you if you're not back,' she added.

The journey from Keswick to Highton was actually a very pleasant drive and Nathan relished the thought of being in the car, on his own, with the magnificent countryside, for a couple of hours. It would be a morning of peace and quiet, and he even had the fleeting thought that he might just misplace more items at the prison in the future. As he slammed the door behind him and shut out the sound of his wife's voice, he smiled to himself and decided that he fancied driving the coastal route. It'd add on a bit of time but secretly, he could do without walking up a hillside with a hangover.

It was a glorious day, and the sun, though lower now as autumn crept up on them, was still ascending over the Yorkshire Dales to the east. It made him remember the time they'd driven with a picnic to St Bees Head to watch the sunset; it was one of the most spectacular views in the whole of the UK, possibly the world. Nathan was a proud Cumbrian, and though not a religious man, he imagined the valleys and hills touched by a divine hand. How else could it have modelled itself on perfection?

But the solitude also brought grief.

Jack Bell had been one of his students, and his death had caused shockwaves amongst them all. Nathan thought back to his first day in the library, thinking himself a lunatic for volunteering for such a task. But he'd never once regretted his decision. His students, young and old, kept him hopeful in many ways: for a better world and a better future. He and his wife had no children of their own, and, at thirty years old, they were faced with IVF as their only option. It had put a strain on their marriage and his wife had become more closed off. Drives on his own had become more frequent; it was his way of forgetting it all.

The A66 was surprisingly quiet for a beautiful October Saturday. The southern Lakes would be rammed on a day like this, he thought. Which is why they preferred Keswick. Bassenthwaite Lake looked resplendent, and he was reminded of the Lakeland poets. Frustratingly, GCSE courses were obsessed with war and conflict, but the A Level course allowed him to open his students' eyes to the wonders of Romanticism, grounded right here in the Lake District. The topic soon made his mind reflective. He gazed at the colours of the trees, so reminiscent of Keats, the bare rock, more emblematic of Shelley, and the bright blue sky so inspiring to Wordsworth. The lines came alive to him and he smiled to himself as he neared the northern edge of the lake, which was dead calm as he spotted people walking around it. It looked like a mirror, and the fells and screes above seemed to flow into it in one continuous stream. It was a vision of gold, claret, green and bronze, a true spectre of Victorian opulence. But he was getting carried away. His visit to Highton this morning was not simply about papers. The police had left him a voicemail: they wanted to talk to him. He was more than happy to vouch for Jack's character. He'd been an exemplary student, so much so that Nathan had arranged to tutor him after his release so he could proceed with his GCSE.

When Nathan got to the Cockermouth junction he said sod it and carried on to the coastal town of Whitehaven, where he'd head to the beach. The detour through St Bees would be worth it on a day like this, and he suffered a brief attack of melancholy as the image of him and his wife holding hands came back to him. All they seemed to do was argue nowadays. They seemed stuck. They both worked hard and Nathan believed they had a good life. But he'd already admitted to himself that he was happier out of the house, in prison even, and today was another example. He looked forward to Wednesdays, and had made a habit of getting to know his students. He spent time sipping tea and chatting to the prison officers too; he'd become familiar with the rhythms and routines of prison life, his wife would say too well, but he couldn't help but feel empathy for his fellow human beings.

He was also a good observer, and had noticed Jack withdraw somewhat just before his release. Maybe he would mention it to the police. All he knew was that it had something to do with that awful character Rickie Burton. He'd asked around, about whether something had happened to Jack to make him so uncharacteristically quiet. A few of the students who knew him well shared gossip with him, and some of it verged on the unbelievable, but none of them knew anything.

The cloud in his head disappeared as he neared the great cliffs and dunes of St Bees Head where Wordsworth had walked with his good friend, the canon of the lovely old church, where Nathan had once sat and contemplated a thesis on the great poet. He stopped the car, turned off the engine, and looked across towards the Isle of Man, and made out the coast of Ireland in the distance. He felt philosophical and wondered if the news about the appalling deaths of the ex-convicts from Highton had affected him more than he realised. It struck him now, in this place of tranquillity, that his affection for Jack Bell was real. Jack hadn't been his most gifted student, but Nathan had touched something in him. A light had gone on for the old man, and that's what made Nathan's job so rewarding. Anyone could revise and work hard enough to get awarded a qualification, but not everyone elicited a dawning invigoration simply from words. Jack Bell spent so much time in the library that Nathan had reckoned they'd have to order more books in. That's why he'd started an appeal at school, for parents to donate books to Highton. The response had been incredible, and had warmed Nathan's heart. A total of 1,293 books had been donated and it was Jack Bell's job to sort them out. It had got him out of his cell and kept him busy.

It had appeared to Nathan that Jack Bell had much to live for.

Chapter 39

The level of activity at Eden House made it feel as though it was midweek. Everybody, bar Kate, was there. There weren't as many uniforms, but Kelly's core team moved around the incident room, going about their jobs with keenness, and a renewed buzz of excitement was notable. They had a name.

Ian Burton.

It was the name given to Emma by the care home in Waberthwaite, and the man happened to share a surname with the convict Rickie Burton.

Kelly wanted to know who he was, and, more importantly, if they were related. They had a sketchy biography and Dan had already been on to the MOD, who confirmed that Ian had served with the Light Infantry from 1999, when he was eighteen years old, and had been medically discharged with PTSD twelve years ago at the age of twenty-seven. Dan had done some sweet-talking and had managed to get some further unclassified information. In 2004 Burton had been the victim of kidnap in Basra, presumed dead, but in fact held captive for almost a year, 309 days to be exact. The exact nature of what had taken place was classified and in the veteran's service files, which would have to be requested through a formal process. Kelly couldn't remember hearing about it in the press. Had he been released, or did he escape?

Military files were not readily accessible to the police, except under section 19 of the Police and Criminal Evidence Act. Without power of seizure, which took time, only a veteran or his or her next of kin could access them. So they'd made a formal request.

Outside his medical discharge and his time in the military, they had little on Ian Burton. The care home had given them a residential address but a squad car had been sent over and reported that no one was home. He wasn't due on shift at the care home until Tuesday, which was three days away. A routine check and search through the national computer didn't have him registered to a motor vehicle or a mobile phone contract.

Kelly had made sure to check Rickie Burton's list of known relatives, but it made no mention of a family member of Ian's age, and Burton was a common enough English name. In fact Rob informed them that over 45,000 people in England had that surname, though it was in fact more popular in the USA. Rob was known for his flashes of nerdiness and he revelled in stats. Kelly thanked him and sarcastically asked for the origin.

'It's Old English, an import of the Normans, meaning enclosure or farm,' Rob said. He winked at his boss, who shook her head. Emma raised her eyebrows, impressed; she was also known for her love of trivial facts.

'Bravo,' she said.

'Their family coat of arms is beautiful, do you want to know their idiom?'

Kelly perched on the edge of a desk. 'I'm all ears.'

'*Vitae lux*. It means light of life.'

'Fabulous, now we've ascertained that Ian Burton is possibly related to William the Conqueror, has anyone got any bright ideas about how to find him?'

'Guv, this is the photo attached to his employment file at the care home,' Emma said. She passed Kelly the image and she stared at his face. She'd been up close and personal with Rickie Burton, whose face was etched in her mind due to his scars, and the way he'd absentmindedly fondled his torn and stubby ear. The man in the photo had a whiff of resemblance, but only insofar as being Caucasian, male and balding. It looked as though it was decades old, too.

'How long has Ian Burton worked at the care home?' Kelly asked. Emma consulted her computer and read out what she had.

'He started there in 2018.'

'This must be an old photo then. I wonder what he was up to between 2012 and then?' Kelly said. 'Right, let's find him. He must exist somewhere. Is he on the electoral roll? And have we tried the passport office?' With no mobile phone, no vehicle and no criminal record, they had little hope of locating Ian Burton apart from waiting for him to turn up to his address, which could be an old one, or work on Tuesday, which, if he was their guy, he probably wouldn't. Dan and Emma spoke in unison. He apologised and Kelly saw the affection between them. Emma spoke.

'No Ian Burton matching his description is on Facebook, Instagram, Twitter or LinkedIn,' she said.

'According to the Electoral Registration Office, there are over eleven thousand Ian Burtons listed on there,' Dan said. 'I've sent his details to the UK passport office but with it being the weekend, the jobsworth on the phone didn't quite appreciate the urgency.'

'Well done, Dan. That's frustrating. We have to be patient. Send an all ports warning in case he tries to leave the country and mark him as wanted on the national police database.'

She walked to a spare whiteboard and rubbed off some old notes.

'Release the photo to the press. Relatives of those he cared for must know him, he has to eat, pay bills and communicate with somebody. Tap into all current colleagues at the care home, all the patients and their immediate relatives. Alert all squad cars within the constabulary on shift to keep their eyes peeled – you never know, we might get lucky. Contact Workington, Whitehaven and Seascale directly. If he's our man, he might like to visit his scenes of crime.' Her phone buzzed and she saw it was Kate. She answered and indicated to her team to get cracking. She walked back to her office and sang Millie's praises.

'Millie has been thrown in at the deep end. She's absolutely lovely with Lizzie! I hope we didn't force her hand,' Kelly said.

'She's already called me, she's thrilled. She can imagine doing something like this and feels as though it's proper work, instead of shifts waitressing for peanuts. She's happy. Thank you, Kelly.'

Her second in command had used her first name in private for a long time now and Kelly welcomed the opportunity to bounce an update off her. Kate listened and offered to work today too.

'I'm reluctant to turn you down, but the rest of the team is in and if you come in too, it leaves me no option to rest anyone,' Kelly said. Then she added: 'Good night?' She couldn't resist.

'It was pretty awesome. He's a gentleman. We laughed, and ate amazing food, and laughed a bit more. His ex sounds like a bitch, his dress sense and manners are impeccable, and he paid.'

'Result.'

'Well, I'm actually in the car already, and don't mind being your wanderer today. It's a day for being out of the office and I've got nothing better to do,' Kate said.

'Okay, great. It's early days, I think the team is holding up nicely so we'll deal with rests somehow. Everyone's heads have lifted a bit this morning with this new lead. It could take us nowhere, but we need to speak to this guy at the very least. How long a drive were you thinking?' Kelly asked.

'I'm listening to Heart 80s and it's a beautiful day, send me where you like.'

'I've got Emma and Dan going down to a care home in Waberthwaite, so I could arrange for you to give Brian Taylor a visit at HMP Highton, it's his duty day and I'm waiting for my answer about a cell search. Ideally I don't want to go above his head with a warrant, I'd like his blessing, though I can't stand the man. I get the impression he's seen enough of me. Maybe you'll have better luck than I did, sweet-talking him, you have a knack with the seniors,' Kelly said.

Kate pretended mock horror. 'Sure. What am I saying? Is he in on a Saturday?' she asked.

'He is today, I checked. He called me late last night and I think he's concerned about how hard we go in, so gently does it. He did consider a cell search, but tensions are high in there and he doesn't want anything kicking off, so we might have to go above his head if you can't talk him round. I also need to know if Rickie Burton has a relative called Ian, and face to face is the only way to get to the bottom of that one. I'd go but I'm chasing warrants and I want to concentrate on Rickie Burton's finances with Rob. It's laborious, but it could be the evidence we need to show he had opportunity and means. Craig Lockwood is aware of the links to Barrow dealers and he's got the drug squad passing him what they know on possible contacts. He's also hauled in the dealer whose mobile was linked to the one in the brown envelope. You might also cross paths with Nathan Appleton, the English teacher who taught Jack Bell. He was contacted this morning and was heading down there to collect something.'

'Well I get all the best jobs. I'm just passing Penrith Castle so I'll head straight out of town and turn the music up,' Kate said.

'Enjoy. I'm jealous,' Kelly said.

She turned back to the room and looked at Rob, who was staring at something on his computer screen.

'Guv, you need to see this,' he said.

Chapter 40

Custodial Manager Liam Fawcett tapped his keys on the open metal cell door occupied by Rickie Burton.

'To what do I owe this particular pleasure?' Rickie asked, smiling with his mouth, but scowling with his eyes. Rickie was a cleaner on the wing. In wider society, of course, one might instantly see this as a manual job and thus one carrying average status, but inside, the opposite was true. It was the cleaner who was given the most freedom and thus had access to the whole wing. Rickie had been the cleaner on A wing for over twenty years. A mop and bucket sat on the floor by the single bed. Rickie didn't share his cell. Liam peered in to the tiny space, about ten feet by seven, and lingered at the door. Beyond was Rickie's private space and a screw only ventured in to break up a fight or conduct a pre-arranged cell search. Spontaneous searches weren't worth the aggro.

'I've got something for you,' Liam said.

Rickie left his bed, where he'd been reading about yoga, and sauntered towards the door. He hung on to the side of his bed and jutted out his chin, to receive whatever information Liam had that might interest him.

'Somebody wants to know if you have a relative called Ian,' Liam said.

Rickie's eye flickered and he fiddled with the skin of his mangled ear. His forefinger caressed the long silver scar and the officer couldn't see it, but his pulse rate elevated slightly.

'Somebody?'

'Coppers. They're also pushing for a cell search. A proper cell search,' Liam said.

Rickie came to the entrance of his cell and poked his head out, looking right and left.

'And just what do they think they'll find?' Rickie whispered. His face was hidden in the shadow of the door, away from CCTV, and Liam's back was to the closest camera.

'Phones.'

'How long have I got?' Rickie breathed.

'Could be tomorrow or Monday. Guv's hands are tied on this,' Liam added.

Rickie nodded, understanding fully what the officer had just given him. He'd presented him with a life-line. A way out of having his world torn apart by the coppers. Much better to divert and take the hit on a lesser crime than go down for your whole livelihood and lose everything. He knew who to rally.

'Leave the officers out of it, Rickie,' said Liam, his mouth barely moving. Rickie's head nodded ever so slightly, and Liam took it as an agreement. Liam walked away, his polished black boots tapping on the newly cleaned floor.

Rickie followed him down the wing and knocked on a few doors. The men were locked inside their cells for most of the day, but that didn't stop them messaging each other through windows using pieces of string, or tapping their walls, or the cleaner speaking directly through the conversation hole. He needed the help of the spice heads and the hooch makers on this one. No fucker was searching his cell without his say-so, and he wasn't about to lose thirty grand on his new stash of wing phones. Highton was about to explode, and Rickie Burton was going to sit and watch.

Chapter 41

'It's the CCTV from the visits room,' Rob said. Kelly pulled up a chair.

'I thought you were working on Rickie Burton's bank accounts?' she asked.

'I was, but there were some transactions that made me do a bit of digging. I started to investigate the cash withdrawals, because it means somebody else has access to his account. The ATM shows up on the bank statement and every machine has a code. These are all from the same one in Whitehaven, always the same amount, and all on visit days.'

'How the hell did do you know how to do that?' Kelly asked.

'The same reason I know how to launder money from lap dance clubs,' he replied, smiling at her.

'It's a good job you're not a criminal, Rob, you'd be so good at it.'

'So I thought I'd check the days and I found this,' he said, sitting back and freezing the frame on his computer.

'Holy shit,' she said.

'I thought you'd be excited,' he said.

In the middle of the visits room at Highton, handing a plastic chair to a prison guard, to make room for a family of four, in full view of the CCTV camera, which had been so cleverly angled as to miss Rickie Burton's visitors, was Ian Burton.

She called Emma. It was now vital they locate their suspect. Emma answered; they were almost at the care home in Waberthwaite. 'Make sure you photograph their winches and find out who manufactures the gloves. I want to know if they contain enough latex to cause anaphylaxis.'

She'd had it confirmed by the histology lab that food and drugs were not the cause of Dean Kirby's anaphylaxis.

'Yes, guv.'

Kelly knew that Emma would be thorough without her vocalising the instructions, but she needed to say them out loud. It was like a checklist in her own mind and helped ease her racing thoughts.

'Ask if he wore a signet ring, too,' she said.

'Yes boss, and the lamps, I've got it all.'

'Of course you have,' Kelly said. They hung up and she called Craig in Barrow. She paced up and down, hand occasionally on hip, gesticulating with it as she spoke. He listened as she listed the developments, one by one. She left Rob and went back to her office, listening to Craig.

'I think in light of this new evidence, your warrant for the cell search won't be a problem. Is it with Carlisle County Court?' he asked.

'Yes, and I agree, it's certainly in the interest of public safety. This removes the question mark over whether the invasion of privacy is merited,' she said.

'I've sent you a couple of photographs of a few local scumbags down here who are linked to those mobile phones found. The IMEIs pinged off cell towers in Barrow three times, and it makes sense that Dean Kirby had communication about whatever he was going to do in Seascale before he left.'

'Interesting that neither man took the device with him when they were supposed to meet,' Kelly said.

'I should think they'd have had new ones,' Craig said.

'Why didn't they destroy the old ones?' Kelly asked.

'Sloppy? Amateur? It looks like neither was the sharpest tool in the drawer,' Craig said.

'Jack was described as backward by one of the inmates,' she said as she sat down to look at the email Craig had sent. 'I'm just looking at those photos now.'

The images were of three separate men, each with a criminal record, each dead behind the eyes, with an unkempt, neglected personal appearance. One in particular caught her attention.

'The second one,' she said. She told Craig, reading the attached name to be clear which one she referred to. 'Check it against the CCTV frame from the Co-op in Workington. Our friend who bought the Snickers bar,' she added.

There was a pause, then Craig sucked in his breath. 'Yup, that's him, he's a known toerag, and a violent one. His name is Kieran Foster,' he said. 'I'll bring him in.'

'I want to know where his pal Ian Burton is,' Kelly said. 'Does he have previous?'

'He's been inside here and there, but I'll have to remind myself of the details,' Craig said. She listened as he tapped on his computer and brought up the criminal record of Kieran Foster.

'Possession with intent to supply, two years in Altcourse, but his remand was at Highton,' he said.

'Bingo,' Kelly said. 'What's his tribe? Any ex-forces?' she asked.

'I'll find out,' he said.

'Thanks, Craig.' They hung up. Now they had two suspects, but Kelly reckoned she knew who the mastermind behind the killings was: Rickie Burton. But she had to prove it. She had a decision to make, but first, she called the number for the army personnel centre given to Dan by the MOD. At the same time, she texted both Johnny and Tom Gorman, asking if they knew a veteran called Ian Burton. Sometimes, word of mouth could prove more powerful than any search engine. She loved HOLMES and would never be without it; however, the knowledge of people was still something that good coppers took advantage of. The world of the army, especially the infantry, was a small place, full of veterans and serving personnel who'd formed bonds akin to brother or sisterhood. They had their own language, their own Facebook groups, reunions and old war stories. If Johnny or Tom knew anyone who had come across Rifleman, and subsequently Corporal, Ian Burton, or Kieran Foster, she'd know soon.

The website for service records said it could take up to six months to retrieve them, but when the call was answered and she explained what she needed, they were more than willing to retrieve a full list of serving personnel linked to ex-soldier Ian Burton. Towards the end of the call, as Kelly was beginning to feel enlivened by the new developments, a text came back from Johnny asking one simple question.

'Why?'

She stared at her phone. Yes or no would have sufficed. Surely, given their recent conversations, it was obvious what she was asking him, and why. Her stomach turned over as she suspected that he did know Ian Burton, and also why she might be asking.

Chapter 42

'Good morning, Jeanie, it's Detective Inspector Kelly Porter.'

'Hello,' Jeanie said. It was curt and guarded. 'I'm off sick,' she added.

'I'm really sorry to hear that. I wanted to ask you some questions,' Kelly said.

'All right,' Jeanie said.

'You were at Highton on Thursday, I missed you.'

'I needed to pick up some personal items.'

'Right. We need to speak to a man called Ian Burton, I wonder if you know him or have seen him visiting Rickie Burton?'

Jeanie paused, and Kelly heard her breathing. The noise could be identified as only one thing: fear.

'The other question is about the emails you received from Jack Bell, especially the one from the evening of his release. Did you see him before your scheduled Saturday rendezvous?'

'No, I didn't,' Jeanie said.

'I'm not judging, Jeanie, your relationship with Jack Bell is your business, but it became my concern when he was killed. In the emails to you he mentioned some lucrative work that he might be pursuing. Do you know anything about that? It could be very important to us.'

Jeanie sighed.

'He was always talking about making it big,' she laughed gently, and Kelly noted real affection in her voice. She had also relaxed somewhat.

'Was there any specific plan? Something for Rickie Burton perhaps? You didn't answer my question about Ian Burton. Is he related to Rickie?'

'I believe that Rickie had a regular visitor called Ian Burton. All visitors are logged in, so he must be accounted for.'

'He isn't – we've already been given a list of the visitors for the last three months. We have CCTV footage of Ian Burton at Highton on the last visit day, with Rickie. But no one called Ian is signed in on that day.'

'That's odd,' Jeanie said. She seemed genuine.

It was clear to Kelly that Ian Burton either had fake ID or the prison was sloppy with who it let inside its walls, and that would be down to the staff on duty and prison policy. The CCTV footage had shown Liam Fawcett in the visitors' room, and he'd explicitly told her that his rank was too senior to be bothered with visit days. Now they'd need to trace every name on the visitors list for that day and see which one didn't exist, as well as who'd signed them in and out.

'Did you supervise visit days?' Kelly asked.

'Sometimes.'

'On any day Ian paid a visit?'

'A couple of times. He was very polite and Rickie was always pleased to see him,' Jeanie said.

'Are they related?'

'I'm not too sure about that.' She was hesitant.

'How are visitors processed for contraband?' Kelly asked.

'I'm not sure I'm allowed to share operational details with you, detective, I'll have to ask the governor.'

'Of course. I'm on my way there now.'

Kelly waited for a moment, undecided about how to proceed.

'Jeanie, if there's anything that you know about Rickie Burton's affairs inside Highton that comes to light in the investigation later, then that could look bad for you. More importantly, it could delay getting answers for Jack. Don't you want justice for him?' she asked.

Jeanie stifled a sob.

'I sense you're scared, Jeanie. What are you afraid of?'

'All of them,' she said. It was a whisper.

'Who do you mean?'

'I'm not part of it, but I know Jack was, and so are some of the others. He said he was doing one last job for Rickie. I pleaded with him not to. I told him it was dangerous. I've already said too much.'

'Jeanie, please. Help me. If there's some kind of cover-up at the prison involving staff and inmates, then it will come out in the end, you know how it works, and you know how it is for female prisoners inside. Perverting the course of justice can carry five years now, and this is a murder investigation.'

'Rickie Burton can make things happen,' she said. Kelly heard her blow her nose.

'You think he's responsible for what happened to Jack and Dean?' Kelly asked.

'Rickie is in charge of all trade inside Highton, and officers get a cut to keep their mouths shut,' Jeanie said. There was bitterness but also a resignation. Kelly made a note to send a squad car to Jeanie Clark's address to keep an eye on her.

'And are you telling me that you weren't included in this list?'

'No. Never. Rickie Burton has some kind of warped sense of chivalry,' she laughed. 'I know it seems ludicrous saying it out loud. He didn't pressure me like he did the others.'

'Pressure?'

'Payment,' Jeanie said.

'How much are we talking?'

'I don't know. It was always envelopes of cash. You'll never find it,' Jeanie added.

'All right, let's backtrack a bit. Is Liam Fawcett involved? The custodial manager?'

Jeanie's voice broke.

'Your disclosure has taken this to the next level now, Jeanie. I suggest you remain at home, off sick, until this is all investigated. I'll arrange it.'

'They know where I live. I know they do because Liam does.'

'All right, take it easy. You're assuming that a prison officer is going to take huge risks to protect a bit of untraceable cash, when he knows that it's Rickie Burton we're after. Do you know what exactly Jack was supposed to do for Rickie on the outside? I presume Dean was involved too?'

'They were to deliver something.'

'Something? Where? To whom?' Kelly was becoming frustrated.

'I can't...' Jeanie said. The woman was becoming so distressed that Kelly knew she'd get little more out of her. If she was to be trusted, though, Jeanie had just solidified their motive for murder. She had to warn Kate. She finished the call with Jeanie and dialled Kate's number. She was almost at Highton.

As expected, her second in command took the new developments calmly.

'Can I be a real pain?' Kelly asked.

'Go on. It's been a lovely drive, I really should come down this way more often,' Kate said.

'There's a garage opposite the turning for Highton, could you pop in and see if they record their CCTV footage? It's a long punt, but it's an obvious place to stop to refuel or pick up some snacks if you're visiting the prison. Ian Burton might have been there.'

Kate agreed and Kelly told her to enjoy the rest of her drive. She ended the call and grabbed her coat, expecting to be out for most of the day. As she went to check out with Rob, she was distracted by an update on her Toughpad, which vibrated in her hand as she went to put it in to her bag.

She opened it and saw that a notification had come through to HOLMES. As she read, a sickly feeling spread through her stomach.

They'd put a nationwide request into the system for any constabularies that might have unsolved murders involving a similar MO to theirs. They'd had two hits. One was last year, in Glasgow, and the other two years ago, in Manchester. The victims were males, with criminal records, and both were involved in running drugs through Cumbria to Barrow.

They'd both served time at HMP Highton.

Chapter 43

Emma drove and Dan sat in the passenger seat. They chatted about the details of the case and occasionally the view, especially which of the peaks Emma had run across, as well as the odd passer-by peering at a map, looking lost. They'd picked up coffees in Keswick and Dan held on to them, passing Emma's to her when she was on a straight stretch and could have a slurp. They hadn't rushed on purpose, taking their time to meander through the countryside. It was an opportunity to be alone together. Their hands touched as he passed her coffee. Emma glanced at him sideways and he allowed his hand to linger.

'I've booked a surprise for us,' he said.

Emma's smile broadened and she handed her coffee back. She concentrated on the road.

'Do I get to know?' she asked.

'Then it wouldn't be a surprise. Are you still free next Saturday?'

'I thought you couldn't get away?' she asked.

'She's going to stay with her mother,' he said. He never mentioned his wife by name. Vocalising her acknowledged her, and that was unnecessary. They'd gone beyond the point where regret or hesitance would change anything. They'd spent the night together last night for the first time. Dan had said he was working late down the coast, and had called his wife to say that he may as well book in to a hotel. In fact they'd stayed at Emma's, going there after the pub, and falling asleep in the early hours after finally satisfying their cravings for each other in her bed, drifting off to sleep in each other's arms and surprising themselves this morning not with regret, but with pure joy.

They were almost at Waberthwaite village.

'This coastline is almost as beautiful as Scotland,' he said. Dan had spent most of his young life in Glasgow, where he was born, never seeing the highlands, but that didn't stop him being proud. He'd visited the northern wildernesses in adulthood and learned how to climb.

'You haven't got a monopoly on breathtaking views, you know,' she teased. 'We have it all here, beaches, mountains, lakes and waterfalls, you name it, the list is endless.'

'Mountains? Under a thousand metres? Hmmm,' he baited back.

She grimaced in mock despair.

A bottleneck of traffic built up close to Muncaster Castle but Emma and Dan were soon through it and found themselves in the bleak wilderness of the foot of Corney Fell. This part of Cumbria was barren and marshy, and in the middle of nowhere. The care home was down a long private approach road and Emma strained to read a sign.

'I think that's it,' said Dan.

Emma put her indicator on and turned off the main road. The home sat in seven acres of gardens and the entrance was quite dramatic, with rhododendron bushes and tall pines on either side. The road swept upwards towards a hill and they could see a small lake. When they neared the top of the small incline, the house revealed itself in all its grandeur, creating an impressive vista. It was of

Victorian Gothic design and reminiscent of the house in the horror film *Psycho*, with its towers and large windows.

'Looks like a looney bin,' Emma said.

'It probably was before care in the community, and all that,' Dan said. 'It's quite stunning architecturally though,' he added.

'Blimey, are you Charles Rennie Mackintosh all of a sudden?' she joked.

'I'm impressed you're familiar with the man himself and his work,' he said.

'I know a thing or two about culture and architecture.'

She followed the signs for the visitors' car park and pulled into an empty spot round the back of the house. There, they saw other temporary buildings and structures, in a bland modern prefabricated style, and they both thought that it was a good job they were added on to the rear and didn't spoil the facade.

A few residents were sat on benches in a large garden, but none of them seemed interested in the visitors. They got out of the car and went to the entrance, their feet crunching on the gravel. They'd been told to ask for the supervising nurse, who was called Peter Fenshaw. There was a reception desk and a bell, and Dan pressed it. The interior was dark and a little unloved. The ceilings were high and the staircases either side wide, but the general splendour of the place had disappeared years ago, taken over by plastic, and chipboard security screens. Maybe it had once been a stately home, or even a hospital. A woman answered the bell and promised to get Mr Fenshaw if they'd wait in the reception area.

Peter Fenshaw was probably in his thirties, and had a strong grip. He greeted them openly and gave the impression he was happy to answer their questions. He was smartly turned out in a well-pressed white tunic which was spotless, like the rest of the man.

'Are you the senior nurse in charge of the place?' Dan asked. Fenshaw confirmed that he was. He also confirmed that he knew Ian Burton well.

'He's a non-clinical member of staff – a carer – and he's been with us for two years. I've been here for four years, so I can tell you anything you need to know,' he said.

Emma sensed that Peter spoke with some kind of tension when he mentioned the care worker.

'What we really need to do is find him,' Emma said. They stood in the quiet foyer; with the door open they could hear the birds singing in the garden. Peter looked concerned.

'What has he done?'

It was very abrupt, and took Emma and Dan by surprise.

'Is he a troublesome employee? That was rather quick there to assume he's up to no good.' Dan said what Emma was thinking.

'He's an ex-soldier who came to us on a rehabilitation programme. It's a bit like work experience for sufferers of trauma. It's run by a charity but paid for by the government.'

'So are you saying that you put up with him? You wouldn't choose to employ him if he hadn't come to you as a charity case?' Dan was blunt.

Peter folded his arms suddenly, indicating discomfort. It looked like he wanted to get something off his chest.

'I keep a close eye on all of my staff, and I would say that Ian struggles with discipline. Ironic, I know. I'm just curious as to what is so urgent.'

'We just need to speak to him,' Emma said.

277

'Well, he's very private. He's not close like the others, I'm afraid I can't tell you where to find him.'

'That's fine, thank you, Mr Fenshaw. We also have a few questions about the kinds of equipment you use here. Clinical equipment,' Emma clarified. 'But first, can you remember Ian wearing a ring like this one? It's quite stand-out,' she added. She showed him a photo of the Light Infantry emblazoned signet ring.

'Oh, yes, definitely. We all know that Ian is a war hero, the older patients love asking him about that. Though I'm not convinced it's true, is it?'

Dan and Emma exchanged a glance.

'He saw active service in Iraq,' Dan said.

Peter raised his eyebrows.

'Do you perform detailed stocktakes, Peter?' asked Dan. 'Do you have stringent controls on what equipment is used and when, and by whom?'

'Absolutely, yes,' he replied.

'Can we see the records?' Emma asked.

'What are you talking about, more specifically?' Peter asked.

'We're interested in where you order your clinical gloves from, and we'd like to look at the winching equipment you use and if you have any lamps like this one on site,' Emma said, showing Peter more photographs.

'Right. Crikey. Well, let's get going, shall we.' They followed him as he showed them through a series of doors, past private rooms, to a large storage facility.

'We have clinical equipment and medication, of course, which is strictly controlled, and then we have general-use items which are kept in a storeroom, so the remedial lamps, gloves and winching equipment would come under that category. Anything involving medication is under lock and key and only I and one other colleague have access to that.'

'Can you show us?' Dan asked.

'This way,' Peter said, striding confidently into the aisles, finding what he needed. He showed them boxes of gloves and Emma took down the details and serial numbers.

'You always use the same brand?' she asked. Peter confirmed that this was the case. He showed them winching equipment, and again they took serial numbers and photographs. Finally, they were shown the remedial lamps and they made notes, taking down all the details.

'How would you know if any of this had been stolen?' Dan asked.

'Stolen?' Peter asked.

'Can your staff just come in here any time they want and use all of this stuff, or is it signed in and out?'

'We do a stocktake every month, so any anomalies would show up then,' Peter said.

'And have they?' Emma asked.

'I'd have to check the computer, but I'd like to think that if we had a thief among us, I'd have been told,' he said.

'All we need is access to your records regarding non-medical kit,' Emma said. 'Are the remedial lamps considered medical?' she asked.

'No, we keep them with our regular stock. Much of the winching equipment is actually on long-term hire, but not the straps, we buy those.'

'From Covey Care?' she asked.

He nodded. 'I think everything is from Covey Care. There are several contractors of medical and clinical supplies that are sponsored by the government and we follow their lead. The storeroom manager isn't in at the weekend so I'll show you where we file everything,' Peter said.

They followed him once more and ended up in a tiny box office at the back of the storeroom. There was a bulky old computer station and a single chair. Between the two of them, Emma was the happiest number crunching and she sat down and watched as Peter logged her in as a guest. She recognised the programme and assured Peter they wouldn't be long.

'Right, can I get you both a drink, or anything?'

Dan turned to him as Emma busied herself at the screen. 'You could tell us what he's like with the patients,' he said.

'Ian?' Peter asked.

'Yes.'

'We call them residents, they're not patients,' Peter corrected.

'Sorry.'

It was clear to Dan that he'd need to push Peter, but he didn't want to lead him too much.

'I'll come with you and grab a couple of coffees if I may?' Dan said, walking from the room with Peter. 'Perhaps you can tell me whether anything comes to mind. For example, has there ever been a complaint about Ian's attitude or manner when dealing with residents? I can reassure you, Peter, this is nothing to do with your home, or any complaint we have received. We're merely trying to get a picture of Ian, and trying to find him. Anything, no matter how small, could help to locate him.'

'Ian is very casual and unsurprisingly dull,' Peter said. 'He does his job and goes home. I'm sorry if that's not what you're looking for.'

They reached the staff kitchen and Peter made them coffee.

'I do wonder why he keeps coming, he's clearly not short of money,' Peter said, stirring the drinks.

'What do you mean?' Dan asked.

'He drives a nice car and goes on lots of holidays.'

'He's single and works hard.'

'Detective, he's on minimum wage and takes home less than a thousand pounds a month,' Peter said.

'Maybe he has a rich relative?' Dan said. Peter shrugged, then showed him the way back to the store-room, where Peter gave his apologies for not being more helpful, and Dan went to see what Emma had unearthed, if anything.

'Hey,' she said, thanking him for the drink. 'Well, it's all going to kick off here. These accounts are a mess. There's stuff going missing all over the place, and it's not just Burton, it looks to me that staff help themselves to kit all the time. Anyway, regardless of that, I've got the items we're after, signed out by Burton, and that's what we came for.'

'Cheers,' said Dan, and they toasted their coffee cups.

Chapter 44

Word travelled fast within the walls of Highton that a sweeping and comprehensive cell search was imminent. The mood on the wings was tense and a rumble of discontent reverberated throughout the prison. Rickie Burton lay on his bed in his tiny cell and planned his next move. All he had to do was let nature take its course and act innocent when it all kicked off. He might even emerge a hero.

He'd started a rumour that certain items would be unavailable as a result of police interference during the current investigation into the deaths of two ex-cons. He'd also mentioned that the police were doing little to solve the crimes but were instead using it as an excuse to target prisoners' basic human rights. It didn't take much copper-bashing to whip up a frenzy of thoroughly fucked-off cons, and he listened as the echoes turned to bangs.

Everyone knew that when a wing kicked off, lock-down occurred almost instantly, so Rickie had made sure that this time would be different. The element of surprise was their ally. He'd made it known that the governor had allowed the police to handle the search themselves, and this had stuck in throats. It was bad enough having a prison officer entering your cell and ordering you about; but a copper, from the outside, with the permission of the governor, was despicably unfair and would not be tolerated.

For the first time in a decade, the two prominent and adjacent wings, A and D, were joining forces, and notes had been passed along pieces of string, transported on pulley systems out of the windows. Three drones had arrived at separate times of the morning, at different windows, manoeuvred and controlled by mobile phone contact with the outside. Equipment was delivered that could be used to build certain items that were vital to tipping the balance during an insurrection: shanks, screw-drivers, nails, bolt cutters, bits of wood to make weapon handles, blades, more mobile phones and toiletry items. The latter was because every con knew that once lock-down happened, they would be seeing no supplies for the duration of their rebellion. If they were successful in their uprising, then they knew that the water and heating would be turned off and conditions would deteriorate quickly.

The ground floors of A and D wings were the best gaffs and held the more senior prisoners, who knew where to get a good crib. Everybody knew that the higher up you got, the shittier the conditions. They were both flanked by the kitchens, another reason why they were prime real estate: they got to the front of the queue quicker. The balcony in between was manned by several junior screws, usually one senior officer and even the occasional custodial manager, like Liam Fawcett. And today, the man himself prowled the corridors, stopping in to check on the lads before they were served lunch. Then it would be time for the staff to have a break, leaving them at their most vulnerable.

The breach of several wings inside a Category A prison was rare. Generally, when riots took place, they were contained, on the roof for example, or barricaded inside one wing. Full-on revolts were almost impossible to pull off because tornado teams were on standby to move at short notice. A tornado team was the name for the highly trained squad on standby to control security emergencies in all prisons. A full breach was considered impossible, due to the many locking systems that were in place between wings and the outside. But even tornado teams had to kit up, mobilise and come up with a plan, and then wait for orders. Plus, Rickie Burton had insider knowledge, thanks to Liam Fawcett, that at eleven o'clock, several security systems were being tested, and it could take a couple of hours. It was a perfect example of institutional stupidity that on the day when fifty new arrivals were delivered to the prison, security work was scheduled. But it was Saturday. The last thing anyone expected was an organised assault.

Intel from the inmates to the prison officers was usually reliable, and no one had reported to Governor Brian Taylor that anything was afoot. Not even Liam knew the extent of Rickie's plans. In fact, Rickie hadn't bothered to inform the bent custodial manager that things had moved exponentially quicker than Rickie had given the impression of. Liam prowled like a cock wanting to mate, blissfully unaware that Rickie Burton had moved so quickly and that a vat of bubbling hot oil of discontent was ready to blow. The threat of a delayed spice delivery, as well as the potential for months on the block, had got hackles up, and after years of injustice, pent-up emotions were on the verge of exploding. Now, all that Rickie had to do was wait for his little seeds to continue their journey from germination right through to sprouting and flourishing;

a process that, in nature, took a whole springtime, but inside HMP Highton might take three hours.

This weekend was different in more ways than one. The fifty new arrivals from Altcourse had caused a stir. Several had been marched, after processing, through A wing, to the chants of *'One on!' 'One on!'*, a terrifying welcome for any newbies on the wings. The whole prison echoed with the chorus and some of the arrivals looked shit-scared, sobbing as they walked, like so many on their first day at a new facility. The ones who showed no emotion were hardened old sweats who knew the score, and they held their eyes unflinchingly forward, and never glanced about the cells as they headed to their final resting place, praying they had an amenable cellie.

Excitement was heightened by the disturbance, and some cellmates had been told to make room for a third. The series of setbacks, delays, frustratingly slow processes, which in themselves made the men feel like idiotic and robotic children, pushed around for the sake of it, had already come together in a perfect storm when news got out of the cell search.

Lunch was served from mobile serveries wheeled on and off the wings by auxiliary staff. On a Saturday, yard time followed lunch; it was a weekend treat, if everything had run smoothly on the previous canteen day. It had, to a point. They had the usual theft, mix-ups and shortages of bags delivered to the lads, but most of that had been sorted out without repercussions or resorting to the block. There hadn't been any violence yesterday, apart from a broken arm on one of the wings, because of an unpaid debt. Child's play.

The mood on the balconies was pregnant with expectation, but it was imperceptible to anyone outside of the loop. The prison officers were looking forward to their own meal. The fact that Saturday lunches were spent away from friends and family was always felt keenly, but there was no animosity, just a silent hope that there wouldn't be any trouble. Both Jeanie Clark and the officer who'd had her lung punctured were still off sick. Tom Gorman was a rookie who'd only just started, and was working his shift on one of the softer wings, which housed financial fraudsters and well-behaved career criminals, and there weren't any replacements. A wing had three POs on duty, D wing had just two. A senior officer sat in the office between them, updating reports on her computer, wearing headphones to drown out the noise of the men during lunchtime. She listened to Coldplay. Liam Fawcett was the only CM on duty and he floated between the office and the other floors. Brian Taylor was the senior manager on duty, and was sat in his office, sulking and moody without his secretary to shout at. He was hungover and furious at the audacity of the young female detective who insisted on sniffing around, but had warmed to another who'd called him just now asking politely to come and have a chat about the English teacher who came on Wednesdays. She sounded much nicer than Detective Porter, more respectful and softer, like a woman should be.

Chapter 45

The foldable tables were in place, and the catering staff was ready to serve. The lads milled about; a sea of grey tracksuits, fooling around, like any school queue of cock-sure adolescent boys, swapping jokes and stories. But there was something else. Eyes darted, fingers fiddled, nods carried warnings and POs were sussed in their positions. Generally the inmates were left alone during chow; after all, this was their Saturday lunch. Not that it was anything reminiscent of meals at home cooked by family. It was the usual shitty slop, dropped in spoonfuls onto waiting trays. The receptacles were like the ones used in nurseries; they had several indents where food could be collected, saving on washing-up, or the complication of carrying more than one plate. In this case, it was about reducing the number of potential weapons available for retribution. The trays were plastic, but that didn't stop them from being broken against the floor and used as a blade.

Liam Fawcett surveyed the floors from the management office. The SO carried on listening to her music, which had changed to Ed Sheeran. Liam whistled and looked forward to his day off tomorrow, when Rickie said it might all kick off. He'd taken him at his word. A thrill of power coursed through him and he smiled gently to himself. He'd been paid well for his intelligence. Cash payments were a regular contribution to his bank account from several sources on the outside, whom he presumed were relatives and associates of Rickie's, employed by the family firm too. He didn't much care where it came from, as long as it was cash, and untraceable. He didn't see any wrongdoing in his actions, he merely saw it as opportunity. He was also keeping the peace inside an institution that society chose to forget. Any other way was not only impossible but incredibly foolish. They simply couldn't keep this place running by legitimate means. They had to have some form of basic human relationship with these men, a sort of transactional insurance, so everybody fitted into their slot, and the status quo remained intact. As long as the governor remained happy looking the other way, and nothing came back to his door, everything ran smoothly.

Liam smiled to himself as he whistled, and thought of the latest cash deposit to his account. He was saving to buy a second-hand Porsche.

–

The hierarchy of reward was fully at play during mealtimes. The cleaners on each wing went first, taking the best-quality food; quality being a suspect verdict on the grey cold mush. That's why canteen Friday was so important. The lads had orange juice, biscuits and UHT cream to add to their princely fayre. Thursdays were the worst mealtimes, because canteen was running low, and most didn't bother. But today, it was a royal feast.

Rickie had already returned to his cell after finishing his food. He'd checked out the mood of the wing as he went. The men ate greedily and nodded to Rickie as he sauntered past. Men began getting up from their seats and watched as the catering staff disappeared to take away the wheelie tables holding the huge pots and trays of food. This was their moment.

Simultaneously, hoodies were thrown over CCTV cameras, and a prison officer was taken wholly by surprise, punched, floored and pinned down. Quickly, his cosh, cuffs and PAVA spray were seized, and his head held firmly against the balcony floor. In a moment, all the officers of A wing were overcome in this manner. The pelargonic acid vanillylamide, significantly more effective than the old CS gas, but allegedly designed to cause less prolonged agony to the victim, was propelled at speed into the officers' eyes and searing screams of pain were muffled by hoodies and fists. Body cameras were torn off chests and smashed against the floor, radios and keys were passed to accomplices. They never saw it coming. The chemicals disabled them instantly and they were easily disarmed. Four men against eighty was no odds to bet on. By the time they recovered, they'd be fawning lambs, at the mercy of the inmates.

The convicts worked in studious and relative quiet, and it was this that caught the attention of CM Fawcett. There was no alarm, no sound of a ruckus, no crash or bang associated with a violent scrap; none of that, just an eerie lessening of ambient noise. Liam spun around in the office and saw that all of the cameras were blacked out.

On D wing, eighty men with intent surrounded three POs. They didn't bother fighting back. All three officers knew the incarcerated men by name and smiled, trying to talk their way out of an alarming situation, while they tried to suss out what was going on. Had somebody been treated unfairly? Was one of the cons facing a stretch in the block unreasonably? They looked at one another, realising too late that the whole wing was unlocked because of chow time. One fell to his knees and begged, another handed over his cosh and cuffs.

'Give us your fucking PAVA,' one con demanded. The officers did as they were told and the spray was immediately turned on them. They fell to the floor and coughed and spluttered, rubbing their eyes in panicked distress. They cried out. The stuff was evil, and the prison population collectively hated it more than time added to a sentence. It made your eyes burn as if on fire, and your throat constrict as if drowning, and, worst of all, it was demeaning. It turned humans into animals, sucking for breath, tormented by those with the upper hand. It felt good to turn it on those in power.

It wasn't a fair fight when PAVA was involved.

The same scenes were replicated in other adjacent wings and word spread throughout the other floors that something was happening. A collective banging rose up and travelled rhythmically through the wings. Catering staff froze and pinned themselves against walls, desperate to escape but finding no way out.

—

In the office of A wing, Liam Fawcett went to hit the alarm, but before he could, the unlocked door was flung open and he lost count of the number of cons storming the small space. A fleeting memory passed through his brain, and that was the work being done on the security codes from around midday today to three o'clock this afternoon: a fact he'd told Rickie Burton.

He'd been double-crossed. The fucking scumbag. But before another thought could appear in his brain, he was overwhelmed by the sheer number of cons storming the office. He heard a brief scream as the female SO was also overpowered, and she landed on the floor with a thud. Men fell on her, but Liam could do nothing. The office held all the keys to every area of the wing, including the exits, and the glass cabinet housing them was smashed with a fire extinguisher. Liam's last thought as he felt knees, elbows, fists and heads rain down on his body was, *what the fuck had he done?*

Chapter 46

Kate Umshaw peered up towards the door. Nathan Appleton followed her eyes. He was a gentle man, with kind eyes and a scholar's hands. It was clear from his reaction that he was unfamiliar with the sound elsewhere in the prison.

The noise was a low hum, but Kate knew that whatever it was, it didn't belong in a secure facility containing a thousand men. In the instant it took her to think this, Nathan had worked it out too and hurried towards the door. They were in the library, apart from the main prison, and behind several security doors. They were alone. Since leaving the house this morning, her brief had grown arms and legs. Kelly had instructed her to have a chat with the teacher who'd had Jack Bell in his class, and she was also there to see the governor, potentially securing his blessing to interview Rickie Burton again. But, now her only focus was the noise coming from the other side of the door.

Nathan was a decent and caring bloke who clearly thought the world of many of his English students, including Jack Bell, who was a keen student and a bit of a class clown. He was always ready with a joke about Shakespeare to lighten the atmosphere if things got too serious. And he looked out for the younger lads.

Nathan had great affection for all his students, Kate had worked out that much. But he was still a civilian working in a maximum security prison, with, she assumed, little if no experience with the criminal underworld. His face confirmed this. He looked to her as if asking what the hell was going on.

The noises grew louder. There was banging, singing and the sound of metal on metal. 'Is that normal?' she asked quietly. Nathan shook his head. She joined him at the door and peered out. The corridor was empty.

'How well do you know this place?' Kate kept her voice low and controlled. She tapped her phone, but she had no signal.

'Fuck,' she whispered under her breath.

'What?' Nathan said.

She realised that any outward expression of her anxiety would cause him to become alarmed, and she needed him not to panic.

'I've got no signal, is it the same with your phone?' she asked. He nodded. 'I was just wondering how well you knew the layout of the prison,' she repeated. A crash caught their attention.

'That's not right,' he said. They closed the door. She kept trying Kelly's number, over and over again. She spotted a phone on the wall and went to it, picking up the receiver. It was an internal link phone with only one button, like those taxi services you get in supermarkets. She pressed it and heard a ringtone. It went unanswered and she replaced the handset.

'Nathan, we haven't got much time,' Kate said. The noises grew louder still and Kate was reminded of the years her children had attended early years nursery. It was the noise of unruliness, the sound of freedom and elation at being wonderfully unfettered.

Some, or all, of the men were free.

She went to the window and peered out. Why wasn't there an alarm? Her next thought was that this probably meant that some or all of the officers on duty had been overcome. There hadn't been time to sound an alarm. It had been planned.

Shit.

She dialled Kelly's number again, and tried 999. Her phone stared back at her impotently, and she felt like smashing it against the floor. Her radio was in her car. She walked around the room, holding her phone up. It was a typically Cumbria problem: shifting geographical pockets with no signal.

'What should we do?' Nathan asked. A loud crash made them both duck.

'Is there another way out?' she asked. He shook his head. 'There's an alarm under my desk,' he said, rushing to it. He knelt down and pressed it, but no sound called out. He bashed it again and again, but nothing happened.

'They must have cut off some systems,' she said.

'Christ,' Nathan said. 'Is it…?'

He couldn't seem to find the words to express himself, which wasn't surprising. Under the circumstances, Kate was finding it tough keeping her cool.

'Indeed. Listen to me. It's very likely that no one knows we're here, and I don't know any con who might want a little story in the library in the middle of a prison break. That's all this will be, some kind of statement over conditions and overcrowding, nothing to do with us.' She tried to reassure him, as well as herself.

His skin turned pale.

'Listen to me, Nathan. Look at me. I'm going to hide my ID. You need to say I'm a teacher too. If they find out I'm a copper, I'm dead. Do you understand?'

He stared at her, wide-eyed. She realised that he was going into shock. It happened. Sometimes, when people found themselves in grave danger, their fear caused them to freeze, and they effectively shut down. Kate had seen it with victims of crime many times. The problem here was, it wasn't that helpful. She needed a clear head to think, and she also needed his cooperation.

She had no choice but to leave him for the time being and try to suss out where they were with reference to the wings. Kate knew enough about modern prisons to know that the chances of a full breach were remote. However, they already knew that certain alarm systems were down. Now, that could be due to maintenance, or planning. Which one could determine if her life was to be cut short today.

The bangs and the shouting grew louder and she checked on Nathan. He'd sat down on the floor and he was hugging his knees. It was a more desirable expression of fear than shouting or screaming in terror right now, because so far they were hidden and safe. She went to the library door again and opened it slowly and quietly, peering along the empty hall. A CCTV camera operated at the end of the corridor and she slipped out towards it, throwing her ID into the waste bin under plenty of paper. She stared up at the camera, and the little green light indicated that it was working. She waved her arms silently, just in case somebody in security was watching.

At last, a piercing alarm ripped through the building, and she heard the sound of metal against metal. She dared to hope that before the security perimeter was put into place, the wings were secured and the library was safe. She tried the door at the end of the corridor and it opened. It was clear to her that this meant that before the alarm sounded, some systems had gone offline and were still disabled.

Fuck.

She looked at her phone, her heart pounding in her chest; still no signal.

The next corridor led to the main quadrant, which was from where the main entrance could be accessed.

She froze.

The sound came closer, working its way around the sharp corners, crudely painted cement floors, and neglected ceilings. It reverberated off electric lamps, and vibrated along filing cabinets, getting louder and louder. Her feet seemed rooted to the ground and her heart beat fast. She thought of her children, and how beautiful they were. Millie's eyes and how excited she was to meet Lizzie. Then Andrew's hands on her last night in her bed. She'd been shamelessly glorious in her desire for him to touch her, and he'd reciprocated with a hunger that made her feel like the woman she'd said goodbye to years ago. Her teeth clenched and her feet suddenly moved and she darted back to the library, running in and slamming the door.

'Help me,' she shouted to Nathan, who looked up at her. It was clear that he wasn't ready to move yet, and so she dragged a heavy desk over to the door on her own. She had no idea where her strength came from but it moved and she anchored her feet against the stained floor, pulling and shoving equally, moving it inch by inch, until it was fully against the door.

Suddenly, Nathan was at her side, dragging another desk, and another, and another. She smiled and nodded to him, breathless, feeling sweat trickle between her breasts. She wiped her forehead with the back of her hand, and they moved eight desks to the door.

Then the banging started.

Chapter 47

Prison officers, cooks, orderlies, and anyone else who had the opportunity, ran towards the central rotunda, from which all the wings led outwards. The cons had nicknamed the area Central Park in a droll nod to the heart of the Big Apple, as if they enjoyed such freedom. Now, Central Park was overflowing with bodies desperate to get out to the perimeter. Not all prisoners wanted to be involved in the riot. As more and more doors were slammed shut, and more POs followed emergency instructions to evacuate, the wings became desolate. The prisoners under Rule 43 – those considered under serious threat from other prisoners, due to the infamous nature of their crimes – were kept in C wing, and that's where a large crowd of the rioters headed now. The POs on C wing had released some of them, but it had to be done under a strict set of rules and procedures. The bloodthirsty gang of insurgents was clearly making its way around the wings, looking for vengeance to assuage their temper, and they were running out of time. Seventeen of the Rule 43 prisoners were escorted towards Central Park, ushered by Tom Gorman and others who'd made it out in time, before C wing became engulfed in men raging with animalistic fury, intent upon unleashing havoc. A wail could be heard from a cell, as five men rushed in to confront a convict inside for buggery of little boys.

He'd been on suicide watch for five years straight. He didn't stand a chance. A home-made shank, and plenty of electrical cord from lamps, made sure that he couldn't move when the handle of a mop was inserted into his rectum.

Prisoners prowled everywhere.

Desks were thrown over the balconies, papers were scattered and burned, windows were smashed, scores were settled, and arenas set up around bare fist fights. Lights were shattered and offices gutted, with computers smashed and chairs barricading the final gateway between the prisoners and the outside world. New arrivals from Altcourse, hoping for a fresh start, were torn between keeping out of trouble or joining in, lest they be seen as a chicken.

The smell of acrid smoke permeated every wing. Rickie Burton sauntered out of his cell and walked along the balcony towards Central Park. The chanting grew louder. 'Fuck the police! Fuck the police! Fuck the police!'

Someone managed to commandeer a sound system inside an office and began broadcasting music. Drill music rang out. The air was thick with floating, burning pieces of paper, fire extinguisher foam and the sound of slamming doors. Men wrestled in it, dropping to the floor, high on spice, while others filmed and streamed live to national newspapers via Twitter.

'Roof! Get to the Roof!'

No one knew who said it first.

Hundreds of men, released from years, months and days of monotonous captivity, ran, leapt, skidded and slid on the detritus. In under an hour, HMP Highton had become a scene of carnage and catastrophe. Men sang football songs, hooch was thrown about and doors were forced off hinges to make sledges for an impromptu race along the wings to Central Park. Those POs caught in the riot cowered in corners, humiliated, stripped and taunted.

Not all joined in. Some of the young offenders sat immobilised in their cells, terrified at what they saw, unable to decide what to do next. Did they act like men and join in? Or did they act like sons and brothers and stay out of trouble? Lay low in their cells pretending their doors were locked, and keep safe? As waves and waves of men swept through to Central Park, they had no choice. Boys as young as sixteen were on remand at Highton because of overcrowding elsewhere. They had no choice but to do as they were told and act bravely, even though inside they were screaming for their mothers.

One man, a known child molester, was dragged to Central Park, where a makeshift kangaroo court heard evidence and mock presentations, and passed its judgement. The penalty was a beating by fire extinguisher. His screams for mercy didn't last long.

–

In the library, Nathan jumped in front of Kate, an act of chivalry so sweet and compassionate that Kate nearly smiled. The tables were pushed further and further into the centre of the room, until finally, there was enough room for men to breach the entrance. They clambered over the barricade and into the centre of the room. Nathan's body tensed and Kate held on to his arm.

'Remember what I told you,' she whispered.

In the time it had taken the men to break in, she'd tried to coach him on everything she knew about hostage situations. It was the mother of all crash courses and she prayed he kept his cool.

'We're teachers! We were planning lessons! Don't hurt us!' Nathan held up his hands in innocence, and Kate did the same.

A huge man stood in front of them and others climbed in behind him. Kate swallowed. These guys had probably not been intimate with a woman for years. All of them held a weapon of sorts. Some held chair legs, others fire extinguishers, and one carried a long blade. She closed her eyes and held on to Nathan for her life.

'What's your name, pretty?'

Chapter 48

In London, news of the riot travelled fast. The chief executive of Her Majesty's Prison Service was alerted and a Gold Command structure was put in to place.

It was pointless mobilising a tornado team now. The prison officers who'd escaped made it abundantly clear that the prisoners had occupied the central rotunda and had access to other facilities. The tide was well and truly with the convicts.

Kelly had approached the prison from the road to smoke bellowing from windows and she tried to remain clear-headed as she witnessed the events unfold. Explaining who she was to officials hastily called to the scene, and other security staff, she'd been invited to the Portakabin, set up on the perimeter of Highton, to help give context to the grave incident unfolding inside. And that's where she'd stayed, watching as the space was made into a command centre. Communications were sporadic. They'd heard titbits from national media who'd been sent videos of prisoners inside. The images of carnage were devastating. No one knew the scale of casualties and Brian Taylor's whereabouts were unconfirmed.

A hostage negotiation team had been mobilised because Kelly's worst fear had been confirmed: they had a teacher and a female police officer inside, alongside twenty-nine unaccounted-for POs, but no one knew their status. Kate had heard nothing from her second in command, and her car was abandoned in the carpark. It was awful news.

On the moors of Hallsenna, it had started to rain, and even the common buzzard, famed for its habitat in the peaty heartland, had given up. Press vans arrived and set up camp as the news spread. Inside the temporary building, taken over by the command personnel, the mood was sombre. A generator had been hooked up and computer terminals put into position.

A grade one governor from HMP Preston, Cassandra Spelling, was placed in charge of the ground operations. It was her job to liaise with London on command issues, and a cross service team would secure a perimeter with the help of Cumbria Police. That was why Chief Constable Andrew Harris had been called here.

Kelly met his eyes as he took off his coat and shook the water off. Kelly had already had a brief strategy meeting with Cassandra Spelling and had got the measure of the woman. She had a history with Brian Taylor, and it was made clear to Kelly that she thought little of him. Taylor had been confirmed on shift, and his car was parked in the car park, so the assumption was that he was trapped inside. Now Kelly tried to work out Andrew Harris's mood. He looked tense, but Kelly figured it wasn't just his role that was making his brow damp.

'Sir,' she said. He nodded and went to Cassandra, who filled him in on the various screens and plans. The woman was a good operator. Kelly respected her already.

'Nice touch,' Cassandra said. Kelly and Andrew followed her gaze and saw on the TV that had been brought into the room earlier that Sky News was reporting from a helicopter. Some of the prisoners had reached the roof and held demands scrawled on sheets and towels.

'Fuck the police!' one read. 'No illegal searches!' read another.

Kelly sighed. 'No one knew about this yet,' she said.

'About what?' Cassandra said.

'Brian Taylor hadn't actually agreed to allow a search, we were working on it – that's one of the reasons why my officer, Kate Umshaw, was here, to discuss it with him, the information must have leaked, which brings me on to another worrying development that only came to our attention this morning.' Kelly had briefed Cassandra on what Jeanie Clark had told them, but Andrew was unaware. She told him now.

'Another of my officers, Rob Shawcross, is piecing together an intricate pattern of transactions in cash, and we have requested bank access to the accounts of Liam Fawcett and Brian Taylor, sir,' Kelly said. Andrew folded his arms and put one hand to his mouth. He watched the TV and shook his head.

'So did the prisoners find out about your search, or did the officers find out about Rob's progress?' Cassandra asked.

'Good question. If Brian Taylor and some of his officers are bent, then we've unearthed something far bigger here than a motive to murder,' Kelly said. 'But, with all respect to both of you, my priority is my officer inside there.'

Cassandra nodded. 'Don't sweat it, my prime concern is save lives first, buy time, then negotiate. Your investigation can wait, frankly,' Cassandra said.

'Agreed,' said Kelly.

'The negotiation team has been handpicked by the chief exec. They have an excellent reputation,' Cassandra said. Negotiation was a delicate affair and took skill. Bags of it. 'The lead, our number one, is called Mike, I'll introduce you when he's ready. They're studying plans of the prison. We're getting ready to drop burner phones in, which we hope will be picked up by prisoners willing to talk. Now, tell me about Rickie Burton. Have we any evidence that he engineered the breach?'

Just then a man entering the small room interrupted them. Cassandra introduced him as the lead negotiator.

'Good timing,' Cassandra said. 'This is DI Kelly Porter and she's probably the only person I trust right now to give me detailed insight into the characters we have inside there,' Cassandra added.

'Good to meet you,' Mike said, outstretching his hand.

Chapter 49

The central rotunda erupted in to a chorus of 'Blood, blood, blood!'

Scores were being settled and vendettas, long simmering behind bars, were being called in and drawn to a close. Much of the action was in Central Park, and took place in the form of bare-knuckle fights, with the odd weapon thrown in for good measure. Of the twenty-nine prison officers still trapped inside, most had either made their way into barricades in the wings for safety, or had managed to get to the outer gates of the long corridors leading away from the centre, to the perimeter. However, a few unlucky ones were cornered. They watched the fighting, assessing their options, which were becoming narrower by the minute, as more and more hooch was consumed.

Their training covered riot situations, and how to react if captured. But nothing could prepare them for the real thing. Reason dictated that few prisoners would want to cause harm to the screws because it would just add more time to their custodial sentence. However, with alcohol and drugs thrown into the mix, predictability and reason got chucked out of the window along with slops and cupboards.

The two officers tied up against a barred door watching the scraps in Central Park spoke to one another quietly.

First, they checked to see if either had suffered injury; then they discussed a plan. They could tell that many prisoners had actually taken the sensible choice to escape the riot situation and had given themselves up to the prison officers and police waiting outside. Only the hard core, or those with no choice because they were trapped, remained behind. Most convicts actually wanted to serve their sentences without incident, and something like what was happening at HMP Highton today wasn't likely to favour their parole hearing. Hundreds of prisoners had walked away from the prison when they could, along with most of the officers, who guided them and encouraged them, loyal to their task, even when faced with tremendous adversity. Many had wounds here and there from knocks and grazes, but, for the most part, they fled in a semi-orderly manner to awaiting buses and makeshift camps, where they would be processed in time, and sent to other overcrowded facilities. News had travelled quickly around the prison that hundreds of Cumbria police officers were now stationed outside, and the perimeter was secure.

Now, inside the central rotunda, the two officers assessed the situation. Their bindings were sloppy and they'd already worked themselves free, but, with a hundred or so Category A prisoners blood baiting and screaming for a victor to emerge from their sporting spectacle, they didn't dare make a move. They were ridiculously outnumbered. Of course, they knew most of the men by name, and also knew that most of them would be unlikely to participate in anything sinister. However, all it took was a few leaders and the rest would be too scared not to follow. Like in a children's playground, the repercussions of being seen to side with the underdog were far worse than nailing your colours to the side of

but that wasn't the point. He was forty-three and had spent most of his life inside. He was about as hardened a con as you could get, but he was still a lad on the inside. That *was* the point. You went inside as a lad and you spent your days as one. They didn't grow up inside. They remained in limbo, holding on, carving out whatever existence they could to keep breathing. He nodded.

'Let 'em through, lads,' he instructed. Not many heard him because they were so focused on the entertainment. Those who did didn't care anyway and moved aside. They'd had their fun spraying them with PAVA, which had thankfully now worn off, and tying them up. The two officers slowly made their way out of the rotunda, towards the offices and past the library. Activity was taking place in every corner of the prison, as far as they could see. They heard the odd howl, as retribution was delivered behind a closed door, and they heard laughing and threats.

Then they heard a woman's voice. It came from the library. They paused and looked at each other.

'Mary got out,' one said.

'So did Pauline,' the other replied, checking the female officers they knew were on duty today.

Baffled, they hoped against the worst. The presence of female officers in a Category A prison was controversial. The majority believed that they provided a calming effect on the prisoners, but recently, with the tsunami of drugs available inside, respect was waning. The officers looked at each other. There was no way either of them could walk past that door and not intervene. Each had a family, each had loved ones at home to go to. They had lives, prospects, possibly other jobs to apply for. Nothing compelled them to pause and interrupt. Nothing except their humanity.

One knocked on the door and the voices stopped.

He took the handle, but before he could turn it, the door had been flung open. Behind it stood two prisoners. Their eyes were red and glassy and the officers hoped that they were just getting stoned. But that still didn't explain the female voice. The officers put up their hands.

'We haven't got any weapons, lad. Look at us, we're in our underwear. We were leaving the premises and want no trouble, but we heard a woman in there and we want to check on her.'

The con was known to both officers and he nodded.

'We weren't doing nothing,' he announced, and opened the door wide. Inside they saw the teacher who came to take classes on Wednesdays, and a woman they didn't know.

'We were taking extra lessons, boss,' one of the convicts said, and the others in the room laughed. The woman's eyes were steely and a quick survey of her attire suggested she hadn't been molested. The teacher looked shit-scared but, strangely, the woman looked calm. The officers entered the library and surveyed the mess. There were piles of books on the floor, cupboards were upended, lamps were smashed and doors off hinges. Smoke billowed behind them and escaped through a window.

'Let us escort them out. Whatever happens here, don't let yourself be caught up in something that you'll regret for the rest of your life,' the same officer said.

'I'm spending my fucking life in here!' another prisoner spat out suddenly, muscling his way to the front. He held an iron bar in his hand and the other lads in the room grabbed various bits of armour. The teacher and the woman flattened their backs up against the wall and watched.

'We're just teachers, please, let us go,' Nathan pleaded. His face crumpled into a vision of terror and anguish. The woman held strong.

'We don't add anything to your cause,' she said. 'It'll look good to the outside if we can walk out,' she added.

The officers waited. They didn't want to overload the pressure and lose it all. Bravado was a powerful force when displayed in front of other alpha males. Should the small gang want to keep the woman for whatever purpose they saw fit, the officers and the male teacher could do nothing about it. Faced with ten or twelve strong and armed young men, intent upon whatever their agenda was in this moment, they stood no chance. The woman knew it. The officers knew it.

Suddenly one of the cons burst out laughing, pointing at the officers' attire, and the others joined in. Even the officers smiled, and attempted to play along to diffuse the potential lethality of the moment.

'Do you think we're fucking stupid? These are hostages, that's what they are,' the con holding the bar said.

The others agreed, and the laughter subsided once more.

'Keep me in here instead, let her go,' one of the officers said. 'What do you want? I can negotiate on your behalf. They'll be dropping phones in, I reckon.'

The atmosphere changed as the prisoners looked at one another.

'We want a kid's play area in the visiting room.'

'We want more yard time.'

'We want dignity.'

'We want better fucking food.'

'We want to get out of the cell for more than an hour.'

The officers nodded, making themselves amenable and sympathetic, the ridiculousness of their semi-nakedness forgotten. The woman watched. The teacher said nothing.

'You can negotiate that without hostages. They'll listen to you. You've made your point. If you harm these two teachers, you won't stand a chance. You know that, I'm just telling you what you already know, lads. But I'm not sure there are others in the rotunda who would understand that. If you protected these two civilians, it'd be remembered and rewarded, I'd make sure of it.'

The men looked around, between one another.

'They're not going nowhere until we've spoken to somebody on the outside. Somebody in charge.' The two officers looked at one another and knew they'd have to stay. A moment passed between them, as if acknowledging to the other that either could leave; it wouldn't be seen as failure or weakness. Self-preservation in a situation like this was understandable. But it was also obvious to both of them that neither was quitting.

Chapter 50

Back in the Portakabin, Kelly was reading the military file that had been emailed to her by the army personnel centre in Glasgow.

Ian Burton had been honourably and medically discharged in 2008, as they'd already learned. That much was straightforward. But as a result of her application, an insert had been included with the report. The details had been declassified.

Corporal Ian Burton had been in charge of a unit of eight men, which had been conducting door-to-door searches in a tiny village near Basra, Iraq, in early 2004. In effect, he'd ignored a direct order to arrest an entire family. Such sympathetic leanings had resulted in Burton being confined to barracks. However, on the day of his ambush, for some reason Burton had been allowed to patrol. He'd disappeared from a position near the village shortly after that, and his men had reported that he'd gone into a building. Upon following him they'd met heavy resistance and gunfire, and retreated, leaving their unit non-commissioned officer inside the building. Burton wasn't seen again for 309 days.

Kelly was transfixed as she read the information, clicking on to subsequent pages, desperate to learn what had happened during those 309 days.

He'd been found wandering near a road twenty miles outside Basra, by a farmer heading to a neighbouring village. He was dressed in local garb, fully bearded and disoriented. The farmer had turned him over to the British, and after a few days, it was confirmed that the man was Ian Burton, missing in action, presumed dead.

Subsequent medical and psychological tests proved inconclusive. The soldier had stopped speaking, and had scored highly on PTSD markers. There was no choice but to send him to rehabilitate at the joint services hospital at Colchester. Kelly turned to the report from that institution and learned that things hadn't ended well. Burton had been violent and abusive, and had to be medicated a lot of the time. He'd eventually discharged himself from the facility and gone off the grid, only to be picked up by the military police in Sussex of all places, a few months later.

It was unpleasant reading, and the young soldier had clearly suffered, but nowhere could Kelly find what had actually happened to him. After years of damage limitation and trying to pick up the pieces of his life and career, Ian was discharged in 2008. Kelly saw that he'd then gone into private military contracting and had been sent right back to the place where he'd fallen apart: Iraq. She couldn't believe her eyes. This guy was damaged, closed off, volatile and dangerously unpredictable, and he'd been hired by a private mercenary company, endorsed by the British Army, and given a weapon.

It was staggering.

His notes didn't finish there. The MOD had clearly kept an eye on him and had taken a keen interest in how he performed in his new career. Kelly wasn't surprised to see that it had gone exceedingly well. Too well, in fact. Burton had become so good at his job of killing any perceived threat to British interests abroad that he became a liability, and had been released from his position two years ago, which meant he was a plausible suspect for the murders in Glasgow and Manchester.

Then the bombshell. Despite Burton being discharged from the military in 2008, they'd still reported on him, and he was investigated by the Royal Military Police on several occasions, with regards to a series of unlawful killings in Iraq between 2008 and 2018. A decade was a very long time, and Kelly noticed that Burton's post-military file was thicker than his the one when he'd been a decorated and respected corporal.

She stopped when a photograph of a body flicked on to the screen. She stared at it; for a few moments she was unable to pull herself away to read the text that accompanied it. When she did, she learned that the photograph was of an Iraqi soldier who'd double-crossed the British, leading to a massacre in a local village. Burton had been employed by a protection company that safeguarded workers who travelled to the oilfields every day. The rogue Iraqi soldier had been taken from his family in the middle of the night. It was unclear how many local Iraqis were involved, but Ian Burton definitely was. Civilians lived in fear of both local Taliban warlords and the British, and they often had to choose sides. It was under these impossible circumstances that the soldier had paid the price.

Burton had taken matters into his own hands and the picture proved it. The soldier was tied to a tree, and his injuries were horrific. It looked as though scores of paramilitaries had got hold of him, but the report stated a suspicion that Ian Burton was involved but was never held accountable due to lack of evidence and credible witnesses.

Kelly was dumbstruck. The guy was a fully paid-up member of the fucking nut brigade, so how the hell had he ended up working in a care home?

The system had made Ian Burton what he was today, but instead of making it right, they'd tried to hide him, and it had backfired. Perhaps the MOD had washed their hands of him. She seemed to remember Johnny telling her that funding for soldiers like Ian Burton was woefully lacking. His record ended two years ago. Had he simply run back to daddy?

She closed her iPad in frustration and listened to Cassandra Spelling barking orders into a phone. Kelly felt the anxiety in her body that came with impotence. Sitting inside this tiny box, waiting for something to happen, was intolerable. She checked the police computer on her iPad and saw that there was no news on the hunt for Burton.

'We haven't had any contact yet,' Cassandra told her. 'But the phones will be dropped in ten minutes. Eventually, they'll make their way to those in charge. They always do.'

'Always? You've had this situation before?' Kelly asked.

'Not exactly – I'm talking about the way these situations pan out in general. It's behavioural science. Most of the men inside will have no desire to carry on this revolt. They'll want out. As time passes, only the hard core will remain, and then we'll find out what this is all about. Our priority is establishing the negotiator cell, but to get close enough, we need those phones to open a channel.'

Kelly nodded her understanding. 'Has there been any word from those officers coming out?' she asked. She knew that Tom Gorman had made it out. What a way to start a new career, she thought.

Cassandra shook her head. 'Not a word about Nathan Appleton, or your girl. I'm sorry. We'll know soon, I'm sure,' she said.

'And the missing officers and the governor?'

'Nope.'

She looked at Chief Constable Harris, who was in deep conversation with the chief negotiator. Andrew shouldn't be here, Kelly thought. But she wasn't about to raise it now. The time necessary to find a replacement as senior as Andrew, together with the paperwork involved, and the sensitive explanations as to why he should be replaced, could mean the difference between Kate surviving and not.

Chapter 51

Ian Burton had been recommended the practice of meditation twelve years ago when he'd left the armed forces. It hadn't gone well. The act of sitting in silence, allowing thoughts and feelings to come and go, but not exploit or live them, was excruciatingly painful. It had proved impossible for him and he'd given up almost the day he started. Why have urges and ambitions if one was not supposed to follow them through? Why else be a part of human existence if not to compete, satisfy and dream? It was all nonsense. His counsellor had recently recommended he give it another go.

He'd never learned the subtle art of controlling one's emotions.

He believed that the pursuance of compulsion was central to the human condition, nothing else. What happened to other people as a result of those desires was immaterial. People got hurt all the time. Families disintegrate, flesh is torn apart and minds shatter; that's life. Only the weak made room for those who couldn't keep up. The earth would be inherited by the warrior.

As a result of his cascading emotions, thoughts also plagued him and made his body twitch. A tiny knot of regret tormented him: he'd let his father down, again. And now he had no choice but to disappear and go to ground.

He was vexed.

It hadn't been his choice to live like this. A feeling of injustice washed over him and he could have screamed out loud with the frustration of it all. They were supposed to be living in a free country. Fat chance of attaining that now the police had been led to believe he'd done something wrong. He thought of his father, incarcerated unfairly, and how he'd wanted to do something to make him proud, and now it was ruined. He'd had a chance to make everything right again, but he'd let everybody down. He never could get it quite right, and always seemed to upset people who wanted to do things another way. He'd proved, time and time again, that his way was effective. People talked when Ian asked them to. He had a rare and exclusive gift for getting information out of people who didn't want to talk, and he felt unappreciated.

His counsellor said that revisiting the past and allowing himself to let go of the trauma was a kind of therapy, but the guy was a hippy. He was some kind of mountain expert who'd found nature after too many tours of Iraq.

He packed a bag sulkily and the overwhelming desire to act out took hold of him. There was no explanation for what went on inside his head when his compulsions took over. They just did. He could taste it, and he could feel it. His body had to move around to expel thoughts of diversion. Did he have time?

It was like an intense craving, one so intoxicating that nothing would satisfy him until he'd seen it through to the end. He wanted – no, *needed* – to consummate his desire. Only that one thing could quiet his head and give him the satiation he required to move on.

It wouldn't take long. He had everything he needed. His father would never know.

The TV mumbled in the background. He had it on to calm his nerves, as he found that silence stimulated him too much. Noise was the balm that could mean the difference between physical action upon his urges and maintaining a quasi-equilibrium which prevented it.

He glanced at the TV and saw men on a rooftop. He stopped what he was doing and walked towards the screen. He turned up the volume. He heard the words 'HMP Highton' and stopped dead in his tracks. The sweater he was holding fell to the floor in a crumpled heap. He trod on it as he moved closer to the set. The men were holding banners and dancing, making silly juvenile gestures for the cameras. Journalists were lining up to give commentary, and Hallsenna Moor was awash with photographers and satellite vans.

He listened, transfixed, as Sky News gave their version of what had happened inside the prison. He began to panic and grabbed his phone, staring at it, not knowing what to do. On TV, prisoners were forcing somebody onto the roof; the man looked vaguely familiar. He was hurt, and he struggled to keep up with the youngsters pushing him to the top of the building.

Then it was announced that the man was Brian Taylor, governor of Highton, and Ian dropped his phone.

The screen went to the female presenter, who was stood in a remote area of the moor, with the prison in view behind her.

Suddenly he forgot about the prison. Instead, he watched as her hair flew in her eyes and she wafted it away with a gloved hand. He studied her face and imagined it pleading with him. He reached out and touched the flat screen, his fingers moving over her soft cheeks. She wouldn't keep still and Ian tutted. He turned his head and he realised that she reminded him of a woman he'd been tasked with protecting in Iraq. He hadn't managed to keep to his task and things had turned out rather differently to how his bosses expected. The woman had ended up dead and thrown by the side of a road, like rubbish out of a car window. The people who did it to her had their reasons. The fact that Ian had allowed it, and participated, never came to light.

But that was years ago. The woman before him now kept a poker face, just like the woman in Basra. She'd enjoyed a rather unchained existence under Saddam Hussein, like a lot of women in modern Iraq. But once the war kicked in and the Sunnis returned to power in many areas across the country, fundamentalist laws set about restricting those freedoms, and women, like the one he saw die, suffered the most. They'd enjoyed having their own motor vehicles, university degrees, businesses and leisure pursuits. Not so after 2003. Swathes of them left, but many couldn't. His ward was the wife of a prominent politician and she was protected to an extent, but after a time, she couldn't be seen as having special privileges. She reaped what she sowed.

The woman on TV continued to talk. Ian had already made up his mind.

He forgot about what his father had told him, and never gave another thought to what might be happening inside the prison. He left his bag unpacked and open on the bed.

He walked out of the flat, on loan as a favour from somebody his father knew. He went to the garage round the back and unlocked the car. He got in and set off, along the A595 from Workington to HMP Highton.

Chapter 52

Rickie sat in one corner of the central rotunda, alone, concentrating on drowning out the noise of the mob. He'd hooked up a radio to a generator. He was waiting for the right time to make contact with the police, so he could play the role of his life: as mediator to the innocent fellas caught up in the dreadful events of the last few hours. Somebody had managed to get a huge flat-screen TV working and images flicked across it, muted by blood sports. He held the radio to his good ear and tried to listen to Bay Radio news. The riot filled every station. A smile spread across his face when it was reported that the governor had been dragged onto the roof. Couldn't happen to a nicer guy, he thought to himself.

He noticed the TV screen change out of the corner of his eye and sat up sharply when he saw a photograph of a female police officer flash up. It wasn't the detective who'd interviewed him, it was somebody called Kate Umshaw. He got off his chair and went across to the set to turn the volume up fully.

'Shut the fuck up!' he bawled at the crowd at the top of his voice. A few fellas turned around and began hushing the others. The two latest competitors, battling it out for kudos and prison status, were interrupted, and those heckling them on peered across to Rickie to see what the fuss was about. Slowly, men began encircling Rickie and the TV screen.

'What's up?' one asked.

'This is what's up,' Rickie said, standing in front of the crowd, pointing to the screen. 'We've got a female copper in here somewhere, hiding out, thinking she hasn't been spotted yet.' Next, a photograph of the English teacher came on screen and Rickie held his hand up for quiet.

'It's saying he forgot something and he came back for it. His wife is distraught.' Rickie feigned sympathy and mimicked a woman crying, rubbing her eyes. The men laughed.

'Who reckons they're in the library?' he said. He'd got their attention. A cheer went up.

'What should we do, Rickie?' one asked.

Rickie took the TV remote and tapped it gently between his hands. He heard a few of the men discussing what they'd like to do to a woman, after years of being denied. It was predictably desperate, and even Rickie closed an eye. His brain worked fast. He'd have to protect this woman if he was to get anything for himself, but how to contain men's urges? They probably didn't have much time to act. He knew how it would go: the police would slowly fence them into a location of their choosing, as prisoners grew weary of the conditions. The Strangeways riot of 1990 had lasted twenty-five days. Rickie hoped they wouldn't have to last that long without fresh water, heating and decent food. He hadn't planned on it. He needed to find CM Fawcett to find out what was going on, and arrange some kind of negotiation.

He asked around to see if anyone knew where the CM was. In turn, men asked one another and finally, someone was located who knew where he was last seen.

'In the SO's office of A wing, Rickie.'

A wing was in the direction of the library. Rickie noticed the stony silence and jutted his chin. 'What?' he asked.

'He didn't make it. He got hit hard, Rickie.'

Rickie tutted. 'Never mind, lad. He was an arsehole anyway.' In fact, with CM Fawcett out of the way, that just left the governor with enough knowledge to allow the truth to surface, and from what he'd heard on the radio, he might not make it, especially with his weak heart.

As if on cue, the electricity was cut. The water pump stopped too and the pipes that had been badly damaged and leaking everywhere stopped their gushing. Next, they'd have no batteries for phones, and no food. Rickie wasn't stupid, he knew that a protest like this could only hold up for a few days. This was no Strangeways, where centuries-old wings, crumbling and lethal, might prevent penetration from outside agencies. Highton had undergone major refurbishment and was now a fully modernised prison. The lightweight material moulded into the walls and floors made it difficult to completely destroy them. Worthy barricades of rubble were therefore out of the question.

His mind whirred. If they could get to the female copper and the teacher before they got out, or were helped out, they might prolong the affair to a reasonable conclusion.

'Let's pay a visit to the library,' he said. They travelled down the long wing en masse, heading in the direction of the library. There was a frisson of excitement, as if they were going out for the evening.

They came to the corridor that housed the library, and Rickie held up his hand for silence as they approached.

He went first and stood outside the library door. He could hear voices within. He banged on the door and went in.

Rickie stood in front of the small group sitting on the ground in a circle as if they were fucking telling bedtime stories. A few of the lads jumped up what they saw him. They were mainly juveniles, and a couple of old-timers, with some seasoned cons for flavour. But not one of them had thought to inform him of their find, and that pissed him off. He spotted the teacher and nodded his head. Behind him crouched the woman.

'You've been missing out, lads. Sky News has just had this lovely lady plastered all over its screens,' Rickie said.

'She's a teacher, boss,' one of the young 'uns said. Rickie laughed hard, together with dozens of others behind who joined him. The woman glared at him, and Rickie was aware of her examining his scars. She knew who he was all right, because she was a fucking pig.

'She's not a teacher, lads, she's a copper.'

Chapter 53

'Who am I talking to?' Mike asked. From the command centre, they'd managed to make contact with a group of prisoners huddled in a toilet block. Kelly and Cassandra stood close to the negotiator and Kelly fought her desperation to butt in.

'Mickey Mouse,' the convict replied.

'I know you're enjoying your freedom, pal. My job, believe it or not, is to find out if anyone is hurt and needs help. I've got nothing to do with the authorities. My name's Mike. How many are in there with you?' Mike said.

And so it began. It was a welcome distraction from the sight of the governor on the roof, being paraded by a handful of men wearing makeshift balaclavas over their faces. They'd be identified eventually from hands, hair and clothes. Whether Brian Taylor made it was in their hands. Kelly didn't like the man but it was still painful to watch. He looked frail and ill, and terrified.

They all listened to Mike. Kelly knew that the process would be excruciatingly slow, and by the time they found Kate, they would have no idea what to expect. She wished it was her on the inside. At least she could try and work on Rickie Burton from the belly of the riot, rather than waiting on the sidelines. So far, Rickie hadn't been identified as one of the men who'd left the premises. So he was still in there, no doubt pretending to be caught up in it all, but proving that in a court of law would be another thing altogether.

Kelly looked at her iPad every five seconds, hoping that somebody in her team would have updated her and found Ian Burton, either by some master stroke of luck or good police work, any would do. She felt so damn useless. Ian Burton wasn't anywhere to be found. It was exasperating. She'd read in his military record that part of training for operations in Iraq was being able to melt into the local population when necessary; it was all part of the 'hearts and minds' campaign that turned to rat shit once civilians started dying in their thousands. In other words, he was a master at disappearing.

'My name's Aaron,' she heard from the speaker. Mike had managed to get one of the lads to open up to him. It was progress. Cassandra ordered his file to be accessed immediately so they could get as much on him as possible, to know what they were dealing with. His details came up on the big screen. Aaron was eighteen years old and on remand for murder. His trial date was set for three weeks' time and he'd served four months already. Cassandra got his details up on screen.

'Aaron Lewis. His sister's ill with cancer, she has regular chemo,' she read aloud. Kelly listened. 'He takes Nathan Appleton's English GCSE class.'

'We need to get the teacher on the phone,' Kelly said. She couldn't help herself. Cassandra could have reacted by calling her out in front of the whole room, but she didn't, instead she validated what Kelly had said and agreed. The woman had nothing to prove and was entirely comfortable with her own command. Often, Kelly dealt with egos that were bigger than the sum of their parts, and it caused problems. Not so with this woman.

'DI Porter's right. That way, we negotiate with an outsider and can leverage getting Kate Umshaw out. Report back,' she commanded Mike.

'You know the English teacher, Aaron? You're in his class, right?' he said. 'Good guy. He's doing his best getting you lads through your GCSEs so you can have a better life on the outside. You have to take your hat off to that kind of thing,' Mike continued.

Kelly listened to his voice. It was velvety and smooth, just the type of voice to catch you off guard.

'We think he's stuck in the library, Aaron. There's a female teacher in there with him. She came to help restart one of his programmes. She's stuck in there too, and we don't know if they're unharmed or need our help,' Mike said.

They heard the young man sigh over the phone.

'They're the good guys, Aaron, like you. We need to know if they're all right,' Mike persevered.

The line went dead.

They waited. Negotiation was a series of interrupted conversations designed to get closer and closer to the subject.

'Did he do it?' Kelly asked.

'What?' Cassandra asked. Everybody looked at her. She noticed that Andrew had been sitting at a desk, not speaking, for long minutes now, contemplating, no doubt, how to contribute without showing too much concern. Kelly turned back to Cassandra.

'Is Aaron guilty? What does his file say? Is he likely to be convicted?' she asked. Cassandra nodded and read further. They knew about his personal and family circumstances, as well as where he went to school and what jobs he'd had, but they hadn't examined his criminal past.

'No previous,' Kelly read from the screen. 'Shopkeeper beaten to death with a baseball bat. Aaron was the only one on the premises when the police arrived. No witnesses. No physical evidence. No CCTV. Full confession, retracted when he saw a lawyer twenty-four hours later. He's a good bet,' Kelly said.

Mike nodded and tried the line again. Aaron answered once more.

'I'm with Doug now,' Aaron said.

'Who's Doug?' Mike asked.

'You wanna speak to him?' Aaron asked.

'Sure,' Mike said.

A much older voice came on the line. They quickly identified the man as a seventy-one-year-old lifer, who was also taking Nathan Appleton's GCSE class. Cassandra had his file come up on screen. She and Kelly speed-read as Mike talked.

'How come you didn't get out, Doug?' Mike asked.

'I'm old and slow, my young man, not like these young 'uns. I was right down the end of A wing, up one flight of stairs, my legs don't work that fast anymore.'

'Sorry about that, Doug. Did Aaron tell you about the teachers stuck in the library?'

'He did. I'm happy to make my way over there, but I can't promise I'll be quick.'

'What are conditions like in there, Doug?' Mike asked.

'Dire. The cells are trashed, there's no water or electricity. There's excrement everywhere. Some of the lads are fighting in the rotunda, I know they're taking bets, settling old scores and the like.'

Doug sounded resigned to the sadness of his reality.

'Have you any idea how many people are hurt? Or if any of the lads need medical attention?' Mike asked.

'I'm not sure. I heard a lot of carrying on down on D wing. I heard some lads bragging that they got to some of the forty-threes.'

Cassandra brought up the list of prisoners at Highton covered under Rule 43; there were forty-seven of them. Only seventeen were accounted for so far. Attacks on Rule 43s were becoming more frequent and they often spent their whole terms in isolation for their own safety. A lot of them eventually committed suicide.

'All right, Doug. Good job. Can you continue to talk? Take the phone with you to check if the two teachers are safe and unharmed. You're probably aware that many of the prisoners are demanding certain changes to the conditions inside. I have to first confirm the status of the two teachers and several prison officers before I'm allowed to proceed. Can you help me?'

'I'll try and get over to the library. What do I do with the phone?'

'It depends on how you assess your safety, Doug. You're a smart guy. Conceal it if you have to and don't compromise yourself.'

'Right, I'll ask Aaron to show me how to turn it to silent.'

The line went dead again.

They were jolted by another of the drop phones ringing, and this time it was a prisoner barricaded inside his cell who'd picked it up from the floor when it had dropped through a hole in the ceiling. Chanting could be heard, and lots of banging and clattering.

'Who am I speaking to?' asked Mike.

A timid voice replied. It was merely a whisper and they could tell the man was terrified.

'I don't want no trouble,' he said.

'Sit tight, we're working on getting you to safety,' Mike encouraged him. 'Are you hurt?'

As the conversation went on, the team tasked with tracing the locations of the drop phones worked on the mobile data and pinpointed this phone to A wing, just off the rotunda. The locations of the two contacts they'd made so far were added to a virtual map, and inform-ation fed into computer software, creating a picture of the inmates left inside, together with where the biggest concentrations of bodies were. Thermal imaging by heli-copter was also expected.

'Can you get out?' Mike asked him.

'No. They've barricaded the rotunda, blocking the way. They're fighting to the death.' He sobbed. 'Some of them have gone to the library, apparently there's a female copper in there.'

'Shit,' Kelly and Cassandra said in unison, as Kelly stared at the TV.

Chapter 54

Ian parked his car along the road from the petrol station. There were crowds of people gathering along the verges. Helicopters hovered overhead and TV vans with huge satellite dishes on top were parked close to the perimeter fencing. People stood outside the petrol station, staring at the prison, hoping to get a glimpse of action. Black smoke billowed from the rooftops of the prison and gently wafted towards the east, tapering upwards until it turned to air. The smell lingered on the downpour, which had lightened. Nothing dampened the fervour of the TV teams and Ian slipped past them, like any other nosy pedestrian looking for the best view.

Then he spotted her.

The woman from the TV. She was stood talking to a man who was showing her a screen. Her concentration showed on her pretty face and Ian stopped by a grassy verge to watch her. The man with her was animated and loud. A few people asked her questions and she ignored them; maybe they knew her, maybe they didn't. Whichever way: she was rude, for sure.

His hood was pulled up over his head, but it didn't prevent the rain from penetrating his clothes as the heavens opened once more. The darts of water pissed their way down across western Cumbria, and out towards the Irish Sea. One could imagine a thousand shipwrecks swaying with the current, a hundred metres down, where sailors and their booty witnessed the song and succour of Davy Jones's Locker.

The woman gazed up to the darkening sky and rolled her eyes. He caught a glimpse of her décolletage and the pale untouched crease of her clavicle. It hinted at shade, and a smooth descent to her sternum, which protected her heart. He'd once seen a surgeon ordered by the Taliban to gut a traitor, but to keep her alive long enough to have full cognisance of what was happening to her. Still she didn't give them what they wanted. To Ian, that was true bravery: facing abject pain and destruction but remaining true to one's core values. The woman never cried out, even when her intestines were removed and placed beside her body. She simply shook, slowly at first, and then violently, as she went into some kind of fit, due to the shock of her organs being exposed to oxygen in such a brutal manner.

Ian thought of her often and wondered if the TV woman would just shake or if she'd cry out.

He sighed with desire. He had to come up with a hook to entice her. But in doing so he also knew that it was highly likely he'd be apprehended. The challenge, and the lure, was to see how far he could get before that happened. The police were otherwise involved inside the prison. His father had made sure of that. He was convinced that his father had started the riot in an attempt to save him by buying him time. It was the singular act of a loving parent.

They'd never exchanged what was commonly known as affection. Ian couldn't even remember a simple smile or word of praise, but that wasn't important, and it had taken Ian many years to appreciate that. Now, his father was displaying the ultimate act of love: protection. The problem was, how mad would he be if he learned how Ian was now jeopardising that? He should be miles away by now, laying low, as his father liked to say. But he also knew that laying low had been the root downfall of the great Rickie Burton. No one could hide forever, so how about exiting this world on one's own terms? That was infinitely more attractive than having one's fate dictated by lawyers or female coppers.

He saw a TV screen behind the woman journalist that caught his eye and he moved closer.

'Excuse me, sir?'

He turned to the young man who was questioning him.

'Sir, you can't go there, spectators have to stay back, I'm afraid,' the kid said. Ian stared at him and noticed the youngster looked nervous. It was a facial expression that gave Ian much pleasure.

'It's all right, she's expecting me, I have a lead for her,' Ian said with admirable confidence. The kid nodded, inexperienced and certainly scared of making a mistake. Ian smiled, which was an unusual sensation for him, and moved towards the TV crew. The screen he'd noticed was filled with the image of a female copper, and as he got closer, he heard that she was trapped inside the prison. Suddenly the journalist turned round and noticed him. She flung her hands up in dismay and searched for the young runner who'd let him get that close.

'You need to stand over there, mate,' she said to Ian. He smiled again, but the woman's face indicated to him that it wasn't a very pleasing smile.

'I know that woman,' he said, pointing to the screen. The female journalist stopped ushering him away and listened, interested in this new development.

'Sorry, what was your name?'

Chapter 55

'Johnny, you need to get home to Millie.' Kelly had called him because she had no choice. Kate's face was all over the news. She prayed that Millie was playing with Lizzie, oblivious to the news channels.

'Kelly, I'm just about to descend,' he said. The line wasn't brilliant. 'The turnout is a bit disappointing to be fair, I thought there'd be more press here,' Johnny said. The wind howled in the background.

'Haven't you heard?' she asked.

'What?'

'There's a full-scale riot going on at HMP Highton. Kate is stuck inside,' she said, breathless, hating herself for breaking the news like this over the phone. But she couldn't leave the command room, it was out of the question.

'What? Where are you? I thought that's where you were heading to meet her?' Johnny asked in alarm.

'I didn't make it that far, but Kate had already gone in to meet a witness we wanted to speak to. Johnny, you have to go and be with Millie. I've got a team of specialist officers going round, and also to her house to check on Kate's other daughters. It's all over the news and I don't want them to find out that way. I'm miles away.'

'So am I, I'm right next door to you at St Bees, remember? Christ, Kelly, it'll take me ages.'

She heard the frustration in his voice and wanted to slam the phone against the table. He didn't appreciate the seriousness of the situation, and, considering what he'd witnessed in his life, it maddened her.

'I'm sorry to put this on you, but I have to be here. I'll send someone from the office, they might get there sooner.'

'Is she all right?' Johnny asked.

'I don't know. We've had no contact, but it's all over the news that she's a copper. We were hoping she'd pass as a teacher, but somehow her profile got out to the media. Coppers are more hated than prison guards inside there, Johnny. I have no idea if she's alive or dead.'

'All right, calm down. Look, now I know why there are so few people here, I think we can with good faith cancel the event. I'll make my way back and I'll ring you as soon as I'm home. Jesus, I hope Kate's okay,' he said. Finally, he was showing some empathy. 'I'll leave now.'

'Do you know Ian Burton? Is he one of your PTSD clients?' There. She'd said it.

'Let's talk later.' He hung up.

Kelly stared at her phone. She didn't need to deal with him being offended right now. Suddenly, she realised that she'd never felt this way about him before. He had been her rock. He'd been there always. And now a feeling of abandonment and disappointment overwhelmed her. She put the thoughts to one side and decided it was time to phone Millie. She could put it off no longer.

She dialled her home number, and Millie answered.

'Hi Kelly! Josie came back early, with pasties, and we're playing trains, well, I am and Lizzie is watching me!' the girl said. Her voice was breezy and bright. Kelly imagined

Kate's voice in her head and what she'd say if she were here right now, facing the dilemmas Kelly was.

'Millie, I want you to listen very carefully to me.'

'What? Kelly, is everything all right?' The girl's tone changed rapidly.

'Listen to me, Millie. There's a situation you need to understand.' Her voice was grave.

'What's it about, are you okay? Is Johnny okay?'

Kelly felt her heart tug. The girl's first thought was of the family she was helping, not her own.

'It's nothing to do with me, or Johnny. It's about your mum.'

'Oh God, I'm going to be sick,' Millie said.

'Millie, stay calm. It's going to be all right. There's been a riot inside Highton prison, and your mum is stuck inside. Her photo has been on the news. I've got officers coming to the house, but I want you to be prepared.' Kelly spoke as quickly and clearly as she could. In her absence, this was about the best she could possibly do.

'What is she doing in a prison?' Millie's voice broke. 'Is she all right?'

Kelly had to tread carefully. 'As far as we know.' She glanced up and caught Andrew's eye. He looked ashen. She also saw how Cassandra looked at him.

'She's investigating a case to do with one of the prisoners. The riot is unrelated and, up until now, no one knew she was in there for work purposes. I don't know who found out and released her photo to the press, but they have.' Kelly waited.

'Can you put Josie on?' Kelly asked. She heard a muffled sound and Josie came on the line. Kelly told her the situation quickly and asked her not to leave the house; Lizzie needed someone with a clear head, and Millie would also need her support.

'There's someone at the door,' Josie said, and hung up.

Kelly stared at the phone. She became aware of Andrew by her side and she turned to him.

'Sir, I think it's time, with respect, that you removed yourself from this incident,' Kelly said. He nodded and looked at his hands. 'Let me handle it,' she added. Cassandra came up behind them.

'Everything all right?' she asked.

'Let me explain, sir,' Kelly said, turning from him to Cassandra. 'The chief constable has been dealing with some tough news. I'm going against the remit of my rank here, but it's my humble opinion that he should go home. I don't think I'm speaking out of turn, but I'm willing to stick my neck out on this one – the chief constable always puts work first. I think we've got this.'

Cassandra looked at Andrew, who smiled weakly, and nodded.

'What are you waiting for? Your DI is more than capable of letting you know the major developments. Go home and take care of yourself.'

He took one last look at the screens and asked Kelly to keep him updated, who, of course, agreed. She watched him leave and knew she'd done the right thing. Then she turned back to the screens.

'So, can we lie about her identity to prevent it coming out that she's a copper?' she asked. Cassandra glanced at her sideways.

'I wish that were possible, but they've clearly got TV working in there on generators. We're working on shutting them down. We can also remove the mobile phone signal intermittently, but we can't compromise the link set up by the negotiating team.'

Kelly nodded. 'Let's have a look at the damage.'

They both turned to the large TV screen. A TV channel was introducing a witness who said he was related to the female copper inside.

'Who the hell is this?' Kelly said to herself.

Cassandra turned to her. 'Who?'

'Him,' Kelly said, pointing. A notification came through on her phone that the specialist bereavement and trauma team was with Millie Umshaw, while another team was tracking down Kate's estranged husband and two other daughters. Kelly could breathe a little.

Until she saw the face of the man pretending to be Kate Umshaw's relative.

Chapter 56

Kate's chest heaved up and down. Since Rickie Burton's arrival in the library the situation had quickly deteriorated out of control.

'Let's fucking do her!' A prisoner leered towards Kate and Nathan stepped in front of her.

'No. I can't let this happen,' he said.

A noise made them all turn towards the door. An old man tottered as he climbed over the detritus.

'Doug!' Nathan said.

'Mr Appleton. Lads, come on now. I can't allow this. You need to leave the lady alone.' He was short of breath.

'She's a fucking copper!'

Doug looked at Kate. Several men were now feet away from her and she felt Nathan's heartbeat, he was so close in front of her. A young man went to Doug and stood beside him. It was a singularly courageous act, which, at first, could have been taken as threatening towards the old man. But Doug put his hand on the boy's shoulder. Another did the same, and another and another, until there was a standoff between those shielding Doug and those wanting the copper's blood.

'Don't believe everything you see on TV, lads,' Doug said.

'She works at my school, with me,' Nathan said. The English students in the room glanced at their teacher and knew he was lying, but it didn't matter.

'I've seen her with Mr Appleton before,' one of them said.

'Me too,' said another.

'I teach history,' Kate said. Every man in the room turned to her and she emerged from behind Nathan, arms by her side.

'I was considering offering a new course because Mr Appleton's has gone so well. I chose a lousy day to come in and look around,' she said. It lightened the mood.

'Don't believe the bitch,' said Rickie. 'We can use her to get what we want.'

Kate looked at him and kept eye contact, unafraid and holding her turf.

'See?' Rickie said. 'A fucking teacher wouldn't do that,' he said. 'She's not scared of me, are you?' His chest jutted out and he went to Kate and stood towering over her.

'Let me talk to the police and I'll prove to you that I am who I say I am.'

'Why is it all over the news?' Rickie asked. Kate looked at him.

'I have no idea. Some clever shit playing around with my photo in his dark bedroom, acting like a keyboard warrior?' she said.

Rickie shrugged. 'The coppers dropped some phones. Who has one?' he demanded. Doug kept quiet. But it rang, and he could no longer keep it a secret. He reached into his pocket, took it out, and held it aloft. Rickie smiled. He held out his hand and Doug passed it to him. Rickie answered.

'Good afternoon. Rickie Burton. No, I have absolutely nothing to do with this shit shower or how it started. All I want is to communicate what the lads are saying, and also to get these two teachers to safety,' he said.

No one in the room believed him.

–

Mike spoke deliberately and slowly. He knew who Rickie Burton was. But he wanted to know that Doug and Aaron were all right, and hadn't been punished for speaking to the negotiating team. It happened. During hostage negotiations, they first had to establish who was in charge. This was proving difficult to do that because the prisoners were holed up in several areas of the building, the main location being the rotunda. His other priority was finding out if the prison officers trapped inside were doing okay, and as well as that, he was asking to speak to Nathan and Kate.

'We were just having an interesting discussion about that. Is she a copper or a teacher?' Rickie asked Mike. 'I think she's definitely a copper, she's trying to negotiate with me. Does she think I was born yesterday?' Rickie carried on. Mike could tell that the prisoner was enjoying the banter and attention. Cassandra nodded to him.

'She's definitely a teacher, Rickie. But I have more important information for you. Your son was arrested outside the prison just now, trying to talk to the press,' Mike said. He waited.

Rickie squeezed the phone in his broad hand. All the weights he'd lifted and pumped above his head, all the dumb-bells he'd forced over his shoulders and up to his chest, all of that seemed so insignificant now, when he couldn't muster the strength to crush a fucking police burner phone. His voice broke.

'Ian?'

'Yes, Rickie. He's in custody, and his arrest is because the police suspect he was involved with the murders of Jack Bell and Dean Kirby,' Mike said. Then he changed the subject, hoping to catch Rickie off guard. 'I have to speak to the two civilians myself, so I can pass on to those who have the authority to grant your demands. Rickie? Are you there?'

Mike listened as a guttural wail escaped from the body of Rickie Burton. It was something that Mike thought he would only ever hear in films, when grown men cried for their very souls.

It was animalistic.

'Rickie?' Mike tried again.

The line went dead. Mike rubbed his eyes and looked at Cassandra and Kelly.

Chapter 57

Cassandra spoke frantically to Gold Command in London, who wanted grab squads to go in. Kelly was busy on the phone, talking to Rob back at Eden House, who was updating her on usable financial evidence as per the financial crime parameters. After his arrest, Ian Burton had been driven back to Penrith and Rob had seen him signed in and placed under arrest. They had twenty-four hours to reach the threshold to satisfy the CPS in order to formally charge him.

'His eyes were dead,' Rob told his boss. 'It's doubtful he understood what is happening to him.'

'Do we have a duty lawyer lined up?' Kelly asked.

'She's on her way.'

'Right, get a mental assessment as soon as you can. The last thing we need is him pleading insanity. We'll find ourselves screwed if they play the PTSD card, because we knew that before apprehending him. Have you made sure his DNA has been sent straight off as an emergency? And who's checking his fingerprints?'

'I am. I already have a match for the signet ring. And yes, his DNA has been sent to Carlisle, marked as urgent.'

'Throw money at it,' Kelly said dryly.

'Indeed, guv.'

'Without forensic evidence, what have we got?' Kelly asked him. She was pinning her hopes on an unrealistic desire to appeal to the best nature of the CPS. But she also knew the answer.

'Not much, guv. We have the signet ring, but he could say that was stolen. We have the care home kit, but just because he signed it out doesn't mean he used it. We have no evidence that he was ordered to do it by his father, and now zero chance of finding physical evidence at Highton. The financial evidence is good, but not water-tight, because everything is in cash. We need more. How are things over there?'

'The place is totalled.' She told him about conditions inside the prison. 'The negotiators had Rickie Burton on the phone and he's basically passing himself off as the saviour of the penal system. That was until he was told that his son was in custody. I think they might have made contact again. Jesus,' she broke off.

'What?' He asked.

'Rob, I have to go, they've put Kate on the phone.'

Kelly spun around. Cassandra held her hand up to hush everybody in the room as the female copper's voice filled the small command space. A collective sigh of relief physically eased the tension in the room. Kelly listened intently. She knew Kate's voice so well, and in many different scenarios. She'd heard her professionally, socially, as a mother, as a dirty-joke-telling friend, tipsy, cheeky and scared.

This was the latter, and Kelly's heart sank.

Mike spoke to her calmly.

'Kate, are you hurt?'

'No.' It was assertive.

'Are you under threat?'

'No.'

'Have you been mistreated?'

'No.'

'Thank you, Kate. Is Nathan Appleton able to come to the phone?'

There was a muffled sound and Nathan came to the phone. He said hello, and Mike asked him the same questions. His voice wavered and shook, as well it might. Kelly wanted to hear Kate again; in fact she never wanted to let her get off the phone, keeping her there as the minutes turned to hours, and the desperate prisoners became more and more disgruntled. She wanted to send in a one-woman tornado – herself – with a semi-automatic police-issued weapon, like the ones she'd trained with years ago, and blast Kate out of there, taking Rickie Burton down at the same time. The romantic vision soon dissipated as reality hit and she concentrated on what Mike was saying.

'Are you going to get us out of here?' Nathan asked.

'Sit tight, Nathan. We are working our hardest to work out how we can get you out of there. You're no use to the prisoners, and their demands are being discussed with the Home Office.'

'Should I tell them that?'

They heard a gruff voice near Nathan ask what he should be asking and to whom.

'No, the most important thing is you do not put yourself in danger, is that understood?'

'Okay,' Nathan said, helpless and afraid.

'I'll talk to Rickie again, now, Nathan, thank you, if he is able? Have you got water?'

'No.'

The phone was passed back to Rickie Burton.

'What are you trying to get him to do? I'm not fucking stupid!' Burton's voice had more control than earlier, but he was still audibly rattled.

Kelly flinched at the anger in his voice. She knew he was scared for his son, and desperate to regain control. Maybe that would work to their advantage, or maybe it would result in him losing all sense of reason and acting recklessly. In other words: the lives of the officers, and Nathan and Kate, were in the hands of this man, and Kelly had to bite her tongue.

Cassandra was back on the phone again to London. Kelly closed her eyes. She didn't want them to rush it. A snatch and grab mission could go badly wrong so quickly, and Kate and Nathan's safety had to be prioritised. Rickie had told them that at the moment, everybody he was aware of was crowded into the central rotunda. But she knew he'd lied. Rushing in now would be a big mistake. She looked at Cassandra, who put her elbows on the desk in front of her, hunched over and closed her eyes. The final tactical decision was hers. Decisions like this could make or break a career, and worse, burn one's name into the public record via *The Sun* and the *Daily Mail*.

All communications were suddenly cut and it was reported by an armed response team outside that a large group of prisoners was leaving the prison with their hands up. The dilemma over Rickie Burton was put on hold as all eyes went to the huge monitors. Cassandra flicked the relevant camera control, and they watched and listened as it happened before their eyes. Kelly did a rough head count; she reckoned over a hundred blokes had left, no doubt having had enough of the initial adrenaline rush, realising quickly that it wasn't worth hanging about to see what happened when they were left with no electricity, no toilet facilities, no clean water and a trashed home. As Kelly had suspected, Rickie Burton wasn't among those who'd left.

Waiting was excruciating. Kelly approached Cassandra and waited until there was a break in proceedings. She perched on the desk next to her.

'I have experience in snatch and grab,' Kelly said. She referred to several courses she'd attended when she worked for the Met. In London, body armour and confined space combat often had to be utilised because many of the places that murderers hid away in were small residential flats. They were a rabbit warren of human delinquency and one had to have a nose for it, as well as the stomach.

'Forget it,' Cassandra said.

'I thought you'd say that. I'll offer my services to the ARU commander in charge. I know him, and last time I looked, he doesn't work for the prison service.'

'He still takes his orders from Silver Command in this scenario, and you know that, DI Porter.'

'Fuck's sake,' Kelly whispered under her breath.

'I heard that,' Cassandra said. 'I know she's not just your second in command. I'm seeing she's your friend. I saw how much she means to the chief constable too. But she's not the only one in there. I'll make the decision to move when I'm happy I've got the best chance of success, I can guarantee you that. Why don't you take a breather and go interview your suspect?'

Kelly looked at the computer screens. She heard Mike's voice again. He was speaking to the old guy, Doug. She closed her eyes hard and wiped away the tears that trickled from them, turning away from Cassandra.

'No, I'm staying,' Kelly said. 'But I'll go and get some air,' she added.

She grabbed her coat and bag and went to leave. Cassandra grabbed her arm.

'I'll get her out,' she said. Kelly wiped her cheek and walked out.

Chapter 58

Outside, Kelly breathed cold air and called Rob again, taking solace in his voice. None of her team would ever guess how much she relied on them for her sanity and emotional wellness. She listened as he passed on the news that Kate was unhurt and she heard the cheer over the phone. She'd read the mood in Eden House as solemn, but now she'd given them some great news. She ended the call and went to the back of the ugly building and found a rock to sit on. It was jutting up from the moor on its own and Kelly sat there, looking at the grey sky, wishing she could do something to save Kate. The black cloud overhead opened again and Kelly looked to the distance, where the cameras and TV crews were waiting for some juicy headlines. Rob called her back.

'I've been talking to the Financial Conduct Authority and they've committed to a full investigation of the various bank accounts linked to Rickie Burton, as well as those of his current wife, several cousins and his son, Ian Burton. I gave them enough to piece together the financing of various well-known family-run businesses across the UK known for their interests in gambling and beauty salons, as well as prostitution and drugs. It's a mighty web, and the information has led to several constabularies sharing information and fitting missing pieces together going back decades.'

'You star,' Kelly said. She allowed herself to half-smile. But her heart wasn't in it.

'Did I do good? Does that deserve a pint paid for by my boss?' he asked. She laughed and it felt good, though short-lived. She wanted to buy Kate a pint too.

'Emma's been studying the CCTV from the garage, sent over by Kate before she went into Highton this morning. They had several stills and full frames of Ian Burton at the cash point and inside on visiting days.'

Kelly knew that he was trying to distract her and she was cheered a little by his efforts.

'Anything else?' she asked.

'The coroner came back to us and confirmed that the burns on Jack Bell were consistent with the remedial lamp used by the care home where Ian worked. We've also found an abandoned transit van, reported in Workington, and we're having the tyres tested.'

'Right. Good work. Tell everybody to keep going. Now we've got him in custody, we need to put together a plan to trip him up and it needs to be watertight. I suspect he's not the type to confess, but I'm hoping to catch him out. Who's the lawyer?'

'She's new.'

'Great. That could go either way. Can't we get someone reliable?'

'Too late, boss, she volunteered apparently. Do you want him warmed up for you? Me and Dan could kick off proceedings.'

'No. I want to wait. Get all the exhibits prepared for the lawyer and email them to me as soon as you can. I need something to tie it all together, which we don't have at the moment. I also want to know how the hell he was employed by a care home, given his military career. Look,

352

Rob, they're talking about sending tornado snatch and grab teams in. I think it's a mistake and too soon, but it's out of my hands.' Her voice wavered.

'Boss, do you want somebody to drive over there? Keep you company?' he asked.

She was touched.

'It's too crowded here as it is,' she said. 'But thank you. I'll let you know when I know anything else. Keep grafting on this, Rob. Thank you.'

'Wait a minute, boss, Emma's telling me something,' Rob halted her. 'I'll put you on speaker phone,' he said. Emma and Dan were only just back from Waberthwaite. 'Boss, Ian Burton was let go from security work after he was caught tying up a high-profile client's daughter,' Emma said.

'What?'

'I spoke to somebody he worked with in Jordan. This was just before he was found a position back in the UK, in 2017. They were working in close protection for a high-profile principal in Amman. He said that Burton was an odd character who he found volatile and rogue, that was the phrase he used. He said the incident wasn't the first time suspicion fell on him and he embarrassed the company.'

'Do you know any more details?'

'Apparently, the daughter later accused Burton of other things,' Emma said.

'Other things?' Kelly asked.

'Apparently it was a game they played, until she got scared and told her mother, and that's when he was sacked and removed. It was all hushed up to protect the daughter's identity.'

'A game?'

'The tying up. It was of a sexual nature, and the girl only told in the end because they were discovered. She was terrified of him.'

'Can we track her down? How old was she?'

'She was thirteen, boss. She committed suicide last year, at the age of sixteen.'

'Jesus Christ. Will the family talk now?'

'I'm trying to find out,' Emma said.

'Well done, thank you. We'll speak later. I'm hoping that Kate will be out soon,' Kelly said.

'How did the press find out she was in there?' Emma asked.

'I have no idea, but when I find out, I'll go for the bastards,' Kelly said.

Chapter 59

'Aaron, Doug,' Kate whispered. The old man and young offender paid attention, and so did Nathan.

'I reckon they'll send in tornado teams soon,' she said.

'What's that?' Nathan asked.

'It's bastards in riot kit.' Doug surprised them with his venomous tone, but Kate reckoned he'd seen enough during his time inside to evaluate the efficacy of full riot kit against offenders desperate to be treated like human beings. Kate made a grimace that kind of agreed with the sentiment.

They huddled in.

They were being escorted along the corridor towards the main prison rotunda. Kate tried to ignore her nerves. Her whole soul screamed with terror and her body wanted her to run for the hills. But she couldn't. They could hear the voices of scores of men, newly intoxicated with their quasi-freedom, and Kate's pulse elevated even higher. The prison was a disaster zone. Nathan took her hand.

'I won't let anything happen to you,' he said.

She was moved. It was a very sweet gesture, but Kate wasn't stupid. Nobody could protect her if a bunch of angry prisoners wanted to take advantage of having a real live woman in their company, especially a copper.

'So, a tornado team is specially trained to quell situations like this. They wear riot gear and have a few more handy weapons than your average POs. It's likely they'll send in armed squads too, at least with blanks, and the fire brigade may be on standby – you'd be amazed at how powerful their hoses are.'

'Is that what's called a Freudian slip?' Doug teased. Kate appreciated him trying to lift her spirits. He was an old-timer, unlike Nathan, and knew very well what she might face.

They chatted easily and Kate reflected on the absurdity of the situation. Aaron stuck close by and she wondered what his story was, he was so young. If she got out of here, she'd put a good word in for both prisoners. And there were others. There were the men who'd kept quiet about her being in the library in the first place. There were the ones who'd stood in front of her when Rickie Burton came sniffing about. They all deserved a mention for their humanity. Just because a man goes to prison doesn't mean that he loses all of his values. Some of them were prob-ably innocent, too. Whatever their backgrounds, Kate was happy that Doug and Aaron were with her now.

The whistles began to reverberate down the corridor as they neared the central rotunda. Kate had never been this up close and personal with cells before. Those beneath Eden House were like hotel suites compared to this. The damage and detritus was staggering. They walked past burning pyres of wood and furniture. The floors were scorched black. Taps drained across the halls, turning everything to a black mush. Glass was scattered across the wing like confetti, and piles of beds, cupboards, doors and desks had been built up to prevent anyone from leaving or gaining entry. She looked around and assessed the situation, in case she could get hold of a phone and communicate the information to a tornado team.

'When they enter, they will shout "get down". It's such a simple thing, but it works, because anyone wanting a fight will stand. We'll hit the deck, and believe me they'll start pushing in with huge force. Anyone standing will be mown down. If you can find a way in to a cell, then well and good, but the important thing is not to give them any reason to use coercion against you. If I'm nearby I'll make myself known to them – they'll know I'm in here and will be looking for me, as well as the POs and Nathan.'

'You know a lot for a teacher,' Aaron said.

She smiled and squeezed his hand. He wasn't much older than Millie. He knew she wasn't a teacher.

'I trained in it, honey. Promise me you'll get your arse on the floor when they come in?' she said. He nodded.

The noise grew louder and Doug, Aaron and Nathan made a blockade around her.

Rickie was chatting to a group of men and turned to see her arrival. The din was deafening now, and Kate saw a look in many of the faces that reminded her of what a criminal looks like when he was charged with a serious offence for the first time: it was an animalistic sense of injustice and arrogance. But it was also mingled with something else: lust. Their eyes were red and wide, probably from drugs, in most cases. She could smell the hooch, and she also recognised the acrid aroma of vomit. Many men were passed out on mattresses, while others danced, some fought and some huddled around the only TV powered by a generator. To most of them the day was just a holiday; some relief from the tedious routine of their isolation.

Rickie approached and Doug got between them.

'I won't have anything untoward happen to this lady, Rickie,' he said.

'Neither will I,' Nathan said, stepping forward. Kate saw Doug's head dip; Aaron watched from next to her. She felt his body shaking and touched his hand.

'It's okay,' she whispered, wishing she could believe her own voice.

'You're a fucking copper!' somebody shouted. The whole place erupted into chants and taunts. The crowd came closer and Kate felt suffocated.

'Get back!' It was Rickie Burton's voice.

'Fuck you! She's getting what's coming,' another said. A few lads rushed forward and managed to get hold of Kate. Nathan jumped on one of them and Doug held on to Kate's arm for dear life. Aaron backed up against a wall. Rickie desperately tried to calm things down but Kate could tell that he'd lost the loyalty of mob.

Nathan disappeared beneath the hoard of men and Doug went down too. Kate frantically searched for them amongst the charging bodies, which seemed to be running in all directions. Her lungs screamed in pain as they were crushed against men's backs and elbows, she took a shoulder to the face and her head seemed to spin out of control. Her vision went blurry and her knees buckled. Somebody pulled at her leg.

She was down. She wriggled violently, hoping no-one could get hold of her, and she clawed her say away from the fighting, on her belly. The noise was deafening. Her leg continued to be pulled by a vice-like grip and it was only when she was clear that she realised that it was Aaron, and he bent low next to her.

'In there!' he said breathlessly. She saw that he was pointing to a cell. She stopped kicking and they squirmed their way to the room. She watched and listened as cracks resonated against the bare plastic walls, and she realised with horror that the noises were probably bones breaking. She looked back and could not see Nathan or Doug. She did spot Rickie Burton, though, who was pinned down underneath a mass of prisoners. Their eyes met and she saw pure fear in his gaze. She looked away and hid with Aaron under a metal bed. He was shaking.

'Are you all right?' he asked her, and she nodded, putting her arm around him, like one of her own children. The noises outside the cell were subsiding and Kate could just see, though the detritus thrown about the cell, what was going on outside. The scuffling was stopping as something else caught the men's attention. She saw that Rickie Burton had regained his footing, though he was bloodied and hurt, he'd managed to divert attention to a new arrival. She watched through the door as a man was brought to the centre of the space, and thrown to his knees. He was pleading for his life to be spared and trying to convince his captors not to harm him.

It was Brian Taylor.

'This was all his plan! He manipulated you! He played you like kids. Don't you see, he *wants* this, he engineered it. Think about it, who told you about the search?' the governor screamed.

Kate watched in horror as the man cried out in terror as he teetered between being spared or being executed. But the situation was beyond her control. She held on to Aaron, and he to her as they watched the crowd murmur amongst themselves.

They were choosing sides.

Chapter 60

The command room became aware of the shifting mood inside the prison via Mike.

'People are coming out!' The communication reached the command room where Kelly and Cassandra stood, arms splayed on the desks in front of them. Kelly wanted to run, but she used all her willpower to stop herself. She had to wait for the armed response units to stand down, and make sure the prisoners gave up their weapons.

They watched the screens helplessly. It was all they could do. No one knew what had happened, and Mike spoke frantically to prisoners who had picked up drop phones and still had them.

'It's over,' one told him. 'The governor's dead.'

Cassandra turned to Kelly and they watched the screens, wildly searching the survivors for signs of prison officers, Kate or the teacher.

Dozens of men were leaving the prison. Most inmates appeared unhurt but some were badly wounded. Reports of fights between those who tried to protect the governor and those who were loyal to Rickie Burton filtered through to the cabin.

Then Kelly saw her.

She looked at Cassandra, who nodded. Kelly sprinted from the temporary suite and pounded towards the stream of prisoners. Kate was with a young man, and they had their arms around one another. Kelly stopped running. Their eyes locked and Kate's face crumpled. The pair halted too, and Kelly saw that the young man was supporting Kate. Kelly charged over to them and stood breathless in front of them, and Kate stumbled towards her boss. The young man smiled at Kelly and she looked at him, then closed her eyes. She held them both tightly.

'What's your name?' she asked the boy.

'Aaron. I found her in the library.'

'We spoke to you on the phone. Well, my colleague did,' Kelly corrected herself. Of course, Aaron wouldn't know how important he'd been, or that a whole command suite was listening to him.

'Doug?' she asked. Kate looked at her and shook her head.

'Nathan?' Both of them shook their heads.

'Rickie Burton is badly injured. It got nasty. CM Fawcett is dead. The governor was lynched. A handful of them are still having a party, but when the majority found out that it was all a plot to save Burton's skin, they gave up.'

'We're hearing reports that Rickie Burton is dead too,' Kelly said. 'Is it true that he was behind it, then?' Kelly asked. Kate nodded.

'It was the governor who pointed it out and swayed the prisoners. I guess he thought it might save his life. Kelly, it was horrible,' Kate said. 'This young man protected me.'

Somebody put a blanket around them and they walked back to the medical tent, set up hastily for casualties.

Kelly noticed movement in her peripheral vision and realised that Cassandra had ordered a tornado team inside. But she no longer cared. Kate was out, and she was safe.

She reflected on the curious situation she found herself in: surrounded by convicts, unshackled and walking in the same direction as them, for the same purpose, and she felt no threat. No threat whatsoever.

'Do you want to speak to Millie? Johnny's with her,' Kelly said. Kate stopped and nodded. She turned to Aaron.

'Millie's my daughter, not much older than you,' Kate said.

Kelly dialled the number and spoke to Johnny. 'She's out, she's all right and she wants to speak to Millie,' Kelly said. She passed the phone to Kate, who took it.

'Millie?' Kate said. Then the tears came.

The phone was passed back and Kelly spoke to Johnny again. She watched as Kate's face changed and the reality of her freedom hit her. Kelly said a quick goodbye to Johnny, but he didn't want the call to end. Before she could hang up on him, like he had done to her, he told her he'd been watching the news and had seen Ian Burton arrested and taken away in a police car. His voice was flat but Kelly knew him well enough to establish that it wasn't due to a lack of emotion, rather the very opposite.

'You asked me if I know him, I do. He needs help, Kelly, not you lot locking him up and throwing away the key. He'll last five minutes inside a prison, and no-one deserves that when they've fought for their country. He went to hell in Iraq, it wasn't his fault. I've been treating him for PTSD for three years,' he said.

Kelly felt sick. Johnny had counselled a monster.

Chapter 61

'Be advised, Mr Burton, that you are being interviewed under caution, and anything you do say might be given in evidence at a later date, should the court require it. You have been arrested on suspicion of murder. What can you tell me about Jack Bell and Dean Kirby?' Kelly asked.

'Never heard of them.'

It was the first time Kelly had heard the voice of the man she believed had killed Jack and Dean, and certainly others too. She pushed the photos of Jack and Dean towards him and watched him. He didn't flinch.

'Nope.'

His accent was neutral. He could have been from anywhere. His dad, Rickie, had a thick northern dialect and he sounded rough and ready, as if he'd lived on the streets, scrapping all his life. But Ian was different.

'Why do you think your father didn't have you recorded as his next of kin?'

The mention of his dead father riled him, which was what Kelly wanted.

'Irrelevant, can you please move on,' the lawyer interjected.

'Do you recognise this?' she held up the signet ring in a see-through plastic bag.

'Where did you find it? I lost that ages ago, or it was stolen,' he said.

'It has your fingerprint on it,' she said.

'It was stolen,' he said.

'You were burgled?' Kelly asked. He didn't answer and the lawyer held her stern gaze, making it clear that she should move on.

Kelly was exasperated, but she also knew that if he was willing to keep up this facade, and keep it going in front of a jury, then they wouldn't get him where they needed him: beyond reasonable doubt. They needed solid evidence of communication between him and his father, and they needed to place him in the vicinity of Seascale and Workington at the right time. Then, and only then, would the circumstantial evidence come together to convince a jury.

'Do you know this man?' she asked, showing him the still of Kieran Foster, the drug dealer from Barrow, the one who'd bought the Snickers bar.

'Nope.'

'That's funny, he knows you,' she said.

'Really? Are you sure he's not just saying that, after seeing my picture in the paper, for some personal gain?'

The lawyer looked at Kelly questioningly. Kelly stared at Ian. The man before her was a narcissist. He'd run away and joined the army, then he'd played God in close protection, then he'd been sent back to his daddy. Any sense of real responsibility had passed him by, and his arrogance compounded the personality disorder. The lies just sealed the deal.

'Why did you take the eyes, Ian?'

'My client isn't on trial, DI Porter,' said the lawyer.

'Did Dean's latex allergy frustrate you, and make you want to hurt Jack more?'

'I have to insist on a new line of questioning, DI Porter. Unless you have some solid evidence to show us.'

Kelly was more used to lawyers letting things go, mainly because they knew half of their clients were guilty as hell. However, this was a new face, and she'd clearly swallowed the manual on interviewing under caution.

'Do you recognise these items?' she said, showing photos of the winching equipment, the lamp and the gloves used at the care home.

'We use them at the care home all the time,' he said.

Kelly reckoned, judging by the pulse in his neck, that his heart rate hadn't gone beyond ninety.

'And this?' It was a photo of the winch strap tying Jack to the chair. Ian twisted his head this way and that.

'Hmmm, it could be from our place, I'm not sure. It's quite dirty,' he said.

'Why didn't you sign in under your real name when you visited your father in prison?'

'He said he didn't want me to, it's a safety thing, he's always tried to protect me from his criminal record, with my military past and all that,' Ian said. He was articulate and in control.

'On that note, Ian, what happened to you between January and December 2004, when you disappeared for three hundred and nine days, near Basra, Iraq?'

'Not much. The family had lost a son, and they kept me living with them to fill a gap, I guess. I was disarmed after a patrol gone wrong, we were sold out by the enemy and I was taken. They were perfectly respectful towards me.'

'But you weren't allowed to leave?'

'No.'

'How did they force you to stay?'

'It might come as a surprise to you, but what the common view of incarceration involves isn't usually correct. Being held in a situation against your will might not always be about violence, although you'd like to believe it is, I'm sure – that would give you the motive you need to prove that I committed some perverse re-enactment, wouldn't it?'

Kelly stared at him. She hadn't had chance to speak to Johnny about his therapy, what it entailed, and what they spoke about. She was too mad at him. She had no idea where the feeling of betrayal came from, but it was there. She couldn't reconcile his work with this man before her. Even after he'd found out who Ian Burton really was, Johnny had still defended him.

'We are aware that you have been receiving therapy for PTSD for the last three years from a counsellor. Mr Johnny Frietze?' She watched him.

'Yes, he showed me your photo. He said images of functional, happy families are therapeutic. Your daughter is so pretty.'

Kelly's nails dug into her fists under the table.

'Did your trauma begin as a result of your incarceration, or was it your work in military security that contributed to it? More specifically the relationship with a minor when working for a family in Amman, between 2014 and 2017?'

No answer.

'What were your movements between midday on Friday fifteenth October and midday on Sunday seventeenth October?'

'Can't remember, I often work nights and sleep all day when I get some time off.'

'I find it difficult to believe that you struggle to recall where you were only days ago, when you remember the kindness of a family sixteen years ago,' Kelly said.

'I think we need to leave it there. If you're not going to charge my client then it's his right to leave, and I'm advising that course of action now.'

Kelly was royally pissed off. The lawyer was technically sound, but very unhelpful.

'Do you recognise this type of phone?' Kelly asked. She showed him a plastic bag containing a Zanco Tiny T1 phone, like the ones believed to have been used by the victims.

'What is it? An MP3?' Ian asked. The lawyer packed her things away, knowing full well that they had little else.

'Turning off the tape at three forty-nine.'

Watching Ian Burton leave custody was one of the worst moments of her career since leaving the Met. But more than that, his smile when he stood up and pushed his chair in made her shiver.

'Oh, I do remember where I was last weekend now. I went walking with Johnny and Tom. It's good for mental health and mindfulness, you know, getting out in nature. You should try it some time,' he said.

Kelly held on to her pen so tightly that she couldn't breathe.

Chapter 62

One month later…

Ted cut into his steak.

'Well rested,' he said. Kelly nodded and smiled. Josie wasn't eating with them tonight. She was out with friends. Her stepdaughter had decided to stay here, with her and Lizzie, after Johnny left. The place was strangely quiet without him. He was never a big creator of noise, or anything like that, it's just that his presence had been felt. He was part of fabric of this place. That's what made it so painful.

It had been a mutual decision.

Millie nannied full-time, and slept over occasionally when Kelly needed her. Of course, Lizzie went to see her father regularly too. He was staying with Tom Gorman in Keswick, in a flat close to the start of many of his favourite fell walks. They'd spoken about Ian Burton a number of times after the events at Highton, and each time it had descended into a bitter exchange as Johnny dug his heels in, insisting that the man needed understanding, not judgement. Kelly balked at the idea of showing a murderer compassion. When she'd asked him to cooperate with the police and tell them all he knew about him, he'd refused, despite knowing that it was an impossible position to put her in – living with someone who could be a witness for the defence. No matter how hard she tried, Kelly couldn't reconcile the two faces of the man she thought she loved. She had to choose between him and her job. The fact that he still considered Ian Burton a victim, combined with his refusal to end the relationship while they investigated him, had been the final straw between them. Johnny and Tom had even continued to walk with Burton, while he was being investigated. They'd pretended that everything was all right in front of the kids, but it wasn't. Kelly had suspected for a long time that his work with veterans took him to some places she'd rather not go. Not if it involved people like Ian Burton. She'd never know for sure if Lizzie had ever been in the savage's company. Johnny said not. She didn't believe him. They'd lost trust, so they lost everything.

In the end, Rickie Burton hadn't had a chance to hide his burner phones, worth a grand each. There was no shortage of prisoners willing to testify against him because the empire had crumbled. A shopping bag full of the tiny handsets had been found in his relatively tidy cell: one of the few left intact in the whole prison. The same couldn't be said about his battered body, retrieved from the rotunda two days after the riot ended, along with the bodies of Nathan Appleton, Brian Taylor, Liam Fawcett and Doug Hopper.

Testing on some of the phones had shown that Rickie had been in contact with the outside on many occasions, and they'd tirelessly pieced together the course of events over countless hours inside Eden House. Kelly and her team had worked out an intricate web of phone networks involving the Burtons, throughout Cumbria, including Dean Kirby and Jack Bell. They'd proven that the phones found in the flats where Jack and Dean lived were bought at the same time and delivered to the same address as the burner phones in Rickie Burton's cell. It was Kieran Foster's address in Barrow. It was also revealed that Foster was a regular visitor to Highton. Perhaps more crucially, a search of the flat where Ian Burton had stayed had led to a bag of washing being found dumped in a wardrobe: the clothes were covered in the blood of the victims. More intriguingly, around £70,000 in cash was also found there and the case for the prosecution was suggesting that it was Rickie Burton's own son who was stealing from his father, not the two ex-cons. Rickie Burton's true motive may never be known, because he'd taken it to his grave, but it was likely that the control he enjoyed inside Highton, thanks to the collusion of the officers, had gone to his head, and he couldn't bear Dean and Jack being free and not at his beck and call. Jeanie Clark had agreed to testify, and she was their star witness.

But in the time it took them to piece together the facts, Ian Burton had been free to roam, for four whole weeks.

Her problem with Johnny wasn't that he'd caused her more work, by lying to her, but more to do with his denial that Ian was capable of killing. The irony of soldiers pleading they were incapable of murder was something that she couldn't come to peace with in her soul.

She'd asked herself many times if love was something that could turn off as quickly as it turned on, and her answer was yes. Should that trust, certainty and sureness, gained through nights sharing the same pillow, holidays nurturing and feeding attachment and devotion, be impacted so crushingly by something that was at odds with everything one knew about a person, then the elusiveness of passion slipped away.

Was she being childish? Selfish even?

She'd questioned herself about whether she was merely throwing her toys out of the pram because Johnny didn't fit nicely into her investigation, and she couldn't control him. But if there was one thing she'd learned from watching people consumed with self-preservation, to the detriment of all else, it was to trust her instinct.

She'd asked him to testify against Ian and he'd said no. And Johnny didn't even keep notes on his clients, he felt that strongly about them being misunderstood. So she'd never know what Ian had disclosed to him.

She could insist that the CPS called him as a prosecution witness, but they wouldn't risk it because he was what they deemed unreliable. A witness on the stand who didn't want to be there wasn't somebody to rest a case on.

Johnny's take on Ian Burton was that he was somebody who had suffered dramatic and acute trauma and needed to be worked with, understood, relieved and given space... not punished.

'No matter what?' she'd asked.

'I did things I'm not proud of on operational tours, Kelly,' he'd said.

'Murder?'

She wished she hadn't asked.

'If ordering smart bombs on villages counts as murder, then yes.'

The CPS had decided, after four weeks of twelve-hour days, of her team building a case against him, that Ian Burton had passed the threshold to be charged with murder, and he was currently on remand, awaiting trial, at HMP Highton. Parts of the prison had been rebuilt, at a cost of £11 million so far, and counting. One sliver of good news was that the case against Aaron Lewis had collapsed. The integrity of the initial investigation had been questioned and he'd been cleared of all charges before he even got to court. He'd been given a second chance.

On days when Kelly found herself driving south along the coast road, past St Bees, heading to the prison to tie up details pertaining to the upcoming trial, she steered herself into the void that this case had created, and noticed that the silence and isolation encouraged reflection on why Johnny had left, and why she'd let him.

The problem with understanding murderers was that it dishonoured the victims. Of course, psychologists and criminologists did valuable work in studying killers, and some of it helped Kelly with her job, but placing emphasis on what Ian Burton needed to heal was a slap in the face for Jack Bell and Dean Kirby, and the others. They hadn't been perfect, far from it, but their lives had been brutally snuffed out, almost on a whimsical habit. Defending serious criminals was an arbitrary process, and everybody had the right to a defence, but explaining away Ian Burton's horrendous crimes as some kind of inevitable behaviour, because of what the army had done to him, was a travesty in her mind.

Because there was one thing that they all overlooked. Plenty of soldiers were harmed beyond repair by the things they had to witness or perform in war, but they didn't all go on to become monsters. And this was what she couldn't reconcile with the man she'd loved. And she'd come to realise that it was so important for her to be able to look her team in the eye, especially Kate, that Johnny leaving had actually brought her relief. It was simpler this way.

Kelly looked at her steak and agreed with her father.

'It is well rested, Dad,' she said.

'It makes all the difference.'

Acknowledgements

Researching this book was only possible because of some very knowledgeable and passionate people. I'd like to thank Dave Part for first bringing my attention to the appalling statistics on re-offenders inside the UK penal system, particularly young men. The input of other professionals was invaluable. Thanks go to Adrian Priestley for answering countless questions, and to Gary Clarke for tightening up my accuracy. To Mike 'Dinga' Dingwall for his expertise and vast experience. To Steve and Jon Doherty for sharing their stories. To my friends in the military world who provided solid and fascinating context, thank you.

I'd like to thank Peter Buckman, my agent, for his constant insight, commitment and advice. Also the team at Canelo, especially Siân and Louise, who backed this book so wholly. The faith in this series never fails to inspire and awe me.

Special thanks goes to my family, Mike, Tilly and Freddie, who have turned into sleuths themselves: you drive me every day. I love you.

Do you love crime fiction and are always on the lookout for brilliant authors?

Canelo Crime is home to some of the most exciting novels around. Thousands of readers are already enjoying our compulsive stories. Are you ready to find your new favourite writer?

Find out more and sign up to our newsletter at canelocrime.com